MADNESS IN SOLIDAR

The Ninth Book of the
Imager Portfolio

L. E. MODESITT, JR.

A TOM DOHERTY ASSOCIATES BOOK
NEW YORK

MADNESS IN SOLIDAR: THE NINTH BOOK OF THE IMAGER PORTFOLIO

Map by Jon Lansberg

A Tor Book
Published by Tom Doherty Associates, LLC
175 Fifth Avenue
New York, NY 10010

www.tor-forge.com

ISBN 978-0-7653-7986-3

First Edition: March 2015
First Mass Market Edition: March 2016

Printed in the United States of America

0 9 8 7 6 5 4 3 2

Praise for *Madness in Solidar*

"Modesitt once again delivers an engrossing power struggle negotiated by a virtuous and talented man committed to achieving the greater good by way of the least harm."
—*Kirkus Reviews*

"L. E. Modesitt, Jr., has long been a pillar of the fantasy genre, for well over two decades. *Madness in Solidar* is proof that the author is still at the height of his creative powers. Highly recommended for anyone who loves to read fantasy novels, *Madness in Solidar* is a must-read for fans of the Imager Portfolio series."
—*Guardian Liberty Voice*

"This is a book that is an enjoyable read and provides political intrigue, betrayal, relationship problems, and friendship to reflect on and immerse in."
—*Deseret News* (Salt Lake City, UT)

Praise for the Imager Portfolio

"The level of detail Modesitt brings to his world-building is, as always, both uncompromising and astonishing. . . . Maybe most important, the intricate look at the history of Lydar/Solidar is unique and fascinating as always. L. E. Modesitt, Jr., combines legends, current politics, and the future (as portrayed in the first three novels in the series) into one of the most complex depictions of the evolution of a fantasy universe ever."
—Tor.com

"L. E. Modesitt, Jr. . . . His name alone makes the promise of engaging adventure, be it of the high fantasy or science fiction variety. As fans following the Imager Portfolio series will readily attest, Modesitt's expert world-building is dense, thorough, deep, and top-notch."
—Mania.com

TOR BOOKS BY L. E. MODESITT, JR.

THE IMAGER PORTFOLIO
Imager
Imager's Challenge
Imager's Intrigue
Scholar
Princeps
Imager's Battalion
Antiagon Fire
Rex Regis
Madness in Solidar
Tyrant's Tools (forthcoming)

THE COREAN CHRONICLES
Legacies
Darknesses
Scepters
Alector's Choice
Cadmian's Choice
Soarer's Choice
The Lord-Protector's Daughter
Lady-Protector

THE SAGA OF RECLUCE
The Magic of Recluce
The Towers of the Sunset
The Magic Engineer
The Order War
The Death of Chaos
Fall of Angels
The Chaos Balance
The White Order
Colors of Chaos
Magi'i of Cyador
Scion of Cyador
Wellspring of Chaos
Ordermaster
Natural Ordermage
Mage-Guard of Hamor
Arms-Commander
Cyador's Heirs
Heritage of Cyador

THE SPELLSONG CYCLE
The Soprano Sorceress
The Spellsong War
Darksong Rising
The Shadow Sorceress
Shadowsinger

THE ECOLITAN MATTER
Empire & Ecolitan
(comprising *The Ecolitan Operation* and *The Ecologic Secession*)
Ecolitan Prime (comprising *The Ecologic Envoy* and *The Ecolitan Enigma*)

The Forever Hero (comprising *Dawn for a Distant Earth, The Silent Warrior, and In Endless Twilight*)

Timegods' World (comprising *Timediver's Dawn* and *The Timegod*)

THE GHOST BOOKS
Of Tangible Ghosts
The Ghost of the Revelator
Ghost of the White Nights
Ghosts of Columbia
(comprising *Of Tangible Ghosts* and *The Ghost of the Revelator*)

The Hammer of Darkness
The Green Progression
The Parafaith War
Adiamante
Gravity Dreams
The Octagonal Raven
Archform: Beauty
The Ethos Effect
Flash
The Eternity Artifact
The Elysium Commission
Viewpoints Critical
Haze
Empress of Eternity
The One-Eyed Man
Solar Express

For my mother,
who introduced me to science fiction and the fantastic
and who made all the books possible

Characters

• REX

RYEN D'REX Rex of Solidar
ASARYA D'RYEN Wife of Ryen
LORIEN D'RYEN Eldest son of Ryen
CHELIA D'LORIEN Wife of Lorien
RYENTAR D'RYEN Younger son of Ryen
CHARYN D'LORIEN Eldest son of Lorien

• HIGH HOLDERS

CALKORAN D'ALTE Vaestora
CAEMRYN D'ALTE Yapres
DELCOEUR D'ALTE L'Excelsis [deceased], father of Asarya
GUERDYN D'ALTE Head, High Holder's Council, Nacliano
HAEBYN D'ALTE High Councilor, Piedryn
MOERYN D'ALTE High Councilor, Khelgror
NACRYON D'ALTE High Councilor, Mantes
RUELYR D'ALTE Ruile
RYEL D'ALTE Rivages
SOUVEN D'ALTE Dueraan
VAUN D'ALTE High Councilor, Tilbora
ZAERLYN D'ALTE Rivages

• IMAGERS

ALASTAR Maitre D'Image
FHAEN Maitre D'Esprit [deceased Maitre of Collegium]
CYRAN Maitre D'Esprit
AKORYT Maitre D'Structure
DESYRK Maitre D'Structure
OBSOLYM Maitre D'Structure
TARYN Maitre D'Structure
ALYNA Maitre D'Aspect

CLAEYND Maitre D'Aspect
GAELLEN Maitre D'Aspect, healer
KHAELIS Maitre D'Aspect
LHENDYR Maitre D'Aspect
MHORYS Maitre D'Aspect
NARRYN Maitre D'Aspect
PETROS Maitre D'Aspect
SHAELYT Maitre D'Aspect
TIRANYA Maitre D'Aspect
WARRYK Maitre D'Aspect

ARHGEN Tertius, Collegium bookkeeper
DAREYN Secondus, aide to maitre
ISKHAR Chorister of the Collegium
ZHELAN Maitre of Westisle Collegium

• FACTORS

BROUSSARD D'FACTORIUS Brick and stone
ELTHYRD D'FACTORIUS Timber, lumber; chief, Factors' Council
KATHILA D'FACTORIA Factors' Council member; spices, scents, and oils
VHADYM D'FACTORIUS Leather and rendering
WYLUM D'FACTORIUS Woolens and cloth

• GUILDERS

GAIROCK Master Stonemason

• OTHERS

DEMYKALON D'CORPS Marshal of the Armies
WILKORN D'NAVIA Sea Marshal
PETAYN D'CORPS Vice-Marshal
CHESYRK D'CORPS Subcommander

KHEL
MONTAGNES
Mont D'Image
Eshtora
Asseroiles
Tacqueville
Moryn
KHELGROR
BOVARIA
Ouestan
Mahrun
Tuuryl
Jovahl
Laaryn
Mantes
Great Canal
Ferravyl
Kherseilles
Alkyra
Ephra
Pointe
Neiman
Kephria
Loha
Westisle
Suemyron
LIANTIAGO
Barna
Sud
Swamp
ANTIAGO
Hassyl

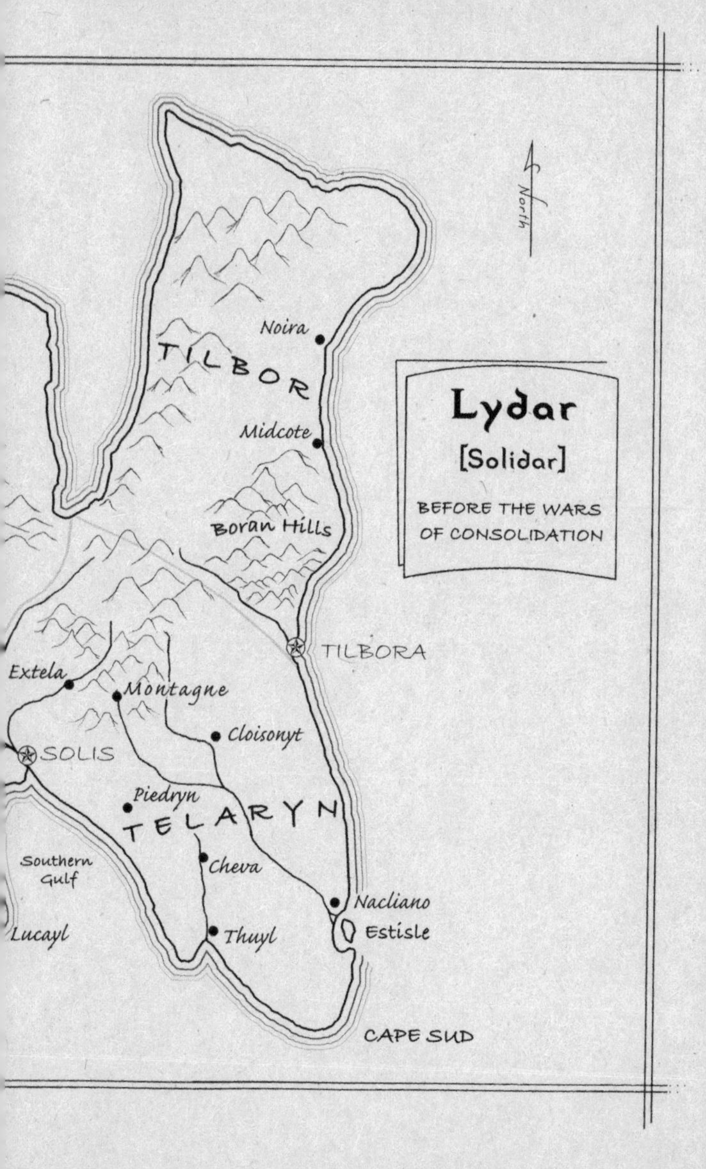
Lydar
[Solidar]
BEFORE THE WARS
OF CONSOLIDATION
North
TILBOR
Noira
Midcote
Boran Hills
TILBORA
Extela
Montagne
Cloisonyt
SOLIS
Piedryn
TELARYN
Cheva
Southern
Gulf
Nacliano
Estisle
Thuyl
Lucayl
CAPE SUD

MADNESS IN SOLIDAR

PROLOGUE (1)

"Five silvers? That's all?" asked the woman in a low voice. "After all the years you devoted to his father?"

"Young master Cerrsyn said that was all that he could spare. The factorage went to his older brother. He got nothing." The stocky man, sitting on the low stool in front of the hearth, stared at the few reddish coals that remained.

The boy listened and watched from where he lay on the rush pallet with its pad of quilted rags neatly stitched together, barely covered by a small and patched woolen gray blanket, his eyes slit so that they would think he was sleeping.

"Like as anyone'd believe that."

"I believe it. He walked from the factorage to the north wharf. I went with him. That's when he gave me the silvers. He got on a schooner bound for Hassyl. He'll be working for his wife's father there."

"Least he'll have a place. Not like us."

"We've the cot, love."

"That and five whole silvers . . . and three young mouths to feed. Some reward for years of service."

"Faerth might take me as a loader."

"At your age . . . how long can you lift bales and barrels?"

"Long as I have to, long as there's no other work to be had. There are . . . other things I can do . . ."

The woman offered a sound that might have been anything.

The boy continued to listen, but neither of his parents spoke, not before he finally slept, restlessly, until much later when a chill breeze blew through the open door, so strongly that the boy had to grab his tattered blanket to keep it from blowing away, not that it was quite long enough to cover both his shoulders and feet, no matter how much he hunched up. He could taste ashes from the small fire that had burned out glasses earlier, even before he had drifted into sleep. He moistened his lips in the darkness. That only made the taste of ashes worse. The door closed, but he could still feel the wind coming through the cracks in the wall and in the doorframe.

"Mother . . ." He tried not to let his voice crack.

"I'm here." She knelt beside him and touched his cheek.

Her hand was even colder than the packed clay of the floor or the stones of the hearth.

"Father?"

"He had to go. He'll be back in the morning. A man had a task."

The boy could hear the way her voice hardened when she tried not to talk about things that worried her. "At night?"

"We do what we have to. Your father will be back. He always does what he says. He always has. He always will. Would that others did."

The boy reached from under the blankets and took her hand in his. "Your hands are cold."

"That's just from seeing your father off." After a time, she withdrew her hands. "Go back to sleep."

This time, he did not find sleep again until it was almost dawn.

1

The two gray-clad imagers sat in the two chairs before the oblong desk. The prematurely gray-haired one glanced at the timepiece on the corner of the desk, and its sands flowing from the top of the glass to the bottom.

"Do you have to go?" asked Cyran, the younger of the two men, if only by a few years, although some silver hairs streaked his blond thatch.

"Not quite yet. I'm supposed to meet the rex at half past eighth glass. He'd be happier if it were sixth glass."

"Is he that early a riser?"

"Supposedly. He always looks tired, even when he's angry, and that's more often the case than not."

"Alastar . . . don't you think you're acceding to his wishes too much? Even Maitre Fhaen . . ."

"He is the source of almost all our funding. That's barely enough right now, as I pointed out at the last meeting of the senior maitres. The drought in the southeast, around Piedryn, and the last rains here and in the west, have halved crop yields, and prices are going up . . . and will increase more. Then there's the small matter that the Collegium's charter is to support the rex, and that means against the High Holders and everything else. In the past, that's meant support against the army High Command as well, but with Demykalon only recently becoming marshal, it's hard to say."

"The word is that he doesn't like imagers."

"That's likely true." In fact, that had been one of the first things Alastar had learned after arriving at Imagisle. "That doesn't mean that Demykalon is that fond of the rex, and these days, Ryen also needs support against the factors' council."

"And everyone else, the Nameless knows," replied Cyran. "That puts us at odds with almost everyone."

"Ryen is far less than he could be, but would you want Demykalon, or any marshal running Solidar? Or High Holders Haebyn, Nacryon, and Guerdyn? Or any factor that you could name?"

"Especially Elthyrd. He's behind some new money-lending factorage, likely another excuse for usury on a larger scale."

"Oh . . . the new Banque D'Excelsis?" Alastar couldn't recall where he'd heard that.

"The word is that he put up the golds to back his son. What about Lorien? Would he be a better rex than his father?"

"Who knows? I've never met him, but it's hard to believe he couldn't do better than his sire, but that's not a certainty. In any event, we shouldn't be the ones making that choice. If it ever came out that we did . . . and it would come out, you know that as well as I . . ." Alastar did not finish the sentence, but he did not have to, he knew.

"It wouldn't be the end of the Collegium."

"If it weren't, it would come Namer-fired close." The Maitre of the Collegium Imago shook his head. "So we'll do our best to keep everyone at bay with everyone else until someone with sense shows up."

"As if anyone with sense would be stupid enough to let it be known," countered Cyran. "Do you know what Ryen wants?"

"No." Alastar stood, letting Cyran know that their talk was over. "I can hardly wait to find out what new scheme or pet peeve he's become obsessed with."

"Better you than me."

"Thank you, my friend." Alastar offered a warm smile, then watched as Cyran left the study. After a moment, he picked up a leather case and riffled through the papers inside, although he doubted that Ryen would wish to discuss what was contained in any of them, unless, of course, Alastar neglected to bring the folder. Then, after donning a riding jacket that matched his imager grays and the gray cap with its polished black leather visor, he made his way out of the study and along the corridor toward the older end of the administration building, that section constructed by the first imagers of the Collegium. *That was a much different time. Much different.*

He still found it almost unreal that he had been the second-highest imager at Westisle less than two months ago, or that Maitre Zhelan had turned down the opportunity to come to head the entire Collegium and had let it be known that Alastar should take the position. The more Alastar heard and saw, the more he understood at least some of the reasons Zhelan had demurred. At least, no one had asked him to go to Mont D'Image, the isolated northern town at the base of the Montagnes D'Glace that housed failed or disciplined imagers. He shuddered at that thought.

Outside the old main entrance, both his escorts were waiting, attired in the standard imager grays, with gray riding jackets and visor caps, given the stiff breeze and almost chill air of midfall. So was his mount, an older but not aged gray gelding, a symbolism that Alastar never voiced, but let others infer.

Although he could have summoned one of the Collegium carriages, he preferred to ride, even though that required two young imagers as escorts. While the two carried blades and truncheons, those were backed by imaging skills ranging from the simple expedient of imaging a cloud of fine pepper around the head of an assailant to imaging something into the body of an attacker.

Alastar looked at the gelding, murmured, "Here we go again, fellow," then mounted and urged the gelding forward. "The north bridge." He looked to the large gray stone dwelling at the north end of the green bordered by stone-paved lanes on each side. Unlike the family dwellings on each side of the green, it was two stories tall and extended a good forty yards across the front with a wide covered porch wrapping around it—a dwelling that would have been far too large for Alastar, a childless widower, were it not for his responsibilities for entertaining those within the Collegium and, occasionally, those from outside, although he had not done that in the brief time he had been on Imagisle. He turned toward the imager on his left. "How are your studies with Maitre Cyran coming, Belsior?"

"Well enough, sir."

"He mentioned that you have a tendency to be . . . excessively enthusiastic in imaging iron darts."

"Yes, sir. He made me understand that."

Alastar smiled at the understatement, knowing that Cyran had made the young man, a solid third, who might someday possibly become a Maitre D'Aspect, image darts until he collapsed, in little more than a tenth of a glass, then walked up to the fallen Belsior and put a sabre at his throat. "He does have a way about him."

At that, Neiryn, the other third, nodded.

Before long, the three were riding across the north bridge over the River Aluse. Once on the west shore, they turned north on the West River Road, threading their way past a wagon moving south and piled with bales of hay.

The shops that lined the west side of the road were neat enough, Alastar reflected, but definitely showed their age, unlike those on the East River Road. As they neared a point opposite the north end of Imagisle, Alastar again marveled, as he had every time he saw them, at the gray stone ramparts that sheathed the entire shoreline of the isle that held the Collegium. He still had a hard time believing that the first maitre had created those walls in a single day, although that was the story. For his own reasons, Alastar was loath to disabuse that rumor, as, he suspected, had been every Collegium Maitre since the first one. *Yet . . . even in a month or a season?*

At the west end of the Nord Bridge, the three turned their mounts onto the Boulevard D'Ouest, another wide stone-paved way said to have been created by the Collegium's first imagers, although the stones showed little if any wear, given that they had been laid nearly four hundred years earlier at the time of the consolidation of Solidar under Rex Regis. Then again, Alastar had to admit that those paving stones looked little different from the way the ones in Westisle had when he had first been an imager primus at that branch of the Collegium nearly thirty years ago.

As they rode closer to the Chateau D'Rex, the shops grew larger and their fronts newer, while the cafés and the occasional bakery sported awnings, although many of those were rolled up, most likely because of the brisk northwest wind. Where the boulevard intersected the ring road around the Chateau D'Rex, Alastar turned south and then took the lane up to the steps leading up to the main portico. At the foot of the steps, he dismounted and handed the gelding's reins to Belsior. "I have no idea how long I'll be here."

"Yes, sir," the two replied almost in unison.

Alastar took the steps, more than a score, reputedly imaged of near indestructible alabaster-like white stone by the Collegium's first imagers. He still wondered why they had not brought the approach lane higher so that there were fewer steps, but he supposed that was so that the grade to the stone plaza at the foot of the steps was gentle enough for wagons and carriages.

One of the guards escorted Alastar from the main entry up the grand staircase to the upper level of the chateau and then back along the north corridor to a chamber almost in the northeast corner, where another guard stood. The second guard rapped on the door. "Maitre Alastar, Your Grace."

"Send him in!"

The force of Ryen's words announced his mood, but Alastar smiled as he stepped into the study and walked toward the massive black oak desk that dominated the east end of the long chamber, on which were piled stacks of papers.

From where he sat behind the desk, the angular and near-cadaverous-looking Ryen glared. A too-long lock of black hair swept almost over his left eye. He wore a gold and gray striped tunic that did not become him over gray trousers, a far more conservative attire than that cultivated by most High Holders. "What took you so long?"

"The half-glass has not yet rung, sir."

"That doesn't matter. It still takes you too long to get here. It's not much more than a mille from Imagisle to the chateau."

"That is as the raven flies. There's no direct route from Imagisle to the chateau. I have to ride north to the Boulevard D'Ouest—"

"You've explained that before." Ryen smiled, the intense glare of the moment before instantly gone and replaced with an expression of total warmth. "We need to do something about that. I will obtain the land, and you and your imagers will build a new boulevard directly from the northern bridge . . . the bridge of wishes or whatever . . ."

"The Bridge of Desires," supplied the Collegium Maitre.

". . . directly to the chateau."

"Just to the ring road around the chateau," suggested Alastar, well aware of the rex's very literal mindset.

Ryen frowned.

Alastar refrained from sighing. "If we build it right to the entry portico, it will destroy your east gardens and make it harder for you and your family to get to the hunting park or the marshal's headquarters or anywhere else. The extra few hundred yards or so won't make any difference in the time it takes to get to and from Imagisle."

"To the ring road, then. But directly there from the bridge."

"Once you have arranged for the land, we will stand ready to begin work on the road. Now . . . what was the matter for which you requested my presence?"

"High Holder Guerdyn has said that the High Holders of all Solidar may refuse to pay their annual tariffs if I increase them in the coming year."

Refuse to pay? Unprecedented as that sounded, it didn't surprise Alastar after the rhetorical rumblings over the past season.

"This year's tariffs?" Alastar knew tariffs were due by the end of Feuillyt, thirty-two days away. "Or next year's?"

"They haven't said. I haven't asked. Yet. It's likely to be this year's tariffs. Why else would they say that now? I have to announce next year's tariffs before this year's are due."

"You *have* to?"

"It's in the codex."

"What if you don't?" *Who could make you?*

"According to the codex, they don't have to pay this year's tariffs until I announce next year's."

"That could pose a problem . . ." temporized Alastar, suspecting that if even a small fraction of the High Holders withheld tariff payments, Ryen—and the Collegium—would face difficult times before long, certainly within months, if not weeks.

"Pose a problem?" snapped Ryen. "There are Namer-fired few golds left in the treasury. They know that. There have been fewer every year by the end of harvest. That's why I need to increase the tariffs. They haven't been increased in years."

"What about the factors?"

"What about them? They don't have to pay, either."

"Could you leave the tariffs at the same level for next year, and say that they'll increase next year?"

"Are you an idiot, Maitre?!! That's how I got into this mess. That's what your predecessor suggested. Then he went and died."

Alastar managed not to swallow. Fhaen had never mentioned tariffs. Then, the former Maitre hadn't mentioned all too many problems. "Is Guerdyn speaking for himself or as chief of the High Council?"

"He can't speak for the High Council until they meet on the eighteenth of Feuillyt."

"Have you heard anything from the other four councilors?"

"Haebyn and Nacryon agree with Guerdyn. Moeryn and Vaun won't oppose me."

"Vaun won't be a councilor after Year-Turn," Alastar pointed out.

"I *know* that. I want you to do something about one of those against me."

"What would you suggest?"

"Whatever it takes." Ryen's smile vanished. "Those insufferable malcontents . . . privileged and spoiled brats . . . all of them . . ."

"That may be, sir, but if any of those three vanish or die suddenly, everyone will blame you. They will as well if any of them takes ill this soon before the High Council meets."

"Then find a way to get one of them to change his mind." The rex's voice turned cold. "Your predecessor was less . . ."

"Less willing to point out the unpleasantnesses? That is true." *And that was one of the reasons why the senior imagers continued to support him until almost the end.*

"I was sorry to learn of his passing." Ryen's voice softened, then turned colder once more. "You know that Demykalon doesn't like imagers, especially when they bring up the unpleasant."

"I'm well aware of the marshal's distaste for both scholars and imagers. Have you talked with him about this?"

"I'd prefer not to use force of arms at this point, or even threaten it. Haebyn and several others would refuse to pay until I put a battalion on his doorstep, and sending a battalion all the way to Piedryn would create problems I don't want to think about."

Alastar nodded. From what little he'd heard about Haebyn, and he had heard a few things, Haebyn never let go of a grudge, at least according to Maitre Zhelan.

"I'd end up having troopers riding everywhere. That would cost more golds. I won't countenance spending golds to obtain them. I won't!" Ryen's voice rose not quite to a shout.

Alastar waited a long moment. "The High Holders might raise private armies in return, and we'd have a civil war on our hands." *And because some of the commanders come from High Holder families, they might well not obey orders to discipline other High Holders.*

"I'm glad you include the Collegium as part of 'we.'" Ryen waved toward the study door. "Let me know when you've taken care of the problem."

"I'll look into it," replied Alastar. "Then we'll see."

"If you don't solve it, I'll have to cut the golds to the Collegium, you know."

"I'm well aware of the source of much of our funding, but at times, tightening one's belt is preferable to slitting one's throat." *Or the throats of innocent students and young imagers, which is more to the point.*

"I won't press the point, Maitre, but an increase in tariffs would serve us all far better than belt-tightening. That would only encourage more attempts to throttle us both in the future."

Alastar nodded, if reluctantly, although Ryen was

doubtless right. He turned and made his way from the rex's study, well aware that Ryen's gaze had turned to the window even before Alastar closed the study door on his way out.

On his ride back to the Collegium, Alastar pondered the situation facing both Ryen and the imagers . . . and the fact that Fhaen had never mentioned the tariff problem.

Once he was back in the administration building, he stopped at the table desk set in the anteroom outside his study and looked at the elderly imager secondus seated there. "Dareyn . . . would you please inform the senior imagers that there will be a meeting in the conference chamber at the first glass of the afternoon. It won't take long, but I expect all of them to be there." *Not that there are that many seniors these days.*

"Yes, Maitre."

"Thank you."

After Alastar returned to the study, his eyes took in the ancient Telaryn sabre mounted on a plaque hung on the wall behind the desk. Not for the first time, he wondered why the most tangible memorial remaining from the Collegium's founder was a sabre, given that the founder had been an imager. With a faint smile, he took his copy of the Collegium's master ledger from the small bookcase behind and left of his desk chair, sat down, and began to peruse the ledger. After that came an examination of the Collegium roster . . . and the revised junior imager training and academic program that he had proposed a month earlier, when he had become Maitre, and oh-so-slowly begun to implement. He was still going over that when Dareyn knocked.

"The others are all in the conference room, sir."

"Thank you." Alastar stood and left his study, crossed the anteroom, and entered the conference room, where he took his place at the head of the long, time-darkened, and well-polished oak table, glancing at the five senior imagers gathered there. Outside of Cyran and himself, there were only four others—Taryn, Akoryt, Desyrk, and Obsolym, all of those four Maitres D'Structure, although the white-haired Obsolym was barely that in terms of imaging ability.

"You're not going to bring up more changes to the academic, physical, and imaging training again, are you?" wheezed Obsolym.

"No, I'm not. I'm going to go over your roles in implementing it." *Since some of you aren't doing what is necessary.* "But before we get to that, I'm going to tell you why." He paused. "I had a meeting with Rex Ryen this morning."

"What did he want?" asked Cyran.

"He wants us to build an avenue straight from the Bridge of Desires to the ring road around the Chateau D'Rex. That was the more reasonable demand. After that, he effectively demanded that we make certain that the High Council does not vote to oppose the increase in tariffs on High Holders and factors that he intends to impose next year. That will require changing one of the probable votes in the coming High Council meeting because the High Council is opposed to paying any increase in tariffs. Ryen doesn't want to announce an increase if they'll vote to withhold their tariffs. They don't have to pay this year's tariffs until he announces next year's, and the treasury is almost empty."

"It's always been almost empty by the end of the year," declared Obsolym. "What about this avenue?"

"I told him we could do the road, but not until he owned the property and had made the arrangements. I also told him it would take weeks, possibly longer. The other matter is . . . more delicate and dangerous. I'd like each of your thoughts on that, especially given the precarious position the Collegium finds itself in." He looked to Taryn, the black-haired Maitre D'Structure to his left.

"Ryen hasn't been the best of rexes . . ."

That total understatement drew a few chuckles, mostly from Cyran and Desyrk.

". . . and he's never been predictable, but he has a point. We're struggling to pay for everything. The factors and the High Holders complain if we use imaging to make anything that cuts into what they do. The army consists of six regiments, or thirty battalions, and the navy is made up of a score of antique warships. Ryen barely rules, but a tariff increase is necessary." Taryn turned his head to the redheaded Akoryt, the youngest man at the table.

"The High Holders won't listen to reason," said Akoryt mildly. "They only respond to force. Force won't work with the factors. There are too many of them, and too few of us to intimidate enough of them to make a difference."

"The factors will follow the lead of the High Holders, though," added Cyran. "Even if they're not happy about it. So far, they have, anyway."

Desyrk cleared his throat. "My brother the commander has often pointed out that force is often the only thing that works. Force will turn everyone against us. That makes all the choices before the Collegium unpleasant." His brown eyes fixed on Alastar, then dropped.

"They are," responded Alastar. "When I was summoned here from Westisle by the former Maitre, I had no idea how much the position of the Collegium here had deteriorated. I have debated summoning several Maitres D'Aspect and perhaps one Maitre D'Structure from Westisle, but, if I did, they would not arrive for more than a month, perhaps not until mid- to late Finitas, and that will be too late for them to help with this difficulty." He paused, knowing what he was about to say would sound like ancient history, but knowing it had to be said. "The first imagers of the Collegium were warriors. They were survivors of prosecution and persecution and murder. They numbered only a handful, but they were battle-hardened veterans who had developed enormous powers, the kind of powers we've not pursued developing to that degree in all imagers. We've neglected them because that kind of upbringing, testing, and training kills nine out of ten would-be imagers." *As it almost has you several times.* "As some of you know, as the senior imager of the Collegium in Westisle, I was criticized because my training methods resulted in greater losses of young imagers, even though what we did there was as nothing compared to what those first imagers endured. If imagers are to survive in Solidar, we must toughen our studies and our training."

"The kind of training you're talking about takes time and patience," declared Taryn. "You're right about how we should train imagers in the future. That was why I supported Maitre Fhaen's decision to summon you, but we have to deal with the problems we're facing now."

"You're absolutely right," agreed Alastar. "We can't rush training of the younger imagers. In fact, their training will have to take longer if it is to be effective. That means we must deal with Ryen and the High Holders by subterfuge, give the impression of greater strength than we have in fact, and create the sense that we are forbearing use of mighty powers in the hope that the High Holders will come to their senses."

"You and Cyran are the only ones with those kinds of abilities, especially at a distance," pointed out Desyrk. "Even you two might be pressed against the latest cannon of the army. Or the focused fire of the heavy rifles."

"When do you intend to make all these changes?" demanded Obsolym.

"We've already started. You know that. Maitre Cyran is working with the most promising seconds and thirds to develop shields and other capabilities sooner in their studies."

"The older way was safer," declared Obsolym.

"Safer for the individual imager at the time, but failing

to develop imaging capabilities to a greater degree has put them more at risk than they ever would have been if we'd followed what I've set out." *Or what we began two years ago at Westisle.* "Something like ten imagers brought Rex Kharst and Bovaria to their knees. Ten. We have close to a hundred, between L'Excelsis and Westisle, and I doubt that any of us could image a fraction of what those ten could do." Alastar was understating slightly, because he and Cyran could do quite a bit more than a fraction, but nothing close to what the structures created by the legendary Quaeryt and even the less legendary Elsior showed was possible. "Now we're faced with a near-impossible situation, and we're in that position because we've pampered ourselves and the young imagers."

"You can't change that overnight," Obsolym pointed out.

"You're absolutely right," Alastar repeated, hating to keep harping on the situation, but knowing that at times repetition was necessary, "but the sooner we begin, the sooner we can begin to change matters, and improve our situation." *If we can hold off Ryen, the marshal, the High Holders, and the factors . . . and possibly even the guilds.* "Now . . . let me go over the outline of the training program . . . and what I expect of each of you. I'm open to any suggestions about improving matters . . ." Alastar had no doubt that the meeting would last at least another glass, but he had to make certain that each senior imager understood not only his responsibilities but also the responsibilities of every other imager.

2

Meredi morning just after seventh glass, a good glass and a half after rising, and after an easy run around Imagisle, Alastar stood in the rear courtyard of the armory, watching as Cyran conducted a training session with imager seconds. A cool wind continued to blow, and Alastar could see a line of gray clouds above the walls to the northwest.

As Maitre of the Collegium, Alastar needed to meet with High Holder Guerdyn, but that required finding out where Guerdyn might be. Whatever High Holder served as head of the High Council could use a comparatively modest but elegant chateau just off the West River Road about a half mille north of the Boulevard D'Ouest. That dwelling, although too small to accurately be termed a chateau, also served as the meeting place for the High Council. Unfortunately, because High Holder Guerdyn had his personal chateau and holding only ten milles east of L'Excelsis, Alastar had to send one of the young imagers as a courier to determine if Guerdyn was at the Council Chateau or at his own holding, and if he happened to be in L'Excelsis, to have the courier request a meeting for the afternoon.

Since worrying would not bring a reply any sooner, Alastar forced his concentration back to the courtyard. Leaning against the stone wall at the west end were wooden targets cut into shapes representing troopers in various positions. Standing to Alastar's right, a few paces from the east wall, were Cyran and seven imagers second, five males and two females, ranging in age from ten to fifteen, not old enough to be men and women, and too old to be boys and girls. The distance from the imagers to the targets was close to thirty yards. A large pile of iron scrap stood in the corner of the courtyard nearest the young imagers, a necessity to keep the seconds from drawing iron from the armory itself, weakening the building or the pitifully few weapons stored there.

"When I point to you," ordered Cyran, "image an iron dart into the target in front of you with enough force to hold. I won't point in order. So watch me." He pointed and snapped, "Beltran!"

A sliver of iron, hardly a dart, appeared in the target opposite the second, wobbling and barely sticking.

"That wouldn't even cause a coney to halt," observed Cyran. "Oestyl!"

A shorter, broader, and younger second concentrated, and a knife-shaped dart bounced off a target, not even the one directly before Oestyl.

"You can make the dart smaller. You don't need a hilt, but you need more power. It would also help if it went where it was supposed to. Julyan!"

Julyan's dart was smooth and deadly and buried itself halfway through the thick plank from which the target had been cut.

"Good! Now you, Celiena!"

The young woman did not seem to concentrate, but a perfectly shaped dart struck the target, but barely hard enough to stick in the tough wood.

"Excellent dart. You need to find more power. Aelbryt!"

Aelbryt's dart looked more like a spear point. It hit the target, held for a moment, then dropped to the stones below.

"You need more power, young man. Much more," declared Cyran.

Alastar walked over to the other maitre. "You'll keep them at it until they're exhausted . . . then bring them back for another session late this afternoon?" His words were barely a question.

Cyran nodded. "They're a bit tired already. They ran a mille first. They'll need to work up to two milles without collapsing. I had them imaging salt mist and fine pepper after that."

"I'll see you later." Alastar left the armory courtyard quietly, still holding full shields, as part of his own efforts to maintain his abilities amid all the politics and planning, not to mention trying to unscramble the finances and administration of the Collegium. As he passed the locked door to the armory, he wondered again why the Collegium even bothered with an armory, or had it just remained from the time centuries ago when a regiment had been quartered on Imagisle? *So many useless remnants combined with an education little more than meaningless memorization of rhetoric and rote imaging.* If it weren't for the fact that imagers needed a strong Collegium in L'Excelsis, where it could effect the rex and the High Council, Alastar would have been tempted to close Imagisle and ship all the imagers to Westisle. But that would just delay the decline of imager power, when what was necessary was to reverse that decline and reestablish the power of the Collegium in L'Excelsis—close to the rex and the High Council.

After he returned to the administration building, he went to the archives, overseen by Obsolym, who was absent at the moment. The archives were one of the few areas of the Collegium that did happen to be well-organized, and Alastar wanted to see what he could find about the past history of the present members of the High Council. Not surprisingly, he found nothing, except their names, as well as the names of every councilor who had served since the time of Elsior. *Elsior, not Quaeryt?* When he returned to his study, he took down the copy of the legal codex of Solidar, supposedly yet another creation of the legendary Quaeryt, and opened it, thinking as he did, *Was there any aspect of the founding of Solidar that wasn't his doing? No man could do all that.*

It took him almost half a glass to find what he sought, and he had barely given himself a self-congratulating nod when Dareyn rapped on his door.

"Imager third Glaesyn is here, sir."

"Have him come in."

The young man who entered was tall and broad-shouldered. From his observations and inquiries, Alastar knew he had an even disposition and was probably unlikely to progress beyond third, even with the more demanding training exercises that Cyran had begun to implement.

"Did you find High Holder Guerdyn, or one of his assistants?"

"Yes, sir. He was at the Council Chateau. He took the message himself. He said he would be pleased to grant you a meeting at half past second glass at the Council Chateau, despite the short notice."

Pleased to grant you a meeting? Not "pleased to meet with you"? Or "honored to meet with you"? "Were those his exact words?"

"Yes, sir. You told me to report back exactly what he said."

"Thank you. You've done well. I'll need you and another third as escorts at a half past second glass. Tell Imager Dareyn that, and have him work it out with Maitre Desyrk."

"Yes, sir."

For the next glass, Alastar pondered how far he needed to go with High Holder Guerdyn, jotting down thoughts . . . and rejecting most of them. Then he walked to the front of the building, carrying an oiled leather cloak in case the growing clouds decided to drop rain on L'Excelsis before he returned.

With Tertius Glaesyn was Chervyt, another third no

longer a student. Chervyt held the reins to Alastar's gray gelding.

"Thank you," the Maitre offered as he took the reins and then mounted. "We'll take the north bridge."

From the time his gelding reached the slightly raised middle of the north bridge, formally called the Bridge of Desires, until he left the bridge and turned north on the West River Road, Alastar studied the buildings to the west of the bridge, knowing that, regardless of what Ryen had said, some of the crafters and owners of other buildings would suffer as a result of the rex's desire for a direct route between the Chateau D'Rex and Imagisle.

Somewhat more than half a glass later, the three crossed the Boulevard D'Ouest. Even from a half mille away, Alastar could see their destination clearly because the chateau stood on a low rise.

"Is that it, sir?" asked Chervyt. "The Council Chateau, I mean?"

"The building on the low hill? It is indeed."

A pair of guards in maroon livery opened the large, wrought-iron, double gates hung on gray stone pillars more than three yards high, then closed them almost silently, except for a slight squeaking. Although too small to be a true chateau, the High Council Chateau was definitely imposing, with a stone wall almost as high as the gate posts surrounding the grounds, a good quarter mille on a side, and with formal gardens on both sides of the stone-paved lane up to the dwelling itself, three stories high, a frontage width nearly twice that of the Maitre's dwelling at the Collegium, with a slate-tiled roof, wide windows on the upper two levels, and a covered entry portico wide enough for two coaches. Alastar had also heard that the rear wing held a sizable ballroom that opened out onto a formal walled garden, but, if so, that part of the chateau was not visible from the front lane.

A footman in the same maroon livery stepped out

from the bronzed double doors at the entry to the chateau and descended two of the four wide stone steps before saying, "Maitre Alastar, welcome to the Council Chateau."

Alastar dismounted and handed the reins to Glaesyn. "You can dismount, but wait here. It may be a while." *And it may not.* He wasn't about to voice that thought as he strode up the steps after the footman and into the circular entry hall beyond the double doors, tucking his visor cap under his arm.

The footman closed the door. "High Holder Guerdyn will be here shortly." Then he departed down the corridor leading directly back from the entry.

The hall itself was spacious, some eight yards across, with a domed ceiling as high as the hall was across. Alastar stood alone in the circular entry hall for only a few moments, just enough to make the point that the High Councilor could make the Maitre wait, before a tall man with gray-shot brown hair and a warm and very practiced smile appeared. Guerdyn wore a gold and black doublet with black hose and shoes, and a black jacket trimmed in gold.

Quite a contrast, thought Alastar, given that he, and all imagers, wore deep gray shirts, trousers, and jackets, with black boots and belts.

"Maitre Alastar . . . I've heard so much about you. I wondered when you might attend to the High Council."

"Attending to the High Council will always be a priority of mine, and to the councilors, beginning, of course, with you." Alastar smiled, imaging a sense of warmth as well. "I would have attended to you sooner, if not for rather more pressing matters at the Collegium."

"Ah, yes . . . the death of Maitre Fhaen. A pity. He always understood the . . . shall I say, delicacy of the relationships between the High Council and Rex Ryen." Guerdyn presented a pleasant smile. "We should continue our chat in the study. It's quite comfortable there."

"Then lead the way." Alastar offered the words lightly.

Even so, Guerdyn stiffened almost imperceptibly, if but for an instant. He turned and walked toward the archway on the right.

Alastar followed, a half pace behind.

Guerdyn did not speak until he stopped opposite the third door on the right and gestured. "This is the receiving study." Two sets of armchairs were spaced in a circle around a low table on which refreshments might be placed, with two higher side tables set between the two chairs on each side.

"From where one can see whom one might be receiving," said Alastar after entering and observing that the windows afforded a clear view of the entry portico.

"It does come in useful at times." Guerdyn motioned toward one chair, then the one across from it, before seating himself in the first.

"All knowledge is useful, and those of us in the Collegium endeavor to understand even that which is never mentioned. It's one of our vices, I fear, you know, knowledge not just for power, but also for its own sake."

"Acquiring some knowledge may be more costly than it is wise to purchase."

"You are doubtless correct in that," replied Alastar as he seated himself across from Guerdyn, not that he hadn't thought of taking one of the other chairs. "The problem there is that one does not know the value of such knowledge until after it has been obtained. While I have the feeling you care little for anything that is not useful, usefulness is often hard to determine in advance."

Guerdyn offered a cool smile. "I do have a fondness for a few items of beauty that may have limited usefulness, but only a few."

"Artworks? Sculpture? Views from your chateau? Poetry?"

"They're few and eclectic. Some day, if you visit my own chateau, I'd be pleased to show you." Guerdyn's smile vanished. "You've been Maitre for little more than a month, and you've not been in L'Excelsis much longer than that. Many were surprised by how quickly you became Maitre, and that you were called here to become Maitre rather than Maitre Zhelan, especially since Maitre Fhaen wasn't that old, as I recall."

"No . . . but he had a progressive flux of the lungs, not consumption, but the results were the same. He summoned me when he realized his days might be limited." In point of fact, Alastar suspected Cyran and some of the more junior maitres, likely pressed by Shaelyt, had persuaded Fhaen to do so, but Cyran had avoided any direct answers to general inquiries, and Alastar hadn't felt it wise to press. As it was, Fhaen had lived only a few days beyond the week after Alastar had arrived. "Maitre Zhelan had long let it be known that he had no intention of leaving Westisle." What Alastar wasn't about to say was that Zhelan had already been feeling uncomfortable about Alastar's greater abilities as an imager, and by refusing the post as titular head of the overall Collegium, Zhelan could maintain his position and allow Alastar to advance without overtly ever admitting Alastar's superiority.

"That hasn't caused a problem? He was senior to you . . ."

"I can assure you Maitre Zhelan is most happy with the situation. If you wish to write him, I am certain he will confirm that. He would confirm that in private with no witnesses."

At Alastar's last statement, Guerdyn laughed softly. "I already knew that. I wondered if you would confirm it."

Alastar shrugged. "I'm not surprised."

"I presume you are here at the rex's behest to inquire about the High Council's opposition to his proposed increase in tariffs?"

"I'm not aware of any proposal. If the rex were to

decide to increase tariffs, it would not be a proposal. It would be the law. As a measure affecting all Solidar it falls under the definition of High Justice under the original legal codex of Solidar."

"So he did instruct you to talk to me about the tariffs?"

"That is obviously a matter of interest to both the rex and the Collegium, but he did not instruct me to see you, or even suggest that I do so."

"Then might I ask what he expects of you and the Collegium?"

"You can certainly ask, but you would know his expectations, far better than I would, since you have dealt with him for far longer than I. What do you think they might be?"

"His intentions are obvious. He wishes to strengthen his position at the expense of both the High Holders and the factors."

"His position or that of Solidar as a whole?"

"Most of the wealth and productive resources of Solidar belong to the factors and the High Holders. Anything that weakens either weakens Solidar."

"You don't consider the small holders, the laborers, or the crafters of the guilds as productive resources?"

"You're sounding very much like an advocate, Maitre Alastar."

"Perhaps . . . but it is a fair question."

"They produce, but they would produce little without what the High Holders and factors do. Higher tariffs would hurt them more than anyone. That is another reason why, if the rex were to propose an increase in tariffs, it would be a poor idea."

"You believe that rather strongly, but . . . as I observed before, if the rex decides to increase tariffs, it is not a proposal. It is the law. Tariffs do not have to be paid, I understand, until he does set the levels for the following year, but there is no provision for withholding of tariffs once the rex does so. How the law is enforced . . . or how lawbreakers are treated . . . is up to the High Justicers. Of course, it might not come to that." Alastar uttered the last few words softly.

"That would appear to be a threat, Maitre."

Alastar shook his head. "The Collegium cannot afford to make threats. If you examine my words, you will find everything I stated is of a factual nature."

"Then you have made a factual threat."

"I have said that, if the rex increases tariffs, it is not a proposal, but a law, and he has the power to make that law to raise golds. Anyone affected by a law who does not abide by it is a lawbreaker. If High Holders break the law, their cases are decided by a High Justicer, not by the rex. If the rex imposes a tariff increase, and High Holders pay it, then it will not come to lawbreaking. How is that a threat?"

"You are fencing with words." For the first time, Guerdyn's voice hardened.

"And you are not?" Alastar smiled gently. "Besides, and more important, fencing with words is far less destructive than doing so with blades or golds . . . or other methods. Isn't that why everyone agreed on a legal codex when Solidar was founded?"

Abruptly, Guerdyn nodded. "That is a very good point. Thank you for bringing it up."

"You're welcome." Alastar immediately worried about Guerdyn's reaction to what he had said. *You've given him a tool, and you don't even know what it is.*

"Now that we've talked around that point," Guerdyn said easily, "might I ask what your plans for the Collegium are?"

"I'm happy to tell you. We're strengthening the requirements for studies and imager training for students, and we're looking into areas where imagers can produce goods that are wanted and necessary, but which do not compete with those produced by either factors or High Holders."

"Admirable goals. The first is certainly attainable. I would be curious about the second."

Alastar laughed. "I'm curious as well. We're not so far along in that, but the last thing the Collegium needs is to compete with either High Holders or factors. First, it doesn't make sense, because there are so few imagers that trying to make something that others can produce by the score seems unwise, and frankly, not terribly profitable. Second, I'd prefer to see the Collegium, the High Holders, and the factors working harmoniously, rather than in competition."

"I fear you have your work cut out for you, Maitre."

Alastar could tell that the two would exchange pleasantries and generalities for a time yet, before Guerdyn signaled that it was time to end the discussion . . . and that was perfectly fine with Alastar, since he had learned what he needed to know—for the moment.

3

After briefly meeting with the senior imagers early on Jeudi morning in the conference room, Alastar returned to his study to go over the list of imagers, both those considered full imagers, and those who were student imagers. *Another thing you should have done earlier . . .*

As he suspected, there were less than a double handful from factor families, and exactly two from High Holder families. The first was Alyna, a Maitre D'Aspect, who was the Maitre in charge of the female students and who also taught mathematics. She had been Alyna D'Zaerlyn. That meant, given her age, that she was likely the sister of the current Zaerlyn D'Alte, rather than of his late sire. The other was Arion, the son of Calkoran D'Alte, still a student, some fifteen years old, although he had enough promise that he was already a tertius, and, if he did not do something incredibly stupid, might well become a Maitre D'Aspect within a few years, if not sooner.

Because Alastar didn't recognize any of the parents of the seven student imagers and the two full imagers from factoring families, he wrote down the names of the nine, then walked out to the anteroom.

"Sir?" asked Dareyn.

"I'd like to find out more about the parents of these students and the two imagers. You can ask the imagers, but I'd prefer you didn't ask the students. They might get the wrong impression."

"I can see what I can find out, Maitre."

"I'd also like to find out, without it coming from me or the Collegium, whether High Holders Haebyn and

Nacryon have arrived in L'Excelsis and where they might be staying. More immediately, send someone to find Obsolym. I'd like to talk to him for a moment."

Dareyn nodded.

Alastar walked back into his study. *Are there any imagers whose fathers are senior officers in the army?* The only way he might be able to find that out would be to obtain the names of the senior commanders, but he didn't want to request that list from Marshal Demykalon, or in any way that could be traced to the Collegium, and he didn't know anyone at the Chateau D'Rex well enough to ask either. He paused. Desyrk had mentioned that his brother was a commander. Somehow . . . trying to get a list that way didn't seem like the best idea. *That will have to wait.*

He'd barely settled behind his desk when Dareyn knocked and then opened the door. "Sir? I thought you should know. One of the imager students, Secondus Dylert, had an accident. He has severe burns on one hand and his arm."

"How is he doing? How did that happen?"

"Maitre Gaellen says he'll recover, but he wants to keep him in the infirmary for a few glasses. It was something about imaging lamp oil."

Alastar shook his head. "I'm waiting for Obsolym. After I meet with him, I'll go over and see Gaellen and the student. Thank you for letting me know."

Dareyn nodded, then closed the study door.

Imaging and lamp oil? Alastar decided not to speculate. He'd find out soon enough.

In less than a tenth of a glass, Obsolym arrived and seated himself in front of Alastar's desk. "You may be getting results with this new training, but one or more of those young imagers will die."

"That's possible, but if I don't, the Collegium will die." At that moment, Alastar wasn't about to mention

Dylert's injury, especially since he didn't know the details. Obsolym would find out quickly enough, anyway, and likely bring it up at the next meeting of senior imagers. "That's not why I asked you here. You've been here the longest, and you're the archivist, and I'd like your thoughts on another matter." Alastar couldn't understand how the old Maitre D'Structure could be a historian of sorts and not understand the lessons of history, but he'd already decided that there was little point in raising that question. "Both Maitre Alyna and Tertius Arion come from High Holder families. What can you tell me about their backgrounds?"

"You don't know about Alyna, sir?"

"If I did, I wouldn't have asked. I grew up in Liantiago, not in L'Excelsis. What is so obvious that I should know and don't?"

"She's a descendant of Quaeryt and Vaelora."

"I wasn't aware . . . they only had daughters, didn't they?"

Obsolym nodded. "Their eldest daughter Chaerilla was a powerful imager, or so it is noted in the archives, and she played a part in putting down the Solian revolt when the High Holders around Solis—"

"Just a part?" asked Alastar dryly. "With her heritage . . ."

"She may have done more, but the Collegium records do not contain any detailed account, only that she and five other imagers were dispatched to Solis by Rex Clayar, and that she and three others returned after successfully dealing with the insurgents. There are detailed records of who obtained the holdings of the rebels, but nothing more about Chaerilla, except that she served for many years as the senior imager."

"Senior imager? The second only to the Maitre?"

"She was the senior imager for three different Maitres, beginning with the last years of Elsior."

Because she thought a woman Maitre would make matters too difficult for the Collegium? "And she only had daughters, too?" That was a guess.

"Two. Apparently, neither were imagers. Neither were their daughters. Daughters seemed to run in the family. One of their descendants married the heir to a high holding and became Vaelia D'Zaerlyn."

"And Alyna is not only the sister of Zaerlyn D'Alte, but distantly related to Rex Ryen?" *And to Quaeryt and Vaelora.*

Obsolym nodded.

"What about Tertius Arion?"

"His father is Calkoran D'Alte. He has a sizable holding in Vaestora—that's a pleasant town well south of Rivages. He's one of the few Pharsi High Holders in this part of Solidar. That's about all I know."

"How did you come to be an imager?"

For an instant, the white-haired maitre frowned, as though the change of subject had been unexpected and not totally welcome. "The same as many, I would suppose, sir. My father was a tinsmith in Tuuryl. He found me imaging holes in tin plate he'd hammered out. Before I knew it, I was here on Imagisle. I can't say I regret it. There have been times . . ." He shook his head. "There are always times."

"That's true. What do you think has changed the most since you came here?"

"Not too much changed until Maitre Fhaen got ill. Then he began to demand more, and he sent for you. They'll change more, won't they?" The last words were more of a challenge than a question.

"They'll have to. The High Holders and possibly even the factors are thinking of defying the rex. No matter how that turns out, nothing will be the same after that. What do you think of young Lorien?"

"The heir? I've never met him. Maitre Fhaen always

said he seemed more sensible than his sire, but that wouldn't be hard, according to what I hear. There's a reason so many call Ryen Rex Dafou behind his back."

"Can you name any factors who have shown an interest in the Collegium in recent years?"

Obsolym frowned, tilted his head, then worried his lips before he finally spoke. "Factor Wylum . . . his son Gherard is a student . . . a secondus . . . Factor Veramur . . . he has a . . . niece . . ."

"Niece . . . as in the daughter of his mistress?" asked Alastar dryly.

"I would surmise so, but Maitre Fhaen never said."

Alastar waited.

"Factoria Kathila . . . her daughter . . . she often inquires."

Alastar did not speak for a moment, considering that out of the hundred or so full factors, those meriting the title Factorius or Factoria, there was only a handful of women. "Why? Don't they speak?"

Obsolym shook his head. "Young Seconda Thelia had a privileged life. Factoria Kathila is on the factors' council."

Meaning that she is very rich and powerful. "What does she factor?"

"Jewels, fine fabrics, oils, scents, all manner of soaps . . . and . . . ah . . ."

It took a moment for Alastar to put the pieces together. "Rendering and tanning? Where she obtains the fats and materials to provide the substance for those soaps, potions, and lotions?"

"Yes, sir."

Most interesting. "Any others?"

"There must be, sir, but I'm not aware of who they might be."

After Obsolym left, Alastar sat at the desk. He'd been so preoccupied with cleaning up all the loose ends within the Collegium in the short period since he'd arrived in L'Excelsis that he'd had little time to learn more about the problems outside the Collegium. *And now it's becoming all too apparent that you should have learned more . . . as if you'd had any time for that.* He took a long slow breath, then stood and left the study, pausing for a moment to address Dareyn. "I'm headed over to the infirmary. I'll be back shortly."

"Yes, sir."

Alastar walked down the long corridor to the old main entrance and then outside, wincing at the odor that assailed him even before he could start to cover the fifty yards or so to the infirmary, a comparatively small structure that held a few treatment rooms, a surgery, and eight other chambers, each of which could hold two beds. What made the stench worse was that the air was heavy and still. Every day the odors escaping from the sewers on the east side of the River Aluse seemed to worsen, while Ryen and the factors' council each insisted it was the other's responsibility to remedy the problem.

The imager second on infirmary duty must have seen the Collegium Maitre approaching, because Gaellen was waiting in the small entry hall when Alastar entered.

"Greetings, Maitre. You're here about Dylert?"

"What else?" asked Alastar, his voice dryly warm. "Or are there more injuries or illnesses you haven't mentioned?"

"Outside of two cases of mild flux, likely caused by eating in the wrong places in L'Excelsis, and Dylert, the infirmary is, thanks to the Nameless, without others who are ill."

"Do you know how Dylert burned himself?"

"I didn't ask. I thought you or Maitre Cyran would be more effective. Besides, if I ask too much, some of them aren't likely to come here when they should."

Alastar didn't like that idea, but he did understand. "How badly was he burned?"

"Not so badly as it could have been. There's one place on the top of his forearm that needed a dressing. We'll have to watch that. One of the junior seconds, Thelia, got most of the burn in a bucket of cool water fairly soon. She made him walk over here with his arm in the bucket. I asked her how she knew that. She said she knew about burns from hot oil."

Thelia . . . the daughter of the factoria? Maybe she isn't so spoiled as Obsolym thinks . . . but what was she doing in the young men's quarters? Alastar repressed a sigh. He'd have to look into that as well. "Where is he?"

"The third door back past the surgery on the left."

"I'll let you know." Alastar smiled wryly, then made his way past the closed door to the surgery and past the open doors of the next two chambers, both of which held imagers, each young man seemingly asleep, although Alastar had his doubts. The third door was only ajar, and he pushed it open and stepped into the room.

Dylert sat in a wooden armchair, wearing only an undertunic, the right sleeve of which had been cut off at mid-biceps. Immediately below the ragged linen, there was a dressing around his arm above the elbow. Below the elbow, Dylert's right forearm was bare, but bright red, as if badly sunburned, and his wrist and hand were also red.

"Maitre, sir . . ." The student imager started to rise.

"Just stay seated." Alastar gestured. "Tell me how you managed to get this burn. The whole story, please, including the parts that might reveal your stupidity. The fact that you're here already reveals that." Alastar's voice remained pleasant, as if he were asking about the weather or what the imagers' dining hall might be serving that evening.

Dylert swallowed. "Ah . . . sir . . ."

"Go on."

"My chamber is on the lower level. It's dark. I had some time before I was to go to exercises with Maitre Cyran. So I took the lamp outside. I know it's not wise to image in the quarters. I imaged oil into the reservoir.

I don't know what happened, but there was lamp oil everywhere, and it caught fire . . ." The student shook his head.

"The lamp wasn't lit, I hope?"

"No, sir."

Alastar nodded. "I think I know what happened. First, you imaged too much oil, and it spurted out everywhere. Second, I suspect you thought of the lamp as being lit when you imaged the oil into it. That would account for why everything caught fire." He paused. "Weren't you told not to image anything without permission?"

"Yes, sir."

Alastar could see that Dylert had almost said more. "But you've done it before, and nothing happened?"

"Yes, sir." The admission was grudging.

More sloppiness. "I want you to remember what I'm about to say. If you don't remember and practice what I'm about to tell you, sooner or later, your imaging will kill you." Alastar paused. "Imaging is controlled by your thoughts and concentration. If you do not concentrate exactly on what you are doing, on precisely the image you need for that imaging, you create great danger for yourself. The errant thought of a lit lamp and a lack of precision in how much oil you needed for the lamp created burning oil over your arm and wrist. You're fortunate that imager grays are thick and that Seconda Thelia knew what to do."

"Yes, sir."

"You are not to do *any* imaging from now on unless a maitre is present. Is that clear?"

"Yes, sir."

"I'd also like to know what Seconda Thelia was doing to be close enough to keep the burn from being even worse."

Dylert flushed. "I didn't know she was anywhere near. I wouldn't have done it if I knew she was."

"*She* was? Or anyone?"

"Anyone, but . . ."

"But especially her? Why?"

"It's just . . . sir . . ." Dylert's mouth moved, spasmodically, before he finally added, "It's . . . she looks . . . like . . . she knows everything . . . and everyone else . . . they're stupid . . ."

"I see." There was obviously something more to Seconda Thelia. *You should meet with her. But then, you should meet with each of the student imagers . . . and before too long.* Along with everything else. "It's clear she knew enough to keep that burn from being worse. It's also clear that you knew what you were doing wasn't something you should have been doing. Where were you? In that grassy space behind the quarters that's surrounded on three sides by bushes?"

"Yes, sir."

"For now, you're restricted to Imagisle. Once your arm is healed, you'll have some extra duties to do."

"Yes, sir."

With that, Alastar turned and left the room.

"What did you tell him?" asked Gaellen when Alastar reached the infirmary entrance. "Besides his being fortunate he didn't kill himself?"

"That he would if he didn't concentrate more when he imaged . . . and that he's restricted to Imagisle."

"In the past . . ."

"*That* will change . . . if it takes locking up imagers in a lead-lined room." Alastar nodded and made his way from the infirmary. He still had trouble believing how far the Collegium in L'Excelsis had fallen in a generation.

Dareyn looked up from his desk as Alastar walked back toward his study. "I have that information, sir."

"Come on in." Alastar had to force pleasantness into his voice. He stopped beside his own desk and turned, but did not sit down. "What have you found out?"

"Both Haebyn and Nacryon have residences in L'Excelsis. I have directions to each."

"Good . . . and thank you. I'd like to have a few moments with Haebyn in the next day or so. I'll draft a polite request, and you can send one of the imager couriers."

"Yes, sir."

"I also need to start meeting with each of the student imagers. We'll start next week with the older thirds . . . no more than a quint of a glass with each . . ." Alastar went on to explain how he wanted Dareyn to explain the meetings to the students . . . and to any other imagers who asked.

Once he finished with that explanation, he picked up the visor cap from the side table, donned it, and headed for the stables. As he strode along the paved walk close to the carriage house, he nodded as he saw the broad-shouldered, but almost squat and stocky figure of Petros, the graying Maitre D'Aspect who was in charge of the stables, mounts, wagons, and carriages of the Collegium. Petros was instructing one of the teamsters about a harness, it appeared.

Alastar waited until the other maitre stepped away from the teamster. "Good afternoon, Petros."

"The same to you, Maitre Alastar. What might you be needing?"

"I'd like you to accompany me on a ride along the East River Road. I need a maitre who's been here awhile and who has a strong stomach. And some other experience."

"Heading south, perhaps?" Petros grinned.

"I had that in mind. I'll tell you more once we're on our way."

Petros nodded. "Do you need your mount saddled?"

"I'll do that myself." Alastar had a little time, and he didn't want to get totally out of the habit of doing so.

A quint later, the two rode across the narrow stone

span of the east bridge, only wide enough for a single horse or a small cart at best, another aspect of the Collegium that Alastar had not had a chance to pursue, since most of the people in L'Excelsis lived on the east side of the River Aluse. *But then, the Collegium gets most of its provisions from the west.* Still . . .

That inquiry would have to wait.

At the east end of the bridge, Alastar gestured to the left. "We'll ride up to the Nord Bridge and then back." The smell of sewage was muted, most likely because the light wind was coming out of the northwest.

"What are we looking for?"

"Where the odors from the sewers are the worst and what might be the causes."

"You know I'm not the most accomplished of imagers, sir?"

Alastar was well aware of that. Petros barely met the standards of a tertius, but he'd been granted the rank of Maitre D'Aspect because of his value to the Collegium in his position as stablemaster, trainer, and quartermaster. "That's not why I wanted you to come. I understand that you were the one who supervised the repair of the sewers for the newer student quarters." "Newer" was a relative term, since those buildings were more than a century old.

"Yes, sir, but I couldn't do the imaging. Not much of it, anyway. Young Cyran did the most."

And he's no longer so young. "I'm interested in your expertise, not your imaging." Alastar guided the gelding to the side of the road in order to avoid a high-sided wagon filled with barrels, most likely either ale or lager, then slowed the gelding as a beggar stepped forward, then scuttled back as he saw the gray imager jackets and trousers. The east side of the East River Road—actually a stone-paved avenue with stone sidewalks—north of the bridge to Imagisle was lined with shops of various sorts, including a milliner, two tailors in the first block, a cabinetmaker with a display window featuring an elaborate sideboard in what looked to be cherry, and several cafés. South of the bridge there were more factorages . . . and an older narrow stone building with barred windows bearing the signboard proclaiming BANQUE D'EXCELSIS.

Alastar reined up at the end of the first block, catching sight of the Yellow Rose, a theatre favored, so he had heard, by the younger merchanters and some offspring of High Holders, perhaps because most of the "productions" featured music and attractive young women who were often less than fully clothed, if tastefully so, according to Cyran. After a few moments, he and Petros continued northward, but even the faint odor of sewage vanished after another block, at which point he turned the gelding back south. Less than half a block past the narrow bridge to Imagisle, he could again begin to smell the odor of sewage. After another block it was almost overpowering. The paving blocks in the middle of the avenue slumped so that those in the middle were almost a hand lower than those on each side. While Alastar could see no signs of liquid, the mortar around the paving stones, where it even existed, was cracked and crumbled, and the odor was even stronger in the middle of the road.

He reined up at the west side of the road and motioned for Petros to join him, then said, "There's likely a problem here. I've done some searches of the records and made some inquiries. The top of the sewers here are only two yards down, if that, and they run down the middle of the road. The tunnel is an oval a yard and a half high and a yard across at the base, where it's flattened into a gentle curve that's almost level except for a slight depression in the center. They're supposed to be flushed all the time using a covered canal that takes water from the river a mille north of the Nord Bridge."

"It looks like the tunnel is leaking and the ground is

sinking. The sewers ought to be deeper, below the cellars of the buildings."

"We can't change that. I was thinking of uncovering them section by section where the odor is the worst and having the imagers repair the breaks and the drains from the buildings and the street. What would you suggest?"

Petros laughed, gruffly. "About what you have in mind, sir. Then you'll see whether it works."

Alastar laughed as well, adding, "No. *We*'ll see. You're going to be with me on this." He studied the center of the avenue. The depressed section of the pavement extended some fifty yards. "Can we do this part in a day, with all the senior imagers and the best five or six Maitres D'Aspect?"

"If you can keep folks away . . . maybe . . ."

"Maitre Cyran and I will also do what we can."

"You might be able to do that. After you do, you may find other leaks farther south."

"Let's hope that they're far enough south that the stench doesn't reach Imagisle." He shook his head. "If it does . . . we'll deal with that." He paused. "We might as well ride farther south, just to see."

The next three blocks showed no overt signs of sewer leakage, and the stench was less farther south, despite the slight breeze from the north.

"We can head back now." Alastar turned the gelding around in front of a large factorage bearing the name Alamara Artisans. He couldn't help but notice that there was no display window and that the single door was stout and brass-bound—and closed.

You can't pursue every strange situation you observe, not when you can't even resolve the problems you have. He resolutely turned away from the brass-bound door and urged the gray gelding northward toward the bridge.

4

Alastar was one of the first in the dining hall on Vendrei morning, after his run and washing up, as was usually the case, and he seated himself at the masters' table. He'd be fortunate if even one or two others joined him, since Taryn was the only other senior master who was not married, and of the eleven Maitres D'Aspect, only five were unmarried, including the only two female maitres. The unmarried status of the two women scarcely surprised Alastar.

He was sipping his tea and waiting for egg toast and bacon that he hoped was not too greasy when Taryn took the seat to his left. Shortly, Shaelyt and Alyna took seats to his right, but Shaelyt left an empty chair between himself and Alastar.

Alastar glanced at the pair of junior maitres and then at Taryn. "I haven't seen them together before."

"They're friends. Nothing more, I assure you."

"That's too bad," murmured Alastar. He didn't have to say why. Every senior imager knew that, almost always, the child of two imagers was also an imager, usually a girl—and female imagers were all too rare.

"You'd do anything to strengthen the Collegium, I think," replied Taryn, his voice low, but with a wide and humorous smile.

"Almost anything . . . almost." Alastar managed not to look dismayed when a server slipped a platter before him with egg toast so brown it was almost black and bacon that was anything but crisp. The small loaf of bread was warm, but might have served equally well as a brick, were there any need to build anything at the Collegium.

"Have you heard anything from His Mightiness, Rex Dafou?" inquired Taryn.

"It's best that reference remain behind closed doors. If junior imagers hear us calling him that, and they do the same . . ." He raised his eyebrows. "We're not exactly in anyone's good graces. I'm not disputing the judgment behind the appellation, just the wisdom of using the term."

"It's used openly by some of the High Holders."

"Did you hear that from Maitre Alyna? Or elsewhere?"

"She has friends her own age who still occasionally talk to her . . ."

Friends her own age . . . Taryn's words took Alastar aback, since he wasn't that much older than Alyna or most of the Maitres D'Aspect, just ten to fourteen years older than the youngest . . . and he was actually younger than Lhendyr or Mhorys or Petros. *Or is it the gray hair that makes them think you're that much older?*

". . . also heard words to the same effect from Tiranya, and I believe she might have heard them from Tertius Arion."

"I have my doubts that he was the source, but if she said she heard them, then I have no doubt she did. It's still not a good idea here."

Taryn nodded, then cut a piece of egg toast, wrapping it around a chunk of greasy bacon before eating both.

A low round of laughter ran along the table occupied by several seconds. Alastar focused on the table, where a thin-faced young secondus with too-long floppy brown hair mimed trying to saw through his chunk of bread, then lowered his knife with a smile of mock despair. The youth's expression was so despairing that Alastar had a hard time not laughing. So he turned to watch as Shaelyt gulped down the last bites of his egg toast and swallowed what remained in his mug, then rose, looking at Alyna as he said, "I need to prepare for the seventh-hour class with the primes and new seconds on government."

"... think about it ..."

Shaelyt smiled and hurried from the dining hall.

Alastar wished he had heard more of what the two had been discussing. He still wasn't convinced they were merely friends. *But that could be wishful thinking on your part.* He looked down at the dark brown egg toast and greasy bacon, and then resolutely took his cutlery in hand and set to eating. When he finished, he made his way back to the kitchen, not really wanting to, but if the cooks were serving him that badly cooked a breakfast, only the Nameless knew what the students were getting.

Shabrena, the head cook, hurried toward him, worry spread across her broad face. "Maitre ..."

"I know you and the others try hard, but egg toast should not arrive looking as though it were almost charcoal ... and if the stoves are that hot, why is the bacon so undercooked?"

"We had ... some trouble this morning, sir. It won't happen again."

Alastar smiled, politely. "Sometimes, those things do happen. We all understand that. They just shouldn't happen often. I'm sure you can make sure they don't."

"Yes, Maitre."

"Good." He smiled and turned.

In the short time between his entering the kitchen and then leaving, a number of primes and seconds had entered the dining hall and seated themselves, one table for primes, another for seconds, and a last one for thirds. The servers provided platters of egg toast and bacon, along with baskets of bread, for each table, replenishing them as necessary. As the number of imagers increased, so did the muted cacophony of conversation.

Alastar smiled faintly, then glanced back at Alyna, who, as the duty maitre for the day, remained at the maitres' table, watching the junior imagers, mostly students, except at the table reserved for the thirds, where perhaps half were unmarried but no longer students. He couldn't help but appreciate her thoughtful study of the students . . . or her infrequent smile.

Dareyn had not arrived when Alastar returned to the administration building, through still air and the continuing stench from the east side of the river. When he reached his study, because it was still slightly before sixth glass, he left the door ajar and proceeded to go through the roster of full imagers, trying to determine who might be better used in a different assignment, or whose duties might have outlived their supposed function. That was time-consuming, because the roster didn't have backgrounds on the imagers, just their name and duty, and quarters assignment. For more information, he had to check the file on each imager.

Every so often he glanced at the glass on the corner of the desk, finally setting aside the roster. He needed to slip over to the studies building to see how Shaelyt was doing. The Maitre D'Aspect was only twenty-three, but he was bright, and at least he understood both the subject matter and the need for a change in the way it was taught, unlike Obsolym and possibly even Akoryt, although Alastar wasn't certain how the quiet Akoryt really felt about most things. Desyrk and Cyran were too busy with other tasks, and instruction. *Not enough maitres, and certainly not enough who truly see how little time we have to make changes.*

When he left the study, Dareyn was seated at his own desk, sorting through the various messages left at the duty desk during the glasses when the administration building was closed.

"Is there anything urgent?"

"No, sir."

"Good. I'll be over observing classes. I shouldn't be too long."

Outside, the stone walks were largely empty, as they should have been, now that the regular day at the Collegium was under way. He adjusted his cap and made his way to the building north and west of the old anomen and then inside and down the corridor to the third door, where he eased it open a crack, peering into the study chamber. None of the primes or seconds seated around the long table looked back at the door, their eyes on Shaelyt, who stood at the far end of the table. Alastar raised a concealment around himself, eased the door farther open, slipping inside and gently closing it. Several of the primes and seconds glanced back at the sound of the door shutting. One second looked clearly puzzled, but quickly turned his head back to the Maitre D'Aspect.

"Looking at the door won't help with your learning, Fherrat," Shaelyt said cheerfully.

The way the young Maitre D'Aspect spoke suggested to Alastar that Shaelyt knew full well what was happening. Alastar just stood inside the room by the door and listened.

"Now . . . back to the question at hand," declared Shaelyt. "Why is Solidar governed the way it is?"

The primes and seconds seated around the long table just sat there. Not a one spoke.

Alastar wasn't surprised. Passive receptivity was the usual reaction to rote learning, and if a question didn't allow for rote regurgitation, most student imagers didn't know how to reply.

"An answer, please . . . or you'll all have to write an additional essay on the question."

"Because that's the way Rex Regis set it up, sir?" volunteered a prime.

"Fair enough. That was almost four hundred years ago. Exactly how many years was it, Fherrat?"

"Sir?"

"Just think about it for a moment."

"Oh . . . three hundred and eighty-nine years."

"Why do we write the date with the numbers followed by the letters A.L.?"

Again there was no answer, and Shaelyt raised his eyebrows.

"Ah . . . doesn't that mean 'After Lydar,' sir?" asked a second, a thin girl.

"It does. Why?"

More silence. Then Shaelyt laughed. "That was a trick question. No one knows, not for certain. We only know that several years after Rex Regis, the dating of documents changed from the traditional means of dating, such as four Vendrei in the year three of the reign of Chayar, to the present system. The story is that Rex Regis realized that, since he had named himself Rex Regis, meaning 'king of kings' in old Bovarian, every rex who succeeded him would also have that title. It's said that Elsior, who was then not the Maitre of the Collegium, suggested the use of the numerals followed by the letters A.L., signifying 'After Lydar,' which was a polite way of saying after the fall of the old ways. In any case, it made sense in practical terms, and it's been used ever since. Why did Rex Regis set things up as he did? Or did he?"

The thin girl raised her hand. "Wasn't there a council of High Holders before?"

"There was. Go on."

"Then didn't he just make up rules for the High Holders?"

"That's close. What is the Codex Legis?" Shaelyt pointed to a second who looked ready to doze off. "Marraet?"

"Ah . . . the what, sir?"

"Codex Legis."

"The code of laws, isn't it, sir?"

"What did it do that was different?"

Again, there was silence.

Finally, another prime spoke. "Didn't . . . isn't . . . I mean, it lists the powers of the rex, and what the High Holders can do, and who pays what taxes."

"That's largely correct. But it does one other thing. It limits the powers of all three, the rex, the High Holders, and the factors. Why?"

Because Bovaria and its domains were largely ungovernable under the old Bovarian system. Alastar waited to see if anyone answered.

No one did and it took almost a tenth of a glass for Shaelyt to work the answers out of the student imagers.

"What did it smell like outside this morning?" asked Shaelyt.

"Awful . . ."

Several of the other imagers nodded vigorously.

"Why doesn't the Maitre of the Collegium just force the rex to fix the sewers?"

When no one answered, Shaelyt pointed to a round-faced boy. "Why doesn't he?"

"I don't know . . . ah . . . because the rex wouldn't do it?"

"Could the rex do it?"

"Not himself, he wouldn't."

"Then how does the rex get anything done?"

"He has other people do it," chimed in a younger student, a prime, Alastar thought.

"How?"

Alastar eased out of the chamber. Shaelyt was making a good start. Getting any thought so soon was an improvement. As he walked back to the administration building, his nose reinforced the point on which Shaelyt had continued the discussion on governing, and . . . and, with the continuing impasse between the rex and the factors over the sewers, why he had resolved to look into the source of the odor. *If you do take imagers over the east bridge and deal with the worst of the problem, won't Ryen see that as a matter of his giving in? Or would the factors see it as high-handed?* Alastar frowned. *Probably both, but you're the one who keeps talking about the need for the Collegium to be seen as independent of the rex.*

Once back in his study, he drafted a polite note to High Holder Haebyn suggesting that a meeting in the next few days might be mutually beneficial, then handed it to Dareyn for dispatch to the High Holder. He debated about whether to meet with the others on the High Council, then decided that for various reasons, he should meet with each. That required three more letters, and additional instructions to Dareyn.

Rather than wrestle with the Collegium ledgers, he walked down the corridor to another small study, rapped lightly on the door, and stepped inside. "Good afternoon, Arhgen."

"Good day, Maitre." The square-faced and graying tertius behind the wide table desk eased several sheets of paper aside and looked up with his always cheerful smile, waiting.

Alastar closed the door and settled into the single straight-backed chair in the chamber filled with file chests stacked against almost every wall. "What do we have in reserve . . . this very moment? In the strong room?"

"Slightly less than a thousand golds. They will barely last past Year-Turn. That is, if the prices of flour, maize, and other foodstuffs do not increase more."

"Which they will. What about meat?"

"For now, that has decreased slightly. The shortage of fodder, you know."

"That means next year meat will be more, and until the next harvest, so will everything else."

"Yes, sir. We have ordered slightly more than twenty golds' worth of supplies, and we will need to pay the stipends to all imagers and to those who work for the Collegium on the eighteenth, and the food costs . . . all in all, operating just the part of the Collegium here in

L'Excelsis takes almost a hundred and fifty golds a week . . ."

The costs of running the Collegium continued to stagger Alastar, but then, effectively the Collegium was paying stipends or wages to close to two hundred people, and feeding almost a hundred of them nineteen meals every week. *And Ryen is supplying most of those golds.*

Not for the first time, nor would it be the last, he knew, came the realization that the Collegium needed more sources of funding—many more. *Along with everything else that you need to address.*

"Where can we reduce what we're spending?"

"We've already cut almost fifty golds a week . . . The cooks are being more careful. As you ordered, we're not replacing anything that is not immediately needed . . ."

Alastar continued to listen as the Collegium bookkeeper summarized the changes already implemented and their results. ". . . the only way you can make more significant reductions in what the Collegium spends is to employ fewer people or cut the stipends to the imagers."

Alastar had already thought about cutting stipends to imagers, but waiting a week or two before surfacing that idea wouldn't make the situation that much worse. "Do you have any ideas about what imagers could create easily that we could sell."

"That wouldn't upset the guilds or the factors, you mean?" Arhgen paused. "I can't think of anything right now."

"Keep thinking about it." Alastar rose. "Thank you."

After he returned to his study, he asked Dareyn to have one of the young imagers who served as a runner find Akoryt.

The red-haired Maitre D'Structure arrived almost half a glass later. "I apologize, Maitre, but I had some of the older seconds out on the river practicing imaging over water."

"No apology is necessary, especially not for that. How did they do?"

"This was only the second time we've done that. It was much better than the first time. *Much* better."

"Good." Alastar cleared his throat. "There is another matter." *There's always another matter.* "We've talked over the problem of golds for the Collegium, and the fact that we depend on golds from the rex. This makes us more and more vulnerable, especially at a time when the High Holders and factors are getting more and more . . . restive. Have you given any more thought to what we might do in the way of imaging that would raise golds?"

"Besides imaging golds and silvers into existence?"

"That won't work here." Alastar tried not to let his voice grow testy as he explained, even though he had done so at least once before. "There's not enough gold in the ground near L'Excelsis, and anywhere there is gold ore, it belongs to one High Holder or another."

"You have mentioned that. One hopes . . ." Akoryt pursed his lips, then went on, "People pay for what they value, fine wines, good lager, fancy attire, good weapons . . . What about rifles? They'd bring a few golds. Or pistols?"

"The Collegium has tried imaging rifles since the time of Elsior, but it's never been that successful. You have to make each part to fit the others, and that means each rifle is unique. If anything breaks . . ."

"Couldn't they image the pieces against a template?"

Akoryt shook his head. "The tolerances are too fine. I can do it. So could you or Taryn . . . and maybe Shaelyt or Alyna or Tiranya . . . but the idea was to develop things that seconds or thirds could image. They can match the shape of knives, but not the tempering."

"There must be something of value."

There is, but it's not something we're about to trust to seconds and thirds . . . "There are many things of moderate value, but finding ones that less experienced imagers can do that won't infringe on the factors and the guilds makes the matter more difficult."

Akoryt frowned, then asked, "What about cheap cutlery? I can't believe the smiths' guild would object to that. Forging little things like that takes great effort, and they can't sell it for much. If they didn't get into doing silver tableware, it wouldn't upset the silversmiths."

"There is an awl and bladesmiths' guild," Alastar said dryly.

"Crockery . . . what about cheap mugs, tankards? There has to be clay in the bottom of the Aluse."

"Actually," replied Alastar thoughtfully, "that might be a possibility. It would also be a good exercise for primes and seconds."

"Exercise?"

"Think of everything that goes into good pottery. The moisture of the clay has to be uniform. It has to be fired at a high heat, and it needs to be glazed." Alastar grinned at Akoryt. "You'd better try it yourself . . . and I'd image it well away from you."

Once Akoryt left the study, Alastar sat behind his desk for a time. While he had his doubts about mugs and cheap crockery, at the very least, perhaps the primes and seconds could create platters and mugs for the Collegium. *What about glassware?* That was another thought. He had the feeling he was missing far too much, but perhaps, if he kept asking enough of the senior imagers, and others, they'd be able to come up with better ideas.

You hope.

5

On Samedi morning, Alastar allowed himself another half glass of sleep, and cut his run to going around the northern half of the isle, so that he did not reach the dining hall until just before sixth glass. He was still the first maitre there, although Claeynd arrived within a tenth of a glass, sleepy-eyed, rumpled, and obviously the duty master. Alastar motioned for the other to join him. "You look a little tired this morning, Claeynd."

"Yes, sir. I don't sleep well when I have duty. Don't know why. Kierstia says it's because I worry, even sleeping in our own bed. Lilabeta's old enough that she sleeps the night."

"No problems, then?"

"No, sir. Quiet as could be when we closed the gates. All the students accounted for." Claeynd smiled faintly. "When I've the duty on Samedi night, that's when I worry. There have been times when an older third wasn't in when the gates are shut. One of them imaged himself a rope and climbed over. Maitre Fhaen wasn't amused. Maitre Cyran suggested no harm was done, seeing as it was but a quint past ninth glass."

"You might pass the word that I'll be even less amused than Maitre Fhaen was."

Claeynd's brow furrowed slightly.

"You're wondering why? Because Rex Ryen has angered the High Holders and the factors, and imagers are seen as supporters of the rex. Being out late, especially alone, isn't a good idea right now, not that it ever was. How are your regular duties coming?"

"There's not too much change, sir. We're working on replacing the cracked roof tiles on the anomen. They say it's older than the Collegium."

"That's what the records show. But it was rebuilt by the first imagers of the Collegium."

"It's a tricky business, imaging out one tile at a time, then replacing it with a new one."

"Just ten of them and a few students built the older part of the administration building, the first twelve cottages, the old student quarters wing, as well as the newer ones, the first two, except they were barracks, the stables, and the Maitre's dwelling . . . and they did it all in a year . . . plus the stone walls around Imagisle and the southern west bridge." Alastar smiled. "That's the level of imaging skill we need to rebuild."

"That's hard to believe, sir."

"There are enough records about what they did that there's not much doubt." *But there are no records about how they did all that.*

Claeynd took a cautious sip from the steaming mug the server set before him. "Maitre Obsolym says that they risked more, and that most of them died young."

"We don't know that they died young just from attempting imaging. We do know that the ones who founded the Collegium survived persecution and war. The strong who work together have a better chance of surviving. Maitre Quaeryt was farsighted enough to get them to do that."

The server slipped a platter in front of Alastar, who looked at the egg toast—only tan instead of dark brown—and at the sausage patty, perhaps slightly greasy, but definitely cooked. He drizzled some of the honey-berry syrup, far more tart berry than sweet honey, over the egg toast, cut a piece of sausage and ate it with a chunk of the toast, then took a sip of the bitter tea. He ate for a time without speaking.

"Is it true that more young imagers at Westisle . . ." Claeynd let his words fade off, as if unwilling to finish the question.

"Some student imagers have died at Westisle. Some have died here. There will always be foolish or careless young imagers. The task of the Collegium is to turn foolish or careless young students into careful and thoughtful imagers. Failure to learn care and thought in imaging may have unfortunate consequences. We try to minimize those consequences, but the task is creating responsible imagers, not excessively protecting those who will not learn or understand."

"Isn't that expecting a bit much, sir?"

"It's expecting a great deal, but the survival of imagers in Solidar is at stake. Do you want to go back to the times before Rex Regis and the establishment of the Collegium, when imagers were hunted down . . . when most were killed as children? If we do not demonstrate that imagers are responsible and valued, there will be no future for the Collegium and for imagers. Right now, we are seen merely as tools of Rex Ryen." *And not very strong tools at that.*

"Yes, sir," replied Claeynd.

Alastar could tell that the younger maitre had his doubts, and rather than press, he merely said, "Just think about what I've said as matters unfold over the next few weeks."

"What's going to happen then, sir?" Claeynd's voice took on a worried tone.

"We'll have to see. In the meantime, just keep your eyes and ears open." Alastar took a last swallow of tea and rose. "Have a good Samedi and end-day tomorrow with your family."

Alastar kept a pleasant smile on his face as he left the dining hall, nodding to the primes and seconds who were dragging into the building and who immediately inclined their heads and stepped out of his way. He worried that Claeynd's attitude was all too prevalent among the junior masters. He had barely stepped out of the dining hall when the odor of sewage and worse filled his nostrils, so strong that he almost retched. *And the rex and the factors are still squabbling over who is to pay for the repairs?* He kept walking.

Dareyn was tidying up the anteroom when Alastar arrived.

"You're here early," Alastar offered.

"I woke up early, and Elmya is visiting our daughter in Caanara. There was no reason to lie around, and there have been some things I've wanted to organize better."

"Far be it for me to get in the way of that." Alastar smiled cheerfully. "I will need you to dispatch some messages in a while."

While Alastar could theoretically have sent one of the imager messengers, what he was ordering would be unpopular, and verbal messages of an unpopular nature had a tendency not to be received, or the recipients somehow "misinterpreted" them. When he seated himself behind his desk, he immediately began to write, first a short note to Obsolym, then an identical one to Akoryt, followed by ones to the other three senior maitres, followed by the same note to several of the Maitres D'Aspect—Alyna, Khaelis, Mhorys, Narryn, Shaelyt, and Tiranya. He decided against including Warryk, because he was recovering from a nasty flux, and Claeynd, because he was the duty maitre for Samedi, although Claeynd could have used the example Alastar intended to set. He wrote a different note to Petros.

When he finished, he took the notes out to Dareyn. "These are to the senior imagers, including Obsolym, and to some of the Maitres D'Aspect. The notes are to be delivered personally. For your information, I've summoned them to meet me here tomorrow morning at eighth glass. I'd also like you to send word to Maitre

Petros to have thirteen mounts ready for me and those imagers by a quint past eighth glass tomorrow."

"It is Solayi, sir."

"That's why I'm delaying the meeting until eighth glass."

"Will you be needing anything else, sir?"

"Not for the moment. At eighth glass, I'm going to see how Maitre Cyran is doing in overseeing weapons training with the junior thirds." Alastar also wanted to continue his review of the imager assignments with Desyrk, but whether he could fit that in depended on how long he watched Cyran's students and whether Desyrk would be punctual in leaving at noon—since noon on Samedi was the beginning of end-day, which lasted until services began in the anomen at sixth glass on Solayi evening.

When he returned to his study, Alastar took out his copy of the master ledger, updated and returned weekly by Arhgen, to go over the Collegium accounts to see where spending might be cut, and just as important, what was being neglected. He had jotted down several areas where he needed to look into changes in Collegium spending when Dareyn knocked on the door, then opened it slightly.

"There's a courier from the Chateau D'Rex, Maitre."

A courier from the rex most likely meant trouble, and Dareyn's absolutely calm tone of voice suggested the old secondus had the same opinion.

"Have him come in, if you would."

Dareyn opened the study door wide, stood back to let the courier enter, and then closed it, leaving the courier alone with Alastar.

The courier—a young man in the yellow-trimmed green jacket and trousers of a chateau guard—stepped into the study. "Maitre . . . sir?"

"Yes? I take it you have a message for me."

"Yes, sir." The guard swallowed.

Alastar had a good idea what was coming. "Yes?"

"Rex Ryen would appreciate your immediate attendance at the chateau, sir."

"Were those his exact words?" Before the stunned guard could reply, Alastar held up his hand. "You don't have to answer that. As soon as I can get a mount saddled, we can ride back together. That might be for the best. If you'd wait out front for me, I'll join you shortly."

"Yes, sir." The courier didn't sound happy.

Believe me, young man, you'll be far happier arriving with me. Alastar stood and walked to the door, opening it and gesturing for the courier to precede him. "Dareyn, send word to the stables that I'll need my horse saddled, and two escorts to accompany me."

"Yes, sir."

Alastar turned to the courier. "I'll meet you in front as soon as my mount arrives."

The courier nodded, almost glumly, then turned and walked from the anteroom out into the corridor, then toward the main entry.

"Did the courier say what the rex wanted, sir?"

"Does he ever let anyone know? I'm just expected to attend him instantly." Alastar offered a crooked smile. "It could be anything. Oh . . . and would you send a messenger over to Cyran to tell him where I'm going to be?"

"Yes, sir."

Less than a tenth of a glass later, Alastar mounted the gray gelding and rode away from the central green on the Collegium beside the courier, with the two imager thirds behind them.

"What's your name?" Alastar asked the guard.

"Llasel, sir."

"How long have you been a guard and courier at the chateau?"

"I was a page for three years. Then I went through rankers' training."

"At the training post to the north on this side of the river? Five milles out?"

"Yes, sir. They said it was once a scholarium. It's where the army trains rankers."

That was something else Alastar hadn't known, that there had actually been a scholarium in L'Excelsis. There was no mention of such in the archives he'd read, but then, he'd only scratched the surface of what lay in the stacks of file chests in the cellar. "Do you know how long ago that was? Did anyone say?"

"No, sir."

"How many chateau guards are there?"

"Three companies' worth. That's here in L'Excelsis. There are guards at all the chateaux the rex owns."

"There are quite a few of those." Alastar had seen estimates that Ryen owned fifteen large estates across Solidar, but those numbers had decreased since the time of Rex Regis, as some had been given to nonruling offspring over the generations.

"I wouldn't know, sir."

Less than a glass later, Alastar and the three others reined up at the white stone steps leading up to the main entrance of the Chateau D'Rex.

"Thank you, Llasel."

"My pleasure, Maitre." The chateau guard eased his mount away.

Alastar dismounted and handed the gelding's reins to Akkard, the older of the two thirds. "Just wait here."

Both imagers nodded, and Alastar made his way up the steps to the entry, where another guard, this one white-haired, accompanied the Maitre through the receiving hall and then up the grand staircase to the second level and back to the closed door of Ryen's private study.

The guard outside the study knocked and announced, "Maitre Alastar, sir."

"Send the good Maitre in."

Alastar concealed the wince he felt at the false heartiness he heard in Ryen's voice, made certain he had a pleasant expression on his face, and stepped into the study. The guard quickly closed the door behind him.

Ryen stood beside the wide desk and its stacks of papers, between the desk and the closed windows to the north. Two other men, much younger, stood on one side of the desk opposite the rex. One was clearly an offspring, because he had the same lank black hair and gray-blue eyes and thin build as Ryen. The other had fine blond hair and greenish gray eyes. He was also slightly taller and more broad-shouldered than either of the others, and he immediately smiled warmly at Alastar.

"Maitre," continued Ryen in his falsely hearty voice, "I thought you should meet my sons. Lorien here"—he pointed to the older-looking and more slender man—"and Ryentar." The rex followed by inclining his head toward the still-smiling younger man, then continued, "And this distinguished personage, my sons, is the new head of the Collegium, Maitre Alastar, and the most powerful imager in Solidar."

Both Lorien and Ryentar nodded politely to Alastar.

"I'm very pleased to meet you, sir," offered Ryentar warmly.

"Likewise," said Lorien cordially, but far from effusively.

"And I, you," replied Alastar.

"You may go." Ryen looked first to Lorien and then Ryentar. "At the stables at noon."

Alastar hoped he wouldn't be spending nearly that long with the rex, but kept a pleasant expression on his face. "Fine-looking young men."

"They are." Ryen laughed. "What else could you say, Maitre?"

"That I was glad to meet them, which I was."

"Sit down."

Alastar waited until the rex was about to seat himself before settling into the chair across the desk from Ryen.

"How are you managing with changing the councilors' minds?"

"I've met with Guerdyn, as a matter of courtesy, and I've requested meetings with the other four."

"That's all? In four days, that's *all* you've accomplished? What are you doing? Sleeping until noon?" Ryen's voice rose slightly and hardened. "In four days? And why meet with all of them? You only need to meet with Nacryon and Haebyn."

"If I don't meet with all of them, it will be obvious that you've already convinced Vaun and Moeryn, and that won't help your cause."

"My cause? I'm the rex! Under the codex I set the tariffs! It's not a cause. It's my right!"

Not if they won't comply. "You told me not to create a direct conflict. If I just barge in on them, that will do just that, and—"

"Four days! Namer-damn you, Maitre! Don't argue with me. Just do what I tell you, or your precious Collegium will suffer."

Alastar did not press his point, but only asked mildly, "Are you telling me to threaten them or remove them, then?"

Ryen glared, and his face reddened. His body shook, and the unkempt lock of black hair slid down across his brow.

Alastar waited, not speaking.

"You don't need to meet with Vaun and Moeryn . . ." Every word sounded hard and forced.

"You don't, sir. I do. Otherwise, they'll feel I'm slighting them, and the Collegium cannot afford that, and neither can you. If they are not amenable to reason . . . well, then, we will have to take other steps, but trying reason first cannot hurt."

"Then get on with it."

"I am, sir." If Alastar hadn't had the fortune and future of more than a hundred imagers and student imagers in his hands, most of whom could not even carry minimal shields, as well as the lives of those who worked for and served them, he might have been tempted to act precipitously . . . *But that's not the way to do it. It's better to work out the problems with Ryen as the foil . . . much better.* Especially since no one, not the High Holders, the factors, the marshal of the army, or the rex himself, either respected or was terribly pleased with the Collegium at the present time. *And you can't blame them . . . unfortunately.*

Ryen shook himself, and then smiled, his voice almost cheerful as he said, "It will be a week or so before I complete arrangements for obtaining the property necessary for you and your imagers to build the direct road to the chateau. I'd like you to have them ready for that task."

"They will be. Building a new avenue will likely take several weeks."

"That long? It didn't take the first imagers that much time."

"You're right, but they didn't have to take down buildings and worry about joining other roads. They just repaved and widened the existing roads."

Surprisingly, Ryen just nodded.

"Is there anything else?"

"Should there be, Maitre?"

"Not that I know of."

"Good. I look forward to hearing of your successes . . . before too long. You may go." The rex turned back to the window.

Alastar let himself out of the study and walked slowly back to the grand staircase and then down to the main level and out to where the two imagers waited with his gelding. *It could have been worse.*

6

Petros was the first imager maitre to appear outside Alastar's study on Solayi morning, simply because Alastar had requested his presence a half glass before that of the others.

"I've got the pack mule ready, sir, with the poles and the cordage, and some shovels and picks. Harrl and Kavan will help, too. If the paving stones are loose enough, they can just lift them away and stack them. That way, the others can do what can't be done without imaging."

"Or without a passel of stonemasons and laborers. What else would you like to bring that I haven't thought about?" Alastar grinned briefly. "Not that I thought about any of that."

"If we forget anything, I can send one of them back here. It's not that far."

"Good enough. I'll see you shortly."

Shortly after Petros had headed back to the stables, Akoryt appeared. "Might I ask, sir . . . ?"

"You might, but I'd rather explain to all of those who will be joining us at the same time. Did you try out the pottery imaging?"

"I did." The junior maitre smiled wryly. "You were right about trying it first. I did manage to work that part out, about not getting it to explode. Now . . . if I were only an artist."

Alastar froze in place, for just an instant. Then he said in a low voice, "How big an explosion did you get at first?"

The young maitre frowned. "Big enough that I'd have

needed a surgeon if I'd been standing within a few yards without shields."

A few yards? Alastar decided he should look into that possibility. "I'm glad you were careful. You'll have to be cautious if we decide to try that approach."

"What approach?" asked Cyran, who had approached from the rear entrance to the building.

"Using imaging so that primes and seconds can create crockery," explained Alastar.

"For training or actual use?"

"Both. If any of it's good, possibly for sale," added Alastar blandly. "If you have any ideas along those lines, I'd be interested."

"I'll have to think about it."

Alastar nodded, then turned as Alyna and Tiranya entered the anteroom. They often came places together, since neither was married and they shared one of the cottages for maitres, although all the others were occupied by married couples. The unwed male maitres had rooms in the small masters' hall to the northwest of the anomen. The two were different in appearance, with the almost petite Alyna having slightly darker skin and light brown hair, set off by black eyes, while Tiranya had mahogany hair, a pale face sprinkled with freckles, and light green eyes. Tiranya was almost as tall as Alastar. That made her very tall for a woman, since only a few of the imagers were taller than the Maitre, although he reckoned himself only as slightly taller than most men. Khaelis and Mhorys followed the women, and then came Taryn, talking quietly with Cyran, followed by Desyrk and Akoryt, and the rest of the junior masters. The last to arrive was Obsolym, if by only a few moments.

Once the masters all stood in the anteroom, Alastar cleared his throat, loudly, and waited for the murmurs to die away. "I'm certain you all have wondered what is so urgent that it demands a meeting on Solayi morning. It is not urgent in that sense, but Solayi is by far the best time to do something that needs to be done, and something that apparently only imagers can do." He kept his voice dry and sardonic as he went on deliberately, looking across the faces of the imagers. "All of you must have noted the stench arising from the east side of the river . . ."

Cyran raised his eyebrows, and Obsolym frowned. Several nodded.

"It appears as though," Alastar continued, "if we wish to continue breathing without retching, we must address that matter ourselves. Maitre Petros and I have discovered where the sewer tunnel may be breached. We need to repair it. That is why I called you all together."

"To fix the sewers the factors have ignored?" snorted Obsolym. "Why should we?"

"Because it will make our life more pleasant. Because it will reduce the animosity between the rex and the factors, and that will remove a problem for the rex. Because it will demonstrate that the Collegium cares for the well-being of others." Alastar smiled coldly and looked directly at Obsolym. "And because I am the Maitre, and I've determined it is necessary."

"You're . . ." Obsolym broke off his words. "Whatever you say, Maitre."

"There are mounts waiting for you all by the stables." Alastar gestured.

Although it was close to ninth glass when the imagers and the two husky laborers reached the part of the East River Road some three blocks south of the bridge where the stench hung over the area, the avenue was almost empty, as Alastar had hoped it would be on a Solayi morning.

While the imagers tied the mounts to various rails and protrusions from the riverside wall on the west side of the sidewalk bordering the East River Road, Petros imaged small holes in the mortar between the paving stones at each corner of an oblong that included the entire area of depressed paving stones, then imaged several others on the sides. His two assistants inserted thin poles into the holes and then strung cord from pole to pole, threading it through a notch in each pole, then looping and tying it. Then they placed poles in the gutter drains that bordered the area.

"We'll start by imaging away the mortar around the stones," declared Alastar when all the cording and poles were in place, enclosing a space almost fifty yards long and five wide. "Shaelyt, why don't you see what you can do? Start with those blocks there." Alastar pointed.

In less than a glass, the junior maitres and the two laborers had removed the sunken paving stones. Several local urchins were watching, if cautiously and from the sidewalks and the porch of a shop that was closed. So was an old woman in faded gray, who sat on the steps of a closed rope factorage, with a basket held together by cloth and cord set beside her sandals.

"Now it gets harder," said Alastar. "Taryn, I'd like you to image out the gravel and soil and pile it outside the cordoned area, at least a yard back. Start at the north end."

Taryn stepped forward, looking at the packed gravel that had underlain the stone, then concentrated. A pile of dirt and gravel appeared in the gutter.

"Don't block the drains, either," Alastar added.

Another pile of dirt appeared at the end of the first pile, but Alastar shifted his attention from Taryn to two patrollers, wearing the brown and yellow of the factors' council. They walked slowly toward Alastar, finally stopping several yards short.

"Ah . . . master imager, sir . . ." began the shorter and older patroller.

"You'd like to know what all these imagers are doing in the middle of the East River Road on a Solayi morning?"

asked Alastar cheerfully. "We're here to repair this part of the sewer, because no one else seems willing to do anything. Do you have any objection to that?"

The two exchanged glances. The older one spoke. "No, sir. How long might this take?"

"We'll have to see, but we chose Solayi in hopes we could finish today."

The two looked at each other again. "You'll put the road back together?"

"We will."

"Thank you, Maitre." The older patroller inclined his head politely, and the two turned.

Alastar strained to listen as the patrollers walked back southward.

"Can't hurt to have 'em try . . . Stink just gets worse . . ."

"If it works . . ."

Taryn managed to create an opening some three yards wide, five long, and roughly a yard deep before he stepped back and glanced to Alastar.

"Desyrk, see if you can deepen that to the top of the sewer."

"Yes, sir." The handsome Maitre D'Structure walked to the edge of the imaged excavation, leaning over and peering down before beginning, but he managed to create a modest pile of dirt and rubble before Alastar could see him pause and rub his forehead.

"That's enough for you now. Akoryt, your turn. Keep deepening what's already there."

Akoryt did somewhat less than Desyrk, but he did manage to image away enough of the overburden that Alastar could see—and smell even more strongly—that there was definitely a problem. First, the sewer wasn't as the records had shown, at least the part that the imagers had uncovered. Instead of being a tunnel cut out of bedrock and sealed or covered, it was a brick-walled ditch roughly two yards high and a yard and a half wide topped with paving stones mortared in place. Rather, they had been mortared, but there were only scraps of the mortar remaining, and there was sewer water outside the ditch walls oozing southward.

"Khaelis, you're next. Extend the excavation to the south. Keep it the same width."

After Khaelis, Alyna stepped forward. As small as she looked to be, especially after the broad-shouldered Khaelis, Alyna removed even more overburden than he had, in fact considerably more than Taryn had, maintaining a determinedly pleasant expression as she did so. Tiranya followed, but she was unable to manage more than about half of what the smaller woman had done, and she was decidedly pale when she stepped back from the edge of the open pit.

More than two glasses passed before Shaelyt stood beside the southern end of the area that Petros had staked, imaging out the last of the mud and gravel. Despite the water that almost submerged the covered ditch, Alastar could see that some sort of work had been done, because there was what amounted to a crude dam on both sides of the sewer ditch designed to funnel the water into another far cruder covered ditch set lower in the ground and headed westward toward the river.

"When you finish clearing that, take a break. I need to look at something." Alastar followed the line of the ditch until he reached the stone wall at the west side of the sidewalk along the river road. He leaned over the wall, ignoring the worst stench he had encountered so far. Three yards down was a gap in the stone wall, and a small stream of liquid trickled out of the gap and down the stones to the marshy reeds growing between the wall and the clearer river water.

He straightened and shook his head, then walked back to the open excavation. "Some years back, someone decided that rather than fix a leak in the sewers, they'd just divert the sewage to the river. We're going to repair this section right." He turned. "Obsolym, can you image one of those paving stones up and to the side? Beginning with the one just this side of that barrier?"

The older Maitre D'Structure nodded, imaging one paving stone, and then another. In all, he removed four before Alastar stepped forward and removed six in a row, then turned to Cyran.

As Cyran imaged the stones off the ditch, Alastar could definitely see the problem, because the ditch was filled with a mixture of putrescence and bones, and at least one set of those bones was human. The sewage ditch wasn't small, but Alastar had trouble imagining how anyone had managed to stuff a dead body into it through any of the drains he'd seen.

The beefy Narryn eased forward to peer down into the ditch, then swallowed and staggered to the river wall, where he promptly retched.

"So much for that," came a murmur.

Alastar thought the comment had come from Tiranya, but when he glanced in her direction, she was listening to Alyna. Even after he looked back to the progress on the removal of the stones, Alastar had the feeling he had missed something. That bothered him. He hated missing anything.

Removing all the paving stones took nearly another glass, and revealed that forty of the fifty yards of uncovered sewer ditch were filled with refuse of all sorts. Alastar didn't even want to consider all that lay entangled in the mess. He just set the imagers to imaging out the refuse into the river.

After inspecting the comparatively clean exposed section of sewer, Alastar could see that the water in the sewer had broken through in several places where the bricks had crumbled and cracked about thirty yards north of the makeshift catchment. He imaged replacements in the areas where he could see obvious breaks, then imaged a coating of glaze along the entire interior walls and floor of the ditch. With that effort, he found himself shaking, and flickers of light crossing his vision.

"Maitre . . ."

He looked to see Alyna at his side, offering a water bottle.

"It's lager. It should help."

"Thank you," he managed, taking the bottle. He shouldn't have tried so much at once, he knew, and he certainly should have brought a bottle of lager for himself. *But you've gotten out of practice at heavy imaging lately.*

Several swallows helped, and he turned to Cyran. "If you could glaze the outside, or part of it."

"I don't think I'll try to do it all at once." Cyran grinned.

After Cyran, Taryn, and Desyrk finished image-glazing the outside of the bricks, Alastar inspected the sewer again, which had filled to a depth of perhaps half a yard with sewage that seemed to be flowing smoothly. He thought about removing the rough exterior catchment and secondary drain, but decided against that and ordered the junior maitres to replace the stones and seal them in place. Once the sewage ditch was completely repaired, with the walls sealed and the stone covering the top back in place, the imagers still needed to return the overburden, as well as add additional fill to replace the dirt that the leakage had carried away. All in all, it was close to fourth glass when the exhausted imagers rode back across the east bridge.

Once back at the Maitre's dwelling at the Collegium, Alastar bathed and changed into a fresh set of grays. He thought the ones he had worn for the repairs smelled of sewage, but wasn't certain, since, even once he'd washed up, everything still smelled of sewage. He also wondered how Alyna had been so quick to see his weakness, and why she had immediately offered her own lager. *Out of concern . . . or for some other reason?* He didn't know enough to judge. That bothered him as well, especially since she did come from a High Holder background.

With almost a full glass before services at the anomen, he decided to spend that time reading more of the Collegium records he had brought from the archives. Part of that effort was based on curiosity, and part on the concern that he didn't know enough about the past of the Collegium. As a younger maitre, he'd never considered that he might become the head of the entire Collegium in L'Excelsis. Consequently, he hadn't studied the background of the Collegium, and even if he had tried, much of that material was not available in Westisle.

Sitting at the desk in his personal study. Alastar turned to the point in the bound sheaf of papers where he had left off reading.

> . . . precedent set by the service of Calkoran D'Alte (the younger) as a Vice-Marshal prior to his time as a member of the High Council in the time of Rex Clayar, Rex Indryen appointed Elloryt D'Tacquel as Marshal of the Northern Army, with the proviso that, should he become Tacquel D'Alte, that appointment would be immediately withdrawn . . .

Alastar fingered his chin, thinking that the infiltration of the High Command by the High Holders had begun soon after Rex Regis—if not before. Hadn't there been a High Holder from Eshtora who had been a marshal for Rex Regis? He continued to read until he came to another interesting entry.

> Rex Indryen did not inform the High Council of the reason for the change in tariff levels, but it appears that the income he received from the silver mine in Tilbor

has dwindled to a mere fraction of its former glory . . . requiring an increase in tariffs to offset that loss in income . . . High Holder Vyncet, as a member of the High Council, objected to the increase, but the Council overruled him on the basis that the government of Solidar could not disallow the replacement of private sources of income with public sources, so long as those funds were employed properly . . .

Rex Regis and his successors had a profitable silver mine?

At that thought, Alastar checked the glass on the corner of the desk. He needed to leave for the anomen if he wanted to talk to Chorister Iskhar before the service. He stood and made his way from the study and then through the main hall to the front door and out onto the wide covered porch. Outside, the wind was brisk and slightly cool, but not chill, and he decided not to go back inside for a heavier jacket.

In less than a tenth of a glass, Alastar was walking through the side door of the ancient anomen and toward Iskhar's study.

The chorister stood from behind his desk. "Maitre. Good evening."

"What will your homily be about?" Alastar grinned.

The sandy-haired chorister of the Nameless smiled back. "If I tell you, you won't stay to hear it. Even if you do, you'll be bored."

Despite Iskhar's youth—he was barely past thirty—Alastar was generally pleased, both with his help in teaching more advanced history and rhetoric to the older students and the insight and practicality of his homilies. Iskhar was also good at counseling student imagers without being condescending or excessively sympathetic. Students sometimes needed that, given that imagers remained mistrusted by most in Solidar, although there had not been a young imager killed, except in the line of study or duty, in more than a generation, but that might have also been due to the two-gold bonus received by the parents of an imager.

"I'm never bored by your homilies."

"That's because I don't tell you what they'll be."

"Your point is well taken. I did have a question for you."

"I thought you might. You're not given to pleasantries for the sake of pleasantry."

Alastar let himself wince. "I suppose I deserve that."

Iskhar laughed.

"Have you heard anything from the other choristers in L'Excelsis about feelings toward either the Collegium or the rex?"

"I don't see the others often. What I have heard is that they're not especially pleased with either Ryen or the High Council. They wouldn't speak to me about the Collegium."

"I'd appreciate it if you'd let me know if you do hear anything."

"I will."

"Thank you. Now, I'll go wait to see how you surprise me with your homily."

There were a handful of primes already in the nave of the anomen when Alastar entered and took a position standing at the side near the front, but several yards back from the simple dais that only held a single pulpit. He continued to observe as each imager and student entered. Interestingly enough, Tiranya arrived with Shaelyt, rather than with Alyna, who accompanied several of the female students. Cyran and his wife Maliendra came, along with Desyrk and his wife, whose name Alastar could not recall.

Almost a hundred were gathered when Iskhar began the service by stepping forward onto the low dais and offering the invocation, "We gather together in the spirit of the Nameless and to affirm the quest for goodness and mercy in all that we do."

Then came the opening hymn, "All Praise the Nameless," followed by the confession.

"We name not You, for naming presumes, and we presume not upon the Creator of all that was, is, and will be. We pray not to You for ourselves, nor ask from You favor or recognition, for such asks You to favor us over others who are also Yours. We confess that we risk in all times the sins of presumptuous pride. We acknowledge that the very names we bear symbolize those sins, for we strive too often to raise our names and ourselves above others, to insist that our small achievements have meaning . . ."

Alastar had always been amused about a confession to a deity who was supposedly without a name, but in fact named as the Nameless.

In the silence that followed the response of "In peace and harmony," Iskhar moved behind the pulpit and looked out at the imagers gathered in the anomen. Finally, he said, "Good evening, and it is a good evening."

"Good evening," came the muted reply.

"All evenings are good evenings under the Nameless, although it is said that Rholan the Unnamer begged to differ, and many of us would agree in our hearts with that sentiment . . ."

Alastar certainly did, although he listened as the chorister stated the point of his homily.

". . . but sentiment should not be the basis of our acts or our judgments. Good feelings can come from either the Nameless or the Namer, and some feelings, such as unselfish love or compassion, spring from the best motive . . ."

Does it matter if the best of intentions spur the worst of actions? Or the worst of intent leads to a better world . . . or Solidar? Iskhar's words led Alastar to consider Ryen.

Thwarting Ryen's desire to raise tariffs would only increase the already nearly unchecked power of the High Holders and weaken Solidar as a whole. Alastar was still pondering those implications as Iskhar brought the short homily to a close.

". . . for while an imager without compassion is an imager without understanding, an imager whose compassion and sympathy override judgment is an imager who cannot be trusted to do what is right and just, for when the currents of feeling are unchecked, so is the power of imaging. Unchecked power used in service of the dictates of feeling can unleash the worst evils, such as righteous revenge, or striking out at those who we feel have somehow dishonored us, or have rejected us in one way or another, yet who have not actually injured anything but our self-respect. Feelings should inform us, even inspire us, but letting them drive us farther only makes us tools of the Namer, who always uses self-pride to turn us from the pursuit of true goodness toward the chimera of self-praise and empty honor." Iskhar paused, then said quietly, "Listen to your feelings, but do not let them become your master, for that way lies the worst of Naming."

Does it, really? wondered Alastar.

Iskhar stood there silently for a moment, then began the closing hymn—"For the Glory."

> *"For the glory, through all strife,*
> *for the beauty of all life,*
> *for all that is and will ever be,*
> *all together, through forever,*
> *in eternal Nameless glory . . ."*

Once the last notes of the hymn died away, the chorister offered his benediction, "As we have come together in the sight of the Nameless, may we go forth renewed in understanding and in harmony with that which was, is, and ever shall be."

When the imagers began to leave, Alastar saw that Khaelis and Narryn joined Shaelyt and Tiranya, while Alyna departed with the four girls.

Instead of going back to the Maitre's house immediately, Alastar took the stone walk north along the west side of Imagisle, into the park-like area comprising the northern quarter of the isle. Although Erion was low in the west, with Artiema almost full there was enough light that he didn't worry about tripping over something . . . or possibly surprising young imagers who might be about. Frowned on as that was, they did have the freedom of Imagisle until eighth glass. At the north end of the isle, the stone river wall rose a good two yards above the ground behind it. Alastar left the walk and stood behind a head-high boxwood hedge. Then he bent over and concentrated, imaging hot ceramic around water.

Shards of pottery splattered against the gray stone wall.

What if you tried that with a bit more water and some iron fragments?

He did, but the explosion was not that much greater. A third attempt, with less water, was even less successful. After almost half a glass of experimentation, Alastar shook his head. Most likely the damage from "faulty" pot imaging would be a few cuts and bruises . . . if that . . . except where those faulty pots were imaged very close to people. At times, that might be useful.

As he walked back toward the overlarge Maitre's house, he thought over the questions of both imager self-protection and channeling imaging into more lucrative pursuits so that the Collegium would not be so dependent on the whims of the rex. Years of quiet experimentation had convinced him that cannon and rifles were far more efficient in killing large numbers of people than was imaging, at least any imaging that he had tried. He still wondered just how great an imager the legendary Quaeryt had really been. Most legends weren't nearly as great and powerful as their legends. *But if he hadn't been* . . . Alastar smiled faintly. He'd never know, not really, and speculating on that wasn't about to help with his very immediate problems.

Under the pearly light of Artiema, he kept walking . . . and thinking.

PROLOGUE (2)

The once-stocky man staggered and nearly fell as he struggled up from the old bench, balancing on his good leg and foot and using the crutch made from the limb of a tree to help himself move toward the front door of the small cot. He looked back. "You watch your brother and sister, now. Keep them away from the hearth."

"Yes, sir."

"Your mother will be back from the inn later."

The boy hoped she would have leftover bread, or scraps. Sometimes she did. Most times, she didn't. He glanced at Mahara and Dyel. The two could crawl, but they weren't walking. They weren't much fun, but he didn't want them to get into the ashes of the hearth. There weren't any coals left.

Mahara was chewing on the leg of a straw figure covered in small scraps of cloth tied to resemble clothing. Dyel was crawling toward the bench that their father had left.

If only they had something to play with . . . a real toy. The boy thought about the merchanter's son he'd seen the day before, who had dropped a shiny blue top from a coach. The boy had picked it up and tried to hand it back, but the coach footman had taken it and wiped it off carefully before returning it. No one had even looked at the boy except the footman.

The boy thought about the top, trying to imagine just what it had looked like. It had only been wood, but painted. If he had a knife, he might have carved one, but the only knife like that was the one his father carried with him all the time. The boy tried even harder to imagine that top, holding it . . . spinning it . . .

For an instant, dizziness washed over him, and then . . . he held something cool and blue in his hand—a blue top! He fingered it. Could he have done that? His eyes watered, and he still felt dizzy. Whatever he had done, he had the feeling he shouldn't do it again. Not soon anyway.

Still holding the top, he watched his brother and sister until the dizziness passed. Then he knelt on the floor in front of Dyel and spun the top.

Dyel gooed and stuck a small hand out, knocking the top slightly, so that it skittered away.

The boy retrieved the top and spun it again.

Even Mahara watched as the two played.

The door opened, and the children's mother stepped into the cot, and the boy grabbed for the top.

"What do you have in your hand? Show me right now."

The boy stood and reluctantly showed her the blue top.

"Where did you get that?"

"I found it in the gutter yesterday. It was all covered with mud." He had found a top in the gutter. That was true. He given that one back. "There was no one around. There was no one to give it back to."

"Likely story."

"I didn't take it from anyone. Honest! I didn't." The boy felt tears running down his cheeks. It was so unfair. He'd just wanted to make his brother and sister a little toy. "They don't have anything much to play with. It's not much, and no one will miss it." That was true.

"No . . ." His mother's voice softened. "I can see you didn't steal it, and if it was in the gutter . . . It could have been anyone's."

"I didn't take from anyone. No one was looking for it."

"You're sure?"

"Yes, Mother. I didn't take it. I couldn't take anything that really belonged to anyone."

She looked at him, then said, "We may be poor, but we're not thieves. We don't take things." She forced a smile. "I have a whole half a loaf of bread, and even some other bits for you three . . ."

The boy looked at the small top. Maybe . . . just maybe . . . he could make other things . . . if he was very, very careful.

7

The egg toast was only lightly browned on Lundi morning. Alastar hoped that was a favorable omen for the day. As Maitre, he certainly could have insisted on having Jienna do the cooking at the residence, but he didn't see the point of that, especially given the parlous state of Collegium finances. He would have liked to have done without a maid as well, but the dwelling was so large that it needed someone to tend to it . . . and Jienna was pleasant enough and good at what she did, even cooking on rare occasions. But he certainly didn't need a full-time cook, not yet, although he might have to reconsider once he got the Collegium on a better footing and he began to do some necessary entertaining. But, for the moment, by eating in the dining hall, he had better control over what the students ate . . . although it had taken three days for the egg toast to appear in proper form.

Alastar took a deep breath as he walked back to the administration building and was pleased to note that there was absolutely no odor of sewage. That had made his morning run much more pleasant. What especially pleased him was that the wind was light and blowing from the southeast, indicating that the repairs had addressed the immediate cause of olfactory distress.

Back in his study, Alastar studied the master ledger, then turned his thoughts to ways of turning the conflict between the rex and the High Council to benefit the Collegium—without the application of what amounted to either extensive covert imaging, which would not remain covert, and overt brute force. He was having little success when Dareyn appeared in his doorway.

"High Holder Haebyn has agreed to see you tomorrow, and High Holder Vaun can only see you this very afternoon, preferably at third glass. Should I send messages to confirm?"

"Please do. Suggest second glass tomorrow afternoon. I take it there's been no reply from either Moeryn or Nacryon?"

"No, sir."

"Then we'll have to wait a day or two before we inquire again."

After Dareyn left, Alastar spent less than a third of a glass jotting down notes on how instruction for imagers in protecting themselves through nonlethal ways might be improved before Dareyn was once again at his door.

"Chorister Iskhar is here to see you."

"Have him come in."

In moments, the sandy-haired chorister, who ranked as a junior master, stepped into the study, carefully closing the door behind himself.

"I take it that you're not here to learn my reaction to your homily," began Alastar, motioning to the chairs. "I liked it, by the way. Thought-provoking, as a homily should be . . . although I'm not so convinced that all feelings, even overpowering ones, are necessarily the tools of the Namer, nor that all rational judgments are superior to feelings." Alastar chuckled. "Then again, your homily might be more appropriate for the students than for a curmudgeon like me . . ."

Iskhar laughed softly. "I have noticed a certain phrase being used by some of the students, to the effect that, if it feels good, one should try it. The implication is that all good feelings come from the Nameless."

"They probably do, but the Namer's not above using

them for his own ends, and the Namer and his tools can also use logic and rationality for the worst of ends. All one has to do is to observe advocates and justicers to see that. But that's not why you're here. What is it?"

"Chorister Lytaarl of the Anomen L'Excelsis visited this morning. He was rather concerned . . ."

"Upset?" asked Alastar.

"Rather." Iskhar spoiled his stern tone with an amused smile. "He wanted to convey to me that Solayi is the day of the Nameless. He said it should not be profaned."

"Especially by imagers, of all people, having the temerity to tear up the East River Road and repair a sewer that was profaning the air along the road and even across the river?"

"Yes, Maitre. He was most . . . voluble, in expressing his opinions."

"I haven't heard from him," said Alastar blandly.

"I didn't think you would want to. I told him that it might be better if I conveyed his concerns to you."

"Was he that upset?" Alastar understood that some people, and more likely choristers, truly felt Solayi was a time for family, reflection, and worship, although most likely Lytaarl would have reversed that priority. "What do you think, Iskhar?"

"I understand his concerns, sir . . ."

"I'm afraid I don't," replied Alastar, knowing he was being deliberately obtuse. "Why couldn't he just thank the Nameless that someone had removed the pernicious stench? Since I seem to be missing something, could you explain what those concerns are, and the basis for them?"

"Many choristers believe that the end-day should be devoted to . . . higher considerations, such as worship and reflection on one's benefits and family."

"Air not filled with odors is a great benefit. Did you mention that to him?"

"No, sir."

Alastar replied sternly, "Perhaps I should." He could only keep a straight face at Iskhar's horrified expression for a moment before he laughed wryly. "No . . . I won't do that. I'd like to, but it would only make matters worse. Tell the most concerned chorister of estimable rectitude that the Maitre appreciates his concerns and that we will not profane Solayi in the future, and that we do not anticipate undertaking any other activities that might reflect poorly on the Collegium's respect for the Nameless . . . or something along those lines." He extracted a gold from his wallet. "Give this to him as a gift to the poor and deserving and as a token of my respect for his efforts to maintain proper respect for the traditions of the Nameless."

Alastar personally hardly had that many golds to spare, and he wasn't about to use any Collegium golds to mollify Lytaarl, but since the last thing he needed was greater irritation of the chorister of the most influential anomen in L'Excelsis, he would part with a gold of his own.

"It might be better . . ."

"No, it wouldn't be. Lytaarl is a most perceptive man. Just from my actions in undertaking the repairs, he knows where I stand. Seeing him personally would send the wrong signal for such a minor affront." *Besides, if he continues to make a fuss after receiving what amounts to an apology in gold, you can make it known that he wanted more than a gold as an apology for doing a good service for the people of L'Excelsis at a theologically inconvenient time.* The factors would understand, and they were going to be the ones who counted.

"You have something else in mind, don't you, sir?"

"I do. I hope it's not necessary."

"So do I, sir." Iskhar took the gold.

"Is there anything else?"

The chorister grinned. "I'll think about a homily on the good side of feelings."

Alastar shook his head as Iskhar left the study.

Second glass neared well before Alastar had accomplished a fraction of the tasks he had in mind. He set aside his draft on physical training for older imagers and made his way to the stable where the gelding was waiting, along with two escorts.

When he reached the stable, he mounted quickly and led the way to the narrow east bridge, and then, once across, turned the gelding north on the East River Road. He took a deep breath, but he could not smell the pungent odor of sewage—other less than admirable smells, but not sewage. He nodded and surveyed both sides of the avenue, taking in the grayish waters of the river to his left and then the buildings to his right, an old, not-quite shabby café with a décor of white and dark brown, including an awning striped in the same colors and a tailor's shop, both probably dating from the time of Rex Hayar, who had decreed that all barges and river merchanting be moved south of L'Excelsis proper. That was also roughly when the old Great Canal had been filled and turned into a paved highway all the way to Laaryn.

Alastar almost snorted. Had Ryen tried something a tenth that ambitious all the High Holders and factors would have been at his throat. *How much of that is because the power of the Collegium and the abilities of its imagers have declined?* The answer to his question had been more than obvious from the moment he had stepped onto Imagisle. *You can't undo the past. You can only hold off the most immediate dangers while you rebuild.* If he could, and some days he wondered about that, especially when he had to listen to Obsolym.

A mille and a half north of the Nord Bridge, he and the two other imagers reached their destination. Vaun had an expansive mansion, if modest for a High Holder, situated in the midst of gardens and grounds enclosed by a brick wall that was itself set back some ten yards from the East River Road. A man in workman's brown opened the iron gates as the three rode up, nodded politely as they rode through, and immediately closed them.

A footman in tan livery, trimmed in black, stood at the front entry. "Welcome to Vaun Hall, sir. The High Holder awaits you."

Alastar dismounted, handing the reins to Chervyt, accompanied this time by an older second, Maercyl, and then followed the footman up the wide steps and through the double doors into the entry hall, positively modest, an oblong space no more than three yards in width and five in length, with simple tapestry hangings on the side wall, each of a stylized tree against a light brown background, bordered in black trimmed in gold thread. The floor tiles were of a translucent amber-colored stone, and the walls of goldenwood. The archway at the rear opened onto a hallway that extended both left and right as well as to a staircase to the upper two levels.

The footman gestured to the left. "This way, sir."

Alastar followed him to the second door on the left, which was open.

"Ah . . . Maitre Alastar, do come in. Might I offer you refreshments after your ride? Perhaps a dark lager?" For all that he was almost as tall as Alastar, the brown-haired Vaun conveyed the impression of a coney—not necessarily scared, but very alert. His nose even twitched as he looked at the Maitre.

"A dark lager would be welcome. Thank you."

Vaun gestured to the footman, and then to the small table, flanked by two chairs, set before a window that afforded a view to the west, mostly of the far shore of the River Aluse. The footman departed silently, and Vaun walked to the table and paused just slightly, enough that he and Alastar sat at the same time.

"You have obviously inquired about my habits, Councilor."

"I could let you think that," replied Vaun, with the hint of a smile, "but I did not have time. The dark lager was a guess. You are known as a man of action, and you are neither young nor old. You are reputed to be the strongest imager of our times, and in little more than a month of taking over a Collegium that has needed stronger leadership than it has had, you are visiting with the High Council. That suggested dark lager." The High Holder shrugged.

"That is still impressive." Alastar had to admit that Vaun's deductions impressed him more than mere preparations might have . . . and if the High Holder lied—and he had inquired earlier, even before Alastar had requested the meeting—that was even more impressive.

"It's been a while since the Maitre of the Collegium has taken the time to visit with the members of the Council."

"Did Maitre Fhaen?" Alastar had found no record of such, and Dareyn had known of no such meetings, but Dareyn had been Fhaen's personal assistant for only the past two years.

"Not in my time on the Council."

The Maitre nodded. *Not in almost five years.*

Vaun looked up as a woman of indeterminate age, wearing tan trousers and shirt, with a black jacket, appeared bearing a tray on which were two crystal beakers, one holding an amber liquid and the other the dark lager. She served Alastar first, and then Vaun, and immediately left, closing the door behind her so gently that Alastar barely heard anything.

"To your presence here," offered the High Holder, lifting his beaker.

Alastar lifted his as well, noting that each beaker bore

an elaborate V cut into the crystal. "And to your kindness in receiving me."

They both drank, more than a sip and less than a gulp, and Alastar set his beaker back on the large coaster where the server had first placed it. "Quite good lager. From your own lands?"

"Hardly. I just buy the best." After the briefest pause, Vaun went on. "I could fence or merely smile. Or we could converse about the lovely weather or how you find L'Excelsis after Westisle. I'd rather not. That would waste time."

"What should I know, then," asked Alastar, "that I likely do not?"

"Besides the fact that Ryen is either deluded or mad, if not both? Or the fact that Guerdyn would rather be rex than head of the High Council? Or the fact that, now that you are here, that will not happen?"

"I think you overestimate my abilities. The Collegium is far more than its Maitre."

"The Collegium is weaker than it has ever been, but it is still strong enough to keep Guerdyn or any small group of High Holders from overthrowing and replacing the rex."

Alastar nodded, thinking about the full implications of Vaun's words—essentially that neither the rex nor the Collegium could afford to antagonize the majority or even a significant minority of High Holders . . . but that Guerdyn was likely to overreach himself . . . unless Ryen did something incredibly stupid. "What about the factors?"

"Yes . . . the factors. They are not as strong as they were in the time of Bovaria, and that is partly because the High Council has chosen in the past to recognize the more wealthy ones."

"That gives hope to those who aspire and weakens the factors as a group."

"Some say so." Vaun shrugged.

"How does High Holder Guerdyn feel about it?"

"He has not said, but his lineage is a long and proud one."

In short, he doesn't like elevating factors whom he sees as having wealth and little else. "And you, you would prefer a slightly stronger and less . . . unpredictable rex, and you would not mind a few more High Holders to replace those who have fallen?"

"I have no objections to those who are wealthy and modest in their pretensions." Vaun offered a smile. "In fact, I have few objections to maintaining what I understand to have been the vision of the first Maitre."

"I must confess I am not certain I have any idea of what that vision was, except a system that balanced the power of the rex, the High Holders, and the factors."

"Precisely. With the Collegium now and again shifting the balance at the edge."

Alastar understood exactly what Vaun was saying. He lifted the beaker and took another swallow. "This is excellent, but I would not expect less of someone who understands so much and can convey expectations through historical descriptions." He paused just for an instant before going on. "Because I am from Westisle and have arrived so recently, is there anything you can tell me about the three other councilors I have not met. I would prefer not to inadvertently bring up some matter that, through my lack of familiarity with matters here in L'Excelsis, I might be commonly expected to know . . . and do not."

"I would doubt you would do anything so obvious as that. Still . . . let me consider." With that, Vaun took a swallow from his beaker, an amber lager, then held the beaker for a time before setting it down. "You might not know that Haebyn had let it be bruited that he might not be averse to being the head of the Council when Ryel stepped down. That was Ryel the elder. He died within weeks of relinquishing his position. That was a loss for the Council."

"Might I ask why?"

"It was not widely known, but the elder Ryel had friendships that provided great insight."

Alastar raised his eyebrows. "Was he close to Rex Ryen?"

"Hardly. They tolerated each other, but . . ." Vaun shook his head. "Enough said."

"Knowing a bit more might be helpful," suggested Alastar.

"To whom?" asked Vaun dryly.

Alastar understood that Vaun had said what he was going to say on the matter of the late Ryel's "friendships." "So, after he stepped down, Nacryon was suggested and then became a member? That is done by petition, is it not?"

Vaun nodded. "Any High Holder may petition to be a member of the Council when a vacancy arises. A petition must have the approval of at least thirty other High Holders from his part of Solidar and five from elsewhere, except there can be no more than five names total from holdings within a hundred milles of L'Excelsis. The other four members of the Council decide from the petitions."

Effectively one High Holder from each of the original five lands of Lydar. "How is the head of the High Council determined? By vote of the councilors?"

Vaun nodded. "Annually, or if any three members request a vote at any time. But there can only be one request in any year, unless a new councilor is selected, and then there can be two in that year. There has, of course, been but one vote and no request for another this year."

"And you will be leaving the Council . . ." Alastar paused. "What would happen if a councilor who was due to step down were selected as the head of the Council?"

"That would count as a new appointment for five years."

Alastar smiled pleasantly. "I'm afraid all of this is new to me. I do appreciate your enlightening me."

"It is my pleasure."

"There are more than fifteen hundred High Holders, I understand. It would seem difficult for you all to know each other."

"I doubt that any of us know more than a hundred or so on a personal basis, perhaps another hundred as acquaintances, and by reputation . . . who knows?" Vaun shrugged.

"Before you became councilors, did any of you know each other?"

"I believe Councilor Haebyn knew Nacryon comparatively well, through their wives' families. That was not known until after Nacryon joined the Council, at least not to the rest of us." Vaun smiled pleasantly once more. "It is refreshing to have a Maitre of the Collegium who is interested in the Council. Do you have any other general questions I might address?"

The way Vaun asked the question was a clear indication to Alastar that the councilor would prefer no pointed questions.

"At this moment, asking about more specific matters might be premature until I've had the opportunity to meet all of the councilors. I am more than happy to answer any questions you might have, or simply to listen, should there be any concerns about which I should know."

"Like you, at the moment, I have no specific matters in mind, although I, for one, am happy to see more of an outreach and an independent view from the Maitre of the Collegium."

That is a definite message. Alastar nodded. "I appreciate your kindness in seeing me, and I trust we will be able to talk on matters as necessary." After the slightest pause, he added, "I would not wish to take more of your time, as I understand you may be traveling . . ."

"You are kind." Vaun rose from the table.

Alastar stood as well. After more pleasantries as they walked back to the entry hall, Alastar made his way out and to the waiting imagers and his mount.

As he rode back toward the Collegium, he considered what he had learned about Vaun as well as what the High Holder had told him. He wasn't in the slightest confident that Vaun would support Ryen, only that Vaun would side with the strongest, just like an intelligent coney . . . and that Vaun had not been pleased with whatever petitioning methods Haebyn had used to get Nacryon appointed as a councilor. He did wonder about precisely what "friendships" the former Council head had enjoyed and would have to keep that in mind.

Dareyn had left for the evening by the time Alastar had unsaddled and groomed the gelding and returned to his study. He could have let Petros's duty ostler do that, but he didn't want to get in the habit of having others do everything routine for him. *At least, not all the time.*

When he sat down behind his desk, for a moment he wasn't certain he wanted to continue working, but he finally picked up his copy of the master ledger and started to leaf through it. One of the entries showed an expenditure of two silvers for a quint of a ream of paper.

Wasn't there an entry for paper just a page earlier? He looked back through the pages, finding expenditures for paper—a silver here, two silvers there, and three in a third place. He set down the ledger, then opened the cabinet beside the desk, drawing out a sheet of paper.

Surely, imaging paper can't be that difficult, can it? He'd seen it made at Westisle, but, for some reason . . . With a smile, Alastar concentrated.

In less than a tenth of a glass, Alastar had fifty sheets

of paper, identical from what he could tell to those used for ledgers and documents. He'd have Dareyn use some of what he had imaged to see how it held up before saying or suggesting anything.

He allowed himself a brief smile . . . and went back to work.

8

When Dareyn arrived on Mardi morning, Alastar handed him fifteen sheets of the paper he'd imaged the night before. "This is some new paper. Try it, and let me know what you think."

Dareyn frowned slightly. "Yes, sir."

"If it works we might be able to save at least a few silvers."

"Sir . . . don't forget that that Tertius Arion will be here at half past seventh glass. He's the first of the older thirds. You did say . . ."

"I did." Alastar didn't want to admit he'd almost forgotten about asking Dareyn to schedule meetings with the older thirds. "Is there one after him?"

"Two, sir. Tertius Nuasyn and then Tertia Seliora. That should still give you time before you leave to meet with Councilor Haebyn."

Alastar plowed through a few more pages of the master ledger before the student imager appeared. Arion definitely showed his Pharsi heritage, if in a handsome way, with a honey-colored complexion, shimmering but well-trimmed black hair, and deep brown eyes. He smiled tentatively, but pleasantly, as he entered the study, inclined his head, and then said, "Maitre."

Alastar motioned to the chairs and waited for the young man to seat himself. "There's nothing to be worried about. I'll be meeting with all the student imagers over the weeks ahead. You're the first because you're one of the most senior students." He smiled. "Tell me a bit about yourself and how you came to the Collegium."

"You must know, sir, that I'm the second son of High

Holder Calkoran, and that I grew up in Vaestora. I was almost twelve before my father discovered I was an imager—"

"Then you knew before that, and you tried to keep it hidden?"

Arion smiled sheepishly. "I didn't want to leave Vaestora. I did read about imagers, and I tried not to do anything stupid."

"Where did you read about imagers?"

"In the old records at Vaestora. The first Calkoran D'Alte was a marshal in Khel. He later served under Commander Quaeryt and was made the High Holder at Vaestora when the previous High Holder died without heirs."

Quaeryt commanded more than imagers? Another thing Alastar had not known. *How much else don't you know?* "Does imaging run in your family?"

"I did have a great-great-uncle who was an imager, sir. His name was Valtyr. There are no others that I know of."

"How do you like the Collegium?"

"I didn't like it at all the first year, but I've come to realize that Vaestora would not have been the place for me." Arion smiled ruefully. "Especially as the younger son."

"In what have you learned the most?" asked Alastar, waiting for the young man's response, and then asking another question. The questions and answers continued for not quite a quint before Alastar showed Arion out. The young man definitely impressed Alastar.

Immediately after Arion left, Dareyn appeared in the doorway. "Before you talk with Nuasyn, sir, you've received a request from Elthyrd D'Factorius for a few moments."

"Did he give any reason?"

"No, sir."

"Eighth glass tomorrow morning, if that's agreeable

to him." Alastar didn't want to slight the head of the factors' council or be late for his appointment with High Holder Haebyn, and it would be too easy for that to occur if he scheduled Elthyrd for any time on Mardi that wasn't already committed.

Nuasyn was a serious-looking young man, sixteen, close to finishing his studies. According to Cyran, his principal tutor, Nuasyn was a solid third with moderate but not outstanding abilities with shields and would probably not show much greater development in imaging techniques. Alastar spent less than two quints with him.

Tertia Seliora was a tall blond young woman. That was surprising to Alastar because he knew Seliora was usually a Pharsi name, something to do with Artiema, the greater moon, and because few Pharsi were blond. She was also shy, having trouble meeting Alastar's eyes, but well-spoken, confirming her background as the daughter of a well-off factor from Montagne.

Somehow, before Alastar knew it, he was riding north for his appointment with High Holder Haebyn, whose L'Excelsis residence was to the north-northeast and required almost a glass to reach. The two-level residence sprawled across a rise in the middle of a hunting park, at the end of a drive half a mille long. Alastar followed the footman, attired in a green so dark it was almost black, into the entry hall just as a chime struck the glass.

Good thing you allowed extra time.

When Alastar entered a comparatively small study, paneled in dark oak, Haebyn rose from a polished table desk, bare except for the single sheaf of papers that the High Holder laid carefully on the wood. "Greetings, Maitre Alastar."

"The same to you, Councilor." Alastar had not realized that Haebyn was young for a councilor, far younger than Alastar.

The High Holder gestured to the small circular table

set before the window. "Would you care for something to drink?"

"If it wouldn't be too much trouble, a dark lager."

Haebyn smiled warmly. "I think we can manage that." He nodded toward the footman, who had remained standing in the study door. "A dark lager and my usual, Ferrik."

The footman nodded in return, then departed, closing the study door.

Alastar let Haebyn move toward the chair on the left and moved to the other. They both seated themselves.

"Are you here on behalf of the Collegium . . . or the rex?" Haebyn's tone was diffident, as if it mattered little to him as to how Alastar replied.

"My first interest is always that of the Collegium." Alastar smiled politely. "Obviously, the Collegium benefits when there is less conflict between the High Holders and the rex, or the factors and the rex, or the Collegium and the rex . . . or the High Holders and the Collegium."

"It does not seem entirely coincidental that you have requested meetings with High Holder Guerdyn and me soon after Rex Ryen indicated he planned to impose additional tariffs."

"No more coincidental than the fact that I've been Maitre for little more than a month and that this is the first opportunity I've had for such meetings."

"What is the situation at the Collegium? There have been rumors . . ."

"There are always rumors. To which of them might you be referring?"

"There are so very many . . ."

Alastar nodded and waited.

At that moment, the study door opened, and a serving girl entered, with a tray on which were a beaker of dark lager and a goblet of a sparkling white wine. Wordlessly she placed a dark brown porcelain coaster on the table before each man and then set the goblet and then the beaker on the appropriate coaster, leaving as silently as she had come.

"To a better understanding between the Council and the Collegium." Haebyn lifted his goblet.

Alastar had the feeling that the toast was as much command as toast, but merely lifted his beaker. "To understanding." He took a sip of the lager, good, but not so good as that offered by Vaun. "Very good."

"I'll take your word. Lager's never been to my taste." After setting his goblet on the coaster, Haebyn cleared his throat. "What is the most interesting is that when Maitre Fhaen selected the second-ranking imager at Westisle as his successor, there was quiet objection until you arrived, and then an absence of opposition. That suggests you are more than you appear . . . although Maitre Zhelan had mentioned that you were gifted. That was some years ago."

"You're obviously familiar with the Collegium in Westisle."

Haebyn smiled disarmingly. "Not really. My father knew Maitre Zhelan from before. I met him as a younger man. He would have been the heir to Dueralt."

"He was the eldest son of Souven D'Alte?"

Haebyn nodded. "Souven the elder, the Nameless bless his passing, had three sons, but I think Zhelan would have made an excellent steward of Dueralt."

"Maitre Zhelan has been most effective in restoring the effectiveness of the Collegium in Westisle. I learned a great deal from him."

"It's interesting," mused Haebyn. "An imager with no background, no education before the Collegium, and no . . . acquaintances in L'Excelsis appears to have calmed the waters by his mere appearance. The only one who appears not to have been calmed is the rex."

"I'm under the impression that he is not the type to be easily calmed."

Haebyn laughed softly. "Such understatement."

"He is rather firm in his beliefs about what should be done."

"As is the Council . . . about what should and should not be done."

"That was certainly the impression I received from High Holder Guerdyn." Alastar thought he detected a slight reaction from Haebyn, but what exactly that meant he had no idea.

"He would know better than I."

"He's been head of the High Council for two years?"

"Two and a half."

"He was raised close to L'Excelsis, I assume, since his holding is near. Do you think that provides an advantage to the High Council?"

Haebyn considered the question before replying. "The advantage is that he has been exposed to more of what occurs here. That could also be seen as a disadvantage."

"He doesn't seem exactly enthralled with the rex."

"Is anyone with a modicum of intelligence? As short a time as you have been here . . . what do you think?"

"I worry that he is perhaps too precipitate in deciding." *And that is a great understatement.*

"Pleasantly and politically said. I suppose that is necessary, given that the Collegium is, shall we say, beholden to the rex."

"Financially, that is so, especially since the factors and the guilds tend to frown on imagers attempting to create anything that might infringe on their perquisites."

"You must have considered that, to say so that openly."

"It is what it is. We are looking into ways to reduce that dependency in a fashion designed not to create difficulties."

"You do not think that might create other difficulties?"

"There are always difficulties. If there is no rain,

crops die in the fields. If there is too much, they rot before harvest. If the weather is perfect, the harvests are so plentiful that the growers make less. If tariffs are too low, Solidár becomes weak. If they are too high, people suffer. If the rex is strong, everyone complains. If he is weak, the land suffers, and people still complain."

"How do higher tariffs do anything but weaken Solidar?" demanded Haebyn.

"If the tariffs are spent wisely, on better roads or harbors, or on port inspectors to make sure foreign shippers pay their tariffs, or on ships to stop smugglers, Solidar benefits. Even if some are spent on wines or fine furniture for the rex, vintners and cabinetmakers benefit."

"Those who pay the tariffs might feel otherwise, Maitre."

"That is true. It's the nature of ruling that those who pay tariffs do not believe they receive value for their golds. That is because they do not reckon what additional expenses they would incur."

"The Collegium receives golds from those tariffs. What benefits does it provide?"

"It saves the lives of people who would otherwise die or live miserably. In turn, they create roads. They balance the power of those who would abuse it. The Collegium has often served as a check on the power of the rex, and such a restraint is far less costly than a revolt against him. The Collegium has built walls against rivers to reduce floods, and most recently, we have repaired a rather grievous break in the sewers in L'Excelsis. We also buy goods from factors and High Holders and crafters."

Haebyn nodded. "It might be said the benefits are sparse, given the costs."

"In this year, perhaps, but what about three years ago, when the river walls kept the worst of the flooding from L'Excelsis. Or when five imagers put down the

Solian revolt and spared the lives of tens of thousands. Only a man excessively concerned about today's coins reckons his losses and benefits in single year . . . or even a few."

"But a man may lose all in a year."

"Only a fool or an imprudent man loses all in a year, and if he does, it is the result of years of foolishness come due."

"The same could be said of a rex."

"It could," admitted Alastar, "but it might be better to guide such foolish rulers than undertake acts that result in deaths and devastation."

"And who might take responsibility for such guidance, so that it might be heeded?" Haebyn's tone held an edge of skepticism, and possibly scorn.

Alastar smiled pleasantly. "Who indeed?"

"Is that a veiled promise, Maitre?"

"I can only promise that the Collegium will not stand by idly if Solidar is threatened, or if the order that has protected generations of imagers is threatened."

"What has that to do with tariffs?"

"Everything has to do with tariffs," replied Alastar, "as we both know."

"The rex has let it be known that he wishes to increase tariffs by a copper on a half silver. That would be ruinous."

Alastar managed to keep his mouth shut. *An increase of one part in five? That would be ruinous . . . and insanely stupid.* "What increase would not be ruinous?"

"A copper on a gold would be the most any would consider reasonable in these times, and many would find that excessive."

One part in a hundred? Equally ruinous from Ryen's point . . . and likely the Collegium's. "Until this moment, I was not aware of either the scope of the rex's proposal or of the likely feeling of the High Council."

"That should surprise me. It does not, unhappily."

Haebyn shrugged. "You might see why the Council is skeptical of what the rex wants."

"I can see both sides on this matter. I have heard that there has not been an increase in tariffs for a good ten years. Did I hear that correctly?" Alastar suspected it had been longer than that, but didn't know.

"Why should there be an increase?"

"With more people and more repairs needed for both the roads and the army, with more ships needed against pirates, more tariffs are required."

"The factors are the ones who demand more ships."

"High Holder Guerdyn seems to think that the same tariff levels need to apply to both factors and High Holders." Alastar was stretching things, but wanted a reaction.

The hint of a frown appeared on Haebyn's face and then vanished. "I thought imagers could create coins."

For a moment, Alastar wondered from where that statement had come, before realizing it was Haebyn's way of avoiding more talk on the issue of tariffs. "Only a limited number, and only if an imager is near a place where the proper ores are in the ground." That wasn't precisely true, but Alastar didn't want to get into details. "Otherwise, no rex or Maitre would ever have had need of tariffs."

"That is a pity."

"It is what it is, alas," agreed Alastar with a slight laugh. "As are so many things." He took another swallow of the dark lager.

Haebyn smiled. "I will not keep you longer. I do appreciate your seeking to meet all the members of the Council." He shifted his weight in the chair as if to indicate he was about to rise.

"I appreciate your seeing me. Your words have given me food for thought."

"I trust that this will not be the last time we meet." Haebyn stood.

"I would hope not." Alastar smiled pleasantly and also rose from the table.

Once he had left Haebyn's L'Excelsis dwelling and was riding back toward the Collegium, Alastar went over the conversation. What he found most interesting was that Ryen had proposed such a massive increase in tariff levels as if it were the most reasonable idea, and that Haebyn had clearly been startled by Guerdyn's insistence on the same tariff level for both factors and High Holders. Alastar thought Guerdyn was right, and he wondered if Haebyn had considered the unrest that would follow if Ryen proposed a higher tariff for factors.

You'll have to see what Nacryon says . . . or doesn't.

Dareyn was waiting when Alastar returned to Imagisle and entered the anteroom to his study, but did not speak immediately.

"What's happened in my absence?" asked Alastar. "You have that worried look."

"The rex wishes to see you tomorrow at eighth glass. I already sent a message to Factor Elthyrd. He was amenable to coming at the first glass of the afternoon."

Likely not happy, but amenable. "Anything else?"

"You have an appointment with High Holder Nacryon on Jeudi morning at ninth glass and with High Holder Moeryn that same afternoon, at third glass. I've rescheduled some of your meetings with students."

Which are going to take longer than you thought with everything else that's happening. "Just work them in as you can."

"That paper you gave me . . . It's better than what we've been using."

"Keep using it, and let me know. It's less expensive, and if it works out, we could save more than a few golds."

"I will, sir."

What else could we image of a common nature . . . ?

wondered Alastar as he entered his study, not quite groaning as he saw the master ledger.

Later, after eating his evening meal in the dining hall—mutton cutlets and boiled sliced potatoes drowned in brown gravy—he returned to his dwelling and the private study there, where he just sat behind the desk, thinking. *How on Terahnar did you end up here, the only person in a mansion that could easily house a score or more?* Even with his comparatively few needs, the dwelling still required a full-time maid and a gardener, not to mention occasional repairs. *And you feel guilty . . .*

Thealia would have laughed, but even then her laugh would have had an edge, something he had realized in the years since her untimely death. Alastar was still pondering over that—and everything else—when he finally fell asleep in the stillness of the spacious bedroom in the Maitre's dwelling.

9

Alastar was at the Chateau D'Rex at a quint before eighth glass, but had to wait in the corridor until two quints past the glass before Ryen summoned him into the study, where he sat, broodingly, behind the wide desk, piled with stacks of papers, stacks that appeared to be the same ones Alastar had seen on his previous two visits.

"Good morning, sir." Alastar checked his shields, in case Ryen became even more volatile than usual.

"It's not morning, except for those who lie in bed. It's midday. It will likely rain later." Ryen smiled broadly. "I expect you to begin work on the new boulevard by next Lundi."

"You have acquired the property or consent for that?"

"I have done everything necessary. Now, you must do what I order."

"If we are to do it properly, I will need a map of which shops and dwellings we are to remove and a proclamation of your grant of authority to the Collegium."

"You're questioning my word? How dare—"

"Sir, I'm not questioning your authority. But when we start to remove dwellings and shops, without an official document, we will face great anger, and people may even attack us. Then we will have to defend ourselves, and people will be hurt. That will take time, and you wish the avenue to be completed as soon as possible. Matters will go far more swiftly with a proclamation and a route set on a map . . . and notices to those along the route."

Ryen glowered. Then he nodded. "I can see that. I

don't like it, but I can see it. You will have the proclamation and map on Vendrei."

"Thank you, sir. That will allow us time to prepare."

"No more about the avenue. It will be called the Avenue D'Rex. How far have you gotten with the High Council?"

"I'm working on that. Just how great an increase in tariffs are you going to propose?"

"Are you planning to be my finance minister as well?"

"You want me to change the minds of High Holders. That's hard to do when I don't know what you want from them. None of them will agree in advance to anything you intend to implement without knowing what it is." *Even knowing, they likely won't.*

"There hasn't been a change in tariffs in fifteen years. My father had a Northern Army and a Southern Army. Now there's just one, and it's the size of the old Northern Army. The factors want warships to stop the pirates in the Southern Gulf. There aren't enough extra golds to build one ship, let alone a flotilla. The factors claim not all goods coming into port are tariffed, and cheaper goods from Jariola and even Ferrum are priced lower. I can't hire more port inspectors without golds . . ."

Alastar listened while Ryen went through a long list of needs, including some, such as refurbishment of the old palace in Solis—or what was left of it—that it would be better not to mention to anyone. When the rex finished, Alastar said, "That's quite a list. How great a tariff increase will that require?"

"Two more coppers for every five collected now. They won't accept that. I've let it be known that I'll accept one."

"That's an increase of two parts in ten."

"They can Namer well afford that after all these years of underpaying. Now you know. No more on that. Just get rid of their objections. Otherwise, what use is the Collegium?"

"We can build roads."

"We'll see about that. Go."

Alastar nodded politely, stepped back, and turned, making his way from Ryen's study. *At least he didn't ask about the sewers.* Yet.

Once he returned to Imagisle, Alastar, from a shielded position, observed Obsolym teaching the younger primes the history of Solidar and of the early years of the Collegium. The older Maitre knew both and presented the information well. After the instruction, he waited until the primes left, dropped his shields, and then said, "That was impressive and well-presented."

Obsolym looked disconcerted for a moment, then smiled, "Thank you, Maitre. I do appreciate your taking the time to observe."

"I would like to have done so earlier, but there has been a great deal to deal with."

"I understand the rex has requested your presence often in the past few days. Has he said more about this avenue? You know that will create great anger among the crafters and factors."

"I know that. I asked him for a regial proclamation declaring his intent and his ownership of the property we will have to raze. I told him that, without those, there would be unrest and possibly violence and that the work would be slowed. He was not happy, but he agreed to provide those."

"They won't be enough."

"They may not be," Alastar agreed. "But we're in no position to refuse."

"I fear you're right." The old Maitre D'Structure shook his head. "He may bring down the High Holders, the factors, and the High Command on himself . . . and us."

"I'm working on trying to obviate the worst possibilities."

"The best of fortune in that," replied Obsolym dryly.

"For all of us," said Alastar with a smile, before turning and leaving the classroom. He still didn't totally trust Obsolym, but there was no secret about what Ryen wanted.

At a quint before first glass of the afternoon, Dareyn announced, "Factorius Elthyrd," and then had to step out of the way as the head of the factors' council marched into the study.

Alastar rose. "Greetings, Factorius."

"I had hoped that we would have been able to meet sooner, Maitre."

The way Elthyrd offered Alastar's title was the second indication that the head of the factors' council was less than pleased, the first having been the frosty glance he had offered when he strode into the study. Alastar gestured to the chairs before the desk and said, "I would have liked that as well, but as head of the Collegium I do answer to the rex, and he insisted on my presence at the chateau this morning."

"And what about yesterday?"

"I had already arranged meetings with members of the High Council. Had you requested a meeting first, then I would have given you the same courtesy." Alastar reseated himself. "You didn't mention the reason why you wanted to meet."

"That should be obvious, I would think, but since it is not as obvious to you as to all of L'Excelsis, apparently, I will be blunt. Might I ask why you took it upon yourself and the Collegium to disrupt a Solayi morning in order to repair sewers?"

"Because no one else was repairing them, and because the stench was affecting large parts of both L'Excelsis and Imagisle. It seemed the civic thing to do. We chose Solayi morning because there are far fewer wagons, coaches, and others using the East River Road then."

"Then when might we expect you to repair the sewers

along the Boulevard D'Este near Nordroad? Or perhaps those near Fedre and Sudroad?" Elthyrd practically glared.

"When might the Collegium expect reimbursement from the factors' council for undertaking what the council has not while the people of L'Excelsis have suffered?" countered Alastar. "And how much will you pay us to undertake those other repairs?"

Elthyrd's mouth opened, gaping like that of a fish out of water, and for several moments, no sound issued from his lips. "You . . . you think you should be paid for such . . . such an affront to the day of the Nameless and a disruption of a peaceful Solayi?"

"You would have been more greatly offended if we had closed off part of the East River Road during a time when factors and shopkeepers were actually using the avenue, and since one needs to see to make repairs, doing so at night was not practical. As for the Nameless, why would there be any objection to work that made L'Excelsis a better place?"

"You have answers for everything, but those answers are not acceptable to the council."

"Why not?" asked Alastar, trying not to overreact, but wondering why the factor was so agitated. "We removed a source of stench and odor, and we did not disrupt business."

"You disrespected the Nameless, and his chorister."

"No disrespect was intended, Factorius Elthyrd. We were trying to remedy something that was making it hard for people to breathe."

"You should have consulted the council first."

Alastar forbore mentioning that Ryen had been "consulting" with the council for weeks, and that nothing had happened. "I likely should have, although I had not realized that resolving a problem would create such consternation. In my newness to L'Excelsis and my ignorance, I had actually thought people would be pleased to have a problem resolved."

"Do not mock me or the council."

Alastar sighed. "Master Factorius, I have not mocked anyone. I attempted to solve a problem no one else has addressed. I had no idea that repairing a stinking sewer ditch would upset anyone."

"I can see that," snorted Elthyrd. "The sewers are the province of the council, but the rex is supposed to provide stipends for the work. He did not do that. By repairing the most odious of the sewers, you have deprived the council of the leverage necessary to obtain not only the golds for repairing those sewers, but those for the others which require repairs."

Alastar saw the conflict. Ryen was trying to use the sewers as another way to force the factors to support increased tariffs, and the factors were using public unrest to put pressure on Ryen for more golds. "I beg your pardon, Master Factor, but I would hope you would recall that I am new to L'Excelsis. While what you have just said makes a great deal clearer, it is not something that Rex Ryen would reveal to me. Yet you are angry at me for not knowing something I would have no way to know in such a short time, and something that I doubt my predecessor knew either."

"That does not speak highly of either of you."

Alastar forced himself not to lash out at the idiot factor. "Had this occurred a year from now, such a judgment would be deserved. It is premature under the current circumstances."

"So what are you going to do, Maitre?"

"To consider what the Collegium can do to rectify the situation, after thinking it over and then consulting with you."

"I hope it gets farther than consideration and thought. That was all Maitre Fhaen ever said."

The time is past for that, unhappily. "I will be in touch with you shortly."

"I do hope so." Elthyrd nodded brusquely. "Until later." With that, he turned and left.

For a moment, Alastar stood there, somewhere between stunned and bemused at the thought that Elthyrd had no concept of what an imager maitre could do. *It's been far too long since the Collegium showed its power.*

"Sir . . . ?" Dareyn peered in through the study door that the factor had left open.

"Yes?"

"Factor Elthyrd left here looking . . . not very happy," said Dareyn warily.

"'Furious' might be a better word. He came in and attacked me and the Collegium for not consulting with the council, and for destroying the sanctity of Solayi. Do you have any idea why he emphasized the sanctity of Solayi?"

"It might be because his brother is Chorister Lytaarl."

Alastar looked hard at Dareyn.

"Ah . . . I thought you knew, sir," offered Dareyn.

"Exactly how would I know?" asked Alastar coolly. "I've never met Chorister Lytaarl, and I'd never heard his name before Iskhar mentioned his concerns on Lundi." His voice softened. "Please remember that I did not grow up here in L'Excelsis. Names and acts that all of you know may be unknown to me. I'd rather be reminded of something I already know than blindsided by something I don't. Please keep that in mind, if you would."

"Yes, sir. I'm sorry."

"You don't have to be sorry. I shouldn't have been short with you, but please volunteer anything you think I should know." After a moment, he asked, "Do you know anything about why the factors and the rex are squabbling over the sewers?"

Dareyn appeared puzzled by the question. "No, sir. Maitre Fhaen never mentioned it."

"Thank you. I'll have to go meet with the factor again, but I don't know when yet."

After he returned to his study, Alastar walked back and forth, thinking. *No one tells anyone anything, as if the withholding of knowledge conveyed power.* He paused. *And it does, if one considers that lack of knowledge will cause difficulties on the part of others. The problem is that one's enemies already have that knowledge, and those who suffer are the bystanders.*

That wasn't the only problem he faced. Another problem was that the Collegium had done nothing of note for years to gain the respect or support of anyone. All that previous Maitres had done was to receive golds from the rex, occasionally support him, but mostly take young imagers and train them, but only to maintain the Collegium. That meant few either respected the Collegium or needed anything from it.

He took a deep breath.

Like it or not, he was going to have to meet with Elthyrd again, and not lose his temper, and offer to repair other sewers, suggesting that the reason for the lack of golds was the low level of tariffs. *And that will infuriate Ryen, especially if it slows building his avenue to the chateau.*

There was also the potential problem of the army command and Marshal Demykalon, one that Alastar hadn't even begun to consider, let alone address, with the likelihood that there were more hidden pitfalls there as well.

10

On Jeudi morning, before Alastar left the Collegium to meet with Nacryon, he made his way to the northwest corner of the administration building where Obsolym presided over the archives. The older maitre looked up. "Good morning, Maitre. What brings you here?"

"You. You've been with the Collegium longer than any maitre. While we do not always see eye-to-eye on some matters, your knowledge and experience are most valuable. So I've come once more to ask you about something. What do you know about chief factor Elthyrd?"

"He's head of the factors' council. He's supposedly a silent partner in the new banque."

"The Banque of L'Excelsis?"

"I think that's what it's called, or maybe Banque D'Excelsis. Maitre Fhaen tried not to meet with him. He found such meetings wearing and wearying, and he could get along with almost anyone."

"I met with Factor Elthyrd yesterday, and I understand fully what Maitre Fhaen meant."

Obsolym nodded and smiled knowingly.

"He expressed some concern that we repaired that section of the sewer without consulting the factors' council. Do you know why the factors would be that concerned?"

"No, sir . . . except maybe they'd hoped to pry more golds out of the rex for making the repairs. That's my best judgment. Maitre Fhaen never said anything about it."

"I suspect you may be right about that." Alastar

shook his head. "Is there anyone that the rex isn't involved in some sort of struggle with?"

"Maitre Fhaen said he was . . . difficult, even as a child."

"What about his children? I've met his sons, but only for a moment . . ."

"Lorien's the heir. He's reserved. Pleasant enough, Maitre Fhaen said. Ryentar is the younger. He takes after his sire. At least, that is what one hears."

Alastar nodded, although from his brief meeting with the two it had seemed the other way around. "What about Lady Asarya? I've never heard a word about her."

"Most don't, sir. She and the rex have separate quarters, so it is said, and . . . well . . . some of the maids are said to be attractive."

That didn't totally surprise Alastar. It was clear Ryen would be difficult to live with. "With what does the lady busy herself?"

"I'd not be the one to say, sir."

The way in which Obsolym offered the statement suggested that someone did. "Who might know more?"

"The only one who might know would be Maitre Desyrk. I understand his brother often attended meetings that Marshal Ghalyn had with the rex."

Although Alastar nodded, he had to wonder just what sort of connections Desyrk had. *You need to look into that.* "I also understand that Chorister Lytaarl of the Anomen L'Excelsis is the brother of Factor Elthyrd. Do you know anything about him?"

"He's said to give a good homily. He's well thought of . . ."

"But?"

"I don't know this for a fact, you understand, but I've heard that he agrees with anyone who can advance his anomen."

"Or his collections in it on behalf of the Nameless?"

"Some have said that."

"What have you heard about the High Holders on the High Council?"

"Almost nothing. Maitre Fhaen indicated . . . it was suggested that he keep a distance from the High Council."

"I appreciate your insights, Obsolym. Thank you."

"My pleasure, sir."

As he walked away, Alastar thought that Obsolym's voice had held a trace of enjoyment . . . and amusement. *So be it.*

Because Nacryon's L'Excelsis residence was well to the east of the city, Alastar and his two imager escorts left the Collegium just before seventh glass, first riding up the East River Road and then east on the Boulevard D'Este all the way out to a small circle that was supposedly called the Plaza D'Nord, where they took the old pike due east for close to a mille, until he saw a brick dwelling on a hillside, rising out of several terraced gardens, and surrounded by a brick wall. The gateposts were also brick, and the gates were open.

Alastar rode up a stone-paved drive that could barely accommodate a large wagon or coach to a flat area with a turnout and a paved area wide enough to allow coaches or wagons to turn and follow the drive up to the paved receiving area. A small roofed terrace, supported by brick columns, flanked the entry to the two-story mansion.

A footman greeted Alastar as he dismounted, and in moments, he was inside the mansion and walking down a short hall to a sitting room, where a man of medium height, likely a few digits shorter than Alastar, and attired in a rich brown jacket over a cream and tan doublet, with hose and shoes that matched his jacket, stepped forward. "Welcome."

"Thank you for agreeing to see me."

Nacryon—blond and green-eyed—offered a warm smile that extended to his eyes. "I'm most pleased you were willing to come here, Maitre Alastar. I must confess I've never met . . . well, I've never even seen a master imager before. But then, we don't see that much of anything in Mantes, and I've only been here in L'Excelsis a few times since I became a councilor."

"You have a well-established dwelling here, though."

"I do. Not through inheritance. It dates back to Bovarian times. The previous owner claimed it once hosted the first Maitre of the Collegium." Nacryon smiled indulgently. "You wouldn't know anything about that, would you?"

"I fear not. Maitre Quaeryt left few records about his personal life or acquaintances. Nor did anyone else, it appears."

"Another mystery in the early history of Solidar." Nacryon gestured to the table set at one end of the sitting room, and an attractive serving girl in a cream tunic and brown trousers. "I've taken the liberty of arranging refreshments, since you would not be back at the Collegium until after noon, even if you left this moment."

"You're very kind."

"Not at all." Nacryon smiled again as he seated himself. "It's in my interest to learn more about you and the Collegium. I can offer you pale or dark lager, ale, red or white wine."

"Dark lager, please."

The High Holder nodded to the server, who slipped away, then continued. "As a young man, I had dreamed of being an imager. I always wondered about why the Collegium so often deferred to the rex when it was so clear that the Maitre and the master imagers were so much more powerful than the rex, or even whole companies of armsmen."

"Did you find an answer to your questions?" asked Alastar lightly.

"Not until I came to L'Excelsis and saw Imagisle. I'm certain you know what I'm about to say. If I'm wrong, though, I'd appreciate it if you'd point out any flaws in my observations."

"I'd be surprised if there are any," replied Alastar.

Nacryon frowned. "Why do you say that? We've scarcely met."

"Because you've thought the matter over, and because it's highly unlikely that the other four members of the High Council would appoint a dullard."

Nacryon chuckled. "Neither did the senior imagers, either."

"Go ahead," suggested Alastar.

"One moment." The High Holder waited until the server set a fluted goblet of a sparkling white wine before him and a tall crystal beaker of dark lager before Alastar. He lifted the goblet. "To a better future."

"A better future."

They drank.

"As I was saying," Nacryon smiled again, "the Collegium must contain several hundred people, perhaps more. There are five senior master imagers, possibly twice that many junior masters, and around a hundred students. I would judge that only three or four of the masters are truly powerful . . ." He shrugged. "So you see . . ."

"Your facts are close to what is," agreed Alastar. "I'd be interested in your conclusions."

"There are many." Nacryon sipped his sparkling wine. "Some might be more applicable than others."

Alastar nodded and waited, taking another sip of the lager, of roughly the same quality as that offered by Vaun.

"The young students might have difficulty protecting themselves. The older imagers have wives and children. Except in Solidar, imagers are still mistrusted. In some lands they are either enslaved in iron chains or killed outright. A prudent Maitre of the Collegium must obviously keep that in mind. To my inexperienced eye, it would appear that past Maitres have done just that.

Past rulers have been careful not to press too hard on the Collegium as well, and to be reasonable in their expectations of the Collegium, the High Holders, and the factors."

"That is also an observation," replied Alastar, "if a most astute one. I still fail to see exactly where you might be headed."

Nacryon laughed again, gently. "I doubt that. The Collegium is not so . . . well-positioned as it has been or might be. The rex is, shall we say, less temperate than he might be. So there will be change. The only question is what sort of change and how it will come about."

"You are very astute, I must say. Oh, and the lager is excellent, also. I notice that you have not mentioned the marshal and the army. They are under the authority of the rex."

"That is true, but those skilled in arms and in command are also practical men."

"And I cannot believe that at least some of the senior officers do not come from a High Holder background."

Nacryon smiled. "There is that."

"You have an idea about what kind of . . . change . . . might occur and how?"

"As the most junior councilor? Hardly. As you yourself said, I have only made observations."

"But most astute ones, and ones worth considering from all points of view, I would say."

"What else would you say?"

"Change is not always what it is thought to be. Nor does change necessarily benefit those who seek it most earnestly."

"The voice of caution, I see."

Alastar shook his head. "Caution is too often cited by those who seek to stop the world in its traces. One cannot hold back a surging current, only channel and direct it. Both those who seek to block it and those who would turn it to narrow purposes usually drown."

"That, too, is an interesting observation, Maitre. Do you have others?"

"Not at the moment."

"What do you think of the lager?"

"Excellent. It has a heft without excessive bitterness . . ."

Although Alastar and Nacryon talked for another half glass, the words exchanged were about wines, lagers, and other pleasantries. The two parted with more warm and polite phrases.

On the long ride back toward the Collegium, Alastar considered what Nacryon had revealed . . . or observed . . . not to mention the veiled threat behind those observations, and the fact that Haebyn or Guerdyn, if not both, had most likely tutored Nacryon in what to "observe."

He also had to deal with Elthyrd. He needed to meet again with the factor and propose that the Collegium, not having any golds, might make other sewer repairs, as well as find out more about where the factors' council stood on tariffs. *You know they'll likely oppose them . . . but still want more warships to cut down on piracy.* That might be, but he still needed to know how firmly the factors felt and whether they'd back the High Holders all the way.

As soon as Alastar rode across the narrow east bridge and onto Imagisle, a junior imager ran toward him, calling, "Maitre! Sir!"

Alastar reined up and took the folded and sealed paper that the youth extended, breaking the seal. The words were simple.

Rex Ryen wants you at the Chateau D'Rex immediately upon your return. His messenger did not say why.

The signature was Dareyn's, and the word "immediately" was underlined twice.

Alastar turned to his escorts. "I'm wanted at the Chateau D'Rex immediately."

Since it was quicker and shorter, he guided the gelding across Imagisle and over the Bridge of Desires and then up the West River Road to the Boulevard D'Ouest. Once he reached the chateau, he dismounted and hurried up the steps to the entry. From there a chateau guard escorted him to Ryen's private study.

"It's about time." Ryen's voice was chill, and he did not look up from where he sat beside the desk.

"I was meeting with High Holder Nacryon."

"You finally got around to that. Marvelous."

Alastar stood before the desk, waiting.

"I don't know why my father or his father ever put up with the Collegium. You . . . you have made things worse. Everything you do makes things worse."

"Might I ask what has troubled you?"

"You don't even know? What stupidity! What inanity! I'm trying to persuade the High Council and the factors to go along with an increase in tariffs, and you do this. Yes, you. I'm talking about your repairing the sewers. I wasn't about to provide the council with any more stipends for roads and sewers, not until they agreed to support an increase in tariffs. Half of what I've given them goes to their own wallets, anyway. They're greedy bastard children of the Namer, every last one of them. You, the head of the Collegium . . . you had to go and undo all the pressure I was putting on them through their own incompetence." Ryen's glare was withering.

Alastar ignored it. "You might have told the Collegium the reason for the stench that made breathing on Imagisle a disgusting and tedious matter."

"I'll tell you what you need to know."

"The less you tell me, the more likely I'll end up doing something else that you won't like. The more you tell me, the more I'll be able to help . . . or at least not get in the way."

"You've already done enough, Maitre. You fixed their frigging Namer-fired sewers . . . and you tell me you can't start on my projects for another week."

"Just three days after we have your proclamation, your map, and your assurance that we can remove buildings along the route."

"Just go. Don't do anything if you can't do it without causing me more trouble."

Alastar did not move.

"You heard me! Go!" Ryen's voice rose almost to a screech.

Alastar didn't trust himself to reply. Besides, in Ryen's mood, saying anything would only have made matters worse. He inclined his head, if only slightly, turned, and left, making certain his shields were strong as his back was to the rex.

From the Chateau D'Rex, Alastar and his escorts rode west nearly two milles and then slightly north into an area of rolling hills in order to reach Councilor Moeryn's L'Excelsis residence, the grounds of which resembled a hunting park. Although perhaps thirty yards across the front, the single-level structure was smaller than any other councilor's residence that Alastar had so far visited. From what Alastar could tell, it was just before third glass when he dismounted on the brick-paved square in front of the roofed entry porch, a space that could only have held a handful of people at most.

A burly man with a reddish square-cut beard stepped out and waited for Alastar to approach. Unlike the other High Holders, he wore a woolen brown tweed jacket and trousers, brown boots, and a pale ivory shirt open at the neck, a space filled with a brown silk scarf. Yet his complexion was more like the honeyed skin shown by most Pharsi. "Greetings, Maitre."

"Greetings to you," replied Alastar, not entirely certain if the man happened to be Moeryn. He walked toward the entry.

"You arrived almost exactly on the glass. I was beginning to wonder if you had been delayed. Come on in. We're not all that formal here." Moeryn, for it had to be the High Holder, looked to the two younger imagers. "If you'll ride to the north side of the house, you can water the mounts there and have some refreshments."

"Thank you, sir," replied the two, almost in unison.

"You're more than welcome. It's a ride out here from Imagisle, and you'll have to ride back." Moeryn grinned, then opened the oiled oak door, and motioned for Alastar to enter.

As they walked through the oak-paneled entry hall, Alastar said, "As a matter of fact, I was summoned rather unexpectedly to the Chateau D'Rex."

"Might I ask why?"

"The rex had some urgent instructions for the Collegium dealing with several tasks we have undertaken, including a repair of a small section of sewers south of the east bridge on East River Road." Alastar kept his expression pleasant.

"I can't imagine . . ." Moeryn shook his head and offered a wry smile. "I hope you don't mind if I include my wife in our conversation. She has always wanted to meet a real imager, and I find that she often has insights that I lack." The High Holder chuckled ruefully.

This man knows his faults, and that may make him more dangerous than he seems. "I certainly have no problem with her joining us." Alastar paused, then said, "You are from Khelgror, I understand . . ."

"Where there are more Pharsi and more imagers except, well, there are very few other Pharsi High Holders. Most of them are near Jovahl or along the coast. That's a far piece from our holding."

The way Moeryn said "our holding" suggested strongly

that the lands had belonged to his wife's family and that he had married into her family, and that he had likely been the younger son of another High Holder. He gestured and turned, leading Alastar into a salon on the west side of the house, a chamber far brighter than Alastar would have thought, given the hangings over the windows, until he realized that the fabric was sheer, designed to block the glare from the afternoon sun, but allow more than a modicum of light. A muscular and not-quite-stocky woman was already standing beside a leather armchair, one of three arranged in a fashion to facilitate conversation, with a low circular table set in the middle of the three.

"Dear," offered Moeryn, "this is Maitre Alastar. Maitre, my wife Thearra."

Thearra, whose heart-shaped face was framed by comparatively short silvered blond hair, strikingly set off by her pale golden skin, inclined her head. "Maitre, welcome to Hillpark."

"Thank you." The way the two had positioned themselves meant that Alastar had to take the dark leather chair facing toward the windows, but when he seated himself, he discovered it had been placed so that the light filtered through the sheer hangings did not strike him directly.

"I presume you are here to feel out how the High Council will react to Rex Ryen's intent to increase tariffs." Moeryn's voice was hearty, but matter-of-fact.

"Rather more to get a better feeling for the High Council and its members, since I had never expected to become Maitre of the Collegium."

"Was that because you were the second senior imager at Westisle?" asked Thearra.

"Frankly . . . yes. I find myself having to learn a great deal more than I'd thought would be necessary." Alastar looked to Thearra, noting that her eyes met his, neither challenging nor deferential. "That, I have discovered, and rediscovered, is the nature of life."

"If one wishes to be fulfilled in life," she replied.

A red-haired young woman, a girl really, entered the sitting room with a large tray on which were three beakers, two pitchers, and three platters.

Thearra stood immediately and set the pitchers on the low table, followed by the beakers, while the girl placed a platter on the table before each armchair. Then Thearra looked to the girl. "Thank you, dear."

"Our eldest," said Moeryn once the girl had departed.

"We're not terribly formal here," explained Thearra.

"We're not formal anywhere except when the occasion demands it," added Moeryn.

"The white pitcher holds amber lager, and the brown one the dark," said Thearra. "There is a sampling of refreshments on the platter—dates wrapped in thin ham, shortbread biscuits, olives, apple slices, and a small loaf of freshly baked dark bread, and some salted almonds. We thought you might need some replenishment."

"I'm certain he does," added Moeryn, "seeing as he just came here after meeting with Rex Ryen."

"Is he really as difficult as Moeryn insists that he is?"

"Let us just say that he has definite opinions," returned Alastar dryly, before lifting the brown pitcher and looking to Thearra, who nodded. He filled both her beaker and his to roughly two-thirds of their capacity before looking to Moeryn.

"I prefer the amber, thank you. Definite opinions." The High Holder chuckled. "A diplomatic way of putting what most would call madness. If he were as diplomatic as you are, he'd have fewer difficulties."

"I don't know about fewer difficulties," said Alastar. "Less unpleasantness, though, I would judge." He took a small swallow of the dark lager. "This is quite good, by the way."

"Thank you. Thearra is the one who takes care of purchasing lager. She has far better taste than I do." Moeryn paused. "Why do you say that he would not have fewer difficulties?"

"There are difficulties with people and their manners, and there are difficulties that have less to do with people, but the way things are. The rex will need more ships if piracy is to be curtailed. That is not a matter of manners and pleasantness, but of golds. High Holders and factors would prefer not to have their outlays increased by higher tariffs. Again, not a matter of manners . . . if you see what I mean. There are other needs, on both sides, of course."

"What you say sounds like a prelude to negotiation," suggested Moeryn.

"I have neither the commission nor the direction to treat with the High Council on any such matters. I'm just trying to get to know the councilors."

"To what end, then?" asked Thearra.

"To determine what is necessary to return the Collegium to its former position of respect." Alastar smiled. "That by itself I find to be a most daunting task." He took another swallow of the lager, and then one of the ham-wrapped dates . . . simultaneously slightly too sweet and too salty for his taste. The olive that followed was more to his liking. So he took another, and then a few almonds.

"Daunting?" asked Thearra. "I fear I do not understand. Do not imagers have considerable powers?"

"Some do. Some do not. Many are students who may develop their abilities after years of training . . . but the greatest warriors were all babes once."

Thearra nodded. "I had not thought of it in that fashion. That does suggest, if I might be so bold to say it, that the Collegium is not so independent as it once was or as many believe it to be."

"The Collegium could be more independent than it is,

were it not for an excess of deference to others that led to the neglect of certain skills. Not those for which imagers are feared," Alastar went on smoothly, "but those that would have provided greater financial independence."

"Meaning that the Collegium needs the rex's golds?" asked Thearra.

"For a time, that is likely to be necessary."

"You find yourselves caught between Ryen and the High Council," declared Moeryn evenly.

"That could happen if we are not careful. That is one reason why I am here."

"Again . . . most delicately and diplomatically put," said Thearra with a smile.

"Hardly delicately, but diplomatically, I would hope," replied Alastar, before taking one of the shortbread biscuits.

Thearra took a small but lingering sip of her lager before speaking again. "You don't look to come from a Pharsi background, but I'd always heard that many imagers did."

From her statement, Alastar understood that there would be no more even indirect talk about Ryen and the High Council. "There is a greater likelihood of an imager being born to a Pharsi family, but there are far more people in Solidar who are not Pharsi, and they occasionally have children who are imagers. From what I know, perhaps one in five imagers has some Pharsi blood in his or her ancestry." He smiled. "Given what is hidden in families, there might be more, but there are definitely fewer Pharsi imagers than imagers from other backgrounds."

"You're from Liantiago, I understand?"

Alastar nodded and took another sip of the lager.

After an additional glass of pleasant talk and refreshments, amid tacit unspoken signals, Alastar finally said, "I've tariffed your hospitality far too long, but I have enjoyed both meeting you both and eating too many of your delicacies, and it is not a short ride to the Collegium."

"Would that you could stay longer," returned Moeryn, rising as Alastar did, "but we do understand."

Thearra smiled and nodded. "I did so enjoy learning about the Collegium at Westisle."

"It was my pleasure."

Once Alastar and the two imagers were on the road and well away from Hillpark, Alastar turned in the gelding's saddle, grinned, and asked Belsior, "Did the redheaded girl serve you refreshments?"

"Why . . . yes, sir." Belsior blushed.

"And she asked you how you liked being escorts or guards for me?"

"Ah . . . yes, sir . . ."

"What else?" Alastar looked to Neiryn.

"Just things about Imagisle . . . whether things had changed much with a new Maitre . . . and if we ever saw the rex . . ."

Alastar prompted the two gently as they rode, thinking as he did that, after meeting all five councilors, he wasn't so sure that the two that Ryen was counting on for support weren't the most unpredictable . . . and potentially the most dangerous.

By the time he, Belsior, and Neiryn returned to the Collegium, the administration building was dark, except for the entry area that held the duty desk. Even after Alastar unsaddled and groomed the gelding, it was too early for the evening meal, but he didn't want to walk all the way to the Maitre's dwelling, wait a fraction of a glass, and then walk back to the dining hall.

He glanced over at the anomen to the west. He could see light there. With a wry smile, he walked to the ancient building, hoping Iskhar might be there. The chorister was, possibly working on a homily for the coming Solayi, with papers and a book on his desk.

"What is it, Maitre?" Iskhar's voice was polite, but formal.

Alastar understood and got straight to the point. "Are there any records from previous choristers that date back to the first chorister of the Collegium?"

Iskhar offered a puzzled expression. "Of course. Gauswn kept very good records."

Gauswn?

"The first chorister of the Collegium."

"Did Maitre Fhaen ever read them?"

"I wouldn't know. He never asked me, but I've only been at the Collegium nine years."

"And you've read them?"

"Chorister Ulrek insisted that I do so."

"Are there any references to Maitre Quaeryt?"

"There are some and quite a few mentions of what Quaeryt did as Maitre, but very little about how he founded the Collegium. Just some passing mentions."

"If you could let me borrow those . . . ?"

"Certainly, sir, but there are three volumes. They're bound, you know. Do you need them right now?"

"No. Perhaps tomorrow?"

"I'll have one of the students bring them over in the morning, if that's all right."

"That would be fine. I won't take more of your time." Alastar smiled. "I wouldn't want you to have to slight your homily."

Iskhar offered an embarrassed smile. "Sometimes . . . well, it's harder. This is one of those times."

"Have as pleasant an evening as you can."

"Thank you, sir."

Alastar headed back from the anomen to the dining hall. He'd still be early.

11

Alastar had no more than reached the bottom of the steps of the Maitre's dwelling on Vendrei morning, for the second time, the first being when he had left on his morning run, when the gray-haired and sprightly Jienna appeared.

"Maitre Alastar, have you thought about the bed linens? Before long, if we don't get more, you'll be sleeping on rags."

Alastar smiled. "I've slept on much worse, but I'll have Dareyn order a set. Just one. The Collegium can't afford more." In actuality, he'd pay for them.

"Two'd be better. The pair would last longer."

"I'll see what I can do . . . and thank you."

"Don't be working until all glasses every night, either."

Alastar nodded. "I'll see what I can do in that regard as well."

Jienna shook her head.

Alastar managed not to grin as he left for the dining hall and breakfast.

The first thing he did once he reached his study after eating was to instruct Dareyn to request another meeting for him with Factor Elthyrd. He'd meant to do that on Jeudi, but what with Ryen's temper, he hadn't gotten back to the Collegium until it had been too late to do that. *You thought you'd have time. Another reminder not to put anything off until later, because there won't be any more time then.* Not the way matters were headed. Then he asked Dareyn to take care of the bed linens, two sets of them, because Jienna would keep bringing it up.

He frowned. There was something else he'd meant to do . . . someone else he needed to talk to, but he couldn't remember who. *Too much going on . . . and you still don't know enough.*

When official studies began on Vendrei morning, Alastar was in the corner of the chamber used by Akoryt, who was conducting a new course of study on the role of law in Solidar. He had raised a concealment, although he had informed Akoryt that he would be observing—or rather largely hearing, since he could not make out facial expressions from where he was positioned, only hear words and sense large gestures. The student imagers with whom Akoryt was working were all older seconds, and the short course of study was designed to refresh whatever they had been taught when they were younger and—equally important—to make them more aware of certain aspects of law. Alastar was well aware of the unevenness of how law applied in practice, and the imagers of the Collegium needed to understand that, as well as the fact that imagers could not afford the slightest impression that they were above the law . . . or that it did not apply to them. He also worried about whether Akoryt was the best senior imager to instruct the older seconds. *But there are so few senior maitres.*

"You are here because it has come to the attention of the Collegium," Akoryt began, "that your earlier instruction on the laws of Solidar was limited to the letter of those laws, how they apply, and the higher standards required of imagers." He paused. "What else do you think you need to know beyond that?"

As with the case of the younger students, there was a long silence.

Finally, one of the seconds answered, in a tone close to a smirk, Alastar thought, "If we knew what we needed beyond that, sir, why would we need to be here?"

"The question was what you thought you might need," replied Akoryt "That suggests the need for thought.

Obviously, your response suggests one answer. What might that be?"

After another long silence, Akoryt said, "Borlan, what does Noergyn's response reveal?"

"That he can't think, sir?"

"Not exactly, but it's close. Let's go back to a simple question. Why are there laws?"

"To keep people from doing what they shouldn't?"

"Don't you all know there are things you shouldn't do? That you shouldn't steal something from someone else, for example?"

"Some people don't know that."

"They don't know it . . . or they think that they can do what they wish, because they're stronger or quicker?"

"They think they can get away with it," offered another voice.

"What do laws provide besides rules?"

"What happens if you break them . . . ?"

"Exactly. Consequences . . ."

After several more questions and responses, Akoryt asked, "Are laws the only rules we have to obey?"

"No, sir."

"That's right. Every group has rules. Some, like the guilds, the High Holders, the factors, or the Collegium, have both formal rules—and these can be spoken or written or both—and unspoken rules. The formal rules are things like laws or regial proclamations, or the written requirements to be a factor or a Holder. But there are also unspoken rules. Those rules must be observed and deduced by each member of the group, and in large part, acceptance and success depend on recognition of and mastery of those unspoken rules. Young people usually understand that such rules exist within their own groups, but many have a harder time accepting that other groups have such rules and that at least some of those rules may differ greatly from the rules they have already learned. Often they get most angry when the rules of those older and more powerful do not follow their preconceptions." Akoryt paused. "Why am I making this point? I don't want a spoken answer. I want you each to write down an answer without talking to each other or looking at someone else's paper. Now . . ."

Alastar eased from the chair and out of the chamber as the seconds bent over their sheets of paper. Like Shaelyt, Akoryt was making a good start.

Once outside the chamber, Alastar dropped the concealment and walked swiftly back toward the administration building. As he neared his study, he could see Dareyn looking toward him. *These days, that's not a good sign.*

"Maitre . . . one of the students brought the volumes you requested from Chorister Iskhar. You also have a message from Marshal Demykalon." Dareyn stood and handed the envelope to Alastar.

Alastar used his belt knife to slit the envelope, leaving the green wax seal intact, then extracted the single sheet and read the short missive.

Maitre—

At the behest of Rex Regis, His Esteemed Grace, Lord Ryen, I would like to request the pleasure of your company tomorrow, Samedi, the thirteenth of Feuillyt, at headquarters in order to discuss matters of mutual interest. I trust that ninth glass will be amenable.

The signature was that of Demykalon, set down in bold square strokes.

"Sir?" inquired Dareyn.

"I'm to meet with the marshal at his headquarters tomorrow morning. It should be interesting." *If that doesn't turn out to be an understatement, you're going to be very surprised.* "We'll need to leave the Collegium just before eighth glass. Have we heard back from Factor Elthyrd?"

"No, sir. Not yet, sir."

"Thank you." Alastar turned and entered the study. The three volumes that Iskhar had sent were stacked neatly on his desk. Each one was more than a handspan thick.

With a rueful smile, he took the top volume, and opened it. The dark brown leather was smooth, as if the book had hardly been read. The first page was blank. The second page held only five words—"NOTES OF A COLLEGIUM CHORISTER"—but those words were written in a precise hand. Alastar turned the page and began to read.

> These writings represent my notes over the time I have been chorister at the Anomen D'Collegium Imago. They do not represent all my notes, for reasons I will keep to myself, but everything within these volumes is as accurate as I know it to be. I do not believe what I have omitted creates a misleading impression for anyone who will later read them. For all I know, no one will, besides my successor, for whom I am compiling these volumes . . .

Alastar continued to read.

> . . . while I sought the Nameless through my younger years, I only found what I sought when the Princeps of Tilbor secured my early release from my position as undercaptain in the First Tilboran Regiment. How was I to know what would follow or that he would create the Collegium and honor me as its first chorister . . .

Quaeryt had been a princeps, an assistant governor? Alastar kept skimming the pages.

> . . . have preached a few homilies with which I was pleased, but doubt any reached the standard of those

offered by the Maitre to his officers and men during the Tilboran Revolt or the Wars of Consolidation . . .

Alastar's eyes again widened. The legendary Quaeryt had been an officer in the Telaryn armies even before the conquest of Bovaria and the unification of Solidar? And he had preached numerous homilies . . . and had possibly been a chorister of the Nameless?

At that moment, Dareyn knocked and then opened the door slightly. "There's a chateau guard here with something that he says he has to deliver to you personally."

For an instant, Alastar wondered what was that important—before he realized that it must be the map and documents necessary for the rex's new avenue. He marked his place with a leather bookmark, then rose from the desk and walked out to the anteroom.

A chateau guard that Alastar did not recognize stepped forward and handed Alastar a dispatch case and a large tubular object that had to be a rolled map. "Maitre, sir, these are from the rex. He said you were expecting them."

"Thank you."

"Ah . . . sir?"

"You'd like a note saying I received them?"

"Yes, sir."

Alastar handed the map to Dareyn and opened the case. There were several documents, all with impressive seals. The first was a proclamation. So was the second. He decided against trying to read them all. Instead, he set the case on Dareyn's desk. Dareyn gave him a sheet of paper, then eased the inkwell toward him, and handed him a pen.

Shortly, Alastar finished the note, let it dry, blotted it gently, folded it, sealed it, and handed it to the guard.

"Thank you, sir."

Once the chateau guard was out of the anteroom, Dareyn looked to Alastar.

"The details for the new Avenue D'Rex, I imagine. I need to see what all this involves."

Dareyn raised his eyebrows, but did not speak.

Alastar gathered the maps and the dispatch case and returned to his study. There, he untied the cords around the map and unrolled it, then studied the purplish lines that Ryen, or someone, had drawn. *It could be worse . . .*

Then he read the various proclamations, wincing at a section in the second one.

> . . . whereas, it is the right of the rex to do what is needful for proper roads and ways, there is no appeal to the decision on the right-of-way. Compensation will be set by the rex and reviewed by the High Justicer of Solidar . . .

And he thinks the factors are unhappy now? Alastar frowned, then looked more closely at the map. From what he could tell, Ryen had actually picked a route that cut through shops and crafters' places, but not touched a single factorage.

He looked at the third document, but realized that it consisted of two sheets, the first being an official notice to a property or shop owner that some or all of his property might be taken for the purpose of a new avenue and that compensation would be paid after the construction was complete, said compensation to be set by the rex and reviewed by the High Justicer, to whom appeals could be made if the property owner disputed the compensation. The notice also declared that there would be imagers of the Collegium working on the construction and that they were agents of the rex and empowered to take all steps necessary to facilitate construction. The second sheet held a listing in very small script of all those provided a notice. Alastar estimated there were more than a hundred names and addresses, vague as some addresses were, such as "corner of cobbler and tent," whatever that meant.

The fourth sheet was a description of the avenue—a stone-paved thoroughfare an even twenty yards wide with a stone sidewalk two yards wide on each side.

Twenty-four yards wide? The last thing we need is to be involved with this right now.

He shook his head, knowing that he'd need to draft instructions and send a note to each of the imagers he'd need to begin the avenue project on Lundi—not all that he'd need, but those for the first day. He also needed to study the map more when he really wished he could resume his reading and search for more information about Quaeryt, but that, like many things, would have to wait. He was still thinking about which imagers he'd need on Lundi when the study door opened.

"Factor Elthyrd will make time for you at second glass, sir, if you will come to the factors' council building."

"Would you send a messenger confirming that?"

"Yes, sir." Dareyn paused. "Tertius Konan is here for his meeting with you, Maitre."

"Thank you." Alastar replaced the documents in the leather-bound dispatch case, rolled and tied the map, and managed a pleasant smile as the broad-shouldered but still somewhat gangly imager third walked into the study.

"Please sit down, Konan. I understand you're from Montagne."

"Near Montagne, sir. A small town called Fharos."

"That's a long way. How did you get here?"

"On horseback, sir. I learned to ride with one of the rex's couriers." Konan's eyes strayed to the founder's sabre, as if he did not relish looking directly at Alastar.

"How have you found the Collegium so far?"

Over the course of the next quint, Alastar found Konan to be reasonably intelligent and remarkably pleasant.

He almost hated to end the conversation, knowing he would soon be heading out to a far less pleasant meeting. He would even have rather read the old journals. *Even? They look intriguing.* With a shake of his head, he rose and headed to the stables.

A fifth before second glass, Alastar reined up outside the headquarters of the factors' council, an ancient and modest building located four blocks north of the east bridge on the corner of the East River Road, just a block south of the "new" Hotel L'Excelsis, an imposing three-story structure that, Alastar understood from inquiries, had replaced a much older hotel some fifty years earlier. At that moment, as he dismounted, he recalled what he had forgotten to do—to talk to Desyrk about what the Maitre D'Structure might know about Ryen and his family. *You should have time after you get back to the Collegium.*

"I won't be much longer than half a glass." Alastar handed the gelding's reins to Chervyt, who was accompanied by Coermyd.

"Yes, sir."

The ancient door creaked as Alastar opened it and stepped inside. It also creaked when he closed it. Two small table desks seemed to fill the small and low-ceilinged entry hall. One was piled high with stacks of papers. The other was occupied by a graying clerk, whose initial annoyed glance was immediately replaced by a smile, one clearly forced, even as he stood.

"Maitre Alastar. Let me tell Factor Elthyrd you are here." He hurried around the desk and toward the door behind him and to his left, which he opened. After a moment, he left the door ajar. "He'll see you now, Maitre."

"Thank you." Alastar walked around the table desk, opened the door wider, entered, and closed it, slipping off his visor cap and tucking it under his arm.

"Good afternoon, Maitre." Elthyrd's thin lips barely moved.

"Good afternoon, Factorius." Alastar seated himself, moving the cap to place it on his thigh, rather than on the factor's desk. "I appreciate your making the time to see me."

"I'm only here on Mardi and Vendrei afternoons, more than enough for the council."

"And the remainder of your time is spent at your own factorage well south of Imagisle on the East River Road?"

"I wouldn't say well south. A mille or so. Close enough to the Sud Bridge. That makes getting wagons to and from the barge piers not that hard."

Barge piers? Then Alastar recalled that Elthyrd was a timber factor, among other things. "You ship timber to Solis by barge?"

"As necessary and what I don't sell here. And the canvas, too. That's a smaller venture. Most ships port now and again there, and that's the cheapest way to get the canvas there."

Alastar didn't pretend to know that much about timber, but he did know at least something about rope and canvas. So he asked, "Is there that much difference between hemp grown in the south and near L'Excelsis?"

"Best hemp comes from old Bovaria. That's here. You didn't come here to talk hemp, Maitre."

"No, I didn't. I came to discuss sewers. The Collegium obviously can't provide golds to the factors' council for sewer repairs. Nor is the rex likely to do so at this time . . . as you well know. He doesn't even have the golds to build the warships many factors would like to have in order to reduce piracy in the Southern Gulf."

"That's what he says."

"It's unfortunately true."

"We're all squeezed, what with the late rains and poor harvests."

From that, Alastar got the impression that possibly the late rains had damaged the hemp harvest . . . or some other endeavor of Elthyrd's. "He's cut the size of the army. He hasn't built any palaces or retreats. No one is complaining about his entertaining at the chateau, except perhaps that he isn't doing enough." The last was an educated guess on Alastar's part, but he did know that the fall and winter social season usually began in early Feuillyt, and he'd seen no signs of decorations or anything of the like at the Chateau D'Rex, and it was approaching midmonth. He'd also received no invitations, and before his death Fhaen had advised him of the role of the Maitre at such events, noting that the Maitre was often invited, and always to the first and last balls of the season.

"He could still spare some golds."

That was as much an admission that Alastar was right as he was likely to get.

"Given that, I had thought that, over the weeks ahead, with the agreement of the factors' council, my imagers could undertake a few more sewer repairs—"

"I'd have thought you'd be all tied up with that new avenue His Mightiness wants."

"That is a larger project and will require some considerable preparation." That was certainly what Alastar planned, especially after seeing the maps and documents sent by Ryen. *And that will create even more impatience and anger at the Chateau D'Rex.*

"I suppose it couldn't hurt," grudged Elthyrd. "No more repairs on Solayi, though."

"We wouldn't dream of that." *Not after the last outburst.*

"I'll have to talk to the others."

"I understand. If you would let me know . . ."

"We'll see. No promises."

"I understand. All of you have a great deal to consider."

"I wondered when you'd get to that. Sneaky way of asking what we're going to do."

"I wouldn't have asked, if you hadn't brought it up.

The High Council believes that the factors will go along with whatever the High Council decides."

"Who told you that?" Elthyrd's face flushed.

"I've had to meet with all the Council members. The Collegium is not on the best of terms with anyone, and I've been trying to assure them of our concerns and goodwill."

"I hope you do better with the High Council." Elthyrd snorted.

"Our intent with fixing the sewer on East River Road was good. So is our present offer."

Elthyrd frowned. "We need more protection against the southern pirates. You really think the rex will put any new golds toward ships?"

"He says he will."

"We'd need more than his word on that."

Unfortunately, Alastar could understand that. "If I hear anything, I will let you know."

Elthyrd stood abruptly. "I'll let you know about the sewers. It won't be before Lundi."

"Thank you." Alastar rose and inclined his head.

"You're welcome, Maitre."

While the factor was not smiling as Alastar left, at least Elthyrd was not frowning.

You'll just have to bring him around . . . as you can.

Once Alastar had returned to the administration building, even before entering his study, he said to Dareyn, "Would you have someone see if they can find Maitre Desyrk?"

"Yes, sir."

"Thank you." Alastar did not close the study door, trusting that Desyrk would not be long, and settled himself, looking at the three volumes of Chorister Gauswn's journals still sitting on the corner of the desk. *You have a few moments. You could read several pages.*

Alastar yielded to temptation and reached for the first volume, beginning to read where he had left off.

. . . should have known that he was more than an imager, that he was blessed by the Nameless to do what no one else could do . . . and bear the burden . . .

At the sound of a rap on the doorframe, Alastar looked up to see Desyrk standing there.

"Maitre? You summoned me?"

"I did. Please come in and shut the door." Alastar closed the journal and studied the other maitre closely as he crossed the room. Desyrk was a handsome fellow in the dark and languid way that some women seemed to favor and had a youthful, almost careless air about him, although he was several years older than Alastar. His brown hair was wavy and slightly longer than Alastar would have preferred, but looked brushed and clean. His grays were also clean and unwrinkled, and his boots polished, almost to a military shine. Alastar gestured to the chairs and waited until Desyrk seated himself, not on the front edge of the chair, but comfortably. "I was talking to Maitre Obsolym the other day, and he mentioned that you were likely the only maitre who might know something about the rex and his family."

"Sir?"

Although Desyrk showed a puzzled expression, Alastar felt the expression was less than fully honest. "Through your brother . . . Something about him accompanying Marshal Ghalyn . . . ?"

"Oh . . . that. Yes, he often helped the marshal . . . Marshal Ghalyn."

Alastar definitely had the feeling that Desyrk was relieved. *Why?*

"I'd appreciate it if you'd tell me what you know about the rex and his family. I've only met his sons once, quite briefly. From what I saw, the elder, Lorien, is in his late twenties . . ."

"I believe so, sir."

"What about the younger?"

"Ryentar is five years younger, or so it's said."

"No daughters?"

"I heard somewhere that Lady Asarya had a child after Ryentar, but that the child lived only a few days. I don't know if it was a son or daughter."

"No one says much about her."

"It's said that she is a very private person, unlike Rex Ryen."

"Was your brother often at the chateau?"

"Not often. Perhaps a handful of times."

"Did he tell you his impressions of Rex Ryen?"

"Not in detail. He did say that Marshal Ghalyn was most careful in how he spoke. You would understand that, I think, from what you have said to us."

"What about social affairs? Does the rex host balls or the like? Who attends them? Does he entertain High Holders?"

"I do not know who among High Holders he might entertain, sir. He does have a year-end ball . . . or he has had one in the past. Maitre Fhaen always went, but he did not enjoy it much, he said. His wife might have, but she died before he became Maitre. The rex has a spring ball, it's also said, but that is more for his sons and their friends."

"What about the Lady Asarya?"

"I cannot say, sir. My brother never mentioned her."

"I take it your brother no longer goes to the Chateau D'Rex?"

"No, sir. Marshal Demykalon takes no other officers with him."

"Has your brother said anything about that?"

"He has only said that Marshal Demykalon has changed procedures."

Alastar doubted strongly that was all Desyrk's brother had said. "Is there anything else you can tell me about the rex or how things have changed . . . or stayed the same?"

"I think I've told you everything I can remember, sir." Desyrk tilted his head as if he were trying to remember, a gesture not totally convincing.

There's something . . . Alastar didn't feel comfortable pressing Desyrk, although it was likely that the Maitre D'Structure wasn't telling everything he knew. He smiled. "That's all. It's just that I've had so little time here in L'Excelsis that I need to rely on what you and Obsolym and other maitres know." He stood. "Thank you. I appreciate it."

"My pleasure to be helpful, sir."

Alastar kept his smile in place until he was again alone in the study. As he reseated himself behind the desk, he couldn't help but wonder about the way in which Desyrk had answered some questions. Alastar was struck by how many times the other maitre had used the phrase "it is said," or something like it. Yet Desyrk had never used that phrase before. *He's hiding something . . . but what?*

Yet another thing to worry about. *As if you don't have enough already.*

12

Under a grayish haze, with a steady but cool light wind out of the northeast, Alastar and his two escorts, this time Belsior and Coermyd, rode toward the army headquarters, located three milles north of the Chateau D'Rex. Alastar had heard that it had once been a high holding, but the original chateau itself was now only one of more than a score of brick buildings. Outside the old gatehouse stood troopers in undress greens, heavy rifles at their sides. They barely moved as Alastar and the two imagers reined up.

"Maitre Alastar, to see Marshal Demykalon, at his request."

"Yes, sir. There's a squad leader waiting to escort you to meet the marshal." The guard gestured, and a trooper rode forward from under the partial shade of an ancient oak that was beginning to shed its leaves.

"Maitre Alastar? Marshal Demykalon will be meeting you at headquarters." The trooper looked at Alastar, but did not quite meet his eyes.

"Lead the way," said Alastar.

When the four rode into the paved courtyard at the rear of the chateau, Alastar was surprised to see an officer in a marshal's uniform riding toward them, followed by another officer, a captain.

"Maitre Alastar, Marshal Demykalon here. This is Captain Weirt. We'll need to ride another mille to the range. We'll be putting on a demonstration. I think you and your imagers will find it most interesting." Demykalon's face was lightly tanned. Under the visor cap, his hair was dark brown with a few streaks of gray. He looked to be ten years older than Alastar.

"A demonstration of what, if I might ask?"

"Some improved weaponry. Let me leave it at that until you can see for yourself. After you do, I'll be happy to answer any questions. By the way, I'm pleased to meet you. I never did meet your predecessor. I understand he preferred to leave the Collegium as little as possible." Demykalon turned his mount and gestured. "Toward the rear gates."

The captain fell in with Belsior and Coermyd, while Alastar and Demykalon rode side by side across the courtyard and through the north gateposts that held no gates onto a paved lane, lined with two long buildings on the right, and three slightly shorter ones on the left.

"The large buildings are the main supply warehouses for this part of Solidar," explained Demykalon cheerfully. "We also have warehouses in Tilbora, Nacliano, Moryn, Solis, and Liantiago. The middle building on the other side is the reserve armory."

"Impressive," said Alastar. "How long have you been marshal? I must confess that, since I came from Westisle, there are simple facts I don't know."

"Just under three seasons. I was army vice-marshal until Marshal Ghalyn took his stipend."

"How many regiments under arms?"

"Eight at the moment. That doesn't include two regiments of naval marines. Three regiments are posted here. The others are in various places, Solis, of course, and Liantiago."

More than seven thousand troopers within three milles of the Chateau D'Rex and five milles of Imagisle? And two more regiments in all than was widely known? No wonder Ryen was having problems with finances!

Alastar glanced at Demykalon's saddle, noting the

empty rifle scabbard. "Have you considered using pistols for close-in fighting?"

The marshal laughed. "The only reliable pistols are single-shot. That's not useful in a fight, and the others could get you killed. Give me a sabre any day."

"But you use rifles for longer range?"

"Call their use for midrange. You'll see."

Less than a hundred yards beyond the last supply warehouse the lane veered eastward around a low long ridge, and then back north again. After riding almost another mille, Demykalon gestured to a lane heading westward through a gap in the ridge, a gap with a gatehouse. Neither of the troopers posted there said a word as the five rode through, but they did present their rifles in salute when they saw the marshal.

Some two hundred yards farther on, where the gap between the sides of the ridge narrowed, a stone wall and a heavy timber gate blocked further mounted progress. Demykalon reined up beside a hitching rail on the north side of the gate and then dismounted. "We'll have to walk up the steps over here."

As he dismounted, Alastar glanced to where the marshal pointed and saw a set of stone steps leading up the side of the ridge to a landing some fifteen yards uphill. After tying his mount, the marshal moved up the steps quickly, with the ease of a man who kept himself in good physical trim. Alastar patted the gelding on the shoulder, then tied him to the rail and followed, keeping pace, but noted, when he reached the landing, that the two young imagers were breathing heavily as they trudged the last few steps. The captain who followed them was not.

"You're in better shape than your escorts," murmured Demykalon.

"We're working on that," replied Alastar in an equally muted voice.

"This way." Demykalon walked along the stone pavement cut into the hillside for another hundred yards, then down three steps and through an archway into a stone-walled chamber.

Captain Weirt remained just outside the archway.

The chamber was small, no more than four yards in length, three in width, and slightly more than two from the stone floor to the heavy roof timbers. There were no windows, just a series of slits at eye height in the west wall. The slits were roughly three digits high and a third of a yard in length.

"Take one of the viewing ports, Maitre, and tell me what you see at the base of the hill."

Alastar took one of the slits near the middle. At first glance, he saw that the ground to the west of the ridge was lower than he had realized, at least twenty yards down from where he stood. He took a moment before finding what he initially thought was a two-wheeled cart, then realized that he was seeing a cannon, but one with a far smaller barrel and bore than the antique bombards that still graced the harbor at Westisle. "Is that a new type of cannon?"

"It is. It's much more accurate, and the rate of fire is faster. We've developed a coarser powder that burns more evenly." Demykalon smiled. "I thought you'd like to see one in action. We're in the process of ranging and testing them. That's why we'll be watching from the redoubt here. That's also why the gunner has a pit and a stone wall there. You can see some sections of stone walls to the west. They're about two-thirds of a mille from here. The proving ground extends almost two milles, but the cannon are less accurate at ranges over a mille. You'll also notice an earthen berm a hundred yards east of the wall sections. It's high enough that the gunners cannot actually see their targets." The marshal turned toward the archway. "Captain, give them the signal to begin."

"Yes, sir."

Alastar watched as one of the gunners took a device, consisting of iron forged into a right angle with another strip of iron, essentially a quarter of a circle, running from a point halfway along the top section of iron to a point roughly halfway down the vertical strip of iron. A plumb bob hung from the upper iron strip. It took Alastar a moment to realize that the device was a gun quadrant, used to determine the elevation of the cannon needed to aim at a particular distance. He also noticed that the gun crew had a choice of bags of powder of various sizes.

The gunner lit the fuse, then ducked behind the wall and knelt with the rest of the gun crew in the brick-walled pit. The first shot was long and high. The gunner looked to the northwest. A spotter used two flags to signal. After several adjustments, the gun crew retreated, and the gunner lit the cannon off. The cannon shell clipped off the top of a section of wall.

The process continued for almost a glass, with the gunner and gun crew aiming at various targets that they could not see, getting signals, and then adjusting the cannon. It seldom took more than three tries to hit the unseen target, success being confirmed by flag signals.

"Have them take a break," Demykalon called to Weirt, who had moved just inside the archway while the cannon fired. "You can see that these new guns are smaller and lighter, but they fire almost as far, and they can be moved into position quickly. They're all cast alike, so that the range tables are similar for each. That means we can be effective with indirect fire with only a few adjustments, especially if we can measure distances in advance."

"Indirect fire?" That was a term Alastar had not heard, although he suspected that was when the gunner could not aim point-blank and had to fire at an unseen target.

"Direct fire is when you aim the cannon directly at

something you can see. Indirect fire is where you want to fire over something and have your shell strike where you want it, such as over a hill, or a wall. Perhaps over a river and trees or walls beyond. These cannon are very good at that. If we used Antiagon Fire . . . well . . . the effect would be terrible."

"Antiagon Fire?" The ancient flame weapon required an imager to make, and one with the skills of a maitre? "There's no record of a request for an imager."

"Explosive shells are almost as good, and far less dangerous to store and handle," replied Demykalon. "We do have a description of the way to create it, though. One of the early marshals thought it might be useful at some time."

Alastar couldn't imagine using shells filled with Antiagon Fire. The fact that Demykalon even mentioned the impact . . . *Except it was a way to get across the effectiveness of explosive shells.* "From your description and the accuracy shown here, I can see that you could concentrate fire on the weakest point, even if you cannot see it. Most impressive."

"They also allow one to inflict fire at one's enemies accurately at over a mille, and from directions it would be hard to determine in a short period of time." Before Alastar could say more, Demykalon went on. "You've seen the new cannon. I don't wish to take that much more of your day. We can talk on the ride back." He smiled and walked toward the archway.

Alastar followed, with Coermyd and Belsior behind him.

"Once we're clear," Demykalon told Weirt, "they can resume testing."

"Yes, sir."

Demykalon did not say more until he and Alastar were mounted and leading the way back toward headquarters. "What do you think of the cannon?"

"I have the impression that you have manufactured

more than the one you were testing, and that the test was largely for my benefit."

"Of course."

"It's obviously an improved weapon, but since there are no other armies in Solidar, why have you manufactured so many? It would appear to me that a naval version would be far more useful, particularly given the rise in piracy in or near the Southern Gulf."

"We do have such a version. At present, we have no vessels designed to use such cannon, but Sea Marshal Wilkorn is hopeful we will soon be able to build warships capable of using it."

"What use might you foresee for these guns?"

Demykalon shrugged. "One can never tell. If a High Holder refuses to do his duty or anyone else who owes allegiance to the rex . . . the cannon would be useful and spare troopers."

"With a great deal more than a thousand High Holders, I doubt you have enough cannon to keep them all in line."

"That may be, but we have enough for more than a few . . . and who would wish to be the first to stand against them?"

Alastar laughed. "You make a very good point. That is often what keeps the peace. At least, previous Maitres have thought so."

"The advantage that an army has, though, Maitre, is that its numbers preclude excessive concerns about those that might be called hostages to fortune."

Alastar understood exactly what Demykalon meant, and while he had a counter, it was best not to offer it. "Very true."

After they had ridden another fifty yards or so, Alastar said, "I understand that Rex Ryen believes that higher tariffs may be necessary if he is to have the funds to construct the ships necessary to deal with the pirates in the Southern Gulf."

"You had mentioned them before. Sea Marshal Wilkorn has hopes for additional warships, and the new cannon would be very effective against both Jariolan and Ferran warships. And pirates, also." The last three words were clearly an afterthought.

"But?"

"To raise tariffs might cause great unrest among the High Holders."

"It might, but continued piracy would increase the unrest among the factors."

"I am certain the rex will consider all matters, as will you if he asks your advice."

"How many of your commanders come from High Holder backgrounds? Perhaps half?"

Alastar could see Demykalon stiffen, if almost imperceptibly.

"All senior officers are trained to act for the good of Solidar, Maitre."

"I see."

"I'm certain that you do." Demykalon smiled. "Do you not think that our new cannon is a most impressive weapon?"

"Your demonstration and explanations have provided a most . . . commanding impression."

"I thought they might."

After those words, the words exchanged on the remainder of the ride back to the marshal's headquarters consisted entirely of cheerful pleasantries.

"What did you think about the marshal and his cannon?" Alastar asked the two younger imagers once they were on the road south from the headquarters toward L'Excelsis.

"He wanted you to see it," said Belsior.

"I wasn't that taken with him, sir," said Coermyd, "begging your pardon. It was like he was almost saying . . . well . . ."

Alastar nodded. "I'd appreciate it if you would not

say much, except that you saw the testing of a new cannon that is more accurate and you had a chance to see Marshal Demykalon."

"Yes, sir."

"We'll be taking the long way back to the Collegium, from the ring road to a point as close to the Bridge of Desires as we can manage. I need to survey the roads and ways there. The rex is considering a shorter route between the Collegium and the ring road around the chateau. We'll likely have to image it into being."

"Sir . . . ?"

"I know. There hasn't been much imaging like that since the time of the first Maitre, but Rex Ryen feels that there should be." *And so do you, if for other reasons, but not in the fashion Ryen would have it done—except . . .* Except Alastar did not yet have more than a sketchy idea of how to deal with building the avenue without turning even more of Solidar—or L'Excelsis—against the Collegium and its imagers.

As it was, before the end of the day on Vendrei, if barely, after he had left Elthyrd, Alastar had sent out notes to Cyran, Petros, and several other Maitres D'Aspect, summoning them to duty on Lundi for the initial phase of a "project commanded by the rex." Most might guess what that was, but there was no help for that. He put that out of mind and concentrated on observing his surroundings, since he still knew so little, comparatively, about L'Excelsis.

Once they reached the ring road, Alastar unfastened the rolled map from behind his saddle and studied it. "Starting at the lane of the apothecaries, just opposite the east drive to the chateau." He looked to Coermyd. "Have you heard of the lane of the apothecaries?"

"No, sir."

The lane of the apothecaries turned out to be more of an alley than a lane, whose paving was as much clay as brick. Alastar thought that many of the shops would have to be removed, and even parts of the adjoining ones. That would require imaging some sort of brick wall where they cut through a shop—if that was even possible—or removing the entire building.

Although Alastar hurried as much as he could, when the three returned to the Collegium it was close to fourth glass, and Alastar was feeling overwhelmed by the magnitude of the project Ryen had demanded. That did not include the potential problem with the Anomen D'Rex, which was less than a block south of the proposed route of the avenue. Alastar worried that, when Ryen saw that, even if he did not happen to attend services that regularly, at least according to what Iskhar had indicated when Alastar had first arrived, the rex might want more changes to the avenue, and that would mean more disruption to the nearby inhabitants. Alastar also clearly needed to talk to Petros, and that meant he'd have to interrupt the junior master's Solayi or wait until early Lundi morning, since Petros had already left his post at the stables.

After unsaddling and grooming the gelding, Alastar made his way to his study in the otherwise deserted administration building, where he took out the first volume of Chorister Gauswn's journals and continued to leaf through it, looking for references to Quaeryt, or anything else of interest that caught his eye. For a while, he just didn't want to deal with the problems of the rex . . . or even smaller ones, like what Desyrk wasn't saying and why Obsolym was so opposed to changing anything.

He leafed through another twenty pages, and while Quaeryt was referenced often, either by name, or by his title, the mentions were matter-of-fact, describing plans for a new building, a change in training or studies, a disciplinary hearing for an unruly junior imager, nothing that was out of the ordinary, nothing that shed any new light on the first Maitre. Then a single sentence leapt out at Alastar.

> . . . while not a word has been said in the years since, I cannot forget what the Khellan Eleni told me, that the Lady Vaelora is more than an imager, more than either Eherelani or Eleni, for all her farsight, and that her judgments are always sound . . .

Eherelani? Eleni? Alastar had never heard either term. Nor had he heard that Vaelora was actually an imager . . . or more than an imager. He had heard of Pharsi farsight, more common in women, but, again, nothing about Vaelora having that talent. He wanted to keep turning the pages, but knowing he couldn't, he marked his place in the first volume and rose from the desk, stretching.

"You can't devote too much time to that, not now." Saying the words out loud didn't assuage his curiosity, but it was time for dinner, not that he was looking forward to what was likely to be some form of leftovers, given that it was Samedi evening, and if he didn't hurry, he'd be late, an example he didn't want to set.

When Alastar reached the dining hall, he was still worrying about the avenue project as well as the question of repairing more sewers—something Ryen would scarcely like—not to mention pondering over the additional snippets of information he had gleaned from Chorister Gauswn's notes and about the encounter with Demykalon . . . and the mention of Antiagon Fire.

The dark-eyed and petite Alyna was already seated at the masters' table, alone, her face pleasantly composed as she surveyed the student imagers, always a sparse group on Samedi evenings, since those with coins tended to frequent cafés or bistros on the one free end-day evening that they had.

"Do you mind if I join you?" asked Alastar, since otherwise he would have left an empty seat between them.

"Of course not, Maitre." The Maitre D'Aspect offered a pleasant smile.

"I thought you were duty maitre last end-day, but then I realized it was Vendrei, but the duty rosters don't usually . . ."

"I agreed to take the duty for Gaellen last Vendrei. He and his wife wanted to go to his brother's birthday dinner. I thought I might be alone this evening."

"All the others who are unmarried are elsewhere this evening?"

"The men? Certainly, but who knows where? Except for Shaelyt. He and Tiranya went to dinner at her brother's house."

"I didn't know . . ."

"They're just friends. It's easier if he comes with her. Expectations, you know."

"You're friends with him as well. Does he accompany you . . ." Alastar shook his head. "That's unfair."

Alyna laughed, but the sound was warm and almost soft, so much at variance with her always-composed appearance that, for a moment, Alastar didn't know what to say, and she replied, "He'd be welcome. So would you . . . or any other maitre I asked, but unlike many High Holders, that cannot happen because my family has never maintained a house in L'Excelsis."

"An old family, tied to its lands?"

She shook her head. "A relatively new family for a high holding. Some four or five generations back, my great-great-grandfather, who established the porcelain works and other establishments, received the lands of a High Holder as a settlement on debts. The former High Holder apparently borrowed from my great-grandfather to pay off what he owed to then–High Holder Ryel, then defaulted and slashed his wrists. My great-grandfather could have taken that name, but with the dishonor . . .

he petitioned the rex to use his own. So we're very recent . . . as high holdings go."

"I heard that the elder Ryel, the one who died several years ago, had certain 'friendships' that were useful to his position as head of the High Council."

"He had more than a few 'friendships.' He was a handsome man, even when he was older. A very striking figure. Years ago, before I came to the Collegium, Father warned my sister off him, even if he had been recently widowed. Father was incredibly stern about it."

"He didn't like Ryel?"

"Oh, no. He thought Ryel was excellent at what he did. He said he would not suit her."

"Did he say why?"

"Only that knowing why would be dangerous for her. He wouldn't say more than that. I've wondered, but my brothers didn't know, either."

As he puzzled over that, Alastar was about to ask whether Alyna would like light or dark lager, when he realized there was but a single pitcher on the table. He decided against asking what it was, since Samedi night was for leftovers. "Lager?"

"Please."

He filled her beaker and then his. "I'm glad that it's the dark."

"There wasn't any doubt of that," replied Alyna. "Shabrena knows you only drink the dark, and it's my preference as well. She saw no point in wasting amber lager."

"You have a certain similarity to one of your forebears, it would appear," Alastar said dryly, "if the histories are correct." He was guessing slightly, but anyone who had been married to Quaeryt and been the sister of Rex Regis had to have had a fair amount of perception . . . and Chorister Gauswn had clearly been impressed.

"Oh?" Alyna looked puzzled.

Alastar wasn't quite convinced by her expression. "You do have a distinguished ancestor, or ancestress . . . and I suspect you know that."

"So I've been told." Alyna offered an amused and wry smile. "I was also told never to mention it. Others from holdings would not appreciate it, and imagers would take it as putting on airs. My mother was right about that. How did you find out?"

"Obsolym told me. Apparently, there's some record in the archives. Are you the only imager in recent years?"

"There is only one other I know of. I had a great-aunt. There were murmurings about her and her mother, but no one would tell me anything."

"What was her name?"

"Aurelya. That's what I was told."

"And no one told you more?"

"Maitre . . . as a daughter in a High Holder's family, when you're told not to ask more, you don't." Alyna's smile suggested more.

"From the little I know about you, I can't believe you let that stop you."

"It didn't. But it stopped everyone else from answering my questions. I can guess that Aurelya was not born . . . on the right side of the blanket, so to speak. Her mother died in childbirth. I did find that out."

"What else did you find out about Aurelya?" Alastar took a swallow of the dark lager, acceptable but not much more.

"There was an imager at the Collegium named Aurelya. She would have been the right age, but Maitre Obsolym said I'd need the permission of the Maitre to know more. Maitre Fhaen would never grant it."

"Quite a hidden history. I'll see what I can find out."

"Thank you." Alyna took a small swallow of the lager.

Alastar was amused at Alyna's approach, and the way in which she had never actually asked him to do anything. "Since you do come from a High Holder background, I'd like to get your views on a few matters. I trust you won't mind."

"I'd be happy to tell you what I know. You must recall that I was only ten when I came to the Collegium, Maitre, and that I was the daughter of a High Holder, and daughters are not told what sons are," she added with a smile that Alastar thought concealed a hint of mischief.

"For which reason, I suspect, daughters are often more observant, even at a tender age."

"What would you like to know?"

"Are not younger sons encouraged toward a career in the army or the naval forces?"

"'Encouraged' might be too gentle a term."

"You mentioned brothers. How many do you have besides the one who is the present High Holder?"

"Just one. He is fortunately occupied in running the main porcelain business. He is rather good at it, as even Zaeryl admits."

"Zaeryl?"

"That was his boyhood name. Now, of course, he's Zaerlyn. I still call him Zaeryl, not that we see each other often."

"You're no longer close?"

"We were never that close, except for a brief time just before I left. He's ten years older; Maraak is eight. I'm the youngest. Then there's Loryna. She's married to Caemren the younger."

Alastar hadn't heard of a High Holder Caemren, but he doubted anyone could remember a sizable fraction of the close to fifteen hundred High Holders. "Is that close to Rivages?"

"His lands are north of Yapres, about halfway between L'Excelsis and Rivages."

At that moment, one of the student servers—a duty reserved as punishment for minor infractions—appeared and set two platters on the table, one before each of them. Alastar surveyed the contents—mutton slices in a tan cream sauce with mushrooms and browned potato cakes and boiled carrots on the side. "Shabrena is good with sauces and gravies."

"You're a practical optimist, aren't you, Maitre?"

"Why do you say that?" replied Alastar, after cutting the mutton and taking a bite liberally coated with the mushroom gravy. He had been right about the sauce. It almost, but not quite, concealed the dryness of the mutton.

"You're the Collegium Maitre. You have no problem in using imaging to repair sewers. You like dark lager, and you can find the one part of a very ordinary meal that makes it better."

"By the way, you were very effective in doing your share of those repairs. You're likely the strongest imager of the Maitres D'Aspect." Alastar suspected she was far stronger than that, but he hadn't had a chance to determine if that might be so.

"Shaelyt may be stronger. I likely have better technique."

"Results—both in terms of the imaging, and in terms of the imager—are what count." *And results matter in everything else, also.*

"You hurried in here. Is that because you're working on obtaining more results?"

"Partly. It's been a long day, especially for a Samedi."

"I doubt you have many short days."

"Not at present. There are too many things that need my attention."

"Like the sewers?" Her voice was light.

"They didn't absolutely need attention, but their repair has made breathing on Imagisle less of a chore."

"For which many of us are grateful."

Alastar found himself not wanting to finish dinner,

yet knowing that he had to return to his study and work out a better plan for creating Ryen's Avenue D'Rex, complete with sewers and accessible drains. He took another sip of the dark lager. "Do you enjoy working with the girls and women?"

"At times. At other times . . ." She shook her head. "What I like the most is teaching mathematics and geometry. Most imagers don't understand how valuable geometry can be."

Alastar smiled. "I think I may have another project for you. Does your geometry include basic surveying?"

"It does. Very basic surveying. It came first."

Surveying before geometry? "How did that happen?"

"Our father insisted that both Zaeryl and Maraak learn the basics of many things. He said that a High Holder who didn't wouldn't remain one, or his grandchildren wouldn't. Zaeryl let me come along, but before long I had to learn some geometry . . ." She shrugged.

"Before you were ten?"

"I was eight. I liked it. I still do."

"I don't want to interrupt your Solayi, but . . ." Alastar went on to describe what Ryen had laid on the Collegium. When he finished, he waited for her response.

"That's . . . rather impetuous, isn't it?"

"He's known for that. There are other matters that make outright refusal . . . a less attractive alternative."

"Because the Collegium needs the rex's golds, and because High Holders don't care for him?"

"Among other things." Alastar didn't want to lay out all his problems. "I'm hoping that you and I and the duty imagers might take another look at the route the rex has laid out tomorrow, but if that would interfere . . ."

"No. I'd like to do something like that."

"Half past eighth glass at the stables?"

"I'll be there."

"Good." Alastar rose. "If you would excuse me . . ."

"You scarcely need excusing, Maitre." Her voice was pleasant, but held a trace of humor.

He smiled, ruefully. "Before all this is over, we both may."

PROLOGUE (3)

In the dim light under the old pier, the boy looked at the dirty copper in his hand. He studied it intently, one side and then the other, back and forth. He hadn't wanted to take it from the hiding place, but he knew that he had to. Even coppers were so hard to come by, and there were so few . . . sometimes none at all.

"It has to be perfect. It must be." He knew too well the dangers of a copper that was less than perfect. That was why he had practiced imaging the drawing on the tattered poster bill he had found in the corner of the alley onto porcelain circles. He'd given two of them to his mother. He'd told her he'd found them in the gutter and that he thought they'd likely been coasters tossed out by some merchant's wife because they were so ugly.

"They are ugly," she'd said.

He put the copper on the flat side of a rock. Then he concentrated, calling up the images of both sides.

A second copper lay beside the first. He started to pick it up, but he could feel the heat. So he waited, glancing up at the pier overhead. There were footsteps, but no one stopped or peered over the side. Finally, he picked up the "new" copper. It looked as dirty as the old one, and from what he could tell there was no difference between the two. He closed his eyes and shifted the coins from hand to hand, but they felt the same.

With a smile, he put the newer one in his single pocket, lined with rags to make sure that the coin didn't slip out, and the cooler one on the rock. He concentrated once more. He managed to do a third copper before his head began to feel light, and he had to sit and rest. Then he secured all four coppers in his pocket and crept along the base of the pier.

He had to walk more than a third of mille to get back home, and every step was an effort. He was tired . . . so very tired, but he kept putting one foot in front of the other until he could see the rear door.

The cot was empty. He dared not take even a deep breath, but tiptoed toward the side of the chimney. He glanced around, looking one way and then another before sliding the brick out and then slipping the original copper back into the small space beside the other one. Then he eased the brick back in place and walked toward the front door.

It opened before he reached it.

"Where have you been?" His mother's voice was hard, the way it got when she worried. Not so hard as it had been for weeks after Mahara and Dyel had died from the flux. She wasn't that way with his father, but he could see the brightness in her eyes when he limped in with his crutch, his battered wooden bowl empty.

"Working. I did some chores, carrying empty pallets on the wharf for a man. He was a quartermaster. That's what he said he was. He gave me two coppers." The boy extended the dirty coins. "I thought . . ."

His mother looked sternly at him. Then the sternness vanished. "You worked hard, didn't you?"

"Yes, Mother." That wasn't a lie. He had worked hard, just not in the way he had said. He was so very tired.

"You should stay away from the south wharf in the future. That's where the smugglers and the rough ones port. That's how . . ."

"I know . . . but . . ." The boy tried to convey the impression that was why he had been there. He had been there, not on the top of the pier, just underneath the shore portion and out of sight.

"We don't need the coppers so much that we'd lose

you." She looked at the coppers again. "You're a good one."

He could see the brightness in her eyes. "Things will get better. They will." Now that he had his own copper, he could make more. He would have to be very careful, he knew. But things would get better. They *had* to.

13

Alastar ended up working well past ninth glass on Samedi evening on a work plan for the new avenue. He then slept later than usual on Solayi morning, three quints later, so that he not only missed his morning run, but did not see Alyna at breakfast. She was at the stables when he walked up under a clear sky and bright sun that made the day seem warmer than it was. He carried the rolled-up map holding the route outlined by Ryen.

Alyna didn't look tired, as the duty maitres often did on Solayi morning. Her grays were pressed and crisp, and she smiled cheerfully. Her hair was largely swept up under the visor cap. From a distance, she looked like a young male imager, carrying a leather case in one hand and holding the reins of a brown gelding in the other.

Alastar saw that his gray gelding was already saddled and tied to a hitching ring at the edge of the paved area outside the stables. He stopped short of the Maitre D'Aspect. "You look like you had an uneventful evening. You usually do, don't you?"

"Why do you say that?"

"You don't put up with nonsense."

"I try. It seems to work." She smiled wryly. "I do have a reputation for being mean."

"Mean? I don't believe that." He paused. "Or is that what the students say when they discover that rules are rules, and most excuses are worthless?"

"Or when they discover that merely trying doesn't give the answers to calculations."

Alastar gestured to the leather case she held. "Surveying equipment?"

"No. I do have some, but you said that we'd only be looking today. This holds map paper, and tracing overlays, along with pressed charcoal drawing sticks."

He unrolled the map. "This shows the route that the rex has in mind. We can likely change it, but if we have to deviate much we'll have to go back to him." He waited as she pored over the map.

"The map doesn't show elevation changes," she observed.

"I've ridden the area, as close to the planned avenue as possible. There doesn't seem to be a great variation, and the western end is higher than the point where the eastern end would intersect the West River Road."

"If you're going to have to image sewers—"

"Even small changes in elevation matter. That's another reason why we're going to need you. You'll likely have to suspend some of your instructional duties while this is going on."

"You're planning on using most of the same imagers who worked on the sewers?" Alyna stepped back from the map, as if to indicate that she had seen enough.

"For the most part." Alastar rolled up the map and then turned as he heard hooves on the pavement. The two duty escorts—Glaesyn and Neiryn—reined up. Alastar watched as Neiryn looked toward Alyna, then stiffened slightly.

"Did you instruct Neiryn in mathematics?" asked Alastar quietly as he turned back to Alyna. "He seems wary of you."

"Not in that kind of calculation. Some years back, he had difficulty in figuring out something else. He thought that all a man needs is a pretty face. Subtlety isn't his strongest point."

It often isn't for any man when a woman is involved.

Alastar just nodded. "We'd better get mounted." He walked to the hitching ring and untied the gelding, then mounted after fastening the map to a saddlebag. He adjusted his visor cap before turning to the escorts. "We'll leave by the Bridge of Desires."

"Yes, sir," replied Glaesyn.

Alastar and Alyna led the way.

Even by the time they were riding up the West River Road, Alastar was still mulling over Alyna's comment about some men feeling they only needed a "pretty face" to appeal to women. *You'll never have that problem.*

More than three quints later, Alastar called a halt on the ring road, facing the narrow lane of the apothecaries. He turned to Alyna. "This is where he wants the avenue to begin."

"Twenty-four yards wide? The lane is no more than five wide, at the most, and the buildings on each side . . ." She shook her head.

"Rex Ryen has declared that the avenue will be built. Supposedly, all those whose properties are affected have been given notice that the imagers have the authority to do what is necessary. He's also informed them that they will be compensated. I also have a copy of a proclamation granting that authority."

"A proclamation may not be enough."

"I doubt it will be. That's why there will be both escorts and imagers. We'll also have to be careful that there are always some imagers fully rested." He paused. "We're going to follow the planned route as closely as we can. I'd appreciate any thoughts you have."

"The entry here should be wider. If the avenue is a direct way to the West River Road, there will be wagons and carriages turning in to it." Alyna smiled. "I assume you want me to write down what I'm suggesting?"

"Please."

"Also . . . what do you plan to do if the area you need to clear ends up in the middle of a structure?"

"I'd thought initially to wall it off, but that would take too much effort. I think we'll just have to remove the entire structure. That will mean providing some notice, at least several days, to people." After waiting for Alyna to take out the case, jot down her notes, and make several quick sketches, Alastar eased the mount toward the lane.

"Sir! Master imager!" A man in the brown tunic of an apothecary hurried out of the first doorway on the left.

Alastar reined up. "Yes?"

"Is it true? Are you going to tear down all the buildings along the lane, just for a road no one will use?"

"The rex has ordered the avenue to be built," Alastar replied. "Most of the buildings along the lane here will have to be removed."

"Just like that? What are we supposed to do?" The apothecary looked to be shivering, but Alastar suspected, given the unseasonable warmth and lack of wind, that the man was holding in anger.

"You'll have to remove your goods and equipment to some other place, and apply to the rex for compensation."

"My father's father lived and worked here. We have no other place." The man's voice rose.

"I'm sorry. But like you, we have no other choice."

"*You* have no other choice? You're an imager. You have choices."

"I do have choices. I can obey the rex, and preserve all the students and young imagers who are defenseless, or I can disobey and leave them nowhere to go and with no one to protect them. Without the Collegium . . ." Alastar broke off as he saw the man was not listening. "You will obey the rex's order. I wish it were otherwise. So do you. Neither of us has a choice."

"If I don't?"

"Then we will do what is necessary to carry out the

rex's order. If you or others attempt to attack, you will be stopped. You may well die."

The apothecary stepped back. "You're as bad as he is. And he is mad, that Rex Dafou." He backed away, his face red and flushed.

You're as bad as he is. The words echoed in Alastar's thoughts.

By the time he and the others were even fifty yards down the lane, his eyes were burning, perhaps from the fumes he had not noticed earlier. *Why not? Because this is the first time you've ridden down the lane when there wasn't a breeze?* He blotted his eyes on his sleeves and looked closely at the old and ramshackle shops and dwellings.

"How can they live and work in places like that?" asked Alyna.

"Because they have no choice. Most people don't. These people," he gestured back up the lane, "live in better circumstances than do many."

"You know that from—" Alyna broke off her words. "I'm sorry. I wasn't thinking."

Alastar had his doubts about that. From what he'd seen and heard from her in the last two days, Alyna was always thinking. But if she had been . . . why had she only partly asked the question? He offered a pleasant smile. "No apology is necessary. I'm certain that most people know that I came from straitened circumstances, as have many imagers." Before she could reply, he said, "I don't see any sign of sewers or drains. Do you?"

"No, sir."

"If we want to build this avenue correctly, that may take more planning. Can you calculate whether we can actually build a sewer from here to the river?"

"I can give you what I think, but I'd have to survey the route to be certain."

"Can you do that? How long would it take?"

"It's over a mille . . . and it can't be done directly, because, if the map is correct, there are buildings in the way. Two or three days, perhaps longer. I can't say for sure."

"I see." After a moment, he added, "Keep that in mind as we follow the route."

"I will."

A quint later, and only about two hundred yards farther east, Alastar reined up facing a two-story structure that stretched across the route on the map. As he was studying the building, checking against the map, a woman in well-washed brown and gray, carrying an infant, walked tentatively toward him, stopping well short of the gelding.

"Master imager, sir . . . ?"

"Yes?" Alastar dreaded what was to come.

"Are you the one? Are you going to destroy our little market for the new street?"

"Where is your market?"

The woman pointed back slightly to the south. "The one with the brown and green awning." In front of the shop were long and narrow tables, with baskets holding potatoes, onions, large cucumbers or green squash, possibly some late beans or something like them. The worn awning barely extended out over the table.

"Sir . . . ?" the woman asked again.

"We may have to. The rex has ordered us to create the avenue. You will be compensated if we do."

"We will lose everything. The rex is not offering enough."

"How do you know?"

"The day my Faerl got the paper, he went to the place to ask. They told him no one would get more than ten golds, and most would get less."

Alastar managed not to frown. Ten golds was not an inconsiderable sum.

"Ten golds is nothing, sir. My father paid fifteen for the shop when there was nothing in it. That was before I was born."

In this part of the city? That brought Alastar up short, although he did not show it. Obviously, property was much more valuable in L'Excelsis than in Westisle. *But then, L'Excelsis is the City of the Rex.* "I hope it is not necessary, but we must follow the orders of the rex, just as you must."

Tears began to ooze from the corners of her eyes. "It is not fair. It is not right. The rex has so much, and we have so little. Now the crops are poor. What the growers ask, we cannot pay. Not and buy what we need to sell." Her voice trembled as she went on. "Please, master imager, take pity on us. You are powerful. We are not." She looked directly at him.

Alastar met her gaze. "We all can only do what we can." He would have liked to have said more, but saying anything that even hinted that he had other inclinations, especially in public, would have been most unwise.

Abruptly, now sobbing, the woman turned and trudged away.

Alastar watched her until she was inside the door that she did not close. Then he turned in the saddle, watching as Alyna sketched out the structure before them. When she finished, he said, "We might as well ride around the building and continue on the other side."

Almost three glasses later, the four rode back across the Bridge of Desires and to the stables, where they reined up. Alastar let the duty ostler and stable boys take care of his and Alyna's mounts, then motioned for her to join him at the end of the paved walk that led to the administration building.

"Now that we've been over the route, what do you think?"

"I'd suggest that you change the route slightly, so that you have a straight road to the Anomen D'Rex. I know it's a little south of the avenue, but . . ."

"You're thinking that if we don't do it that way, once the avenue is finished, and he sees how close it is, we might have to make changes?" Alastar had already considered that, but wanted her opinion.

"It did occur to me. It also might be better to change the road around the anomen square there to an oval and widen it to match the width of the avenue. Coaches and wagons wouldn't get too crowded and slowed that way."

"You're right about that. This might take longer than the rex has in mind. But if that's what it takes to do it correctly . . ." Alastar shrugged. *You're going to be treading a narrow and dangerous path either way.* But then, the reaction of the apothecary and the woman produce vendor suggested that there was going to be a strong reaction once the imagers started to work in earnest—and Alastar wasn't looking forward to dealing with that at the same time as he had to deal with Ryen and the High Holders and factors.

"You're concerned about how people will take it?" asked Alyna blandly.

"I'm concerned about everything. I'll need to warn the rex, but I can't say that I'm not worried about his reaction."

"Does he react as . . . violently . . . as it is said?"

"At times. At other times, no, at least from what I've seen so far. Is that the way most High Holders view him? As violent when crossed?"

"I haven't been close to many actual High Holders, except my brother. When you're a girl of ten, you don't see them. Your family doesn't want you seen, because the only question is whether you'll be bright enough, but not too bright, and pretty enough to marry well. I saved my father and brother that dilemma."

"Very few daughters of a High Holder are as bright as you, and fewer still are talented enough to become maitres." Alastar wasn't about to mention that she was attractive, because that would have been most untoward, given his position—and that he was widowed and thus single.

"You're most kind, Maitre."

Alastar grinned at the honeyed, and patently false, tone. "I'm not kind at all. I'm being accurate. You're likely too bright to make a good wife for most High Holders, and the fact that you're a Maitre D'Aspect and probably already know enough to become a Maitre D'Structure before long speaks to your imaging ability."

"How do you know that?" Her question was direct, but neither challenging nor obsequious.

"I watched you image sewer repairs." He paused. "Thank you again for accompanying us today. I'd like you to bring your surveying equipment tomorrow. Tell Dareyn, first thing in the morning, to post on the board that your mathematics instruction will be postponed until further notice. Will you need a packhorse?"

"I can manage without one."

"Then I will see you later, or in the morning." Alastar watched for several moments as she walked north toward the quarters cottages. Then he headed to the administration building. Once in his study, he spread the map on his desk and considered what Alyna had suggested and how he could handle matters in a way that minimized difficulties for the Collegium. He frowned and began to study the map thoroughly. Finally, he concentrated, blotting his forehead after a copy of the map appeared beside the original.

He compared the two, but so far as he could see, they matched. After using some map-tracing paper and a charcoal stick to overlay a rough approximation of what Alyna had suggested, he found himself considering his conversations with her, and during their survey of the proposed route. In two days, he had talked to her more than the total of all interactions with her over the time since he'd arrived at Imagisle. There was something different about those conversations with her, and it wasn't because she was a woman. *Or not primarily.*

But what? After a moment it came to him. While she had been most respectful, she had not been ill at ease or in awe of him. She had just talked to him.

Alastar smiled wryly, realizing that was exceedingly rare. Almost no one seemed completely at ease in talking to him since he had arrived at the Collegium. He just hadn't seen it in that way. *But then, she is the daughter of a High Holder, and a rather practical one, it appears.*

Before he knew it, or so it seemed, he was standing in the anomen at services, listening as Iskhar launched into his homily.

"We're all familiar with Naming, aren't we?" asked the chorister, obviously rhetorically. "The arrogation of words over deeds? The pride taken in burnishing one's name and reputation with words. Or even endless repetition of one's deeds in an effort to exalt one's own name and reputation." Iskhar paused. "I have a question for all of you. Can an act or action, in and of itself, be Naming? Even if one never speaks of the acts."

Alastar's immediate thought was, *Of course it can.*

"I see more than a few nods out there," Iskhar observed with a smile. "Let's take that a step further. Can an absolutely selfless act, one which confers no benefit to the doer, not even kind words spoken on one's behalf, can that still be Naming?" Without much of a pause, the chorister went on. "That all depends on the motive of the doer. If a selfless act is done solely to prove one is better than another, it is merely a hidden form of Naming. If such an act is undertaken to make one feel better, then it is a form of Naming, if not one of the more egregious forms. If that act is undertaken out of guilt, or in recompense for an ill done to another, it may not be Naming, and it may indeed be necessary, for many reasons, but it is the very least one could do . . ."

As Iskhar went on, Alastar had to think about the chorister's words.

Nearly two quints later, after the service, he waited until the others had departed and then approached Iskhar.

"Very thought-provoking, Iskhar, but I think you were a bit hard on guilt. Don't you think that, without guilt, the world would be a worse place? Is guilt that prompts good acts necessarily Naming? At what point does such guilt pass from past atonement to merely doing good? Can you honestly judge that it never does?"

For a moment, Iskhar looked surprised. Then he chuckled. "Maitre, perhaps you should give a homily."

"I think not. I'm more comfortable in posing questions. But then, that might also be a form of Naming, especially if I ask them out of pride."

"Your thoughts are most provocative, Maitre. I would be happy to listen to them at much greater length."

"That may have to wait until I am more settled in as Maitre." Alastar did not bother to keep the dry tone out of his voice. "Then . . . then we might have some interesting talks."

"I will look forward to that."

After leaving the anomen and Iskhar, Alastar did stop by his study in the administration building to pick up the first volume of Chorister Gauswn's journals. Once he was back at the Maitre's residence, he settled himself in his private study and began to continue his reading. As before, pages went by without more than a casual mention of Maitre Quaeryt. Alastar's eyes were burning, and he was about to stop for the evening, knowing that Lundi would be a very long day, when he finally came across another interesting passage.

> . . . overheard a conversation that again suggested how the Nameless works in directing the ways of men. Maitres Khalis and Lhandor agreed it was for the best that the Maitre had offered the blade of Erion that had saved him to the Council of Khel . . . and that the Eleni

had accepted it as a token of faith, as if true faith requires such tokens . . .

Alastar kept reading, but there was absolutely no explanation beyond the words, and he could not recall having heard of a blade of Erion or reading about it. *Why would the chorister mention a blade of Erion? Was it something taken from Khel and then returned? How could it have saved Quaeryt's life? And why did Gauswn even mention it? Was it a quiet way to allude to more about Quaeryt? Why didn't he ever say more?* Alastar chided himself, noting that he was less than halfway through the first volume of three, and that there might well be much more later, although he had a feeling that there just might not be.

With no ready answers to his questions, he slowly closed the book, imaged out the two lamps, and made his way from the study up the stairs. He was tired, and he was not looking forward to Lundi. Not totally.

14

While Alastar slept decently, he woke early on Lundi, did his run, then washed, shaved, and dressed quickly before making his way to the dining hall, where he also ate quickly, and then walked through a blustery wind to the armory. There, he found Cyran.

"You look serious, Alastar."

"Very serious. I'm going to have to disrupt your schedule. I'd like you to accompany me and the survey team. Alyna and I spent more than three glasses yesterday looking over the route for Ryen's new avenue. It's not as easy as Ryen's map makes it look. We'll need Alyna to survey the route before we start. There will be more people who are unhappy when they see us preparing the route, and I have the feeling that I'm not going to be able to spend much time directing either the surveying, or the construction, when we get to it."

"I'll do whatever you need, but I don't know what I can add."

"Between you and Alyna, I'm sure you can work it out."

Cyran frowned, then offered an ironic smile. "You need me to keep the shopkeepers and imagers in line, and her to supervise the actual imaging. Is that it?"

"She'll do the surveying, today and tomorrow, possibly Meredi and even Jeudi. After that, she and Petros may be able to oversee the imaging, and you can make certain the work isn't disrupted and that no one is hurt. I still have to see what can be done about the rex's tariff problem with the High Council, especially since Marshal Demykalon is most supportive of the rex." *More accurately, so unsupportive of the Collegium that he would relish any excuse to level Imagisle with his new cannon.*

"I can do that."

"Good. We'll be leaving at half after seventh glass." With a nod, Alastar headed back to the administration building, glad to see that Dareyn was already at his desk.

"Dareyn. You've been here awhile. Do you recall an imager by the name of Aurelya?"

"Aurelya? That sounds familiar, but I can't place it."

"Could you have Obsolym find out? I'm taking out a surveying party of imagers and escorts to do some preliminary work on the avenue that Rex Ryen has ordered. If I can manage it, I'll be back by midday, but that's not certain. You'll have to reschedule some of those meetings with students. Oh . . . and would you send a messenger to High Holder Guerdyn with a request for me to meet with him this afternoon at third glass, or even fourth, if he can't accommodate me at third? I'll be back when I can be, but it won't be before noon. Is there anything I need to do before I leave?"

"No, sir."

"Good." With that, Alastar straightened his visor cap and headed to the stables. Alyna was already there, as were Petros and Cyran. Before long Shaelyt, Khaelis, and Lhendyr arrived. Khaelis glanced around, as if puzzled.

"You're right, Khaelis," said Alastar. "We don't have enough imagers for heavy road imaging. We won't be doing any of that today or tomorrow. Late in the week, we may begin on the preliminary work on the edge of the ring road to set up the entry and the width and starting points." *As much as to show Ryen we've begun work as anything.* "Maitre Alyna will be doing the surveying. Petros will be studying the buildings and the existing roadbed. Maitre Cyran and the rest of you will be there in case the people whose shops and homes may have to be removed get too angry. I picked you because you've all got very strong shields. We don't want anyone hurt . . ." Alastar went on to describe the general approach to the day's tasks.

When he finished, and the imagers were readying their mounts, he walked over to Alyna. "How accurate can you be?"

"More accurate than just looking and guessing," replied Alyna. "Quite a bit better than that, but not as good as a real surveyor. I just have the old-fashioned surveying equipment—surveyor's cross, merchet, a brass yard chain, a compass, some angle plates, and a water level. They're already packed behind my saddle. To be really precise, especially over longer distances, I'd need a telescope diopter, but I didn't know enough geometry or optics to image a copy of the one Zaeryl had."

Telescope diopter? Alastar had no idea what a diopter even was. "Imaging was how you got everything, even the yard chain?"

"The chain was hard work at the time." Alyna smiled. "That was when Father discovered I was an imager. He thought I'd taken it. Less than a week later, I was at the Collegium."

"What? Ten years ago?"

"You're kind. More than fifteen. We're starting at the ring road?"

Since Alastar had already said that, he understood that Alyna did not wish any more questions about her age or past. "We are." He smiled, then half-turned. "Everyone! Mount up!"

"You want me in the rear?" asked Cyran quietly.

"Please, along with whichever junior master you think will be best."

"Khaelis, then."

In a matter of moments, Alastar and Alyna mounted and then led the survey party from the stables toward the Bridge of Desires. Three-fifths of a glass later, Alastar reined up on the ring road, some fifty yards north of the lane of the apothecaries. A scattering of wagons, coaches, and single riders were visible on that part of the ring road that he could see, roughly a third of it. Finally, he turned to Alyna. "What do you think?"

"About what?" Her voice was pleasantly matter-of-fact. "You haven't told me what you're considering."

"A more gradual approach to the avenue, as you recommended."

"I'd like to do some measurements first. Anything I say now would just be a guess."

"Then start measuring. Have Lhendyr hold your mount."

Alyna nodded and turned the brown gelding. Alastar rode toward Khaelis and reined up. "I trust you can image and use shields while holding my mount?"

"Yes, sir."

"Good." Alastar dismounted and handed the gelding's reins to the young Maitre D'Aspect, then walked toward the narrow lane where he stood watching as Alyna took her yard chain and began to measure the width of the lane proper.

Before long, three men approached Alastar as he stood on the narrow sidewalk of the ring road on the north side of the alley-like lane. He made sure his shields were a full strength, then smiled pleasantly and waited.

"Master imager . . . ?" offered the oldest and shortest of the three.

"Yes?"

"That . . . imager, the one with the chains . . . ?"

"She's taking measurements before we begin work on the avenue that Rex Ryen has commanded us to build."

"You're going to tear down our shops . . . just like that?" asked the brown-bearded man who looked younger than Alastar. "Take away everything we've got?"

"Not just like that," temporized the Maitre. "First we have to measure . . ."

"Comes to the same thing!" snapped the third, a burly bald man with a gray mustache and square beard. His faded gray tunic and trousers were spotted with stains.

"There's nothing we can do to stop this . . . this unfairness?" asked the older man.

"You could petition the rex," Alastar said. "It was his decision, not mine."

"Ha!" snorted the bald man. "Easy way to lose your life, too. Don't notice you telling him it's a bad idea."

"You're right. I did tell him that he had to do it under the law. That way, you'll get some compensation."

"It's not enough," said the brown-bearded man.

"It's not fair."

Alastar just waited.

After a time of silence, the older man asked, "When will you start tearing things down and building?"

"We'll have to finish measuring and surveying. That will take at least a day or two. It could take a little longer. It's hard to tell. We'd rather not remove anything we don't have to."

"What about right here?" demanded the bald man.

"To get an entry to the avenue . . . we'll have to remove the two corner shops for certain. How much beyond that, that's what we're trying to find out."

The bald man clenched his fists.

"Don't even think about it, Amarr," declared the older man. "There are three imagers besides the master here, all looking at you."

"You aren't losing everything," said Amarr bitterly, glaring at Alastar.

"No . . . every one of us lost everything we had when people found we were imagers. Some imagers are the children of High Holders and wealthy factors."

"It's not the same . . ." Amarr did not say what he

might have as he saw something in Alastar's eyes. Abruptly, he turned and walked away.

For some of us, it isn't. But the apothecary didn't need to know that.

As Alyna continued, Alastar walked over to the still-mounted Petros, who raised his eyebrows as if to ask why he was necessary.

"You're here to look at all these buildings and to think about what we'll need to do once we image away all or parts of them . . . and what immediate imaging might be necessary to keep things from falling down around us and anyone else."

"We're really going to do this, sir?"

"We don't have much choice. Our only choice is how well we do it."

Petros nodded, almost sadly.

Alastar kept watching everything that he could, well aware that more than a few pairs of hidden eyes were on him and the other imagers.

After more than a quint, Alyna approached. "Would you hold the chain for a moment while I do some figures?"

He nodded. The chain, fine as the links were, was heavier than he realized, and that meant Alyna was stronger than she looked, because she'd showed no strain at all. Alyna took out the leather case from one of her saddlebags, and used it as a writing—or calculating—board. In less than a tenth of a glass, she returned.

"What do your calculations show?" he asked.

"If you want an easier entry to the avenue, angling it, say, at a little more than thirty-five degrees, you'll have to start the cut back from the ring road something like forty yards from where the entryway will meet the new avenue. Where your curb intersects the curb of the new avenue will be about thirty yards back from the ring road. That means taking out almost three shops on each side, because you'll also need room for the sidewalk."

Alastar had known that making the entry onto the new avenue easy would take space. He just hadn't calculated just how much. "We'd better measure that and see what it looks like."

"I can do that. I've got marking chalk. Do you want me to use that?"

"Please. Make the marks clear but not huge."

She nodded.

When Alyna finished, and marked the positions with a chalk stick on the wall of the shop on the north side of the lane, Alastar nodded sadly. *Three shops will have to go, definitely. All the more reason to make this very deliberate.*

After that, Alyna used the surveyor's cross and measuring staff, brass-tipped at the bottom, and with a brass graded notch or slot at the top, as well as the chain, with which Shaelyt helped her, to survey and measure the lane. Then, in places, she used a water level—essentially a miniature brass trough little more than a finger's width, but a hand high and a third of a yard long with measuring grooves cut along the inside.

From the lane, the slow process continued eastward.

As noon approached, Alastar rode over to Cyran. "I'm going to turn this over to you. I've got to go meet with High Holder Guerdyn. Just let Alyna survey the route. Quit around third glass, at a place that's convenient for her to stop taking measurements."

"Third glass?"

"We don't need to be in a hurry to start tearing down shops and dwellings." *For more than a few reasons.*

Cyran offered an inquiring look.

"Don't ask," said Alastar dryly. "Make sure no one gets hurt." Then he rode over to Alyna, who looked up as he reined the gelding to a halt. "I need to leave to deal with another item of interest to Rex Ryen. Maitre Cyran will be in charge. You can ask him or Petros, or anyone else for whatever assistance you need. If I don't see you late this afternoon, you can tell me what I need to know in the morning."

"Yes, sir."

As he rode back to the Collegium, accompanied just by Shaelyt, Alastar thought over how the surveying had gone. It seemed to him that he could leave much of the road building to Petros and Alyna—and their protection to Cyran. Despite his best efforts, because he had to take side streets, it was almost two quints past noon when he reined up at the stables and turned to the Maitre D'Aspect.

"Shaelyt, for now, you can keep up with your instructional sessions, at least until Maitre Alyna finishes surveying the route. That's likely to be several days."

"Yes, sir."

Alastar dismounted, handed the gelding over to the duty ostler, and then walked back to the administration building. As soon as he entered the anteroom, Dareyn immediately announced, "High Holder Guerdyn will see you at half past third glass. He only has a half glass."

"Thank you. That should be more than enough. Do I have any student imagers coming?"

"Secondus Gherard will be here at first glass, and then Seconda Linzya after him. Also, Arhgen asked if he could have a few moments."

"Send for Arhgen right now. I doubt I'll have time later."

"Yes, Maitre." Dareyn hurried off.

Alastar barely had the master ledger out when the Collegium bookkeeper appeared.

"Maitre." Arhgen looked distinctly distraught.

"Did I overlook something, or has something come up?"

"Minister Salucar's steward sent this." The bookkeeper extended a single sheet of paper.

It took Alastar only a moment to read the words.

Please inform Maitre Alastar that Rex Regis, His Grace Ryen, has informed the Minister Salucar that the Collegium's monthly stipend will be half that of the usual until the matter of future tariffs is resolved.

"I can see that the minister did not wish to inform me of that," said Alastar, adding sardonically, "I can't imagine why."

"Yes, sir."

"According to the ledger, we have enough to get through the end of Ianus. That's if we don't cut spending more. Is that about right?"

"I'd want to check again, sir . . ."

"It's close enough. Hold off on purchasing anything except food and produce until you check with me. And urgent fodder, if Petros says he needs it."

"Yes, sir."

"I'd also like your suggestions about what we can do without for the next few months. By tomorrow sometime, if you can."

"Yes, sir." Arhgen bobbed his head.

As soon as the bookkeeper left, Alastar leafed through the ledger and jotted down several notes to himself, setting them aside when Dareyn announced the first student imager.

Secondus Gherard entered immediately, a chubby boy who clearly hadn't come into his growth yet. He had bright green eyes set in a round face and a mouth more suited to pouting than smiling.

"Good afternoon, Gherard. Please take a seat."

"Good afternoon, Maitre. Yes, Maitre." The second looked at Alastar, but did not quite meet his eyes as he took the chair farthest from Alastar.

"You've been here over two years, haven't you? And you come from a factoring family."

"Yes, sir."

"How have you found the Collegium?"

"It's the Collegium, sir."

"What exactly do you mean by that?"

Gherard squirmed slightly in the chair. "Where else would an imager go?"

"Where would they go elsewhere on Terahnar? What happens to them in other lands?"

"Ah . . . some places they get killed, they say. In Jariola, they belong to the Oligarchs . . . I think."

"If they're fortunate. You never answered the question about how you found the Collegium."

"It's . . . it's the Collegium."

Alastar was definitely getting the impression that young Gherard wasn't thrilled to be at the Collegium and that he didn't want to say so, but didn't want to lie, either, not out of any moral sense, but simply out of fear. "What does your father factor?"

"Sir?"

"I asked what your father factors. Your father is Factorius Wylum, is he not?"

"Yes, sir. He's a woolen and cloth factor. He has a spinning mill north of here. He sends the cloth down to his warehouse on his wagons."

"You lived in a large house, perhaps on a hill to the north of L'Excelsis?"

Gherard frowned. "It was a nice house. It's east of here."

"Do you go there when you can?"

"Yes, sir."

"Does your father send a coach for you?"

"No, sir."

"Your mother, perhaps?"

Gherard swallowed.

Alastar waited.

"Ah . . . yes, sir."

"What kind of imager would you like to be?"

"I don't know, sir. I'm just learning." Gherard paused, then asked, "When will I be advanced to being a tertius?"

"When your imaging skills meet the standards for becoming a third."

"But I'm a better imager than some of the older thirds . . ."

"Some of the thirds obtained that position because of their skills and value in other areas. They will likely never become maitres. You have shown no other talents, and your imaging skills alone are not yet sufficient for you to become a tertius."

"That doesn't seem fair, sir. I'm a better imager than some thirds, and I'm only a second."

"Those thirds served the Collegium for years with both imaging and other skills. You're still a student, and your imaging skills are not as good as those of other students who are thirds."

"I can image more. I know I can. The maitres . . ."

"They won't let you do more? That's because trying to image too much before you are ready is dangerous. It could kill you. Before there was a Collegium, most imagers died young."

Gherard appeared ready to argue, but did not, his lips forming into an expression just short of a pout.

"When your skills improve, you will become a tertius. According to Maitre Shaelyt and Maitre Alyna, you need to practice more—within the rules." Alastar paused, then asked, "How are you doing in your other studies?"

"I'm doing best in language . . ."

After another painful tenth of a glass, Alastar released young Gherard, withholding a sigh of relief after the second departed. He offered a pleasant smile to Seconda Linzya as she entered and took the chair directly across from Alastar. Like Gherard, she did not quite meet Alastar's eyes at first. Unlike him, after a moment she did, and he noted that her eyes were pale gray, almost overshadowed by her thick jet-black hair, short-cut as it was.

"How are you finding the Collegium, Linzya?"

"I like it, sir. The food is good, and Maitre Tiranya is nice. She's strict, but she explains things. So does Maitre Alyna, but she works mostly with the thirds. I've learned all my letters. I can even give a copper or two to my ma."

"She lives in L'Excelsis?"

"In Caelln, sir."

Alastar had not heard of the town. "Is that far?"

"It's south of here, sir, mayhap five milles, on the river. My da's a boatman."

After a quint with Linzya, once she left, Alastar was feeling slightly better. Gherard had definitely left a bad taste in his mouth, yet he worried about that hint of defiance he had seen. He checked the student roster. Obsolym was Gherard's preceptor. *That attitude? Coincidence?* Alastar shook his head, thinking about the difference between Alyna and Gherard. *Then again, you didn't know Alyna when she was Gherard's age.* He still didn't believe she'd been like that. *But you don't know.*

Over the next two quints, he considered what he might say to Guerdyn, but in the end, decided that he would have to see what the High Holder said and how he acted. Then it was time to leave, and he hurried out to the area in front of the administration building, where his escorts, this time Belsior and Akkard, were waiting with the gray gelding. Once they were riding toward the Bridge of Desires, Alastar motioned for them to move up beside him.

"How did you two find the Collegium when you came?" Alastar looked first to Akkard.

"I hated it. I missed my family. My mother. I never saw much of my father. He's a farrier, and he spends most of the week traveling to where there are horses needing shoes."

"And now?"

"I like it. I'm working with Arthos in the forge, and I'm learning about imaging metals, or shaping them. I can't create metal from nothing, the way he can, but I can image a piece into something. I even made a decent pair of candlesticks last week. It wore me out for two days."

"What about you, Belsior?"

"I didn't even have a name. Belsior was what Maitre Fhaen named me. I was just 'boy.' "

Alastar waited.

"My ma—my mother—she served at the inn. That was up in Talyon. She never said who my father was. Maybe she didn't know. When the innkeeper found out I could image—I tried to make a copper for her—he blindfolded me, tied me up, and carted me down here for the gold he got from the Collegium. It was the best thing that ever happened to me." Belsior grinned. "Even if it turned out I'll never be a great imager."

Alastar smiled. "You'll do just fine." He couldn't help but think of the diverse places from which they all had come, and the differences in upbringing even among those from similar backgrounds.

They reached the Council Chateau before third glass. Alastar had to wait in a small sitting room until almost half past the glass before the same footman who had escorted him before appeared and led him to the receiving study. This time Guerdyn wore a silver and black doublet with black hose and shoes, and a black jacket trimmed in silver. He stood by the window and turned as Alastar entered. He gestured to the chairs around the low table, then stepped forward and seated himself. "I apologize, but our time will be limited, as I informed your imagers."

Alastar sat down quickly in the armchair across from the High Holder. "I do understand."

"Rather than assume I know why you are here, might I inquire?" Guerdyn's tone was condescending.

"You might indeed," replied Alastar cheerfully. "You understand that, recently arrived as I am from Westisle, there are certain procedural matters of whose practices and niceties I am unaware. In brief, not being from L'Excelsis, I have no idea how the Council operates, except in very general terms. In the case at hand, if the High Council does consider tariffs to be a problem, might I ask exactly how the Council will address the matter. Procedurally, to be precise."

"I do appreciate your interest in the matter." Guerdyn smiled smoothly, although his eyes remained cold. "I also understand you have met with each councilor, and each has confirmed that you did not attempt in any way to suggest in the slightest how the High Council should address the matter of tariffs. Your words, or the lack of such words, convey an understanding of the restraint necessary for a Maitre of the Collegium. On the other hand, your very presence . . . that might present a problem."

"A single imager who represents but a double handful of full imagers and a few students?"

"Your modesty becomes you, but we all know that small numbers of imagers have brought great power to bear."

"Only for the greater good of Solidar."

"'Greater good'—that is a phrase subject to interpretation."

"It is indeed. I would interpret it as meaning that all would prosper, if in different degrees, as opposed to a prosperity where one group, or two, prosper at the far greater expense of others. That is the definition under which the Collegium has always operated."

"No one's prosperity should be held hostage to another," declared Guerdyn. "When a 'greater good' is invoked that costs one group to benefit another, that is theft, nothing more."

"Not necessarily. You may be tariffed. Those tariffs may seem to benefit others, because a road is improved, a bridge built, a warship constructed to stop piracy . . . or the marshal of the army may build new cannon. The foundry where those cannon are cast purchases iron pigs from you or another High Holder. The workers at the foundry buy goods from shopkeepers, many of whose purchases result in greater sales to you or large factors." Alastar watched Guerdyn, especially as he mentioned cannon, but the High Holder showed no reaction to that reference.

"That may be, but the benefit is diffuse. The cost is immediate and direct."

"Any ruler, even the High Council, must balance immediate costs against long-term benefits." Alastar smiled. "I'm not telling you anything you don't know. So what is the procedure?"

Guerdyn straightened himself in his chair. "The Council, as you must know, will meet here at the first glass of the afternoon on Meredi. We will discuss any matters that any member may wish to bring up. How we proceed depends on what the majority determines is necessary."

"But any single member may bring up any matter?" Alastar wanted to be clear on that.

"Certainly."

"And should the Council find itself opposed to something . . . then what?"

"Then, as in the past, we will convey our views to the rex. If he is wise, he will heed them. Should that occur, I would trust that the Collegium would also consider what might be the wisest course for the rex."

"How could the Collegium do otherwise?" asked Alastar. "At times, however, determining the wisest course is not so obvious as others might think."

"In matters such as tariffs, the High Holders and factors do not differ greatly."

He really believes that! "I could not speak to that."

"Word is that you met with the head of the factors' council."

"I did," replied Alastar, making his tone as wry as possible. "We discussed repairs to the sewers of L'Excelsis and the fact that it would take either many golds or much imaging to make all the repairs necessary. And the fact that imagers should not make such repairs on Solayi."

The faintest hint of a cool smile appeared and then vanished before Guerdyn spoke. "Do you think you could convince the factors to stand against the High Council?"

"I've made no attempt to convince any factor of anything, except that the Collegium did not mean to upset the chief factor by repairing sewers on Solayi."

The High Holder frowned. "He was upset by that?"

"Quite upset."

Guerdyn shook his head. "Are there other questions of procedure you might have?"

"Of procedure . . . I think not. Not at this time, anyway, but you have been most kind."

"Then . . ." Guerdyn stood. "I do not wish to seem inconsiderate, but . . ."

Alastar stood. "I do understand, and I appreciate your making time to see me. I will not keep you from your other obligations." He inclined his head slightly.

Guerdyn returned the gesture, then walked toward the study door and opened it. The two left the study, and the High Holder accompanied Alastar as far as the entry hall.

"A pleasant ride back to the Collegium, Maitre."

"Thank you." Alastar nodded again, then turned and made his way out and down to where Akkard and Belsior waited.

As Alastar rode back south on the West River Road, he was still worrying about what he should do about the forthcoming High Council meeting, as well as how the surveying of the avenue route was proceeding, and about what Factor Elthyrd might decide.

When he finally entered the administration building and stepped into the anteroom, he found Desyrk pacing around the anteroom. Yet when Desyrk looked up, he squinted, almost as if he did not see Alastar that clearly, before hurrying toward him. Alastar especially did not like the worried expression on the face of the Maitre D'Structure.

"Maitre . . . ?"

"Come on in." Alastar gestured toward the open door to his study, then looked to Dareyn. "Is there any word from Cyran or Alyna?"

"No, sir."

"Thank you." Alastar waited for Desyrk to enter the study, then closed the door and motioned toward the chairs. "What is it?" He seated himself behind the desk.

Desyrk took the middle chair, but sat forward. "We had a problem . . . Taurek."

"He's a tertius. You said he had great potential."

"He does, but he has a temper. He's had trouble before. This time . . . I was talking about technique. I had just said that substituting strength for technique could get them in trouble. One of the other thirds—I didn't see who it was—made a snide remark under his breath, something about most bulls who were obstinate got gelded. Someone else snickered, and then Taurek clamped shields around Bettaur. For a moment, I didn't recognize what happened, because Bettaur wasn't moving . . ."

"Until he started turning red?"

"That's right. I ordered Taurek to drop the shields. He didn't even hear me. I imaged ice water over him, and then he tried the shields on me. I managed to turn them on him, but barely. He was mad, and he is strong as a bull. I had to hold them until he passed out."

"How is Bettaur?"

"Scared, but he'll be all right."

"Taurek?"

"I blindfolded him, and chained and cuffed him, just in case. He's in the iron-and-lead-lined detention room. He's still angry."

Alastar took a deep breath. "I don't recall anything about Bettaur . . ."

"He's from a small-holder family in Tuuryl."

At least he's not a High Holder or a factor's son. "We'll have to hold a disciplinary hearing in the morning. It's obviously too late today, and it won't hurt Taurek to get a taste of the discipline cell. Set it for eighth glass. Maitre Tiranya will need to be on the panel. Neither Cyran nor Alyna can be. Gaellen and Obsolym . . . and Akoryt. I'll act as justicer, since you can't. You'll have the students who observed it all there to tell what they saw?"

"Yes, sir."

"Were there any other witnesses?"

"No, sir."

"Is there anything else I should know?"

"Not that I can think of."

"Then that's all we can do about that tonight. Make certain someone keeps checking on both Bettaur and Taurek. Even if they look fine . . ."

"Yes, sir."

Once Desyrk had left and closed the door, Alastar took a deep breath. *What next?* He didn't even want to think about the possibilities.

15

The first thing Alastar did on Mardi morning, after his run, cleaning up, and breakfast, was to find Cyran in the armory.

"You have that look of a maitre looking for another master to deal with a problem." Cyran laughed.

"I do indeed. You're going to have to take over supervising the surveying party today."

"You mean for all of the day instead of just half?"

Alastar nodded. "How did the rest of the afternoon go?"

"There were no problems. I just listened to Alyna and kept order. I had the feeling you didn't want people working particularly late. We started back a little before third glass."

"How far did Alyna get?"

"About a third of the way. I think there's a part that's going to be trouble, but you'll have to talk to her about it."

"I'll do that later. I've got to deal with a disciplinary meeting."

"Is this to do with Taurek?"

"Unfortunately. Has he been difficult before?"

"He hasn't needed a disciplinary session. It's been close. He has trouble containing his feelings, and he says exactly what he thinks. He doesn't have much tact." Cyran frowned. "That's not right. It's more that he doesn't even know what tact is."

"I'll keep that in mind. Now, I'll see if Alyna's at the stables."

"I'm sure she is," replied Cyran. "She likes doing things."

With a nod, Alastar turned and walked swiftly from the armory. As Cyran had predicted, Alyna was indeed at the stables and had already saddled the brown gelding. She offered a pleasant smile as he neared.

"Good morning, Alyna. How did the surveying go yesterday?"

"Slowly. There's also an area where you'll have to run the sewers well away from the avenue because there's what was once a small valley . . ."

Alastar listened as she explained, then said, "Cyran will be in charge again today. I have to preside at a disciplinary meeting."

"Taurek? I heard he was in confinement."

"That's right. There's another matter. I've been meeting with the student imagers as I can . . ."

"I heard. Tiranya said you met with Linzya."

"She's apparently come a long way."

"Very long. She told Tiranya you were very stern. Stern in a nice way, though."

"She's very enthusiastic about the Collegium and very positive about you and Tiranya."

"More likely positive about Tiranya and accepting of me."

"She said you explained things patiently and well."

Alyna looked slightly surprised. "She did?"

"She did." Alastar paused. "I'd like to ask you a question. You don't have to answer it, but I'd appreciate it if you did. Did you find it hard to adjust to the discipline of the Collegium? When you first came, I mean?"

Alyna opened her mouth, then closed it, shaking her head and laughing softly.

"I take it that the adjustment wasn't difficult."

"Discipline at home was absolutely firm, and the punishments swift and very certain. The Collegium was certainly not any more demanding, and the punishments less so. The only things I missed were my brothers and sister . . . and my parents . . . and maybe the food. But I could image . . . after a while, that is, and I'd worried about that for over a year."

The punishments less so? Alyna's upbringing had been very strict, particularly for the child of a High Holder. "I take it your household was stricter than that of other High Holders?"

"Far more so, from what I overheard."

"That's a loss for High Holders and a gain for the Collegium." He paused momentarily. "I'd appreciate it if you'd continue to keep very good notes. I may have to explain some of the difficulties to Rex Ryen . . . and thank you."

"You're welcome."

By the time Alastar reached his study, Dareyn was already in the anteroom. "Good morning. Did you find out anything from Obsolym about that older imager—Aurelya?"

"I did, sir. She was the senior imager when Elestor was Maitre. She was at least a Maitre D'Structure. Obsolym said she might have been more powerful than Elestor. He also said that Elestor never disputed her, and always took her advice. She was very quiet. Looked a bit Pharsi, but she never said."

"What else?"

Dareyn shrugged. "There's not much else. Her husband was a Maitre D'Aspect, but he died in the first mess at Estisle, the one where the local council head started burning books because he said they were the tools of the Namer. She didn't go. Might have been because her son was born about then. When the second burning occurred, she did go. There's not much about what she and the three with her did, but Estisle and Nacliano pay their tariffs and still send a token of fifty golds a year to the Collegium."

That was something else Alastar didn't know. "What happened to her?"

"She died in her sleep, several years before I came here, sir."

"And her son?"

"He wasn't an imager. His name was Rousel. He went into trade. Woolens, maybe."

Alastar concealed a frown. Usually, a child of two imagers was also an imager. "Did Obsolym say anything else?"

"No, sir. There's a file on her in the locked section."

"I'll look at it when I have time." Alastar looked up as he saw Desyrk walking toward him. "How are Bettaur and Taurek this morning?"

"Bettaur's fine, except he's worried about speaking before five masters."

"He should be. While there's no excuse for what Taurek did, nasty comments also don't have any place in the Collegium."

"You're thinking of reprimanding him?"

"And assigning him some messy cleanup duties." Alastar hadn't forgotten being the smallest and youngest student imager at Westisle.

"They're just boys. And Maitre Fhaen . . ."

"What about Maitre Fhaen?"

"He said that we needed to remember that."

That's not what he was going to say. But Alastar doubted that he would get a straight answer, not from the stubborn set of Desyrk's jaw. "I don't think you understand. Allowing hazing and nasty teasing is an invitation to revenge. Taurek's obviously not the subtle type, but what happens when the smallest and weakest boy grows up to be a talented imager? What happens if he's particularly subtle as well . . . and holds a grudge? And can wait . . . and wait? Or what happens if that youngster can't wait and hurts or kills the son of a powerful factor or High Holder? Good, no . . . excellent manners are a necessity, at all times, even when no masters are watching, especially among the younger students and the older ones who deal with them. Once the students get older and begin to understand what imaging can do, they tend to become more aware. Part of our job is to make certain they do. Just what would have happened if Bettaur had made that comment after dinner in the darkness while they were walking back to their rooms?"

Desyrk didn't quite meet Alastar's eyes.

"We can't afford to lose a single imager to another imager's anger. We lose enough from mistakes in imaging," Alastar added. "And I seriously doubt that the student imager who 'ran away' the month before I arrived did any such thing. You have all the other witnesses?"

"Yes, sir."

"Now . . . if you'll set up the conference room for the meeting, and have the other maitres who will hear what happened join me in my study when they arrive."

"Yes, sir."

As Alastar walked into his study, he was not quite seething, both at himself for getting irritated at Desyrk and at Desyrk for not understanding. *But then, too many of the senior maitres don't seem to understand just how precarious the situation of the Collegium is—even after you've explained it more than once. It's as though, because nothing this dangerous has ever occurred, they can't even see that it's dangerous.* He didn't have long to consider that, because Tiranya and Obsolym arrived in less than a tenth of a glass, and they had barely entered his study when Akoryt followed.

"This about that boy Taurek?" asked Obsolym. "He's been trouble since he got here."

"From the initial report from Maitre Desyrk, apparently there was more than one side to the altercation. It happened while he was instructing."

"I wondered why you were heading the meeting,

rather than him," said the oldest maitre. "He usually acts as justicer."

"I'd just as soon have had him doing it, with everything else that's going on," said Alastar, not exactly truthfully.

"Who else will be on the panel?" asked Akoryt quickly.

"Gaellen," answered Alastar.

"He's usually early to everything," observed Tiranya.

Another two quints passed before Gaellen hurried into the study, breathing heavily. "I apologize, Maitre. One of the cook's assistants cut herself when another spilled boiling water . . . I had to clean and stitch the wound."

"Those things happen." *Especially when everything else is not going well.* "Let's go into the conference room and get ready." Alastar left the study, followed by the others, and crossed the anteroom to the conference room. The conference table had been turned and placed at one end of the chamber. Behind it were five chairs. Alastar took the center seat, with Obsolym to his right, Akoryt to his left. Tiranya sat to Akoryt's left, and Gaellen to Obsolym's right. Glaesyn and Neiryn stood flanking the closed doors. There were two empty chairs set against the wall on the right side of the chamber, midway between the table and the door.

Once the five maitres were seated, Alastar said, "Bring in the offender."

Neiryn opened the doors.

Desyrk led Taurek into the chamber. The student wore a thick black blindfold, and his hands were manacled behind him, so that he could not lift his hands to remove the blindfold.

"This hearing is in order," Alastar announced. "Taurek, Imager Tertius, step forward."

Prompted by Desyrk, Taurek stepped forward. He was almost as tall as Desyrk, and broader across the chest.

Indeed, almost bull-like, thought Alastar before asking, "What is the offense reported?"

"The student imager raised shields around a classmate," began Desyrk. "He refused to drop those shields when ordered by a senior maitre. He almost suffocated the classmate to death, then attacked the senior maitre with shields before he was restrained."

Alastar could feel a tenseness from the maitres seated beside him.

"You are charged with three offenses, Taurek," Alastar declared, "attacking a classmate, willfully disobeying a maitre, and attacking that maitre. Do you dispute those charges?"

"Not the charges, sir. I ask for consideration of the circumstances."

"That request for consideration is noted. Please seat the offender."

Desyrk guided Taurek toward the two chairs, where Taurek sat, leaning somewhat forward on the chair, given that his hands were manacled behind him. Then Desyrk returned to stand before the conference table.

"Maitre Desyrk, please describe exactly what happened."

"Yes, sir." Desyrk began. "I was instructing the lower-level thirds in the use of technique in imaging. I was having them image copies of intricate figures, and I had made the comment that there was no substitute for technique. I then said that substituting strength for technique could get them in trouble. Tertius Bettaur made a remark I was not meant to hear to the effect that most bulls that were strong and obstinate got gelded, like some thirds might."

"Were those Bettaur's exact comments, to the best you can remember?" asked Alastar.

"Yes, sir."

"Go on."

"Then a number of the other thirds snickered. Taurek squirmed in his chair, and his face twisted. Bettaur didn't move at all. Then Bettaur began to turn red, and I realized that Taurek had clamped shields around Bettaur. I ordered Taurek to drop the shields. He didn't. I don't think he even heard me. I imaged ice water over him, and then he tried the shields on me. I managed to collapse his shields back on him. I had to hold them until he passed out. I immediately sent Orlana to fetch Maitre Gaellen, but both students recovered before he arrived."

"Did either student say anything after they recovered?"

"Bettaur said that Taurek was always losing his temper and that he couldn't take a joke."

"Was that all he said?"

"That was all he said. Taurek said that Bettaur was always setting things up to trick and tease him, and that he'd had enough of his—Bettaur's—pretended innocence. Bettaur started to say something else, and I told him to be quiet."

"Why did you say that?"

"Because I could see that he was likely to say something else to irritate Taurek, and Taurek was still upset."

"To your knowledge, is this the first time that Taurek has attempted to use imaging against another student or maitre?"

"It is."

"Is it the first time you have observed taunting or untoward behavior on the part of Bettaur?"

"I have heard murmurs before, upon occasion, but I could not determine what was said, or by whom. Most of those times, I could see that Taurek had some reaction."

"How many times has this happened?"

"Not that often. Perhaps half a score."

"Did you say anything on those occasions?" pressed Alastar.

"Not for the first time or so. After that, I immediately said that murmurs and other comments were not appropriate to an instructional period."

"You were not able to determine who made those remarks?"

"No, sir. They usually occurred when I was working with one student on something or not looking at the students."

"Do any of you have any questions?" Alastar looked first to his left and then to his right.

"If I might," offered Tiranya.

Alastar nodded.

Tiranya looked squarely at Desyrk. "Did you talk this over with other maitres to see if they had observed this behavior in their dealings with students?"

"I didn't think it was appropriate. That would have been asking about gossip."

"Thank you," replied Tiranya.

"Are there any other questions?" asked Alastar.

"Just two," replied Akoryt. "You said that Taurek had not used imaging against any of the other students. Had he ever acted physically against them?"

"Not that I ever saw."

Akoryt nodded. "You said that right before Bettaur turned red, Taurek squirmed and his face twisted. Do you have any idea why?"

"No, I don't. I thought it was because he was getting angry."

"Did you talk to him after you restrained him?"

"He said he wanted to explain. I told him it was too late for explanations and that he could explain at a disciplinary meeting. He said that I would have done the same thing. I told him not to say another word until the meeting."

"That's all I wanted to ask," said Akoryt.

As usual, there's more here than meets the eye. "You may take your seat, Maitre Desyrk," said Alastar. "We'd like to hear your side of the story, Tertius Taurek. You may remain seated. Please begin by addressing what happened with Bettaur in the imaging instruction. You can offer additional explanations after that, if you feel it necessary."

"Yes, sir." Taurek paused. "At first, most everything happened the way Maitre Desyrk said. Except after the maitre talked about technique being more important than strength, Shannyr whispered that I'd rather be strong like a bull. Then Johanyr snorted like a bull, and Bettaur murmured that was why they gelded bulls, and he . . ." Taurek swallowed. "He used shields . . . well, like he was trying to . . . to make me an ox. He's always doing sneaky things like that. That's why I try to carry shields all the time, but that's hard, and I was tired. I didn't think he'd do something like that, not in front of a maitre. It really hurt. He didn't just jab. He kept squeezing. So I put my shields around him, but he wouldn't stop, not until he turned red. I knew Maitre Desyrk wanted me to stop, but Bettaur didn't stop. As soon as he did, I dropped the shields around him. It was either a moment before or a moment after Maitre Desyrk dropped the ice water on me. Then Maitre Desyrk put shields around me, and they hurt where Bettaur had hurt me even more. I tried to stop him, but . . . I couldn't."

Alastar watched Desyrk, but the Maitre D'Structure's face revealed little. *That's not good, not at all.* "What happened after that?"

"When I woke up, I was blindfolded, and my hands were shackled behind me."

"Do you wish to offer any additional explanations?"

"Yes, sir."

"Go ahead."

"I'm not quick with words, sir. I believe people when they say things. Bettaur would say things, like Maitre Obsolym said he would be late to his session, and we don't have to be there until a tenth past the glass. Then when I turned the other way, he and the others sneaked around the building and were there on time. I was only a little late, but I was late, because I was looking for them. Then a month later, Bettaur says the same thing. I don't believe him, and I go to the room, and Maitre Obsolym is still working with the primes, and he gets gruff for my walking in, because he'd told the others to wait a tenth of a glass . . ."

Alastar listened to another five examples laid out by Taurek, where the student imager claimed that he'd been set up or tricked, to the point where he never knew whether what the others said was so, and that led to his questioning various maitres because he never knew something to be so unless he heard it himself.

". . . I've forgotten a lot of the little things Bettaur and the others did, but it was always something . . ."

Alastar looked to his left. "Are there any questions?" He looked to his right. All he saw were headshakes.

"That will be all for now, Taurek. You're to remain here and be silent."

"Yes, sir."

"Summon Tertius Bettaur."

This time, Glaesyn opened the door, and Neiryn stepped out, returning almost immediately with Bettaur, who could not have presented a better physical example of a young imager—muscular, but not overly so, and well-proportioned, slightly square-chinned with a slight dimple, a straight nose, a fair but not pale complexion, fine blond hair, and brilliant blue eyes.

"Step forward, Tertius Bettaur," Alastar said.

Bettaur did, inclining his head politely.

"Tell us what happened yesterday when Maitre Desyrk was instructing you and the other thirds in imaging technique."

"We arrived at first glass, Maitre. Everyone was there before the bell rang the glass—"

"Who were the other student imagers?" interrupted Alastar.

"There were just five of us. The others were Johanyr, Klovyl, and Shannyr . . . and Taurek, of course."

"Go on."

"Maitre Desyrk showed us an object. I don't know how to describe it, Maitre. It had angles, and curves. It was hollowed out, and had an oval wooden top . . ."

Alastar refrained from nodding to himself as he took in Bettaur's pleasant baritone voice.

". . . with an octagonal base. It looked to be entirely of wood, but parts were painted different colors. One part was red, and the curve—it wasn't a semicircle, but an arc—it was gray . . . the maitre let each of us examine it, and then he put it on a stool in front of us. He said that, in a few moments, each of us would have to image the best copy of the object. He started to talk about how important technique in imaging was. He said we had to concentrate on the image we intended to image into being. He said being a strong imager wasn't enough. Then he said that strength without technique would get an imager into trouble. Shannyr murmured that he'd rather be strong like a bull. Johanyr snorted like a bull. I said there was a reason why they gelded most bulls."

"Did you say anything else?"

"No, sir. All of a sudden there were shields around me. I couldn't say anything. The next thing I knew, Maitre Desyrk was looking down at me and asking if I was all right."

"Did you touch or jab Taurek?"

"I didn't lay a hand on him, sir, the Nameless knows."

"How did you get along with Taurek?"

"We didn't, not really, sir. He was always doing stupid things. I just tried to stay out of his way."

"You didn't play pranks on him, then?"

"Oh, sometimes, but I played pranks on others, too.

Just little things, like telling him Maitre Obsolym had delayed an instruction. I didn't think he'd believe me. Maitre Obsolym never delayed an instruction."

"What about Maitre Shaelyt needing a left-handed pair of scissors?"

"There aren't any left-handed scissors. I thought he'd know that."

"Actually, there are, and Taurek knew that."

"Oh . . . I really didn't mean any harm, sir."

After several questions from Akoryt and Gaellen, Alastar said, "You may return to the anteroom. You're to stay there until the meeting is over and you are dismissed."

"Yes, Maitre." Bettaur inclined his head politely, turned, and left.

The next student was Johanyr.

After Johanyr's statement, almost identical to that of Bettaur, Alastar asked, "Did you snort like a bull after Maitre Desyrk said that strength was not enough?"

"No, sir. I might have coughed. I don't remember."

Again, Johanyr did not quite meet Alastar's eyes. Alastar could also see the rigidity and even a slight trembling of anger in Taurek's form.

Shannyr's statement, and then Klovyl's, echoed, close to word for word, that of Johanyr, and their answers to questions were almost identical.

When Klovyl left the conference room, Alastar gestured to Neiryn and Glaesyn. "Escort Tertius Taurek out into the anteroom and remain with him. Maitre Desyrk, please remain here."

Alastar saw Desyrk's face stiffen.

After the conference room door closed behind the three thirds, Alastar turned to Desyrk. "Has Taurek complained to you about Bettaur in the past?"

"He did, several times. He said that Bettaur was doing sneaky things, and jabbing him when no one could see. I never saw anything that he complained about, and he couldn't explain more than that. I asked him if Bettaur or the others had physically abused him. He said that they had not. I told him that I couldn't do much if they weren't hurting him, and that he'd have to find a way to deal with it. Boys have always been boys." Desyrk looked boldly at Alastar.

"That's true enough, but when those boys are almost grown men and they're imagers, telling them to work it out is akin to lighting a torch in a gunpowder magazine. You're relieved of your duties as discipline master and preceptor . . . and as an instructor until I review those assignments. You may go. You're not to leave Imagisle until we talk further."

Desyrk stiffened, as if he'd been slapped. "I did my duty—" His voice contained a petulance that Alastar had not heard before.

"The fact that this incident happened right in front of you is proof you did not. There will be no discussion of this right now." Alastar's voice was like ice. "Go."

Desyrk tightened his lips, then turned.

Doesn't anything work right here? Even as Alastar thought that, he realized it was unfair and inaccurate. Some things did work. It was just that too many did not.

"Weren't you a little hard on Desyrk, Maitre?" asked Obsolym after the door closed behind the departing maitre. "You know, he doesn't see that keenly, not beyond five yards."

"He never mentioned that," Alastar replied.

"He wouldn't. He's too proud," said Tiranya.

"That's part of the problem, too. If he couldn't see what Bettaur was doing and refused to listen to Taurek, he let his pride get in the way of his duty." Alastar turned back to Obsolym. "Do you really think I'm being too hard. Think about the implications. Very carefully."

The silence in the conference room stretched out.

Finally, Alastar cleared his throat. "Do any of you

have any information that bears on what we have heard?"

"I do," said Tiranya. "On two occasions as duty maitre, I observed Bettaur and several others making comments to which Taurek reacted by either flushing or immediately turning away. In both instances, I asked Taurek what it was about. He said that Bettaur was up to his usual tricks, but he was unable to explain what those tricks were. I asked Bettaur, and he offered the statement that he hadn't meant to upset Taurek. The second time Bettaur said that, I told him that I didn't expect to ever ask him again about his words upsetting another student. The last incident I observed was in Agostas."

"Thank you," said Alastar. "Might I ask what Bettaur's subsequent interactions were when he saw you were duty maitre?"

"After that, his behavior was exemplary whenever I saw him. Whenever he came into the dining hall, he made a point about smiling at me."

"Anyone else?" asked Alastar.

Gaellen nodded. "I don't know if it was an accident or one of the 'tricks' that Taurek mentioned, but last Juyn, Taurek came to the infirmary with a burn on the back of his hand. He said that when he'd picked up his mug at breakfast, it split and spilled hot tea on his hand." After a moment, Gaellen said, "That's all."

"So they teased him," declared Obsolym. "An imager needs to be able to withstand that. He still broke the rules, and he attacked a maitre. We can't allow that."

"You're right about that," Alastar agreed. "But we also can't allow a clique of junior thirds to take control of anything, especially when we're training them to become stronger and better imagers. I'm appalled at the surreptitious use of shields to torment and harm another imager, and in a way designed to make him appear to attack a maitre when he was trying to escape excruciating pain. That kind of planning bespeaks a cruel and devious mind."

Alastar was surprised when Obsolym actually nodded.

"I don't like the control that Bettaur has over the other three," said Tiranya.

"So how can we handle this?" asked Akoryt.

Alastar smiled grimly and began to explain.

When he finished, he looked to Obsolym. "Does that meet your criteria for appropriate discipline?"

"It does, Maitre. I'm sorry it's necessary, but . . . I have to admit that Maitre Desyrk should not have let matters get this far." The words seemed almost to have been dragged out of Obsolym.

"Akoryt? Gaellen? Tiranya?"

The other three nodded.

"Maitre Tiranya, would you have the escorts bring in all five thirds?"

"Yes, Maitre."

In less than a tenth of a glass, the five thirds stood in a line before the table.

"Tertius Taurek," began Alastar, his voice cold. "From your actions, it is clear that you did not consider the consequences of those actions. Attacking any other member of the Collegium with the intent to inflict severe harm or death can be punished by death. As Maitre of this Collegium, I have the authority to condemn you to death. You did not consider this. The circumstances of your provocation indicate that your intent was not murder, but uncontrolled anger. You have been warned about this. You did not consider that, either. You were in effect goaded by other students, but you did not describe the extent of that goading, and you did not bring it to the attention of any maitre in a fashion that could be addressed."

Alastar then looked at the handsome Bettaur, forcing

his voice into the same cold impartiality as he spoke. "Tertius Bettaur, you are far from without guilt and complicity in this matter. You have manipulated words and shaded the truth. You have in effect hazed a fellow student, seemingly with the intent of goading him into breaking Collegium rules. You employed covert imaging in doing so as well, and that is against Collegium rules, to an extent that your acts fall under the provisions dealing with harm to other imagers. The same rules apply to you as to Tertius Taurek. You committed an offense that can be punished by death. You knew that your acts were against Collegium rules. Your twisting of words and truth and your attempts to conceal what you did is proof of that. In addition, you have persuaded others to assist you in this goading and teasing.

"Tertius Johanyr, Tertius Klovyl, and Tertius Shannyr, you allowed Tertius Bettaur to persuade you to assist him in acts that are against both the rules and the spirit of the Collegium.

"Therefore, the following disciplinary sentences are necessary. Tertius Taurek, you will be confined to a disciplinary cell for the next two weeks. Thereafter you will be restricted to Imagisle until Avryl thirty-fifth. You will have additional special assignments, as determined by the Maitre. Failure to meet the terms of this discipline will result in a hearing to determine whether you are fit to remain an imager."

Taurek swallowed, as well he might, reflected Alastar, because if the disciplinary panel and the Maitre agreed that an imager was no longer fit to be an imager, there were only two possibilities—death or being blinded and being exiled to Mont D'Glace.

"Tertius Bettaur, for your lack of concern for others, for your willful twisting of facts, and for your willingness to harm another, you will be confined to a disciplinary cell for the next two weeks. Thereafter you will be restricted to Imagisle until Avryl thirty-fifth. You will have additional special assignments, as determined by the Maitre. Failure to meet the terms of this discipline will result in a hearing to determine whether you are fit to remain an imager."

Bettaur's mouth opened, if momentarily. Then he clamped his mouth shut.

"Tertius Johanyr, Tertius Klovyl, and Tertius Shannyr, you will be restricted to Imagisle until Avryl thirty-fifth. You will have additional special assignments, as determined by the Maitre. Failure to meet the terms of this discipline will result in a hearing to determine whether you are fit to remain an imager.

"Whether any of you understand it or not, every imager's fate is tied to every other imager's fate. The Collegium cannot afford the pettiness and scheming we have uncovered here. Nor can the Collegium allow individual imagers to take justice into their own hands." Alastar paused. "The discipline applied is effective immediately. Maitre Akoryt and Maitre Obsolym will convey Tertius Bettaur and Tertius Taurek to disciplinary quarters. This meeting is concluded." Alastar stood, then turned and said in a low voice, "Akoryt . . . before you deal with Taurek . . ."

"Yes, sir?"

"Thank you for asking questions about the way Taurek looked. I didn't catch that, and it was important."

"Good observation," added Obsolym.

Alastar thought the redheaded maitre looked slightly embarrassed and added, "That was a good example why we need to work together." *And Desyrk's failures that led to this hearing are an example of what happens when we don't . . . and he doesn't understand.* Alastar feared that he never would, either. "Once you have Bettaur confined, I'll need a moment with you."

"Yes, sir."

As the two Maitres D'Structure left, with their charges, both Gaellen and Tiranya moved toward Alastar.

"You've handled disciplinary hearings before, haven't you?" asked Tiranya.

Alastar nodded. "The senior imager at Westisle was usually the one who acted as justicer." He waited for Gaellen, who clearly had something on his mind, to speak.

"I've been thinking about that burn Taurek suffered. Looking back, I can't believe I didn't see what seems obvious now. Do you think . . . ?"

"I think most young imagers are decent at heart," replied Alastar. "But they want friends; they want to belong, and someone who is talented, handsome, and manipulative, like Bettaur, can lead them astray. When that happens, the leader often focuses on someone else who is different, lacking in some way. Taurek isn't as dense as Bettaur wanted everyone to believe, but he's socially less adept, and he has great difficulty speaking up for himself, despite his size and physical strength. That makes him a target. We have to watch the ones like Taurek, because they can either become the bullies or the bullied, and neither situation is good where developing imagers are concerned."

"What will happen now, do you think?" asked Gaellen.

"Bettaur is the one to watch. From my experience, he'll want to get even, and he'll play the perfect student until the right opportunity presents itself."

Tiranya nodded. "Like he did with me."

"You had an idea about this from the beginning, didn't you?" asked Gaellen. "Did you know about Taurek?"

Alastar shook his head. "What I knew is that, in this sort of situation, where there's a group and someone on the outside, in eight out of ten cases, the one who gets caught doing something wrong is usually the victim, who's had enough and is lashing out because they can't take it anymore. And that's exactly what a cunning plotter like Bettaur has in mind."

"You don't care much for him," declared Gaellen.

"I don't care for anyone who wants to succeed by hurting others, rather than triumphing through positive efforts. Especially within the Collegium, we need each and every imager to be the best they can be, and we need to work together, not at cross-purposes." Alastar grinned, self-deprecatingly. "End of homily. Now, we all need to get back to work."

Alastar had no more than left the conference room than Dareyn approached.

"While you were conducting the hearing, sir, the rex sent a messenger. He would like to see you immediately. Your horse and escorts are waiting. Factor Elthyrd also sent a message. He will be available after second glass at the factors' building."

Alastar thought about putting off that meeting, but then remembered that Elthyrd only liked handling the affairs of the council on Mardi and Vendrei. "If you'd send a messenger saying that I'll be there at half past two."

Dareyn nodded.

"I'm going to wait a bit until Maitre Akoryt gets back." Alastar hoped that wouldn't take too long, but Ryen would be angry in any event, simply because Alastar wasn't immediately available, and Alastar needed to tie up one loose end. "Also, will you post a notice that for the next week, Maitre Desyrk's instructional sessions will be canceled."

"Yes, sir."

Fortunately, Alastar had to wait only a tenth of a glass before Akoryt returned, and he used part of the time to gather and roll up the imaged copy of Ryen's map, since Alyna had the original. Although he had no idea if that might be what the rex wanted to discuss, he wanted to be prepared for that possibility. He stood as Akoryt entered the study.

"Sir, you wanted to see me?"

"I did. First, though, how is Bettaur?"

"He doesn't understand that he did anything wrong. Other than that . . ." Akoryt shrugged.

"I was afraid of that. We'll have to be very careful once he leaves confinement. That wasn't the reason I wanted to see you. I need you—the Collegium needs you—to take over Desyrk's duties. I realize I'm asking a great deal, but it's something I can't do."

"I'm the most junior Maitre D'Structure . . ."

"You're also perceptive, and that's going to be even more necessary. Obsolym isn't temperamentally suited to the position. That leaves you and Taryn, or one of the junior maitres."

Akoryt nodded slowly. "I'll do my best. If I'm not doing what you need, please tell me."

"I will." Akoryt's words confirmed to Alastar that he was the best for the position. "You'll make mistakes. We all do. The only question is whether we learn from them." Alastar smiled. "Thank you. I do appreciate it. If you will excuse me, Rex Ryen has once more summoned me."

Akoryt offered a faint smile. "Better you than me, sir."

Alastar followed Akoryt from the study and then continued out of the building to where Belsior and Chervyt were mounted and waiting with his gelding. While they made good time, it was still just before noon when Alastar strode up the chateau steps and was escorted to Ryen's study on the second level.

The rex was seated behind his desk. He did not rise, but glared at Alastar. "You took your sweet time to get here."

"I came as soon as I returned to my study and received your message. I can't stay in my study and run a Collegium."

"Hmmmphh."

Alastar approached the desk, but did not sit until Ryen motioned for him to do so.

"I could see your imagers yesterday and today. They were there, but nothing happened. That isn't progress."

"There is an old adage that applies to cabinetmakers and other builders. 'Measure once, cut twice. Measure twice, cut once.' We've been studying the route for days, and we're surveying it now."

"You don't need to survey it. I gave you the route. Just get on with building it," snapped Ryen.

"Sir . . . there are no sewers along that route. We need to know the grades and how to slope the avenue so that the sewers we will build with the avenue will drain properly."

"Sewers? I didn't say anything about sewers . . ."

"No, sir. You didn't. That isn't your task. It's ours. You like things done correctly. If we image an avenue without sewers or one with sewers that won't work, the avenue will stink. An avenue named after you should not stink."

Ryen opened his mouth and then closed it. Finally, he said, "You do have a point."

"There is also one other matter about the route . . ."

"What about the route?"

"The route you outlined passes less than a full block from the Anomen D'Rex. If we angled the avenue from the ring road to the anomen square and then constructed an oval road around the square, and then angled the avenue to the Bridge of Desires, the ride or drive would only be a few moments longer, but you would have a direct route to both the anomen and the Collegium, and imagers would still be able to reach the chateau easily."

"Let me see the map."

Alastar stood and unrolled the map, spreading it on the desk.

Ryen studied the map, frowned, then said abruptly, "For once you're telling me how to make something better rather than how hard it is to do what I want. That makes sense."

"You do know that the apothecaries and others are already complaining about the route and that they will not be adequately compensated—"

"Let them complain. People always complain. That's not your business. Your task is to complete the avenue." Ryen smiled. "I understand Marshal Demykalon demonstrated his new cannon to you. Marvelous weapons. They can destroy the strongest stone structures even across hills and rivers, even in the dark, I understand, if they're properly ranged and laid."

Alastar definitely understood the not-so-veiled threat . . . and the fact that, while imaging shields might stop rifle shots, they would hardly suffice against the direct impact of a cannon shell, especially if the imager happened to be asleep. "They looked to be quite effective."

"I'm certain they are, from what the marshal and Subcommander Chesyrk showed me." Ryen smiled again. "You can go now."

There was something about what Ryen had said, but Alastar couldn't place it. Still trying to connect the words, he leaned forward and caught the map that Ryen casually pushed in his direction, then rolled it and tied it. Although Alastar inclined his head before leaving, the rex did not turn in his direction.

Alastar had just barely reached the bottom of the grand staircase when a woman's voice stopped him.

"Maitre Alastar, I presume?"

He stopped and turned.

The woman who stood there could have been no other than Lady Asarya. She was tall, almost as tall as Ryen, with silvered blond hair that was swept back. The teal-green tunic and trousers she wore set off her gray eyes and fair and still unblemished complexion. Her knee-high riding boots were of polished gray leather. Her face was slightly narrower and longer than ideal, but she was definitely an attractive woman, although her voice was deeper than Alastar would have expected from her appearance, not that he had any real reason for that expectation. "Yes . . . and you are Lady Asarya, I presume?"

"Most perceptive of you. I had heard, indirectly, that you were."

Behind Asarya stood a single chateau guard, his eyes moving from the rex's wife to the Maitre and back again.

"Perception can be helpful, as can any skill."

"You didn't ask what I might require of you," she said with a smile.

"That would have had implications I'd rather avoid."

"You are cautious." She paused. "There are times when caution is more dangerous than being impetuous, you know?"

"If one is wise enough to recognize those times." *And people, especially those trustworthy enough not to take advantage of that impetuosity.*

"Wisdom can be the most foolish of virtues."

Alastar smiled. "I bow to your wisdom, Lady."

"You could be a dangerous man, Maitre." Her smile was warm and friendly, the kind that came from years of practicing sincerity, Alastar suspected.

"Except that there is some flaw in either my being or my knowledge, if not both. How would you suggest I remedy that?" Alastar maintained a pleasant expression, not attempting a smile of sincerity, which would have been unmatched by the feelings behind his face.

"That, Maitre Alastar, is entirely up to you." Another smile appeared, slightly condescending, before Asarya said, "It has been a pleasure to meet you. Until our paths cross once more." She offered a nod of dismissal.

Alastar inclined his head in return. "Good day, Lady." He did not look back as he walked to the chateau entrance and then down the outside steps toward the waiting pair of imagers. He could certainly see why Ryen and Asarya might not have shared quarters for years—if indeed that rumor was true.

Rather than ride directly to the Collegium, then wait for less than half a glass before setting out for his meeting with Factor Elthyrd, Alastar led his escorts along the route that Alyna was surveying. Once he located Alyna and the surveying party, less than a third of a mille from the Bridge of Desires, he rode to where she had positioned her surveyor's cross and reined up.

Alastar could see a smear of charcoal across the left side of her forehead, just above and to the side of her eyes. Somehow, it made her look both competent and . . . he couldn't say what. So he smiled.

"What is it, Maitre?"

"I thought you'd like to know. The rex agreed to the change you suggested. Will you need to resurvey that part of the route?"

She shook her head. "It seemed better to survey both possibilities. So I did. Not that I don't appreciate the word, but you didn't need to chase us down."

"I'm glad you already surveyed both. As for chasing you down, I have to return to the Collegium. You'll both likely be gone when I get back from my next meeting, and there's something else you need to know." Alastar motioned for Cyran to join them and waited until the dark-haired Maitre D'Esprit arrived. "The disciplinary hearing this morning revealed that Desyrk had neglected certain aspects of his duties as justice and preceptor of students. I relieved him of his duties and restricted him to Imagisle until further notice. I thought you two should know, and I'd appreciate it if you, Cyran, would let the other maitres here know as well."

"I'll take care of that. About the students involved?"

"Bettaur and Taurek. Bettaur had been using imaging to bait and torment Taurek. So there was guilt on both sides. For that pair, two weeks' confinement, restriction until the first day of summer, extra duties, and reevaluation for suitability if either causes more trouble. The other three, restriction until the first day of summer, extra duties, and reevaluation for suitability."

"Commander Taurran won't be pleased about that," said Cyran, "not when he finds out his son was set up."

"That's Taurek's father?"

Cyran nodded. "He's stipended off, though he might . . ."

"Have friends still in the army? It's probably better I didn't know." Alastar frowned. "None of the other maitres mentioned it."

"Desyrk is likely the only one who'd have a way to know. Besides Maitre Fhaen. And me, of course. He has—or had—the student records, and his brother's a subcommander . . . or he was last time I heard." Cyran paused. "I can see that about Bettaur, but that's in hindsight."

"Desyrk knew, I think, even about the extent of Bettaur's scheming, much as he protested. I can't see why he didn't say more."

"Could be that there's bad blood between Desyrk's brother and Commander Taurran."

"That shouldn't enter into Collegium affairs."

"Just like tariffs shouldn't?" asked Alyna sweetly.

Both men laughed.

"In any event," Alastar said to Cyran, "you might talk to Akoryt about it. He's agreed to take over Desyrk's duties, at least for now. That's all I needed to tell you two for now. I'm off to see Factorius Elthyrd once more."

"I think I'd definitely prefer to assist Alyna with surveying than do that."

"So would I," replied Alastar, "but I'll leave you two to handle it."

As he expected, riding the last third of a mille to the West River Road took two quints, but crossing Imagisle was faster, and he actually arrived at the factors' council building only a quint past second glass.

Elthyrd saw him immediately, and Alastar sat in front of the factor's desk, wondering what Elthyrd and the factors' council had decided.

"You understand, Maitre," began the factor, "the council is not terribly pleased that you alleviated a certain pressure on Rex Ryen."

"I understand that, but I must tell you, in equal frankness, that His Grace Ryen, Rex Regis, does not seem to respond to pressure of any sort, except negatively."

"Ah . . . that is something the council also considered, and we will accept your offer to repair the worst of the problem areas with the sewers. But not on any Solayi."

"Is Samedi acceptable?"

Elthyrd nodded.

"We also cannot work on them all immediately, perhaps one location a week."

"We understood that as well." Elthyrd extended a single sheet of paper. "There are four locations that have caused difficulties. We have listed them in order of probable difficulty, but we would leave the order of repair up to the Collegium. We would expect to be informed when and where you will begin each."

"Of course. It will not be this week. We will have to investigate them all to determine what needs to be done, and in what order makes the most sense." Alastar took the paper, quickly looking over the locations. All four seemed to be fairly close to the East River Road . . . or not too far from it.

"We understand that." Elthyrd cleared his throat. "Then there is the tariff matter. Not only I, but others have heard that you have talked to some of the members of the High Holders' council."

"I have, but my purpose was to meet them, since I

knew none of them, not to influence any specific decision." *Except through my presence.* "Because I am not from L'Excelsis, I thought it necessary. High Holder Guerdyn was the only one who actually brought up the tariff matter. He seems to assume that the factors would back whatever the High Council decided."

"You mentioned that before."

"I did. I thought it was important."

"I also heard that you visited the army headquarters on Samedi."

Alastar understood what Elthyrd was suggesting—that anything outside of Imagisle that Alastar did, and perhaps even what happened on Imagisle, would come to his attention. "I was requested by Rex Ryen to meet with Marshal Demykalon." That might not have been technically true, but it was close enough. "The marshal had me watch a demonstration of a new lighter and more accurate cannon that could be used to great effect anywhere. He said that they had developed a version for warships as well."

The factor offered a wintry smile. "That's one of the more informative things you've said. I take it that even the strongest imager could not withstand a cannon shell?"

"Nor could any pirate vessel, if Rex Ryen had enough tariffs to build the ships to carry them. As for imagers . . . that's not something any imager would wish to test, not any that I know," Alastar said dryly. "It is fair to say that, if any imager could, there would certainly only be a few, at most."

"You're in a rather intriguing position, Maitre. It will be interesting to see how matters turn out."

It's all too likely to be far too interesting. "We all do what we can."

"If there's nothing else . . ."

"Not unless . . ."

Elthyrd shook his head and rose.

Alastar stood and inclined his head. "Thank you. I appreciate your understanding and that of the factors' council."

Elthyrd smiled as Alastar left the study.

As Alastar rode back toward the east bridge and Imagisle, he considered just how much friendlier Elthyrd had been . . . and the fact that Elthyrd had brought up the tariff matter, although he had ignored Alastar's comment about the need for warships to carry the new cannon. *Maybe the factors aren't in such lockstep with the High Holders.* But then, it could be for another reason . . . one not any more helpful to Alastar and the Collegium. *And that's far more likely.*

16

Alastar was at the stables Meredi morning immediately after breakfast and before the group surveying the route of the new avenue departed. He stood in the light wind, more chill than he'd thought, given the clear skies and bright morning sunlight, waiting less than a quint before Alyna arrived.

She smiled pleasantly. "You look like you're waiting for someone. Cyran or Petros?"

"You, actually, and I suspect you know that."

"I was the other possibility, but it would have sounded self-centered to include myself."

Again, Alastar caught a glimpse of humor in her eyes and expression. "After you've finished today, will you be able to sketch out the new route and where the sewers should be?"

"If you don't want too detailed a map, I can have something by tomorrow afternoon."

"I'd appreciate that. Please be careful. I have the feeling that the people along the route may get more and more unhappy as time passes." Alastar paused. "I know you and Cyran can more than take care of yourselves, but it would be best if you could avoid having to do so."

"Avoid what?" asked Cyran as he walked toward Alastar and Alyna.

"Having to use force on anyone who gets upset about the new avenue."

"You two are better at that than I am." Cyran grinned. "I'll take my lead from Alyna."

Alyna raised her eyebrows, slightly darker than her

light brown hair, with an expression that suggested Cyran would scarcely take his lead from anyone.

Alastar repressed a smile. "I'll leave you two to work it out. I'm certain you'll manage." He turned and began the walk back to his study.

As was often but not always the case, Dareyn was already in the anteroom.

"Good morning, Dareyn. How are you doing this morning?"

"I can tell winter's coming."

"It's more than a month away."

"That's by the calendar, sir, not by the weather."

"You may be right. It was colder out this morning than it looked," Alastar admitted. "Desyrk should be in his cottage. Send a messenger informing him he's to be here to meet with me at half past seven."

"If he's not there?"

"I need to know immediately." *He should be, if he has any sense.* "One other thing. What do you know about Bettaur's background?" From Bettaur's demeanor, speech, and bearing, Alastar had his own ideas, but he wanted to see what others knew. All the Collegium records showed was that he had been admitted six years earlier.

"Nothing, sir. He came before I began to assist Maitre Fhaen."

"Did Maitre Fhaen seem to take more of an interest in Bettaur?"

"Not that I—" Dareyn paused. "Come to think of it, he did meet with him more often than with the other thirds. Not a lot more, and it wasn't regular-like."

Almost as if someone had requested information about Bettaur, and that means someone important. "Is there anything else?"

"I can't think of anything more, sir."

"Thank you." The first thing Alastar did after settling behind his desk was think about Bettaur. *Should you talk over his background with him?* He shook his head. Bettaur was safe enough from meddling in the detention cell, and talking to him right after disciplining him would undermine the very punishment he'd received, but he made a mental note to do so once Bettaur finished his two weeks in the disciplinary cell.

After that Alastar began to go over the possibilities for dealing with Ryen . . . and Marshal Demykalon. He didn't like any of them, especially since it was clear that Ryen expected Alastar to change the Council's likely decision and build an avenue through a populated area in a way that was already upsetting all too many people and that Demykalon would appreciate any excuse to target his new cannon on Imagisle. If the Collegium didn't accomplish Ryen's ends, the rex was rash enough to allow Demykalon to do just that—and that might even temporarily strengthen Ryen's position with regard to the High Holders and factors, assuming he was mad enough to turn the army on the High Holders. Over time, however . . .

Alastar shook his head, but then caught sight of the founder's sabre. *Is it there as a reminder that at times force is the only solution?*

Promptly at half past seventh glass, Desyrk walked into the study and sat down in the chair across the desk from Alastar, even before the Maitre could finish gesturing to the chairs.

"Good morning, Maitre. You requested my presence. I am here."

"Good morning. Have you thought over what occurred between Bettaur and Taurek?"

"I have."

"What are those thoughts?"

"I understand your concern for Taurek. I believe you are being unrealistic. Boys, and men, have always followed the strongest. By protecting students like Taurek from what occurs naturally, you will not save him, but only weaken the Collegium more. I've seen that over the years."

Alastar didn't care for the implication that Desyrk had seen more, nor for the tone of voice, but he replied, keeping his voice even, "Infants will freeze if you expose them to the elements. Smaller children will starve if they have to compete with older children for food. By the logic of your argument, we will have no Collegium left. What you are ignoring is the fact that the physical ability of young imagers develops before their imaging skills do. What you are also ignoring is how few imagers there are. Your approach would kill off those imagers who are slower to develop in one way or another at a time when we need every imager. In addition, you fail to understand that, if Taurek had not been handicapped by partial supervision, and been left unsupervised totally, he would have been free to deal with Bettaur directly, and Bettaur would likely be the one dead or crippled."

Desyrk's face expressed puzzlement and doubt.

"Taurek is physically stronger. He is already a slightly more accomplished imager. He can protect himself adequately, even if he does lack certain personal skills, against any of those who tormented him. What he couldn't protect himself against was manipulation by a group."

"You can't protect them from each other," declared Desyrk.

"I don't think you understand. Without the support of the other thirds Bettaur gathered, he would not have fared well against Taurek. You allowed that group to pick on Taurek until he felt he had no choice. What exactly did you think would happen?"

Desyrk did not respond.

"What did you think would happen?" Alastar asked once more.

"Men always have had groups. Young men are no different . . ."

"It depends on the group." Alastar knew that trying to get Desyrk to understand was likely to be futile, but he felt he had to try. "The whole purpose of the group Bettaur formed was not to improve the group. It wasn't to make them better imagers. It was simply to get Taurek into a difficult situation and to reinforce Bettaur's dominance. If you will, Taurek was the designated enemy whom Bettaur used to unify the group and reinforce his control. And you're absolutely correct. Young men without strong supervision do this all the time. That makes it neither correct, nor the best way in which they should develop." Alastar looked at Desyrk, taking in the almost clenched jaw, the fingers gripping the wooden arms of the chair in which he sat, and overall stiffness. He waited to see if Desyrk would say anything.

The Maitre D'Structure remained silent.

"Do you have any questions?"

"Just one." Desyrk's voice was even. "Might I ask when I might expect to be returned to my position, or one similar?"

Possibly never, with that attitude. "I've canceled all your instruction sessions for the remainder of the week. That will give you some time to reconsider the matter in light of what I have just told you. It will also provide me and the senior imager with time to consider in what other capacity you would best serve both your interests and those of the Collegium."

"I see."

Alastar doubted that. "There's little more to be said now. I'll let you know on Lundi." He stood.

"Thank you, sir." Desyrk's voice was almost without emotion as he rose.

Alastar watched as the Maitre D'Structure departed, then waited for several moments.

How can he think that way? Alastar shook his head. Most people did think that way, unable to look beyond the letter of the rules or what they believed. That was exactly the problem. *And the fact that Maitre Fhaen and his predecessor weren't able or didn't see the need to show the Maitres of the Collegium the costs and dangers of thinking that way.* A wry smile crossed his face. *And how do you know your way is better?* Alastar didn't. *But what Desyrk was doing wasn't working.*

He walked out of the study.

"Maitre Desyrk didn't look pleased when he left," ventured Dareyn.

"I doubt that he was. I couldn't find a way to get him to understand that allowing bullying or cliques created by students is not in the best interest of the Collegium."

"That might be because he comes from a military family. Army officers don't like those who stand up to authority. The most successful junior officers are those who develop friendships with others and never say anything against senior officers where anyone can hear. They never disobey, and they never question."

"And they always maneuver to make those who are different or who question stand out unfavorably?"

"So it's said."

"Was Desyrk's father an officer, too? Someone said his brother is."

"His father was a major."

Alastar nodded slowly, then shook his head. Deciding what to do with Desyrk could wait, especially since Alastar knew he wouldn't be as dispassionate as he needed to be if he made any decision at the moment. "I'll need my horse and two escorts for a ride in half a glass. I need to look at places where the sewers need repairs."

Dareyn smiled knowingly and nodded.

A little over half a glass later, Alastar rode out over the east bridge, a chill wind, stronger than earlier in the day, at his back. Accompanying him were Akkard and Belsior. At the east end of the bridge he turned the gelding north on East River Road. Factor Elthyrd had listed four locations where sewer repairs were necessary. Alastar had decided to start with the one farthest from Imagisle—on Nordroad two blocks north of the Boulevard D'Este.

Two quints later, Alastar and the thirds reined up on the east side of Nordroad, little more than a block south of Hagahl Lane. While there was a definite odoriferous stench, it did not seem nearly so strong as the one that had engulfed Imagisle. Part of that might have been because of the cold wind. Alastar surveyed the area. To his left was an imposing three-story dwelling constructed of yellow brick, while across Nordroad to his immediate right were two matching dwellings faced in gray stone. Each had black shutters and black double doors festooned with gleaming brass door handles and boot plates. Not a single dwelling was other than well-kept and stylish.

Alastar nodded, then turned to Akkard. "We'll take Nordroad south to the next location." He urged the gelding forward.

Two glasses later, the three rode back over the east bridge. Each location did in fact have problems with sewers or sewage ditch drainage, but two were located near the residences of factors and two near the largest factorages that Alastar had seen in L'Excelsis.

As Alastar reined up outside the Collegium stables, he decided that the sewer repairs could be done without undue haste or perhaps with deliberate care. In the meantime, he needed to consider what duties he could assign to Desyrk and how to shift some of Akoryt's duties to others. He also couldn't help but wonder exactly what the High Council had decided and how the High Holders intended to oppose Ryen. *They will oppose him. The only question is how.* Once they did, Ryen would be furious and ask Alastar how the Collegium could possibly have let it happen. *As if we had any choice except assassination or blackmail through the threat of assassination or something worse.*

Between one thing and another, Alastar found himself occupied until close to eighth glass that evening when, sitting in his study in the Maitre's house, he finally finished reviewing the Collegium expenditures that could be reduced, a listing developed with Arhgen.

He was tired, but he wasn't in the slightest sleepy. So he picked up the heavy volume that contained the words of the first chorister of the Collegium and continued from where he had left off. For a good twenty pages, he came across little that was of more than passing interest before a particular entry jumped out at him.

> . . . When the Maitre came back from the Chateau D'Rex and met with the imagers, he said very little, except that Lord Bhayar told the Maitre that the death of Chorister Amalyt was inconvenient. Then Lord Bhayar again requested that the Collegium assist with the repairs to the Anomen D'Excelsis. The Maitre agreed. He also said that the Collegium would now be willing to make the repairs before the new chorister took over the anomen . . .

. . . *would now be willing?* That suggested that Quaeryt had been less than pleased with Chorister Amalyt, whoever he might have been. Alastar reread the words and those following, but there was no further explanation. He continued leafing through the thick volume until he reached another section.

> . . . The Maitre gave the homily last evening. He is a far better speaker than any chorister anywhere in Solidar. His words are well-chosen and to the point. Those of us who heard him in the old days wish he would speak more often. I have asked occasionally. His answer is always the same, that a lost one shouldn't be more than an infrequent speaker in an anomen of the Nameless. He is more than that, but after Rivages, it is clear that,

for his sake, and that of the Collegium, his great deeds be allowed to fade from memory. He is far greater than Rholan, but Rholan will be remembered because, in the end, his success was less than complete, unlike the Maitre . . .

For his sake and that of the Collegium?

Alastar kept reading until his eyes burned, but he could find no other reference in the pages he perused to what Quaeryt's great deeds might have been, or what had happened in the old days . . . or even anything more about what Chorister Gauswn had known about Quaeryt. As for the phrase "a lost one," Alastar had no idea what that meant, except that Quaeryt possibly wasn't the strongest believer in the Nameless. *But allowing his greatness to be hidden . . . or was he greatly flawed and that needed to be hidden as well?*

He finally set aside the book, then imaged out the lamp wick, and walked through the darkened house up to his bedchamber.

17

Alastar was still worrying on Jeudi morning when Dareyn stepped into his study, walked to the desk, and extended a cream-colored envelope. "This message arrived by a private courier."

Alastar took the envelope and studied it. The outside was inscribed:

Alastar D'Imagisle
Maitre, Collegium Imagio

Alastar did not recognize the seal impressed on the tan-colored wax, but then, there were few he would have known. He took his belt knife and carefully slit the envelope so as not to break the seal, then extracted the single sheet and began to read.

Maitre Alastar—
The High Council met on Meredi. High Holder Guerdyn proposed that the Codex of Solidar be changed to state that no increase in tariffs may be imposed without the consent of the High Council of L'Excelsis. While I cannot speak for others, it is most likely that a great many, if not most High Holders, may not pay tariffs this year until this matter is resolved. The High Council has sent suggested wording to Rex Ryen. In view of your interest in the matter, I thought you would like to be apprised of this.

With great regard,
Vaun D'Alte

Alastar winced. *Now* he knew why Guerdyn had appreciated his mentioning the codex. But why had Vaun sent the message? High Holders never did anything without a reason, and Vaun certainly impressed Alastar as being very deliberate.

"Sir?" prompted Dareyn.

"Let me know when the courier from the rex arrives."

Dareyn offered a quizzical look.

"Before eighth glass, I'd wager. If you'd arrange for my mount and escorts, also."

As Dareyn left the study, Alastar thought over the short missive, and what it said . . . and what it did not. Vaun hadn't said that the High Holders wouldn't pay their tariffs, only that most would not until the matter was resolved. Given the geographical spread of the High Holders, and the size of Solidar, Alastar would have thought that there would have been hundreds who had no idea what the High Council was doing and that they would be submitting their tariffs to the regional governors of Solidar, and that those tariffs would wend their way toward L'Excelsis. But the wording of Vaun's missive indicated that most High Holders would not be submitting tariffs. *And that means the High Council had already laid the plans to withhold tariffs.* Given the size of Solidar, that had to have been arranged weeks, if not months, earlier, and that suggested very strong opposition to Ryen's proposed increase. What made that worse was that, in all likelihood, those nearest to L'Excelsis would be most likely to withhold their tariffs, and those would represent the golds Ryen was expecting the soonest.

The courier from the Chateau D'Rex arrived little more than a quint after Alastar had read Vaun's message, and Alastar and his two imager escorts—and the courier—arrived at the Chateau D'Rex at two quints past eighth glass.

When Alastar entered the rex's formal study, Ryen was standing before the closed windows on the north side of the chamber. He turned, and even before Alastar finished closing the door, stated loudly, in words as much accusation as declaration, "I told you to change their minds! You didn't. You failed."

Alastar stopped several yards short of the red-faced rex. "You also said that I wasn't to do anything that would threaten or kill them. Exactly how was I supposed to persuade them in less than two weeks when you haven't been able to get tariffs increased in years? Why don't you just inform them that the increase will take place?"

"Then they won't pay this year's tariffs, you idiot!" Ryen's face turned even redder. "You get them to change their minds . . . or . . ." The rex offered a raised clenched fist. ". . . or I won't have any need for a Collegium and all the golds you cost me."

"Without a Collegium, you'll be at the mercy of the High Holders and the factors, just as Rex Kharst was."

"With the Collegium, I already am! Change their decision . . . or don't bother coming back here. Ever!" Ryen's voice finished with a high-pitched yell that filled the study with its echoes. "Then you'll see what use I have for you. Get out of here, and do something useful!"

Alastar's first thought was that the most useful thing he could do would be to remove Ryen. His second thought was that doing so would not address the roots of the problem . . . and would result in turning the new rex and Demykalon immediately against the Collegium while not gaining any real support from either the High Holders or the factors.

"As you command, Your Grace." Alastar turned and walked toward the study door.

"Stop! You don't leave without my permission!"

Alastar turned. "You ordered me to leave and do

something useful. Then you told me to stop. Which do you wish?"

"Don't fence with words, Maitre!"

Alastar waited. Saying anything would merely enrage Ryen even more, now that he was truly behaving like a Rex Dafou.

Abruptly, Ryen shook his head. "Go. You know what I want, and you know what I'll do to your beloved Collegium if I don't get it." His voice was not a scream, but loud and cold.

Alastar inclined his head, then turned and departed.

At least, Alastar reflected ruefully on the way down the grand staircase and out to where his gelding and escorts waited, *he didn't go on about the avenue . . . or the sewers.* That would come later, assuming that Alastar and the Collegium survived the conflict over the tariffs.

After he mounted the gelding, Alastar gestured toward the ring road and then to the northeast. "We're heading to the Chateau D'Council next."

Chervyt and Glaesyn exchanged uneasy glances.

Alastar did not respond. While he had no idea whether Guerdyn would be at the Chateau D'Council, it wasn't that far out of the way from the route he'd be taking back to the Collegium, and he doubted that the head of the Council would be far away at the moment.

The two guards in maroon livery opened the wrought-iron double gates without even inquiring then closed them behind the three imagers. The sound of hooves echoed in the silence of the cold fall air as they rode up the stone-paved lane to the three-storied structure and reined up under the covered entry portico. The same footman who had greeted him every time before stood at the top of the steps.

"Maitre, High Holder Guerdyn said you might come unannounced. He will see you for a brief time."

Alastar nodded in reply, then dismounted, handed the

gelding's reins to Chervyt, and walked up the steps and then into the chateau after the footman.

Guerdyn was waiting in the study, this time wearing a red and black doublet with black hose and shoes, and a black jacket trimmed in red. He stood beside one of the armchairs set in a circle around the low table. "I thought I might see you after you were summoned to the Chateau D'Rex," Guerdyn said dryly. "I assume that His Grace Ryen, Rex Regis of Solidar, was not in the best of temper."

"Your dear ruler, Rex Ryen, has just learned that the High Council intends to flout the codex and deny him an increase in tariffs that has been overdue for years. Why indeed might he not be in the best of temper?"

"Maitre . . . do not try my patience. I have had the kindness to see you."

"High Holder, do not try mine. If I determined you would see me, I would see you."

Guerdyn frowned. "I take it that you will support the rex, then?"

Alastar sighed, loudly. "Both the High Council and the rex are behaving like unruly second-year imager students. Neither of you is looking at the needs of all Solidar. The rex wants too high an increase in tariffs, and you want none, and the only possibility you will grant is too small to pay for what Solidar needs. You're both angered when anyone points that out."

"As I have told you, Maitre, the High Council sees no need for additional tariffs at this time. What need do we have for an army of eight regiments when there is no one to fight?"

"There is a need to fight Southern Gulf pirates and smugglers who cheat both the factors and the rex," suggested Alastar mildly. "And it appears that there is a possibility of fighting rebellious High Holders."

"The army would not take up arms against any High Holder for merely refusing to pay tariffs."

"Some officers might, if they learned that their positions and careers were to be destroyed as a result."

"There is small chance of that." Guerdyn shrugged. "Even so, that is a risk we will take."

Meaning that your sympathizers control the regiments here in L'Excelsis. "I've just come from the rex, as you clearly know. He has threatened to destroy the Collegium if I cannot persuade the High Council to stop opposing an increase in tariffs."

Guerdyn raised his eyebrows. "Do you think that will change the Council's decision?"

"The way matters are going . . . no, I don't. I did think you should know what he said and obviously meant, however."

"Then . . . what is your purpose in informing me and the High Council?"

"I thought you should know exactly where the Collegium stands," Alastar replied. "It is often useful to know matters such as that."

"That could be termed a veiled threat, Maitre."

"It could. But a truly wise man would consider it as a statement of fact, and then make future decisions based on that fact."

"Fact or not, it changes little."

"I thought as much, but I did wish you to know."

"I know, and the High Council will know. That does not put the Collegium in the best light."

"At present, it appears there is little light cast upon anything. We will endeavor to do so."

Guerdyn gestured lazily. "You will do what you think best. So will the High Council."

Alastar smiled politely. "I thank you for your time, High Holder Guerdyn, and I bid you good day."

"I could offer a similar pleasantry. I won't." Guerdyn's face was impassive.

Alastar inclined his head, then turned and walked from the study. When he reached the entry hall, the footman opened one of the bronzed doors and nodded, but did not speak. After mounting the gelding, Alastar rode down the paved lane, intently studying the walls and the approach to the Council Chateau, as he had previously.

Once he was back at the Collegium, he sent for Akoryt, then drafted a missive to Factorius Elthyrd, informing him that the Collegium would repair the damaged sewers near Nordroad and the Boulevard D'Este on Vendrei. After having Dareyn dispatch the message, Alastar studied the Collegium roster for the short time while he waited for Akoryt.

Akoryt arrived at a quint before the first glass of the afternoon, easing almost cautiously into the Maitre's study and closing the door. "Sir?"

Alastar set down the roster sheets, motioned to the chairs in front of the desk, then waited for Akoryt to seat himself. "I take it that you're somewhat familiar with the abilities of some of the student imagers? As well as of some of the maitres?"

"Somewhat," answered the redheaded maitre cautiously.

"Once Maitre Cyran returns, I'd like you two to determine how many imagers we have capable of combat and concealment if Rex Ryen should order the armies against us, or if Demykalon does so on his own."

Akoryt looked intently at Alastar, not even trying to conceal his surprise. "Sir . . . are things that bad?"

"Not yet, but they may get much worse. I'd like you not to mention that to anyone but Maitre Cyran. I'd like whatever you can give me by seventh glass tomorrow morning. I also need you to work out a plan that would move all students and staff at the Collegium to the north end of Imagisle in less than a quint."

"Into the park area there?"

"Along the stone revetments against the river. Again, please don't mention this to anyone except me. You'll also need to decide what masters will be in charge of instructing and informing what students and staff. I hope neither will be necessary, but mere hope is a poor plan for dealing with possible attackers."

Akoryt nodded. "By tomorrow as well?"

"Yes. You can improve it later, but we'll need an immediate plan by then."

"Yes, sir."

Alastar offered a crooked smile. "I know you don't need this on top of everything else. If you need the time, you can cancel any or all of your remaining instructionals this afternoon."

"I only have the one in a few moments, and it would take as much time to cancel it and explain than to do it. I might cut it short."

"As you see fit. That's all I have for you . . . as if it isn't more than enough."

As soon as Akoryt left, Alastar began to write. When he finished, he read over the short letter.

Councilor Vaun—

I appreciated your counsel and thoughtfulness. In return, I thought you might like to know some information that I passed on to Councilor Guerdyn, in the unlikely event that he has not had the time to relay it directly to you.

The rex is adamant that the High Council must change its decision. He has also declared that if the Collegium cannot persuade the Council to do so, then he will destroy the Collegium. Given that the marshal of the army recently invited me to a demonstration of his new cannon, such a declaration cannot be easily ignored. Obviously, this places the Collegium in a difficult situation, and I would be interested in any helpful thoughts or suggestions you might have about how we might bridge the gap between the rex and the High Council. I look forward to any thoughts you might care to share.

When he finished the short message to Vaun, he then wrote similar letters to Haebyn, Nacryon, and Moeryn. Then he had Dareyn arrange for them to be dispatched by messenger.

The next step was to determine what imagers would be best for the sewer repairs and send messages to them, telling them that their presence would be required for such repairs on Vendrei and to make the necessary arrangements.

When the surveying party returned to the Collegium, Alastar was at the stables to meet them. He looked at Cyran, then Alyna, and waited until all of the imagers were looking at him. "There's been a slight change of plans. Tomorrow, we'll be taking a break from surveying to do another sewer repair, this one requested by the factors' council . . ." He went on to explain.

When he finished, he could see Cyran nod knowingly. Alyna maintained a pleasant expression, but Alastar thought there was a certain concern behind the facade. *But is that really what she feels . . . or just what you want to think she does?*

For the remainder of Jeudi, Alastar wrestled with the possibilities of what Ryen and the High Council might do and considered what additional steps he and the Collegium could take.

At eighth glass he was still pondering, if seated behind the desk in the private study of his residence. *Ryen isn't mad, even if they call him Rex Dafou. He's impatient, intolerant, easy to anger, and self-centered, but he's right about needing control over the High Holders. He's also anything but stupid. So why is he pressing you so much on this? And what can you do? If you remove him immediately, everyone will know who did it, and there's no telling what Demykalon will do. There's also no telling what his son Lorien will do . . . except he's unlikely to defy the Council if he becomes rex right now. And why is Guerdyn being so adamant? You've sug-*

gested that the Collegium might pose a threat to the High Council, and Guerdyn's reaction was to suggest indirectly that Ryen has no support except for the Collegium. It's almost as if they're both trying, in different ways, to destroy the Collegium. Or are they trying to remove you because you're trying to return the Collegium to a position of greater power?

What if you do nothing? Will Ryen turn Demykalon on the Collegium? Even if he doesn't, he'll cut off your golds. Then what? Without using force, we'll be in isolated enclaves with fewer members every year. In a few years, imagers will be hunted again. And if you use force without provocation . . .

The best tack to take is to publicly try to persuade both the High Holders and the rex to come to an agreement about how much tariffs will be increased. Very publicly. And then . . . Slowly, Alastar nodded.

At that moment, there came an insistent pounding on the front door of the Maitre's residence. "Maitre! Maitre!"

Alastar bolted from his chair and hurried out into the front hall, where he slid the bolt back and then opened the door. Tertius Arion stood there.

"Maitre Taryn sent me, sir. It's about Secondus Gherard."

"What about him?" Whatever it was, it couldn't be good.

"He's dead. Maitre Taryn said you needed to see for yourself. So did Maitre Obsolym."

Dead? Did the poor idiot try to prove he was a third? After all that you warned him? Alastar fastened his tunic and stepped out into the cold air, following Arion down the west side of the lane past the cottages and to the quarters for the students.

"In the back courtyard garden, sir."

Alastar saw Taryn first, holding a lantern. A few yards away stood Obsolym with another student. A figure lay sprawled on his back perhaps a yard from one of the stone benches. Young Gherard was definitely dead. His face was still half-contorted in an expression of agony.

"Thank the Nameless you're here," said Taryn quietly, stepping toward Alastar.

"What was he trying to image?" asked Alastar.

"That." Taryn pointed to the stone bench, on which rested two objects, side by side. At first glance, they appeared identical—a decorative figure with four legs supporting a pentagon, out of which rose three coiled solid tubes that rose a sixth of a yard, where they were topped by a small triangular pyramid.

Alastar couldn't help but frown. "Those look like Desyrk's models, the ones he uses to teach thirds how to concentrate. That shouldn't . . ." He stopped as he realized what Gherard had attempted. Desyrk had imaged his models out of wood, and then imaged paint of various colors on various sections, so that the triangular pyramid on top was painted gold, while the twisted coils beneath were silver, and the pentagonal base was black, while the four angled legs were brass-colored. "He should have known. I even warned him about trying to do too much before he was ready."

"You should talk to Borlan," suggested Taryn.

In the dim light of the lantern held by Taryn, Alastar could see the worried face of the young second, standing beside Obsolym, whose face showed no expression. Alastar took a slow breath and walked toward the second. "Borlan? What can you tell me about what happened?"

"I didn't have anything to do with it, sir. I didn't." Borland's eyes met Alastar's, then darted away.

"No one said you did. I need to know how this happened." Alastar waited.

"I saw him—Gherard—after supper. He had the model. He said it was just a model, but he was going to show the Maitre. He said he was going to image it better than any third could. I told him he shouldn't, and he shouldn't have taken it from the instruction room . . ."

How did he get it from there? Did Desyrk leave it out?

"He said . . ." Borlan's voice caught, and he swallowed before going on. "He said that he'd image it better than anyone. I didn't know he meant . . ."

"That he was going to try to image real gold, silver, brass . . . and black onyx, all at once?"

"No, sir. We're not supposed to image by ourselves. I just thought he was going to do it with wood. I told him he shouldn't. He told me to be quiet, or he'd image something where it'd hurt me . . . I got worried, and I ran to find Maitre Taryn. I knew he was the duty maitre. The maitre came quick, but we were too late . . . I did what I could, sir, I really did."

Given that Borlan looked almost a head shorter than Gherard and was thin as well, Alastar had no doubts. "I know you did. Sometimes, we can't stop people from doing things they know aren't good. Is there anything else I should know?"

"I don't think so, sir. I told you what happened."

"Thank you." Alastar looked to Obsolym. "Can you add anything?"

"No. I'd been working late, and I'd just left the administration building when I saw Taryn and Borlan running this way. I thought I might be of help." Obsolym shook his head. "It was too late."

Alastar nodded, then moved to the bench. He lifted the original model. *Definitely painted wood.* He set it down, then lifted what Gherard had imaged. Despite its comparatively modest size it must have weighed almost half a stone. Gherard had only tried for gilding the pyramid, but the stone pentagonal base, the brass legs, and especially the silver coils . . . *Far too much even for some junior maitres, at least right here.*

"We'll need to take him to the infirmary for tonight . . ." Alastar nodded to Taryn. *It's going to be a long night, and tomorrow will be worse.* He thought about asking more of Obsolym, who had been Gherard's preceptor, but decided that could wait until morning.

18

Despite the fact that dealing with Gherard's death kept Alastar up past midnight, part of which was the problem that the records Alastar could find had no home address for Gherard's father, Factorius Wylum, Alastar rose early on Vendrei because he had called a meeting of the senior imagers as early as possible. He didn't expect any response to his letters to the High Holders, if he received any at all, until late on Vendrei, or even on Samedi, and he hoped to start the imagers he had picked on dealing with the one sewer repair before he went to pay the unhappy call on Factor Wylum.

Alastar looked down the table, taking in Cyran at his right, then Akoryt, Obsolym, Taryn, and Desyrk. "This meeting will be short. I wanted all of you to know the circumstances surrounding the death of Secondus Gherard. It's likely you all know something about what happened. What you may not know is what led up to this tragedy. As you know, I have been meeting with student imagers . . ." He went on to describe his meeting with Gherard, and then the subsequent details of what had occurred the night before. ". . . and as with the incident involving Bettaur and Taurek, this unhappy event with Gherard is a direct result of a student with too much arrogance and too little understanding of the dangers and costs of imaging. It also reflects too little respect for the words of the maitres who instruct them. I would like each of you to consider ways in which the Collegium can temper this arrogance without destroying self-confidence and what additional instruction or demonstrations might be useful in getting students to understand the true dangers of thoughtless imaging. We will talk about this next week, after we all have had a chance to reflect on the matter."

"Had I been conducting instructionals," Desyrk offered smoothly, "it would have been more difficult for Gherard to obtain the model he attempted to duplicate in real materials."

"Those models are kept on the high shelf, as I recall," returned Alastar. "The study chambers are not locked, nor is the building locked until curfew. Gherard did not take the model until after the evening meal, at which time you would not have been present. There is no blame on you for using such models, nor on the fact that you did not teach yesterday. Gherard would have obtained the model, or something similar in any event, and, given his attitude, the results would likely have been similar."

"You don't think you were too hard on the boy?" asked Obsolym.

"He doubtless thought so. I told him that he was not yet skilled enough to become a tertius. I never said a single word that would have indicated that he would not have become at least that. I also clearly told him that trying to do more than he was ready for was dangerous and could kill him. He was much more interested in being a tertius than in obtaining the skills that merit the appellation."

"That's always been a problem," said Taryn. "At least, Maitre Fhaen said that on more than one occasion."

"Another form of naming," murmured Akoryt.

"Thank you," said Alastar warmly. "That's an excellent point, and I will talk to Chorister Iskhar about a homily along those lines. There's also another issue. According to the Collegium records, the factor disowned his son when he entered the Collegium. Since I was not here at the time, and there is nothing in Gherard's records, does anyone know whether that was strictly for reasons of law and inheritance, or because Factor Wylum was displeased with his son?"

"If there's no entry to the contrary, it's usually only for reasons of law. That's especially true in the case of the eldest son," replied Obsolym. "Gherard was the eldest son."

"Thank you."

"It would have been even uglier," said Obsolym, "if he'd tried that in his quarters. I've always said that the lead was a bad idea."

Why is he bringing that up? Alastar caught himself and replied quietly, but firmly, "The lead lining of their rooms remains a good idea. It is there to protect them from each other. It won't protect them from themselves. Gherard's problem wasn't lead; it was that he didn't listen, and he paid the price for not listening. All of you need to use this as an illustration of why it is important for student imagers to follow your instructions and those of other maitres in regard to imaging." He paused, then added, "One thing we have to remember is that almost all young people believe that somehow they are different from us and from their parents, and that the cautions and restrictions we apply are stupid and willful, and that they really know better."

"You're not giving them much credit, Maitre," said Desyrk.

"And after what happened right before you, Desyrk, you're giving them far too much." After just a moment, Alastar added, "That is all for this morning. There will be a work party doing some sewer repairs, and I will be paying a call on Factor Wylum."

From the conference room, Alastar returned to his study, from where he retrieved his imager gray riding jacket and gloves, and then made his way to the stables. All those maitres picked for the sewer repairs were already there, as was Belsior, since Alastar wanted one escort for his visit to Wylum. All the imagers began to mount up as he walked toward the gray gelding.

Once Alastar was in the saddle, Cyran immediately eased his mount toward Alastar. "If you wouldn't mind . . ."

"Not at all. I already thought that we could use the time to go over a few things." Once the group had crossed the east bridge and headed north on the East River Road, Alastar turned in the saddle. "You had a few concerns about the meeting?"

"You didn't have to tell everyone what happened in the meeting you had with Gherard," said Cyran quietly.

"Yes, I did. This is the second time in a week we've had a problem because student imagers have had an exalted opinion of themselves and their position and abilities—and a lack of understanding of the dangers of imaging. If I'd not mentioned it, what happened with Bettaur and Taurek would just be regarded as an unfortunate incident, not a Collegium-wide problem."

"Neither Desyrk nor Obsolym see it the way you do."

"Do you?"

"I think it's a problem. I'm not sure it's as widespread as you fear."

"It doesn't have to be widespread to be a serious problem," Alastar replied. "Not when we're talking about what an imager, even a student imager, can do to others . . . or himself."

"There's another problem. That's Desyrk. He was almost sneering the entire time you were speaking."

"I can't exclude him from meetings of senior imagers without removing him from duty or reducing him to a Maitre D'Aspect."

"And those require a meeting of all senior maitres," finished Cyran.

"Precisely."

"That comment about your paying a call on Factor

Wylum means you're going to leave Alyna in charge of repairs and me in charge of security, doesn't it?"

"It does. I also don't want to be away from the Collegium for too long, not with the problems over the tariffs." *And a few other matters.* "I need a few words with Alyna, if you wouldn't mind."

"I thought you might." Cyran grinned, then eased his mount to the side of the road and motioned for Alyna to ride up beside Alastar.

"Yes, Maitre?" asked Alyna once she joined Alastar.

"Once I point out where the sewers need repair, I'll be leaving you in charge of directing those repairs, as well as doing your share of that imaging. Cyran will watch for any possible difficulty. I'd like you to push everyone to do a bit more, so that they're all tired by the time you finish." *That also might press them toward increasing their strength as imagers.*

"I can only suggest for Taryn."

"Suggest cheerfully," replied Alastar dryly. "On another matter . . . do you know if your brother will withhold his tariffs if the High Council declares that all High Holders should do so?"

"I've heard nothing from him. He would be loath to go against the High Council unless he had a good reason."

Alastar nodded. "I'd appreciate it if you would continue to practice shielding whenever you can, and to carry shields against both imaging and weapons, especially when you are away from the Collegium."

"I've been doing that for the past week."

"Can you tell any difference?"

"I'm already stronger. It does make a difference."

"Can you suggest that to Tiranya?"

"I already have. She thinks I'm being too cautious, but she's doing it. Mostly, anyway."

"Thank you."

"You're very worried, aren't you?" Alyna's voice was low.

"More than I'll say openly," he admitted.

"I won't say a word."

"I didn't think you would." He paused. "Did you ride a great deal as a child?"

"All the time. It was the only way I could keep up with my brothers."

"What about your sister?"

"She rides well enough, but she never enjoyed it the way I did."

"I envy you," Alastar said with a soft laugh. "The first long rides I took were on the way from Westisle to L'Excelsis. I was sore for days."

"You ride well now."

"I look like I know what I'm doing in the saddle now. You ride well."

"Thank you."

Alastar thought he detected a slight hint of a blush, but he wasn't certain. "I'm just observing what I see. Were you also tutored in the womanly arts?"

"Singing and playing the clavecin?" Alyna laughed. "I cannot carry a tune, and my skills at playing are similar to the way you describe your riding. I worked hard enough that I would not disgrace myself if I had to play . . ."

Three quints after leaving Imagisle, Alastar was almost sorry when he reined up a half block short of Hagahl Lane on Nordroad. "This is one of the places where we need to make repairs. This will be the only repair for the day . . ."

"Not nearly so bad as the last," murmured Cyran, almost under his breath.

". . . and you can see where the sewage backs up from that drain and flows along the gutter to the next drain. Maitre Alyna will be in charge of who does what, while Cyran will make certain that those actually working on the repairs are undisturbed." Alastar nodded to Alyna and then to Cyran. "I will see you all later back at the Collegium." He gestured to Belsior.

The two of them rode south on Nordroad, past the center of L'Excelsis, where it became Sudroad, and then to Fedre, following it west to the East River Road, where they turned south and continued for slightly more than three blocks, until they reached Wylum's factorage. The brass letters set against the black background of the sign over the entry read WOOLENS AND CLOTH.

Alastar dismounted and handed the gelding's reins to Belsior. "This might not be brief, but I doubt it will take that long." He walked to the black-painted door, and opened it, stepping into an open space filled with large racks holding bolts of what appeared to be various types of woolens. An empty cart stood before one of the racks.

A thin young man, vaguely resembling Gherard, turned and saw Alastar. He froze in place for a moment, then stuttered, "Just a moment, sir." With that, he turned and hurried toward the back of the factorage.

Alastar could hear words being exchanged, but could not make out exactly what was said.

Several moments later, a tall square-faced man with thinning brown hair and broad shoulders, but with a solid midriff as well, walked from between a set of racks and stopped some two yards from Alastar. "I know why you are here, Maitre. You don't have to explain. My son is dead. He died because the Collegium failed him. Why didn't you inform me last night?"

"By the time I was informed it was late, and, frankly, since the Collegium does not keep records of the domiciles of factors, I came first thing this morning."

"Oh? Then how did I learn?"

"How did you learn?"

"I was informed by someone at the Collegium who obviously knows more than you. That, too, I find disturbing. Not nearly so disturbing as losing my son to the carelessness of the Collegium. I was under the impression that sending my son to the Collegium was in his best interest and that he would be safe there. Clearly, I was mistaken."

"No, you were not mistaken," Alastar replied quietly. "Before there was a Collegium, less than one in ten imagers lived to adulthood. Imaging is incredibly dangerous, and it is easy to make fatal mistakes. Your son attempted a kind of imaging he had been told repeatedly not to do until he was more skilled. We cannot watch every student every moment of every day. Even a student who was with Gherard told him not to do what he was trying. Because your son was bigger and stronger and a better imager than his peer, the other student could not stop him. So the student ran for the duty maitre. The maitre hurried, but arrived too late. Your son died for the reason many young people die—because he did not listen to those older and more experienced. This is worse for imagers, because there are more ways for the young to do stupid things that are fatal, especially if they ignore warnings and instructions."

"Excuses are all very well, but he was in your care, and he is dead."

If you hadn't instilled all that pride and arrogance in him, he would still be alive. "He is dead. I cannot change that. He has been at the Collegium two years. I also cannot change what he learned or did not learn before that."

"I cannot believe you're blaming him."

"He was told repeatedly not to try what he tried. He was told what would most likely happen if he did—"

"Most likely? Then if it does not happen to all young imagers, why did it happen to him?"

"Some few young imagers who image foolishly only injure themselves. Most who ignore the rules do end up killing themselves. I personally told him that he was not ready to accomplish greater imaging only a few days before he did just that."

"Why would he have done that? Why?"

"He told another student imager he was going to

show the maitres how wrong they were. That was when that student ran for help."

"Who saw all this? I have only your word."

"The student who was with Gherard saw it. He was in tears because he could not stop Gherard. The duty maitre saw the results."

"Just what was this . . . imaging he tried?"

"He tried to image an intricate figure out of gold, silver, brass, and black onyx. Even imaging a single gold is dangerous for most maitres. Not a single junior maitre would have attempted what Gherard did. There is a very good reason why the Collegium needs golds from the rex."

For a moment, Wylum looked puzzled. Then he shook his head. "Excuses . . . excuses."

"Factorius Wylum, the Collegium needs every imager it can train. There is no way I would *ever* countenance anything that increased the threats to a young imager. Learning how to image properly is dangerous enough. Every Maitre of the Collegium has felt this way. The Collegium has been able to reduce the threats so that most young imagers do in fact survive and prosper. I cannot tell you how sorry I am that your son was not one of them. But do not ever discount the dangers facing an imager as a mere excuse." As he spoke, Alastar tried to image the impression of both sadness and absolute certainty.

The taller factor almost seemed to wilt in front of Alastar, but then straightened. "That is all well and good, but you have not lost a son."

"No, I have not. I lost both my wife and my son. She died because she was with child and did more imaging than she should have, and that imaging inadvertently killed them both."

Wylum looked to speak, then shook his head. After a long moment, he finally spoke. "You can understand my grief."

"I understand your grief. Perhaps you can also understand why I would never have allowed your son to endanger himself and why not only I, but his maitres, tried every way of cautioning him against trying to do too much."

"He . . . was strong-willed . . ."

Alastar nodded again. *Will alone is not enough, not for an imager.* Perhaps not for anyone.

In time, Wylum looked at Alastar. "Despite what I said, you were kind to come. I thank you for that."

"I wish most deeply I had not met you this way, Factorius Wylum."

"That makes us a pair, Maitre. I will send a wagon immediately."

Alastar was glad not to have to ask whether the family wanted to handle the memorial services or leave it to the Collegium.

"He will be ready."

Wylum nodded.

"I would not impose more." Alastar inclined his head, then seeing Wylum's nod in return, turned and left the factorage.

By the time he reached the Collegium, it was two quints before noon. After arranging for the transport of Gherard's body, by a quint past the glass, he was immersed in a pile of maps, looking to see what they might indicate about the area around Imagisle. After another half glass, carrying several rolled maps, he left the administration building and walked to the stables, where he commandeered Tertius Neiryn as an escort, saddled his gelding, and then mounted.

First, he and Neiryn rode to the north end of Imagisle. There Alastar dismounted and tied the gelding to the hitching rail at the end of the lane. From there he made his way up the stone steps on the east side to the upper walk that ran immediately behind the stone river wall. He studied the back side of the stone ramparts that looked like the prow of a vessel facing into the River

Aluse. The grassy ground behind the gray stone walkway was slightly more than a yard lower than the stones of the wall itself, each massive stone close to a yard in thickness, and extended back at the same level for about three yards before sloping down to a point a yard and a half lower. The lower ground was park-like, with old oaks, winding walks, and a pavilion surrounded by a waist-high hedge. There were stone benches along the walks, but not placed in any pattern Alastar could discern. He walked the entire north end of the isle, studying everything, with Neiryn following, and then back to the gelding.

"We'll take the Bridge of Desires," Alastar announced as he mounted.

As they crossed the bridge, Alastar studied the West River Road to the south, especially the area along the river between the two bridges linking the isle to the west bank of the river. Then he and Neiryn rode north. Alastar rode slowly on the river side of the road, stopping occasionally, and using a black pastel crayon with a fine point to note something on the writing pad he carried. Less frequently, he unrolled a map and compared it to what he saw. When they neared the Nord Bridge, he needed to slow or stop less frequently.

The two continued north on the West River Road until half a mille past where the paved road turned away from the river. There Alastar reined up and surveyed the welter of houses and shops to the west and northwest. Turning to Neiryn, he said, "We can head back now."

The return to Imagisle was not as deliberate as the ride out, but Alastar did stop several times, particularly near what appeared to be an abandoned, or at least disused, mill of some sort.

When he returned to the anteroom outside his study, just after fourth glass, he found Obsolym there, apparently finishing a conversation with Dareyn, since Dareyn immediately said, "Here comes the Maitre now."

"Very good." Obsolym turned to face Alastar.

"You wanted a word with me?"

"Just a few moments."

Alastar motioned to the study, then walked into it, with Obsolym following. The Maitre D'Structure closed the door after he entered.

Alastar did not sit down. He'd spent almost three glasses in the saddle and felt more like standing. "What is it?"

"I wondered how matters went with Factor Wylum."

"He wasn't happy, understandably. We talked for a short while. I made arrangements with him to send Gherard's body to his factorage, as he requested."

"Is there anything else necessary?" asked Obsolym.

"Only to find out how Factor Wylum learned of his son's death almost before I did, since there is no home address for the good factor in the file on Gherard."

"He knew already?"

"He did." Alastar had no doubt that Obsolym had been the one to inform Wylum, since he had been Gherard's preceptor, but Alastar wasn't about to make an accusation.

"I see. I wonder how that happened."

Alastar smiled. "So do I. Is that all you wanted to know?"

"Yes, sir. Thank you."

As Obsolym left the study, Alastar couldn't help but wonder why the other maitre had let Wylum know. Because he believed that Alastar was being too hard in what he asked of students and senior maitres, or because he had other ambitions . . . or just to make life difficult for Alastar? Then he started back to work correlating his observations with the maps. That lasted for less than a quint before Dareyn announced, "Maitres Cyran and Alyna to see you."

"Have them come in." Alastar stood.

Some sort of dust streaked the trousers of both imagers, and Alastar had to admit they looked tired as they walked into the study. "Were you able to deal with the problem, or will you have to go back?"

"We managed, once we figured out the problem . . . or Alyna did." Cyran gestured to Alyna. "You can explain."

"I just noticed that the sewer water ran past two of the drains," Alyna said, "and then went down the third, mostly anyway. I thought that we ought to see what was wrong with the drains first." She offered a rueful smile. "Some idiot poured mortar down two of the drains and some down a third, just on the west side of the road. Or something like it. The sewer ditches themselves were fine, except backed up. Imaging out chunks of stone took most of the day. We only had to replace two small sections of the ditches where we couldn't separate the mortar from the ditch walls and pavement covers."

"They all seem to be working now." Cyran paused. "If you wouldn't mind, Maitre. I did promise . . . Alyna can explain . . ."

"You can go. If there's anything else, we can talk in the morning."

Once Cyran had left, Alastar said, "I noticed that the water ran past the drains, but I thought that was because the sewer itself was plugged up."

"That was my first thought, too. But I didn't want to image huge holes in the pavement if we didn't have to. I decided that, even if the sewer was plugged, we'd still have to clean out the drains. So I had us start with the drains. I was fortunate. At least, less unfortunate. Imaging out solid mortar is definitely hard work."

"Thank you. That's for both the ingenuity and the work." Alastar smiled warmly. "I do appreciate it. Is there anything else I should know? Did anyone complain?"

"No one seemed to pay much attention, except for the last two glasses, when we had to block almost half the road. The only thing that looks different is that the pavement we replaced looks newer."

"A few weeks, and no one will even notice, even if the stones stay a different shade."

"They're close to the original."

"I'll be interested to see how your imaging feels by Solayi."

"In addition to carrying stronger shields?"

Alastar nodded. "You've already had a long and hard day. I don't want to keep you."

"It has been a long day . . . but it was good to fix something." She smiled. "Thank you."

"The thanks are all mine."

After Alyna had left, Alastar just stood by his desk, not really quite sure what he was thinking, except that her smile had definitely had an unsettling effect on him. *Because you're hoping?* He shook his head and went back to work on the maps and what he had discovered.

Later, after eating in the dining hall, Alastar returned to his study in the administration building. There, he picked up the second and third volumes of Gauswn's journals and carried them back to the Maitre's residence, where he set them on the desk and then sat down, thinking.

What else can you do about the standoff between the rex and the High Council? You can't have the Collegium seen as beginning anything. That would undo everything that it stands for, and it would rekindle the distrust and hatred of imagers. He shook his head. *But doing nothing for fear of that is what led to the present situation.*

Finally, he took out Gauswn's journal and finished the last twenty pages in the first volume, and started the second volume. After reading another twenty pages and finding only passing references, or day-to-day activities of Quaeryt being mentioned, he closed the heavy volume and sat silently at the desk for a time.

For so many mentions, there's so little that really says anything. He smiled wryly. *Isn't that true of all of us? The Maitre did this. He did that. He said this. He said that . . . and little of that says much about the man . . . or the imager.*

At last, he rose and imaged out the lamp.

19

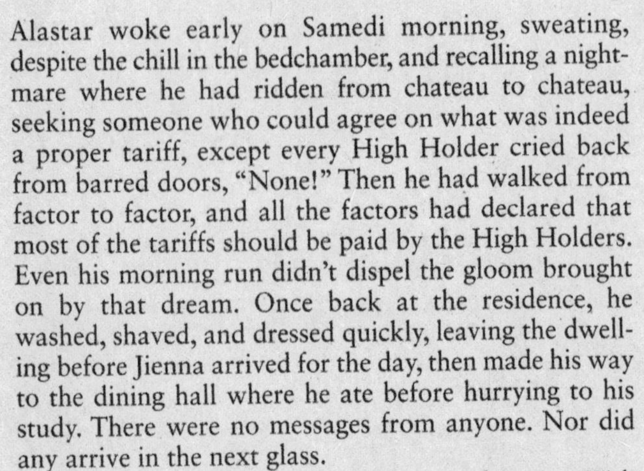

Alastar woke early on Samedi morning, sweating, despite the chill in the bedchamber, and recalling a nightmare where he had ridden from chateau to chateau, seeking someone who could agree on what was indeed a proper tariff, except every High Holder cried back from barred doors, "None!" Then he had walked from factor to factor, and all the factors had declared that most of the tariffs should be paid by the High Holders. Even his morning run didn't dispel the gloom brought on by that dream. Once back at the residence, he washed, shaved, and dressed quickly, leaving the dwelling before Jienna arrived for the day, then made his way to the dining hall where he ate before hurrying to his study. There were no messages from anyone. Nor did any arrive in the next glass.

You can't just wait for something to happen. With those thoughts in mind, he made his way to the instructional building, where he heard a lutelin being tuned. Curious, he eased down the hallway to the chamber from where the sound came.

After raising a concealment, one that also blurred the door, he entered the chamber. None of the students noticed, since they were facing Shaelyt, although the junior maitre paused for an instant before continuing.

". . . ah . . . sometimes, ah . . . as I was saying, songs tell us things that the histories or even the stories handed down don't. I'd like you all to listen to the words of this one." Shaelyt strummed the lutelin and began to sing.

"Rex Regis was a warrior, and a mighty man was he,
He broke the holders of the hills, and he made them die and flee,
His armies swept Bovaria and set all her people free,
Then conquered Khel and Antiago, to rule from sea to sea,
But few among the armies knew his line was solid Pharsi
Praise your Hengist or your Caldor, any warrior you can see
But none's as mighty as Rex Regis, the Yaran who was a Pharsi . . ."

As the young maitre played and sang, with a pleasant but not outstanding voice, Alastar watched the seconds. The body positions suggested puzzlement.

"Have any of you heard that song?" asked Shaelyt when he finished.

"No, sir." That response was unanimous, not surprisingly, even to Alastar, who had never heard the tune, and he'd overheard many, especially as a boy in Westisle.

"You can hear why. It's not that good a song, but it was sung hundreds of years ago. I doubt that it was that popular even then, but I found a copy in the archives. More important, why did I sing it in a study session about the history of Solidar?"

There were no answers, no words from the student imagers.

"What do you think about Pharsis?" Shaelyt pointed to a slightly rotund second.

"They lived in the west. In Khel, when it was separate land. Rex Kharst killed most of them."

"So why are the Pharsis important to the Collegium?"

"Some imagers are Pharsi, aren't they?" asked the sole girl among the students.

"Yes, they are, Linzya. Why might that be?"

The lack of replies suggested more blank faces.

"Borlan? Do you know Tertius Belsior?"

"Yes, sir."

"Do you know where his name comes from?"

"Elsior, sir. He was a great imager in the old days, and he was the second Maitre of the Collegium."

"He was also a Pharsi. So was Quaeryt, the first Maitre. So, as the song shows, was Rex Regis."

"They all were?" Borlan's face showed considerable surprise.

"There are other names that also have a Pharsi origin . . ."

Alastar slipped from the chamber. Much as he'd enjoyed Shaelyt's way of getting into the contribution the Pharsi community had made to the creation of Solidar, he was getting worried . . . even though he had the feeling that he'd hear little from anyone until Lundi . . . if then.

As he walked back to the administration building, he could feel that the winds of the past few days had died away, but also noted that the sky was becoming overcast, although, without a breeze, the day felt only chilly. When he reached the anteroom, Dareyn looked up from his desk.

"You received a letter from Factor Elthyrd. I left it on your desk. I didn't know when you'd be back. I didn't think you'd be long."

"I was observing a lesson. Is there anything from anyone else?"

"No, sir."

That concerned Alastar, but there wasn't much he could do about that. So he walked into the study, opened the single envelope on the desk, and began to read even before he sat down.

Maitre Alastar—

I must say that the factors' council was pleased with the speed with which the Collegium addressed the first of the locations requiring repairs to the sewers. The fact that the imagers managed the repairs with minimal disruption to wagons and coaches traveling Nordroad was also noted favorably.

I also trust it will not be too long before the Collegium can proceed with the other repairs that the council brought to the attention of the Collegium.

Alastar smiled sardonically at the last words of the missive, then sat down to write an immediate response. *Since you have the time and it will serve another purpose.* He wrote deliberately and cautiously.

Dear Factorius Elthyrd—

Thank you for your missive about the recent sewer repairs.

As I indicated when we last spoke, when we can get to the next repairs will depend on other commitments, since, as you may have heard, Rex Ryen and Marshal Demykalon have a considerable difference of opinion with the High Council over the level of next year's tariffs, and the rex has made a number of demands on the Collegium recently. You may rest assured that we will indeed complete the repairs you suggested, but the timing will depend upon other events over which the Collegium has no control.

Alastar looked over what he had written, then decided against adding more, and signed the letter. After letting the ink dry and then blotting it, he folded it, put it in an envelope and sealed, before taking it out to Dareyn.

"Please, have this dispatched back to Factor Elthyrd, at his factorage, not at the factors' council."

"Yes, sir." Dareyn smiled faintly. "And no, sir, there aren't any more messages."

"Thank you." Alastar had the feeling that the remainder of Samedi would be long and uneventful, but that lack of happenings was likely the calm before the tempest.

20

With all his worries, Alastar didn't sleep late on Solayi, but woke as early as he did during the rest of the week. When he entered the dining hall for breakfast, he was surprised to see Alyna there—until he realized she was seated with Tiranya, who was the duty maitre. *That makes sense, since they share a cottage.* He debated taking the seat beside Tiranya, to show impartiality, then decided to be selfish, and moved to the seat beside Alyna.

"Good morning," he offered cheerfully. "You wouldn't mind if I joined you?"

"Not at all," replied Tiranya almost forcefully and with a wide smile.

"Please do," added Alyna quietly.

"Thank you." Alastar eased into the chair.

"We'll likely get better fare now that you're here, Maitre," declared Tiranya. "That's for certain."

"I fear it will take more than my presence," he replied with a laugh.

"The food has improved since you arrived at the Collegium," said Alyna.

"Not nearly as much as it needs to, but I'm glad to hear that my presence has had a beneficial effect in some areas." He reached for the sole pitcher, then paused as a student server hurried forward with a second one. "Let me guess. There's only pale lager in that one."

Alyna smiled mischievously. "How did you ever calculate that?"

"It wasn't with geometry." Alastar glanced at her beaker, noting that it was empty, then took the new pitcher and filled her beaker before his own. He couldn't help smiling as he set the pitcher down.

"I would have asked . . . if you hadn't shown up when you did."

"But you're saving the requests for when they're absolutely necessary? Is that something you learned young?"

"Of course . . . and thank you."

At that moment, two servers hurried up with a plate for each of the three maitres, set them down, inclined their heads respectfully, if quickly, and headed back to the kitchen, as if they did not wish to remain. One of the three was Shannyr, which might have explained both the quick service and departure.

Alastar noted that the cheesed eggs were solid but not firm and only held a touch of brown. The small loaf of dark bread was still warm. The strips of ham were crispy on the edges but not burned. *Definitely an improvement.*

"Will we begin actual imaging on the avenue tomorrow?" asked Alyna.

That was something about which Alastar had very mixed feelings, but he only said, "Unless something comes up to make that infeasible."

Tiranya swallowed quickly and looked past Alyna to Alastar. "Maitre, that sounds ominous."

"It does, doesn't it?" replied Alastar. "I didn't mean it to sound that way." *Even if it's likely true.* "The rex wants his avenue built. The factors want their sewers repaired . . . and then there are the priorities within the Collegium. I don't want to cancel too much instruction at any one time."

Tiranya nodded, looked briefly at Alyna, then turned back to her plate and took another mouthful of eggs.

"Nicely done," murmured Alyna in a dry voice so low that Alastar could barely hear it.

He managed not to choke on the lager he had just swallowed. At the same time, he wanted to smile. He liked Alyna's understated humor. *Because you like her . . . or just the humor?* He broke off a chunk of the dark bread and ate it, finding it warm, but not quite so moist or sweet as he would have preferred.

"When will you have us do another sewer repair?" asked Alyna.

"Not for at least a week. We've repaired the two most critical places." *One critical to the Collegium and one to the wealthier factors and their wives.* "I worry about the apothecaries and others once we begin to remove buildings. What reaction have you seen when you've been surveying and measuring . . ." He shook his head. "I'm sorry. Surveying includes measuring."

"That doesn't require an apology," replied Alyna.

"It would if I'd said it," quipped Tiranya.

"You're not the Maitre," said Alyna, her voice false-honeyed.

How many ways can you take that? wondered Alastar, immediately deciding to return to his previous inquiry. "Did anyone appear angry . . . or worse?"

"More unhappy, I think. One man muttered to another about even imagers would be sorry, but that was only once."

"For everyone who said something, quite a few more likely thought it," mused Alastar, before finishing his eggs and the last scrap of the crispy ham.

"They wouldn't act against imagers, would they?" asked Tiranya.

"It depends on how angry they are. Very few in generations have seen what an imager can do. The problem is that, if they do, we may create even more difficulties for ourselves." *Unless you can set it up so that it's clearly someone else's doing and fault, and that doesn't seem possible . . . yet.* Alastar took a last swallow of lager from his beaker and set it on the table.

"Would you mind if I walked with you?" Alyna asked even before Alastar thought about rising and leaving.

"Not at all . . ."

Alyna turned to Tiranya. "I'll see you at services, then."

"If there aren't any problems," replied the younger maitre.

"I'm sure you can handle them." Alastar stood, hoping at the same time that there wouldn't be, given that the Collegium already faced enough difficulties.

"Tiranya definitely can," added Alyna.

When the two left the dining hall, Alastar could see that, while they had been eating, the clouds had thickened into a blackish gray. A gusty cold wind battered them as they walked in the direction of the administration building and, beyond that, of Alyna's cottage to the northwest. They had just gotten halfway across the green when an especially strong gust of wind whipped past them. Alastar could see rain sweeping toward them, like a wall of water so heavy that he could barely see his residence to the north.

"You'll never make it to your cottage without being drowned." He touched Alyna's arm and pointed to the administration building. "We can wait out the storm there. Downpours like this don't last that long. Not usually."

"Just like Ryen's tantrums don't last long—usually?"

"I'd wager on the storm being more reasonable."

"I wouldn't wager against you."

Even so, hurrying at a pace just short of a run, the two reached the door as the deluge struck, but the projecting roof kept them from more than scattered droplets. Alastar closed the door quickly against the pressure of wind and rain, then turned to Alyna. "We can wait in my study until it subsides."

"Or until it's clear it won't end any time soon?" Alyna smiled humorously.

"Either way, it's your decision." He began to walk down the hall toward the Maitre's study.

"Even though you're the Maitre?"

"Especially since I'm the Maitre. There's too muc temptation." As soon as he'd said those words, Alasta wished he hadn't phrased the thought quite that way yet all he could quickly add was, "In power, that is."

"You almost had me worried," returned Alyna dryly.

"Should I be glad or concerned?"

"There's no good answer to that, dear Maitre."

Alastar laughed. "I suppose not." He crossed the dark anteroom and opened the door to the study, which was not that much brighter, given the gloom of the storm beyond the windows. After motioning for Alyna to enter, he followed her, then took the end chair in front of the far end of the desk and turned it, before gesturing to the others and waiting for Alyna to seat herself. He couldn't help noting the grace with which she did.

Feeling slightly awkward after sitting down, Alastar finally said, "I was surprised to see you at the dining hall this morning until I saw that Tiranya was the duty maitre."

"I don't always accompany her, but the food has gotten better lately. I was hoping you'd be there."

"You had to know I would be there."

Alyna laughed softly. "I had good odds. I wouldn't have come just because she had the duty . . . but it provided an excuse in case you did eat at the same time." She smiled wryly. "I like hearing what you have to say."

Alastar had the feeling that was not all. "That makes two of us. I like what I say too. Too much, I fear, and too many other maitres, unlike you, seem reluctant to say what they think." He paused. "What did you want to know? I'm assuming that was one reason why you were there."

"A few things. How much danger does the Collegium really face? I received a letter from Zaeryl yesterday, sent by one of his private couriers. He said that Guerdyn and Haebyn have sent out word not to submit tariffs until Ryen agrees not to increase the levels. He also said

. . . e High Holders will take steps against anyone . . . pports Ryen in that."

. . . not-so-indirect reference to the Collegium, I take

. . . And the army High Command, I would guess. Zaer- . . . not thrilled with anyone, right now, not Ryen, not . . . uerdyn and Haebyn . . ."

"But he's not willing to defy the High Council, not openly?"

"He didn't say that." She offered a wry expression. "He didn't have to. He's very cautious." She looked at Alastar and waited.

"Danger? That's the problem. I don't know. It all depends on just how determined the High Council is, how reckless Ryen may be, and to what length Marshal Demykalon will support him. The more I talk to Guerdyn and Ryen, though, the more worried I get."

"You've tried suggesting some sort of compromise?"

"Twice. The first time the idea was absolutely rejected. I haven't heard on the second time, but that silence suggests that Ryen, at least, will reject the idea. He insists that tariffs have to be raised to pay for what Solidar needs."

"Do you think he's right?"

"He is. The army is half the size it was in his sire's time, not that we need that large an army, but we do need a larger and stronger navy, and there are no funds for that. Ryen says that he doesn't have enough funds for road and bridge repairs—"

"Didn't the Collegium do that once?"

Alastar shook his head. "All the stone-paved roads in Telaryn were created and paved in the old way. Quaeryt and his imagers did resurface a number of ways here, such as the East and West River Roads, and the ring road around the Chateau D'Rex, but there have never been that many powerful imagers in all of Solidar since then."

"Why not, do you think?"

"Something about the times . . . and Quaeryt, I think. According to the stories, he created the entire stone river wall on the north end of Imagisle in one imaging. He also destroyed the entire palace complex of the Autarch of Antiago during the battle there."

"You're from Westisle. Did he?"

"There's a sunken park there now. Whatever he did lowered a square of ground three quarters of a mille on a side almost ten yards."

"Ten yards?"

"It's as though he imaged out that from under the palace and let the whole thing drop. Maybe he even took what he imaged and dropped some of it on top of the palace."

"No one could do that."

"No one today could do what they did then. They rebuilt the walls of the Chateau D'Rex. You can't even scratch them with a sharp blade. It will likely stand forever."

Alyna shook her head. "You hear the stories, but . . . you saw that park. No one thinks about the walls or the roads that don't seem to wear out here in L'Excelsis."

"There aren't any records, either. I've been reading the journals of the first chorister of the anomen at the Collegium. He was an undercaptain in the Telaryn army who served under Quaeryt in putting down the Tilboran Revolt . . ." Alastar went on to relate what little he had learned about the first Maitre. When he finished, at least as far as he had read, he added, "It's still a mystery why he didn't want anyone to know all he did. For that matter, it's clear, at least from the Collegium archives, that Vaelora didn't either . . . unless she told things to her daughters that have come down through your family." Alastar looked to Alyna inquiringly.

"There's nothing that I know of. I did ask Father about her, but he said there was nothing, either. I think he was telling the truth about that."

Which suggests that he didn't always tell the truth about everything. Alastar just nodded, before asking, "Do you have any thoughts about that?"

"Some wives heed their husband's cautions," Alyna said with a shrug, not quite convincingly.

"I get the impression Vaelora wasn't that type. She married an unknown imager well before . . . well, he was princeps of Tilbor."

"That's not a bad match for a junior daughter. She was the youngest."

"I think there was more there." As the pounding of the rain began to subside, Alastar looked to the window. "It won't be long before it's over . . . or maybe only a drizzle." He turned back to Alyna. "The way you say that . . . you . . ." He wasn't quite sure how to finish the sentence.

"Before it became obvious that Father didn't have to worry about a match, I was told quite often that I could not afford to be picky."

"Why not? You're intelligent and attractive."

Alyna stiffened almost imperceptibly, and Alastar realized she was also blushing, although the slight honeyed shade to her skin meant that the flush was not obvious to anyone not looking closely. After a pause, she said, "Thank you. You're kind."

"Perhaps, but I'm also accurate."

This time, Alyna was the one who looked to the window. "Thank you for spending the time with me. I'd never heard most of that. You make it more interesting the way you say it."

"You're being kind."

"Perhaps, as you said a moment ago, but I'm also being truthful."

Alastar wanted to sit with her and talk more, but it was clear his observation about her had somehow distressed her. He rose. "The rain has almost stopped. I'll walk with you to your cottage and then keep going to the residence."

Alyna also stood and smiled gently. "I'd enjoy that."

They walked from the study without speaking and from there out of the building and into a fine misting rain that was so light it barely felt like precipitation, except that the air was even colder than before.

Belatedly, Alastar realized that what he had thought to be mist was actually tiny ice particles. "The first sign of winter."

"It's too soon for winter here."

"But it's already snowed in Rivages?"

"It has, according to Zaeryl."

When they reached the door to the cottage, Alyna turned. "Thank you again. I did enjoy the morning."

"So did I."

Alyna smiled warmly, then turned and entered the dwelling.

Alastar looked at the closed door for several moments, then continued northward toward the residence. The air seemed even colder.

He spent the afternoon checking his notes and maps, and, after that, even trying to figure out what he might say to Ryen—assuming he talked to the rex any time soon—and began to develop a series of plans for what he and the imagers could do.

Finally, it was time for the evening services. As was his custom, he took a position near the front but against the wall, standing, as all did, except for the truly infirm, for whom there were benches. From there, he could observe what maitres attended. Student imagers were expected to attend, unless ill.

Iskhar's homily was one of his less inspiring, dealing with the giving of gifts and how doing so could be a form of Naming. Alastar saw the validity of the point, but the presentation left something to be desired. After the service, Alastar waited until the anomen was almost empty before approaching Iskhar.

"You have that look, Maitre," said the chorister humorously.

"I do indeed. If you are so inclined, I would like you to think about giving a particular homily. You may have even given one like it in the past, since I understand that Maitre Fhaen and I shared a certain concern. This past week it became obvious—again—that too many students are more interested in attaining a higher rank, being a tertius or a junior maitre than in obtaining the skills that merit the appellation. Maitre Akoryt rightly called the arrogation of position over accomplishment another form of Naming."

Iskhar raised his eyebrows. "Is this because of the matter with Gherard?"

"It is. I met with him before he attempted his ill-fated imaging, and he was far more concerned about why he wasn't a third than he was about improving his skills as an imager."

The chorister nodded. "That has often been a problem. I have mentioned that in the past, but not recently."

"If you could address it once more, before long, I would appreciate it."

"I can do that."

"Thank you."

When Alastar returned to his residence, through air cold enough that his breath was visible, the rooms felt emptier than usual. He knew he wouldn't be able to sleep, not immediately. So he went into the study and took out the second volume of Chorister Gauswn's journals and began to read.

After almost another hundred pages, when his eyes were blurring, and he was about to close the volume and head up to his bedchamber, he came across another few lines.

On Jeudi evening Moriana and I had dinner at the Maitre's house, and she sat across from Lady Vaelora. During the main course, a superb fowl dish with alternating slices of dark meat and cheese with an orange glaze, a dish from Khel, Moriana mentioned that there were times when she wished she had the vaunted Pharsi talent of farsight. Lady Vaelora raised her eyebrows, but did not reply immediately. Moriana said it would be useful in avoiding danger. To that, Vaelora said quietly that the gift never allowed that; it only allowed one to prepare, if one could even determine what that danger might be, or if it happened even to be a danger. With those words, she smiled. So did the Maitre, knowingly, but neither would say more . . .

Alastar frowned. He remembered reading something about Vaelora being more than just the sister of Rex Regis, but, for a moment, he didn't recall where. Then he realized that it had been an earlier entry in Gauswn's journals, where the chorister had called her an Eleni or something like that and said she was more than an imager.

More than an imager? He shook his head. *You've read enough.* After marking his place and closing the volume, he imaged out the lamp and made his way to the stairs, thinking about what Alyna had said earlier about Vaelora . . . that there were no tales about her, either, even from her daughters.

But why? He wondered if he would ever find out. Then he yawned as he started up the stairs.

21

By Lundi morning Alastar had decided to accompany the imagers to begin actual imaging of Ryen's new avenue. Also, rather than make an immediate decision about new or different duties for Desyrk, he included the Maitre D'Structure in the work group to see what happened and how Desyrk reacted. He then canceled the instructionals for those imagers he'd picked for the road work—Cyran, Desyrk, Alyna, Shaelyt, Petros, Khaelis, and Narryn. That didn't include the thirds accompanying Cyran. Alastar didn't like being away from the Collegium with so much undecided, but he left word with Dareyn to send a messenger if anything happened and to send all messages to him immediately. He still worried as he rode across the Bridge of Desires beside Cyran.

"How do you want to handle people if they try to stop the imaging?" asked Cyran.

"Use shields. Anchor them to your saddle, and then move forward slowly. That should push them away."

"What if they use weapons?"

"Still use shields and truncheons, if they have to. Sabres as a last resort. If someone gets really unruly, then confine them in shields until they can be tied up—that's what the rope I had you bring is for—"

"I thought that might be the reason."

". . . and then we'll need to turn them over to the patrollers." Alastar belatedly recalled that he had not seen a single patroller when he'd been working with the imagers on the streets, except for the first sewer repair. "Have you seen any when Alyna was surveying?"

"Not a single one. It could be that they think there won't be trouble around us."

Alastar wasn't so sure. From what he'd seen, city patrollers were not all that they could be and had a tendency to avoid areas where there was a likelihood of great violence while maintaining the peace in areas where the effort was less. That wasn't surprising, since they were essentially paid by the factors' council, and the factors liked order around their homes and factorages, not that such areas were prone to either excessive crime or violence.

When Alastar did not reply, Cyran laughed. "No offense to you, but I hope I'm right."

"So do I."

Later, as Alastar and the imager work party turned off the West River Road and rode away from the river along the Boulevard D'Ouest, he could see that the streets were still damp from the intermittent rains. The air held a damp and bitter edge, but that would have been worse if there had been any wind. They reached the lane of the apothecaries just after seventh glass.

Once there, Alastar gathered the imagers. "We'll begin by removing the first three shops on each side of the lane starting from the corner and working east. Next we'll place the curbs. After that, we'll image the sewer ditches and covers in place, followed by the drains just inside the curbs . . . then the paving stones, with the sidewalks for the last. Just doing the entry to the new avenue will likely take all day . . . if not longer. We won't do anything until Maitre Alyna has marked out the new curb and entry lanes." Alastar turned to Cyran. "You and the thirds need to make certain the shops are empty. If they're not, tell them they have a glass to carry out everything. After that, they'll lose anything that's left there."

"I'd wager most of them haven't moved anything."

"That's their problem. They've been given ample

warning." Alastar had to admit that he was getting tired of everyone's problems. Ryen had problems. The army had problems. The High Holders had problems. The factors had problems. The apothecaries had problems . . . and where they lived and worked was a stenchpit. Most likely the guilds had problems. And, of course, the Collegium had problems. *You're not being fair.* He knew he wasn't, but no matter what he tried to do to improve matters, no one was happy. In fact, most of those involved just got angry and angrier.

Alastar remained mounted, with Neiryn mounted beside him, and watched as Cyran, Akkard, and Glaesyn dismounted, leaving their mounts in the hands of Shaelyt and Petros. Then he turned to Alyna. "How do you plan to proceed?"

"We'll measure with the chain, and then mark out the curb with a chalk line," said Alyna. "When that's done, we'll measure and chalk out where the sewer ditches will go. Then the lines from the drains to the sewers."

Alastar smiled. "You'd better get started. Neiryn can hold your mount."

After dismounting, Alyna handed the gelding's reins to Neiryn, then unstrapped the surveyor's staff and other equipment. Once she had everything assembled, she checked several sheets of paper, folded them, and slipped them into her heavy gray jacket. She walked toward the narrow lane, where she set up the staff.

Alastar glanced across the lane to where stood the same three men who had approached him during the initial surveying—an old and short man, the brown-bearded man younger than Alastar, and a burly bald man with a gray mustache and square beard. Before long several others joined the group, then a few more.

Alyna chalked a line down the middle of the lane, extending it from a point even with the curbs of the ring road eastward into the lane some thirty yards into the lane. Then she began to measure the distance from the chalk line to the north, and, without looking at Alastar, continued laying down the measuring chain and chalking its course on the stone.

Alastar noticed that the ring road curbs appeared as though they had been but recently laid, although they supposedly dated to the time of Rex Regis.

Before long, the group on the south corner of the lane and the ring road had grown to almost a score of men, and Alastar still didn't see Cyran and the two thirds. *You'd better stop this before it gets ugly . . . or uglier.* He turned in the saddle. "Neiryn, stay here and watch Maitre Alyna. She's too busy to be aware of anything unforeseen."

"Yes, sir."

Alastar turned the gray and rode across the end of the lane, reining up just short of the group standing there.

The burly bald man with a gray mustache and square beard, Amarr, as Alastar recalled, stepped forward. "Master imager, this is wrong. You're coming in here and taking everything we have."

"Rex Ryen has offered compensation," said Alastar.

"Rex Dafou . . . mad as spooked coney," called someone from the rear of the group.

". . . about as much sense . . ." muttered someone else.

"I know it's not as much as you'd like," Alastar said loudly, "but the rex didn't have to offer anything. Not to build a new road."

"He didn't have to take our shops," declared the oldest and shortest of the original three.

"You're going to tear down our shops . . . just like that?"

"You'll have to move now," Alastar said firmly, knowing that he couldn't let the anger turn into action against him or the other imagers.

"You can kill us," stated the young brown-bearded man. "That's what it'll take to move me." He looked around. "Don't know about the rest of you. Might as well take a stand, rather than lose everything we've got."

Alastar extended shields a yard before his mount and two yards on a side, linked to his saddle, then eased the gelding more to the left before moving forward. The shields pressed against the men, forcing them to move back and south along the sidewalk and the edge of the ring road.

". . . imager bastards . . ."

At that instant, the brown-bearded man turned and ran back and then around the unseen shields, well into the ring road, narrowly escaping being hit by a wagon stacked with barrels, then sprinted in an arc back toward Alyna. As he ran, he drew a long knife or short sword.

She stood there, watching as if calculating, then nodded. Abruptly, her attacker pitched forward, slamming facedown on the paving stones, the blade skittering from his hand across the road. Surprisingly, at least to Alastar, the man staggered to his feet and drew another blade, shorter, clearly a knife, but only took one step before Neiryn's truncheon cracked into his skull. He pitched forward and did not move.

"Amarr!" Alastar called, reining the gelding in. "You—just you—can go drag your friend away. The rest of you back off."

The burly Amarr looked at Alastar, then circled around him and the gelding and made his way to the fallen apothecary. "Come on, Jaimyt . . ." Suddenly, Amarr looked up from the inert form. "He's dead! You imagers killed him."

"No," replied Alastar. "He ignored the commands of the rex, and he attacked an imager carrying out those orders. He tried twice. No one gets a second chance at attacking an imager. Now drag him away."

Instead, the burly man lifted the corpse over his shoulder and walked south on the ring road, toward the next alley. The rest followed, many looking back over their shoulders.

Neiryn eased his mount up beside Alastar. "I'm sorry, sir. I know you said to be careful. I didn't think I hit him that hard."

"You might not have. Hitting his head hard on the pavement twice might have done the same thing. You did what you were told to do, and that was to protect Maitre Alyna while she was working." Alastar offered what he hoped was an understanding expression. "Just keep doing your duty."

"Yes, sir."

As Neiryn rode back closer to Alyna, Alastar kept looking to see if any of the earlier group returned. The lane remained empty, and he could see no one but imagers at the entry to the lane. Alyna had returned to marking where the curbs would run, although Alastar knew she could only chalk until she reached the wall of the first shop that needed to be removed.

Alyna had clearly used shields set well away from her to trip the attacker. That showed far more ability than a Maitre D'Aspect. The way she'd defended herself had also been designed to make it seem as though her attacker had merely tripped. Alastar wondered about that, especially given her abilities.

Cyran and the two thirds emerged from the third shop on the south side of the lane and walked slowly toward Alastar and the other imagers.

"Four of the shops are empty—both of those on the corner. The second one on the north side seems almost abandoned. It didn't look to be a working apothecary. The last of the three on the south side hasn't been emptied, but there's no one inside."

Alastar nodded. "We'll take them down one at a time." He gestured for the imager work party, except for Alyna, to ride closer to him, then began to explain. "We'll start by removing the ground for the approach, then the first shops on each side. I'll begin the building removal with the first shop on the south side so that you can see how I'd like you to proceed . . ." As he explained, he studied the faces of the imagers. Desyrk avoided looking at him directly, but seemed to be paying attention.

Less than a quint later, Alyna chalked the curb lines to the point where they stopped at the walls of the first shops. Then she carried her equipment back to her mount and looked to Alastar, as if to suggest that until the shops were removed, she could do no more.

Alastar wasn't certain exactly how much he could do, or what might have been left in the shop. For that reason, among others, he had all the imagers move well north on the ring road before he began to concentrate on the shop on the south side of the lane, concentrating on removing it, and adding the stone curbing along the line chalked out by Alyna, with a paved sidewalk behind the curb, even though he'd thought that would come later.

Dust rose, then vanished, leaving a cleared and open space, with the curb in place and open ground where the angled approach to the avenue would be. The first thing that Alastar noticed was that the rear of the building on the other side of the alley to the south was decrepit and ugly. Almost without thinking, he imaged a neat stone facade . . . and his head felt like he'd been hit with a club.

For several moments, Alastar just sat in the saddle, his head throbbing as he saw little besides flashes of light before his eyes.

"Maitre?"

For an instant, the word didn't mean anything. Then he looked through the flashes to make out Alyna reaching up from where she stood beside the gelding and extending a water bottle. He wondered how she had gotten so close.

"It's dark lager. It should help."

He didn't argue. He took the water bottle, uncorked it carefully, and drank slowly. Within moments, the worst of the light flashes had subsided, although his head still ached. He looked down at Alyna. "Thank you."

"Keep it. I brought two."

"That merits double thanks." After another swallow of the lager—more than welcome—Alastar gestured to Desyrk. "Remove what you can of the building on the north corner."

Desyrk nodded, but did not speak. He eased his mount closer to the building, closer than Alastar would have wished.

Because he needs to see more clearly?

More dust and grit rose from the north corner. When it cleared, Alastar saw that Desyrk had managed to remove the west and south walls and perhaps a third of the roof and the space behind them. As he continued to watch, more of the roof collapsed, as well as part of the floor and the interior supports, leaving rubble partly on the cleared area and behind it.

"See what you can add, Khaelis," Alastar said.

In less than half a quint, between Khaelis, Shaelyt, and Petros, the ground where the first shop on the north side had been was clear.

"Maitre Alyna . . . if you would chalk in where the sewer ditches should be . . ." Alastar paused. "Chalk a square a yard on a side where they begin. That way, if necessary they can be linked to another set of drains."

When Alastar finished speaking, Cyran gestured to the west. A chateau guard rode along the ring road, then headed toward the imagers, as if he had not expected to see them. Tertius Coermyd moved to intercept him. Alastar watched as the guard halted and said something, and then as Coermyd turned his mount and rode toward him, reining up a few yards away.

"Maitre, sir . . . the guard says that Rex Ryen wants you at the Chateau D'Rex immediately."

"Tell him you and I will be with him in a few moments. Cyran, you're in charge, but Maitre Alyna will direct the imaging until I return. If the rex requires me for an extended period, do not proceed farther than creating the avenue to the point even with the end of the shops to be removed. If the imagers become too tired, you can stop work at any time."

"Yes, Maitre." Cyran nodded.

Alastar took another swallow from Alyna's water bottle, then turned his mount toward the chateau guard.

Less than a quint later, he was walking into the chateau study he had seen all too often over the past two weeks.

"Why can't you be here this quickly all the time?" demanded Ryen from where he sat behind the desk piled with papers, some of which Alastar thought had not been moved since his last visit.

"Because I'm usually not working with imagers just off the ring road. Your courier happened to see the imagers and came to see if I happened to be with them. I was."

"Oh . . . the new avenue. It's about time." Ryen's voice was dismissive, but he looked directly at Alastar with an icy glare. "You're doing better on that, late as you are, than getting the High Council to stop opposing my tariffs. What do you have to say to that, Master Maitre?"

That I'm getting tired of your stubbornness and tantrums. "I'm working on it."

"Working on it? Do you call suggesting I might compromise working on it?" Ryen's voice increased in pitch and volume. "Why did you make such an idiotic Namer-blessed suggestion?"

"To see how they would respond."

"I frigging know how they'll respond! The same way they always have! By refusing!"

"I wanted to see if there was any possibility of you and the Council coming to an agreement."

"The only agreement I'll accept is what I told you, a copper on a half silver."

"They won't accept that."

"You had better make them see reason, Maitre. That's all I have to say."

"You're not willing to—"

"How many times have I told you? It's a copper on a half silver!" Ryen's voice rose to a high-pitched yell. "I'm not bickering like a tradesman. I'm the rex, and they will pay!"

"How many dead High Holders are you willing to accept?"

"However many it takes," replied Ryen, not quite shouting. "They've gotten away with trying to thwart me at every turn long enough."

"You expect the Collegium to take the blame for those deaths?"

"Why not? You've taken golds from every rex for nearly four hundred years." Ryen gestured toward the study door. "Go. I don't want to hear from you again until the High Holders agree to the increased tariffs and start submitting this year's payments." Ryen's voice turned low and hard. "If I don't have an agreement by Meredi at fourth glass of the afternoon, I'll assume you've taken their side and will act accordingly."

"Meredi?"

"You've had more than enough time. All the members of the High Council are in L'Excelsis or close by. I'm tired of your stalling and everyone thinking that they can do as they please. That includes you. Now . . . get out of here!"

Now what? Alastar thought about using imaging on Ryen right there, then decided against it. *There must be another way . . .*

"Don't even think about ignoring me, Maitre," Ryen

added after Alastar turned to leave the study. "You may escape my wrath, but your precious Collegium won't, no matter what happens. And if anything happens to me . . . you won't have a Collegium!"

No matter what happens . . . you won't have a Collegium?

"Make those high-handed bastards submit!"

Alastar waited until Ryen stopped shouting before he opened the door and stepped outside.

The guard posted outside kept looking straight ahead, as if ignoring both the Maitre and the rex.

Alastar walked resolutely toward the grand staircase, thinking. *If you don't get an agreement, the Collegium will be attacked, most likely with Demykalion's new cannon. If you resolve the problem by removing Ryen, the same thing will happen. And if you start removing High Holders, who knows what will happen?*

"You're rather pensive this morning."

The low female voice told Alastar that the woman who stepped out of the side chamber, quickly closing the door behind her, was Lady Asarya. While she wore a tunic and trousers, both were black with silver trim and tailored to show a very feminine figure. Her boots were black as well, and a silver scarf was loosely draped around her neck.

"I am at times. So are you, I imagine."

"What was His Mightiness screaming about now?"

"He's less than pleased with the High Holders' refusal to accept his tariff proposal, as I'm certain you know."

"No, Maitre, I do not know. We talk—I would not call it conversation—as little as possible and as seldom as practical . . . as I'm most certain you know."

Alastar still had his doubts about her lack of knowledge, but he nodded. "I did know that you have had separate quarters for some years."

"Separate lives, except when required. Just how unreasonable is he being?"

"He's doubtless correct about the problem. As for the solution . . ." Alastar shrugged. "The Collegium and I will do what we can to see if we can persuade the High Holders of the seriousness of the problem."

"Do you think that is even possible?"

"Everything is possible until it is not," he replied with an ironic smile.

At that moment, the door to the chamber opened, and Ryentar stepped out and joined his mother. "I wondered who might be here that so engaged you." The younger heir wore a dark blue tunic and gray trousers.

The words alone told Alastar that both Asarya's initial approach and Ryentar's "curiosity" were planned.

"Your father apparently persists in his delusion that he can bring the High Holders to his way of thinking by the volume of his voice." Asarya's words were quietly sardonic.

Alastar nodded. "He was quite vocal."

"He often is," she replied. "Has he attempted to browbeat you into bringing some form of imaging against the High Council?"

"He believes they're unreasonable."

"What do you think, Maitre?" asked Ryentar, offering a serious but friendly expression. "Are they?"

"From their point of view, they believe they are reasonable. And they are, that is, if one believes that they should determine tariff levels and not the rex, which they do."

"And how will you resolve this?" asked Asarya.

"By attempting to develop a compromise acceptable to both."

"That will be most interesting," observed Asarya. "Neither knows the meaning of the word."

"Life is often interesting, Lady."

"Since you are determined to reveal little, Maitre, we will not delay you longer. Perhaps in the future, when this contretemps is resolved, we might share refreshments."

"She has a delightful dark lager," interjected Ryentar, "although I prefer the light myself."

"I appreciate your interest and kindness, Lady, Lord Ryentar." Alastar inclined his head.

"Interested I am. Kind? That depends. Isn't that true of all of us?" Asarya's smile was enigmatic. "Good day, Maitre."

"Good day."

Alastar made his way down the grand staircase, musing about exactly what Asarya had in mind, but suspecting whatever it was might not be in his interest . . . or the Collegium's.

In half a quint, he was reining up at what would be the beginning of the new avenue, but even before the gelding came to a stop, Cyran rode over to join him, a grim look on his face.

"Maitre, we have a problem."

The way the Maitre D'Esprit said "Maitre" suggested to Alastar that it wasn't a small problem. "What is it now?"

"Desyrk . . . somewhere in the dust that rose when we took down the last of the shops . . . When it cleared, he was gone. He had to have used a concealment, but the dust covered the fact that he had vanished."

"That's my fault." Alastar couldn't say he was surprised. He'd actually half-expected it, and he'd been watching Desyrk. He just hadn't thought he would be summoned by Ryen so early in the day, and he'd forgotten to tell Cyran his suspicions about Desyrk. "I thought he might try, but I neglected to tell you before I left to see His Mightiness. That was why I had him image first. He could have done more than he did, but he was holding back. That was why."

"I wish I'd known."

"It's probably better you didn't. You'd likely have had to kill him to stop him, and only the Maitre has that power . . . and even then, if I'd done it, I'd have faced a hearing to determine if the act was justified." Alastar took a deep breath, then pulled out the bottle of lager, uncorked it, and drank, taking a deep swallow. After slipping the bottle back into his saddlebag, he said, "Desyrk's actually a smaller problem than the one our dear Rex Ryen has created."

Cyran raised his eyebrows.

"We have until Meredi, by the fourth glass of the afternoon, to reverse the decision of the High Council or face Ryen's wrath."

"What does that mean? Really?" asked Cyran. "I mean . . ."

"He'll likely cut off all golds to the Collegium. He's already cut what he sends in half. We might be able to image some things . . . but I don't know that I'd want to eat anything I imaged. Nor would that be good for the horses. He could blockade Imagisle. With concealments, we could get out, but bringing in supplies would be difficult. He could do worse than that. Remember Marshal Demykalon doesn't like imagers."

"You really think he'd send the army against us?"

"Who knows?" lied Alastar. "He is Rex Dafou, remember?"

"He'd be . . ."

"Mad? Exactly. But we know he already is. Can you finish up the work here, just to the end of where you removed the shops?"

"I don't know. Some of the imagers are getting tired."

"Do what you can. Push them some. Just not enough to drop them."

"I can do some imaging as well," added Alyna.

Alastar was surprised, because he hadn't seen her approach, but then she'd walked over to join them, and they were mounted. "As much as you can, but not quite as much, comparatively, as I tried." He kept his tone wry, ignoring the puzzled expression on Cyran's face. "Also, once you get back to the Collegium, would you stop by my study? It will only take a few moments."

She nodded. "I can do that."

"Thank you." Alastar looked to Cyran. "Do what you can. Don't leave a mess."

"You don't think—"

"Who knows?" repeated Alastar. "It may be better this way, in one fashion or another." He smiled ironically. "I'll see you both back at the Collegium." He turned the gelding and gestured for Coermyd to join him as he began the ride back to Imagisle.

When he finally returned to the Collegium, he left the gelding with the third and hurried to his study. Once there, he immediately sent for Akoryt, then turned to Dareyn. "Send a third or someone you trust immediately to Maitre Desyrk's cottage. I need to know if he's there . . . and if his family is as well."

"Sir?"

"I'll explain later. Please just do it. Let me know what you find out as soon as you can."

After Dareyn left, Alastar took a quick look at his maps, then glanced at the master ledger before shaking his head. *Running short of golds is the least of our immediate problems.*

Akoryt arrived in half a quint, carrying a leather folder as he entered the study and seated himself with a worried expression. "Sir, you sent for me?"

"We're facing a possible attack on the Collegium." Alastar waited for the impact of his words to sink in.

"I don't understand, sir."

Alastar thought Akoryt did, but was asking for an explanation. "It's simple. If I don't get the High Council, before Meredi evening, to agree to Rex Ryen's proposed new tariffs and to agree to pay this year's tariffs, then we face the wrath of the rex. If I do what is necessary to obtain that, we'll likely face other forms of attack."

"By Meredi evening?"

"By fourth glass. The rex has never been especially patient," Alastar said dryly. "I'd also like you to use older seconds and thirds to do some scouting, especially areas within a mille or so of Imagisle, and I'll need a constant watch over army headquarters to see if Marshal Demykalon moves troops or wagons anywhere. He might act against the Collegium or individual High Holders. Or he might not act at all. We need to know which of those possibilities takes place—or doesn't—on a continuing basis until this tariff mess is resolved. Oh . . . to complicate matters, it appears that Desyrk vanished from the imaging party working on the new avenue while I was meeting with the rex."

"Desyrk . . . he can be . . . overly proud," ventured the red-haired maitre.

"Can't we all? But there's a difference between excessively proud and stupidly proud. Do you have that plan for moving students and staff completed?"

"A draft of it, sir." Akoryt opened the folder and extended several sheets. "I brought the two in case that was what you wanted."

Alastar took them. "Excellent."

Akoryt handed over three more sheets. "The assessment of imaging abilities is problematical for some of the seconds and thirds. My best guess, really."

"Your guesses are far more likely to be accurate than mine. You've been here far longer and worked with more of the students. Do you have copies of these?"

"Yes, sir."

"Then I'll keep these. I'll go over the movement plan tonight. If I have any suggestions, I'll let you know. There will be a meeting of the senior imagers at seventh glass tomorrow. Bring your copies with you. Do you have any questions?"

"How likely is it that we'll be attacked?"

"I can't say, but it's likely enough that we need to

expect it will happen. We can't afford not to be prepared. Anything else?"

"No, sir."

"Then I'll see you in the morning."

No sooner had Akoryt left the study than Dareyn hurried in. "Sir, Maitre Desyrk's cottage is empty. I mean, the furnishings are there, but his wife and their son are gone. So are most of their personal things."

Alastar nodded. "That's about what I thought. Desyrk raised a concealment and sneaked away from the work party this morning. Oh . . . tell Arhgen that he's not to pay Maitre Desyrk's stipend. Better yet, write a letter to him as bursar for my signature saying that." Alastar didn't think Desyrk would attempt to collect, but it was clear that Desyrk might try anything. Besides, some things needed to be in ink.

"Yes, sir."

Alastar went back to work, outlining the other preparations necessary to deal with possible contingencies.

Slightly past second glass, Cyran walked into Alastar's study.

"How did the avenue work go?"

"We finished what you wanted." Cyran offered a crooked smile. "It wouldn't have happened without Alyna. She's got the strength of a Maitre D'Structure. Maybe more."

"Why isn't she one, then?"

Cyran shifted his weight from one foot to the other. "I don't know . . . not exactly. Maitre Fhaen . . . I overheard him say he wasn't about to have another Aurelya in the Collegium."

"Aurelya, the woman who was the senior imager? I take it Fhaen wasn't happy with her?"

"He couldn't stand the thought that she was as strong an imager as he was, well . . . until she died, suddenlike. That's what I heard."

Alastar had always gotten a cold feeling when he heard about someone dying suddenly around imagers. He did this time as well. "I see. I'm afraid I do." *And I don't like what I see . . . Again.* Abruptly, he wondered if the feelings against strong female imagers might have been why both Rex Kharst and Rex Regis had wanted Khel under their rule . . . and why Vaelora apparently never revealed the extent of her abilities. *It's suggestive, but you'll never know.*

"Would you recommend Alyna for Maitre D'Structure?"

"Yes, sir. So would Akoryt and Taryn. They never understood why she wasn't."

"Then I'll tell her when she comes in."

Cyran grinned. "She came with me. She's waiting in the anteroom."

"Don't you tell her. There are Namer-few good things I'm getting to tell anyone these days."

Cyran's grin faded. "What about tomorrow?"

"I'd like to plan for a half day of work on the avenue, but we'll be having a senior imagers' meeting at seventh glass. That's another reason why I wanted to know about Alyna."

"She'll do well. She might be as good as me before long, now that . . ."

"Now that she doesn't have to conceal her abilities?"

"Something like that."

"If there's nothing else, I'll see you in the morning. You might think of anything that would help defend Imagisle."

"Against what?"

"Anything that the army, the rex, the High Holders, or the factors might decide to do once they learn that Ryen won't support us."

"You're not asking a lot." Cyran made a wry face.

"It's what we face. Until tomorrow."

As Cyran left, Alyna entered the study, gracefully closing the door behind herself.

Alastar waited until she sat down before he spoke. "I'd like to thank you again for the very welcome and necessary dark lager this morning. How did you know that it would help?"

Alyna smiled. "I learned about it a long time ago, before I was even aware I was an imager. Zaeryl used to carry it with him whenever he rode. He said it was liquid bread, except better. That made sense to me. Imaging takes strength, and I never did my best when it had been a long time since I ate. So I made a habit of carrying it." She shrugged. "That's all."

"I doubt that, but I won't press. I'm grateful, and I think I'll follow your example from here on out. Now, there's one other matter . . ." He smiled. "You're to attend the senior imagers' meeting tomorrow at seventh glass."

"I'm not a Maitre D'Structure."

"You are now."

"How can you say that? You can as Maitre, but . . ."

Those words were the first Alastar had heard from Alyna that showed even the slightest hint of being disconcerted. He couldn't help but smile slightly. "I trust Cyran. He is a Maitre D'Esprit. He told me that what you did today was at least Maitre D'Structure level, and I saw what you did with that hidden shield at a distance. You've certainly been at the Collegium long enough, and acted responsibly the whole time. And the Collegium needs your intelligence, as well as your imaging abilities, recognized among the senior maitres."

"Much of it is technique."

"The result counts, whether it's great ability with less technique or great technique without quite so much raw imaging power." Alastar had no doubt about her having great ability, but because that feeling was based on his sense of what she could do, rather than on long direct observation, he did not say more about her ability. Instead, he smiled again. "I will see you in the morning, and I would welcome any additional thoughts you might have about the situation involving the rex and the High Holders."

"I'll have to think about that. Is there anything else?"

"Not right now. I won't keep you." Once more he regretted his wording, but simply added, "If there's anything else, I'll let you know tomorrow."

"I'll be here."

"Good." His eyes did not leave her as she left. After the door closed, he went back to work.

When he went to dinner at the dining hall, the only maitres there, as usual, were single Maitres D'Aspect—Shaelyt, Warryk, and Khaelis. Neither Tiranya nor Alyna was there, but they were there only infrequently. Alastar sat at the masters' table with Taryn, who was the duty maitre, leaving several seats between them and the other three.

Taryn set down his beaker of pale lager. "Maitre, I understand that someone tried to attack Maitre Alyna."

"One of the apothecaries. She used shields, as I instructed, to drop him to the pavement. He tried another attack, and Tertius Neiryn used a truncheon on him. He hit the stones again. He didn't get up."

"The word is that Desyrk deserted."

"That's right. He used the dust raised by the removal of some shops to raise a concealment and sneak off. Do you have any idea where he might be?"

"He's got a brother who's a senior officer at headquarters. He's a subcommander, I think. I don't think he's got any other family, anymore. His aunt died last year, he said."

"Do you know if he and his brother were close?" Alastar knew that Desyrk and his brother talked some, because Desyrk had mentioned it in one of the senior imagers' meeting.

"They talked. That's all I know."

"Why do you think he left?"

Taryn snorted. "He was one of Maitre Fhaen's favorites. When you came, that stopped. Then you disciplined him. That should have happened years ago, but Fhaen liked him."

It would have been nice if someone had mentioned it to you. But that was often the way it was, Alastar knew, finding out something too late, because no one wanted to say anything bad even when asked or because they thought it didn't really matter.

"Maitre Alyna has all the qualifications to be a Maitre D'Structure. Why wasn't she made one?"

"Most likely because she wouldn't sleep with Fhaen. With her brother being a High Holder, he really couldn't make her, and she had better shields than Fhaen, but he could say she wasn't qualified as Maitre D'Structure." Taryn laughed softly. "Could be that she had to have those shields." He paused. "Are you going to . . ."

"I already have. It will be announced at the senior imagers' meeting tomorrow at seventh glass. I'd appreciate your not saying anything until then."

"I won't." Taryn smiled. "It's not as though I'll see Cyran, Akoryt, or Obsolym much before then anyway. They stay away from here after work."

The two talked over a dinner consisting of a casserole that likely combined items left over from previous meals, but Alastar had to admit that Shabrena was good with sauces. He didn't learn anything else new during the remainder of the meal, but did get a better appreciation of the comparatively young Maitre D'Structure.

After leaving the dining hall, he walked along the green to the Maitre's residence through a cold mist that came off the river. Once in his private study, he considered the costs of the various options open to him in dealing with Ryen's ultimatum. In the end, though, it appeared that which ones were most feasible would depend on what happened on Mardi . . . and Meredi.

Tired as he was, Alastar wasn't sleepy, and in hopes of either finding out more about Quaeryt or reading himself into a dozing state, he opened the journal at the point he had bookmarked and began to read. He immediately came to a startling section.

> . . . Maitre Quaeryt preached the most eloquent, moving, and thoughtful homilies I have ever heard in my blessedly long life. Yet on many occasions, it was clear that he was less than comfortable doing so. It was not until he was much older that I dared to ask him why. His answer was simple. I remember the words clearly. "Gauswn, you believe in the Nameless. I can only claim to believe in the major principles of the Nameless." While he never said that he doubted the existence of the Nameless, his words and actions suggest that he did. When I look back on his early homilies, or those few he has delivered at the Collegium, I realized that he never spoke directly about belief in the Nameless, but only about adherence to behaviors in accord with the Nameless. Why did he give homilies if he did not believe? I can only surmise that he believed in the principles about which he preached, regardless of whether the Nameless existed or not.

A chorister of sorts . . . who did not believe?

That thought kept coming back to Alastar through almost another glass of reading, perhaps because the next fifty pages were exceedingly boring, with mention after mention of Maitre Quaeryt, all of which were routine and unrevealing. He finally went up to bed and managed to drop off sometime close to midnight, worrying about Ryen and the High Holders . . . and exactly what treachery Desyrk had in mind, because he had no doubts that the errant Maitre D'Structure had something in mind that would not bode well for either Alastar or the Collegium.

22

The first thing Alastar did on Mardi morning was to dispatch a messenger to the Chateau D'Council, requesting yet another meeting with High Holder Guerdyn, and one to Factor Elthyrd requesting a similar meeting early on Meredi morning. Then, at just before seventh glass, Alastar escorted Alyna into the conference room that held the other senior imagers—Cyran, Obsolym, Akoryt, and Taryn.

"I'd like you all to welcome Maitre D'Structure Alyna."

"It's about time," said Akoryt warmly.

Alastar noted that even Obsolym nodded, and not grudgingly.

Alastar sat at the head of the long table, another reminder that there had likely once been far more senior imagers, and cleared his throat before beginning. "As I've mentioned to some of you, Rex Ryen, our dearly beloved ruler, has declared that if I fail to change the decision of the High Council of the High Holders by fourth glass tomorrow afternoon, he will regard the Collegium as having sided with the High Holders, and we will feel his wrath. You may know that Maitre Desyrk has abandoned the Collegium for reasons he has not made known to me, or, so far as I know, to anyone. Did he say anything to any of you?" He looked down the table.

Obsolym moistened his lips, then said, "Several days ago, he said that he felt you had no understanding of the Collegium and that he hoped he was not here when that became apparent."

"Did he say anything else?"

"No. Nothing that I heard."

"He obviously planned his departure in advance because his family is also gone. Does anyone know if his wife has relatives in L'Excelsis?"

"She was a major's daughter. That's all I know," said Taryn.

The others shook their heads.

"Now . . . we need to get back to the tariff problem," declared Alastar. "For better or worse, Rex Ryen is known to be a man of his word. That suggests that we most likely won't see anything happen until at least fourth glass tomorrow. Maitre Akoryt has been sending out trusted seconds and thirds as scouts to see if Marshal Demykalon might be moving army companies anywhere in preparation for attacks on either any High Holders or on the Collegium." Alastar turned to Akoryt. "Have you heard anything?"

"Late yesterday afternoon, one of the thirds saw four wagons headed out from army headquarters. They were heavy. They took four dray horses for each. A mounted squad went with them. What was in them was covered with canvas. The third followed them. He used a partial concealment." Akoryt looked apologetic. "That was the best he could do."

"A blurring shield?"

Akoryt nodded. "He didn't want to go too far, but he followed them far enough that it was unlikely they were going toward Imagisle. They were headed out the Boulevard D'Este, and at the Plaza D'Nord, they didn't turn on Saenhelyn. They took the pike away from L'Excelsis."

Toward Nacryon's chateau or Guerdyn's . . . or both? "Did they see anything else?"

"No, sir. Not so far. I had them all report back by seventh glass, though. There aren't that many thirds, even older seconds that I can use."

"We may want to post one near the Nord Bridge and the West River Road."

"I have a second there now, sir."

"Good. Change them every three glasses, and have someone there until close to ninth glass tonight."

Akoryt nodded.

"Maitre Akoryt has also developed a plan for moving everyone on Imagisle to the north park, if the marshal begins an attack with cannon or if it appears likely. I've had copies made for each of you . . ."

"There's no shelter there . . ." began Obsolym, before breaking off his words. "Do you really think Demykalon would carry out orders against us?"

"From my one meeting with him, I suspect he would enjoy doing so."

"He's also not fond of High Holders," added Alyna, "according to a letter I recently received from my older brother."

"High Holder Zaerlyn?" asked Cyran.

Alyna nodded.

"Perhaps I'm missing something," said Obsolym, "but couldn't the Collegium work out something with the High Holders and require the rex to accept it?"

"Anything the High Holders would accept without our using force," replied Alastar, "wouldn't raise tariff payments enough to support the Collegium without cutting the amount that goes to the High Command. The marshal doesn't like imagers anyway . . ."

"I see. That . . . does pose a problem."

"What about the avenue work?" asked Cyran.

"I'd like you and Maitre Alyna to take a smaller party and extend the new avenue another fifty yards, a hundred if you can, but not to work much past ninth glass, noon at the latest." Alastar saw Obsolym's brief puzzled frown and added, "Should we be attacked, it's important that we not be seen to have given any provocation to anyone, and our continuing work on the avenue is evidence of our good faith. For the same reason, I'll be making another call on High Holder Guerdyn before Ryen's deadline, hopefully today." Alastar turned to Akoryt again. "You estimated that, besides the senior imagers, we have roughly thirty imagers capable of some level of imaging combat at a distance of fifty yards or less. How many of them could image iron darts or the equivalent across the river?"

"No more than fifteen at most. That's a guess."

"Why that distance?" asked Obsolym.

"Because I would guess that, if Demykalon actually attacks, he'll attempt to use his cannon on the bridges, then use rifles against anyone trying to cross what bridges remain or any that we image into being. That will limit the number of imagers who will be useful to those who can image at a distance, maintain shields sufficient to withstand bullets, or who can hold a concealment while doing other imaging."

"Ryen and Demykalon could be bluffing," suggested Obsolym.

"They could be," admitted Alastar, "but that's another reason why we can't afford to act first. If they're not, we have to be able to react quickly."

"What did the Collegium do to deserve this?" asked Obsolym.

"Absolutely nothing," replied Alastar dryly. "Unfortunately, the Collegium has not exercised any visible power, nor has it recently, until the past few weeks, done any imaging of any noticeable benefit outside of Imagisle. We're no longer regarded as either helpful or something to be feared."

"But we're imagers . . ."

"It's been a long time since any imager has demonstrated openly great power. People forget quickly . . . or they believe that today's imagers don't have the power of the great ones of the past. In any event, we are where we are, and that's what I wanted all of you to know."

"What are you going to do now?" asked Obsolym.

"Go over preparations; talk over the avenue work with Cyran and Alyna; and then meet with High Holder Guerdyn as soon as I can."

"You said they won't accept any increase."

"That's what he says, but we have to try to change their minds without actually using force." *Until they do.* "In the meantime, I'd like you, Taryn, and Akoryt to try out the movement plans Akoryt has worked out. Change them if there's a problem. What's important is that if there is an attack, we need to get all those imagers and others who cannot fight away from the buildings and then to have an imager party at the Imagisle end of each bridge in case Demykalon does send troops across. I have my doubts that he will, but it's better to be prepared. Are there any questions?"

There were no further questions, and in moments, only Alastar, Cyran, and Alyna remained in the conference room.

"There's not much else besides what I said earlier," Alastar began, "except I want you to be careful and keep an eye out for anything or anyone who might be a danger."

"I'm not quite sure why—" said Cyran.

"Why we need to keep working on the avenue? First, it's good hard imaging that will strengthen those doing it. Second, we made a commitment. Third, even if it was Ryen's idea, it was a good one. Fourth, we need to be more visible all the time so that we don't get put in another position like this ever again. Fifth, we're showing we're working while they're arguing and maybe doing worse."

Cyran turned to Alyna. "You see why I usually don't argue with him."

"Good words can hide a bad idea," replied Alastar. "What's wrong with what I said? If you think so, let me know what."

"Will anyone really care?" asked Cyran.

"Most won't. Not right now. I'm thinking about what happens if we're successful. If we fail, it won't matter because there won't be a Collegium before long. If we're successful, we have to have everyone understand that we only do drastic things when we're threatened or endangered, and even then, we don't forget our obligations."

"Do you think they'll remember?"

"They will if we keep reminding them, quietly and persistently . . . and if every young imager is trained to understand that."

Cyran looked to Alyna. She nodded.

The Maitre D'Esprit grinned sardonically. "Then I guess we'd better start in on reminding them."

As soon as Alyna and Cyran left the conference room, Dareyn hurried over.

"You have a message from High Holder Guerdyn. He said to tell you that, although there's nothing to discuss, except the rex's acceptance of the Council's terms, he can spare a half glass at the first glass of the afternoon."

"Send back a messenger saying that I'll be there."

Once the messenger was off, Alastar took a walking tour of the east side of Imagisle, checking the width of the river as he did. Even so, he had time to work on other preparations, and then ride to the Council Chateau and arrive half a quint before first glass.

He had to wait until nearly a quint past the glass. That didn't surprise him in the slightest, since he doubted Guerdyn wanted to see him . . . and likely wanted to put a certain arrogant Maitre in his proper place.

When the footman finally escorted Alastar to the study, Guerdyn rose almost languidly from behind the desk and only walked to a point barely even with the wooden front. He wore black hose and a red and black doublet.

"Good afternoon," offered Alastar with a pleasantness he did not feel.

"Why are you even here? I did say that there was nothing to discuss . . . or didn't you get that part of the message?"

"I got it. That's one reason why I'm here. The Collegium is still attempting to find a middle ground."

"There is no middle ground, as you put it. The High Council will not accept any increase in tariffs. Neither will the High Holders. The ones who have to come to agree are the rex . . . and you, Maitre Alastar."

Alastar smiled coldly. "I don't think you understand, Guerdyn. Ryen is prepared to bring force against the High Holders if you do not accept his higher tariffs. He has new cannon and more than seven thousand troops here in L'Excelsis."

"And you will not stop him? How very kind of you to inform us."

"Why should we? The High Council certainly won't support the Collegium willingly, and there aren't enough golds in the Treasury to pay the army, the Collegium, and everything else that is required."

"Then all of you should require less." Guerdyn made a sound between a sniff and a snort. "You can bluff all you want, Alastar. We will not accept any increase."

Alastar pointed to the crystal vase on the side table. "Is that terribly valuable?"

"Not especially. It's Council property."

"Good." Alastar concentrated. Instantly, the vase vanished, and five crystal knives were buried in the marble of the table.

Guerdyn looked amused. "Parlor tricks."

"Look at your jacket."

Guerdyn looked down. A sixth dagger rested in a strap directly above his heart.

"Be careful," cautioned Alastar. "It's sharper than any blade you have. You might notice that the knives are buried in the marble tabletop. Marble is much harder than flesh."

"I have no doubt that you and other imagers could kill me. Then what? That won't change the minds of the others. You don't dare kill enough High Holders to change everyone's minds. None of you have the nerve. And if you did, all Solidar would turn against you."

Alastar remained silent. *He's half right.*

"You see? If you intended to kill me, you would have."

"Are you going to agree to an increase in tariffs?"

"Of course not. Why would we? Now that I've made that clear . . . again . . . either kill me, or I'll show you to the door."

"I can find my own way." Alastar paused. "Tariffs will be higher, and they will be paid."

"Words, Maitre. Words. Only deeds change what is."

Alastar smiled. "You're right about that, but you've forgotten one thing. Good day."

Guerdyn didn't say a word as Alastar left the study.

Cyran was waiting when Alastar returned to the administration building at two quints past second glass.

Alastar looked from Cyran to Dareyn. "Find Maitre Alyna and have her join us."

Then he motioned for Cyran to go into the study. "I'll be with you in a moment." Turning to Dareyn, he asked, "Have we heard from Factor Elthyrd?"

"He will see you at his factorage at eighth glass tomorrow morning. I have directions in case you haven't been there."

"Thank you. I haven't. I've always met with him at the factors' council building. Send Maitre Alyna in when she arrives."

Dareyn nodded.

"What happened?" asked Cyran after Alastar entered the study and seated himself behind the desk.

"What I expected, but I'll wait until Alyna's here before we get into that. How did the work on the avenue go?"

"We actually finished almost a hundred and fifty yards by ninth glass. It looks good. Very good. Alyna's a strong imager."

"I believe you suggested that. Did you see any patrollers or chateau guards?"

"Not a one."

"What about troopers? Did you see any, especially around the Chateau D'Rex?"

"I can't say that we did."

"Any large covered wagons?"

"No . . ."

"I suspect that's how Demykalon is moving cannon. Or something else equally disturbing."

"I still don't see how this makes sense."

"I'll tell you both in a moment . . ." Alastar looked up as the study door opened.

Alyna walked in. "I came as soon as I got word." Her steps were graceful but determined.

Alastar managed not to smile as he gestured to the chair beside Cyran. Once she was seated, he began. "Thank you. This won't take long. Not too long." He paused. "Everyone thinks of Ryen as Rex Dafou, the mad ruler. They're wrong, but it's not in our interest to correct them. Ryen is anything but mad. He's egotistical, short-tempered, highly irritating, and has a great number of other unpleasant traits. But he's not mad. He's been unable to get an increase in tariffs for years, but he's finally come up with a plan to get them."

"Why now? Why not earlier?"

"Because of Demykalon and me. Maitre Fhaen was likely ill much longer than he let on, and he simply would have refused any demand from Ryen to force the High Council to accept higher tariffs. Even Fhaen would have refused to kill High Holders to that end . . . and there was no way Ryen could force Marshal Ghalyn to move against the Collegium, not with Fhaen being a cousin of sorts."

"How did you know that?" asked Cyran.

"Fhaen told me. He said he could trust Ghalyn, but not to ever trust Demykalon. He wouldn't say why." Alastar looked to Alyna. "You wouldn't know, would you?"

"No. Zaeryl doesn't trust him either, though."

"The problem facing the Collegium is simple . . . and impossible. As I hinted this morning, if we act against the High Holders without provocation, before long no imager will be safe. If we don't act, then no imager will be safe from Ryen's wrath, not with Demykalon just wanting an excuse to strike at the Collegium."

"We might as well act, then," said Cyran.

Alastar shook his head. "The Collegium can survive Ryen's wrath, but we cannot survive if all the factors and High Holders are against us."

"He's right," said Alyna. "High Holders would understand and accept an attack in return. They might not like it, but they would come to accept it, especially if the attack were directed at individuals who created harm."

"So we have to wait until we're attacked? Students . . . staff . . . innocents . . ." Cyran shook his head.

"There are less than five hundred people on Imagisle," replied Alastar. "A few more than a hundred imagers, and maybe thirty-five to forty are good enough to inflict damage on attackers, and that's if they're close. There are fifteen hundred High Holders in Solidar, and Demykalon has something like seven thousand troopers just outside L'Excelsis, less than three milles away."

"Then why don't we remove Ryen? He's the problem."

Alastar shook his head. "The problem is that, while he flies into rages, and can be mad, intractable, stubborn, and stupid about some things, he's also right about the High Holders. Remove him now . . . and Lorien will be in a worse position . . . and so will we."

"Then . . . what do you propose?"

Alastar told them.

When Alastar finished, Cyran swallowed. Alyna nodded sadly.

"That could be a high price," Cyran finally said.

"It will be, but that way everyone pays, and that means we can survive. We can take some steps . . ." He went on to describe the precautions he had already begun to implement.

After they left, Alastar took out some of the paper he'd imaged and began to write a letter to Factor Elthyrd, one that he would deliver personally. He tore up three drafts before he had something that he liked.

Factorius Elthyrd—

As you may have heard, matters dealing with tariffs have not gone well. I have thus far met with High Holder Guerdyn upon three occasions, attempting to see if some middle ground might be reached that would be acceptable to both the High Holders and the rex. At my last meeting, yesterday, High Holder Guerdyn insisted that no middle ground exists, and that the rex would have to accept that, regardless of the needs of anyone else, including the factors, the Collegium, the guilds, or the merchants who need protection from pirates. He also said that if tariffs were insufficient, then everyone else would just have to do with less.

Although it is true that Rex Ryen wishes to impose higher tariffs than necessary to resolve shortfalls, the failure of the High Council to recognize the need to fund the real needs of Solidar remains a vexing problem. Of concern to the Collegium is that in our efforts to suggest a middle ground, and one that would benefit the factors and merchants of Solidar, we may well have angered both the head of the High Council and Rex Regis as well. We trust that neither will behave intemperately, but should they do so, the Collegium will be forced to act in its own interests and in the interests of all those others, including the factors, to assure that neither the rex nor the High Council will do so again and to further assure that a middle course of moderate action is adopted and carried out.

In the interests of moderation and compromise, I remain

Alastar D'Imagisle
Maitre D'Image

He reread the letter, then folded and sealed it, and went on with the other preparations for what he feared was inevitable, beginning with a short meeting with Obsolym, and then one with Cyran, and finally with Petros.

By the time he finally reached the residence, well after dinner, he was tired, but hardly sleepy, and he took refuge in reading a few more pages of the chorister's journal. Four pages were almost enough to make him sleepy, showing just how tired he was, when he came across the first interesting words in more than a hundred pages.

. . . the problem with great power, the Maitre said, is that, to be believed, it must be exercised. If it is not exercised, people forget its greatness, but when it is exercised, they complain that they did not know. Or they say that they had no idea how great it was. He also said that unless future Maitres understood that and used great power occasionally, the Collegium would eventually fail . . .

Alastar leaned back in his chair. *How could someone so great and so perceptive be totally forgotten? Even by the imagers who followed?*

After a time, he marked his place and closed the journal.

23

On Meredi morning, Alastar ate as soon as the dining hall was open, although he knew that Shabrena would have served him whenever he appeared, but he disliked taking advantage of his position unless it was actually necessary . . . and not a personal convenience. As soon as he downed the last drops of his second mug of hot tea, he rose, straightened the heavier gray imager jacket he had chosen because of the colder weather, and made his way to the armory, where he hoped to find Cyran.

The senior imager looked away from the rack of sabres that would likely never be used in any full battle and toward Alastar. "I can't say I'm happy with your plan, especially heading out and working on the avenue first."

"Only for two glasses. Then you head back, unless I send word for you to return earlier. You'll take Alyna, Taryn, Shaelyt, Mhorys, and Narryn, and three thirds. After whatever work on the avenue you can do, you all come back to the Collegium. Eat and take a break until sometime before fourth glass, then lead your group, except for Alyna, who will be with my group, out over the old south bridge, under a concealment until you muster somewhere just south of there. Check with me before you leave so that I can tell you what else we've found out."

Cyran nodded.

Alastar waited, then asked, "Do you have a better idea?"

"No. That's one of the reasons I'm not happy. It seems . . . wrong . . . when you know what's going to happen . . ."

"What happens if we act first? Or if it's a bluff to get us to act first?"

"I know you're right, but I don't have to like it."

"Make sure you're ready if Demykalon sets up any other forces to the south."

Cyran nodded, then asked, "You're sure Akoryt can handle matters here? Obsolym is senior, you know?"

"That's a risk I'll take. Akoryt is a stronger imager, and he won't dither. I've put Obsolym in charge of dealing with the staff in the outlying areas because he knows them better. He seemed fine with that." *How fine is another question, but it's better than the alternatives.* "We'll move the rest of the mounts and imagers we need well before fourth glass."

"Do you really think Demykalon will take out the bridges?"

"I don't know, but it's the first thing I'd do. If he doesn't, we'll have more options." *But less visible provocation.*

"I still don't like this."

"Neither do I, but we won't know until something happens. All we know now is that Demykalon sent what appear to be cannon and troopers east in the direction of the chateaux of Nacryon and Guerdyn. If Ryen only attacks the High Holders and didn't plan anything against us—or Demykalon didn't—and we act, then how long before there are no imagers to speak of left in Solidar?" asked Alastar, adding in answer to his own question, "A generation at most."

"But you want me and Alyna to head out and work the roads . . ."

"That's something that needs to be done." *For other reasons as well.* "And it's also a way to have imagers off Imagisle in case Demykalon doesn't respect Ryen's deadline."

"I can see that."

"But you don't like it, and neither do I."

"We agree on that." Cyran offered a crooked smile.

After leaving Cyran, Alastar returned to his Collegium study. Once there, he left the door open and settled behind his desk . . . waiting, first for Dareyn, then for Akoryt. After that, he'd have to ride to Factor Elthyrd's factorage, thankfully not that far away.

Akoryt appeared even before Dareyn.

Alastar motioned the red-haired maitre into the study. "Leave the door open."

"Yes, sir."

When Akoryt settled into the chair in front of the desk, Alastar could see the circles under his eyes. "A long night? Have your imagers discovered anything?"

"More than either of us would like," replied Akoryt. "At least five canvas-covered wagons have left the army High Command. So have at least two companies of troopers, never more than a squad at a time. There are two wagons and a squad of troopers in one of those areas off West River Road that you marked off on the map, the point that juts into the river about half a mille north of the north end of Imagisle. Another wagon and more troopers are in the old rendering yards just north and west of the Sud Bridge."

So much for Demykalon ignoring Imagisle. "Could they tell what's in the wagons?"

"No. Not without revealing themselves. They're not that good with concealments. But the wagons were heavy like the others, and each took four dray horses."

"That sounds like cannon and ammunition to me."

"That was my thought."

"Have you arranged for Khaelis, Lhendyr, Warryk, and three thirds to be ready to ride out with me and Maitre Alyna this afternoon?"

"Yes, sir. They'll meet at the stables at three quints before fourth glass."

Alastar nodded. "There's one other thing. You need

to talk to Petros about moving the remaining mounts if there's any hint of an attack."

Akoryt smiled faintly. "I already did, sir. He'll have them saddled as well."

"Good. I'll need you to keep me informed about any other movements of Demykalon's forces. Interrupt me if necessary. Is there anything else I should know?"

"Probably, sir." Akoryt smiled. "But I don't know what it is. If I find out, you'll know."

Alastar couldn't help but smile in return. "Then go and find out." He followed Akoryt out of the study because he had seen that Dareyn had arrived.

"Good morning, sir."

"Good morning," *although it may not be so good an afternoon or evening.* "I've asked Maitre Akoryt to find out more about several urgent matters while I'm visiting Factor Elthyrd. Whenever he returns, assuming I'm back, even if my door is closed, please interrupt me and let me know when he's here. Also, in case I'm not here later today, you're to make sure that everyone is out of the administration building by two quints before fourth glass, and they're not to return until tomorrow morning. The only one who can change or modify those orders in my absence is Maitre Akoryt."

"What about Maitre Cyran?"

"He can also, but it's unlikely he'll have returned to Imagisle by that time. That's why Maitre Akoryt will be in charge in our absence."

"Do you really think someone's going to be dumb enough to attack the Collegium, sir?"

"They're not stupid. It's just that they don't understand what imagers can do." *Or will.* "Because they don't, they just might. It would be better if they did understand, but if they did, we wouldn't have to be so worried."

"Maitre Fhaen worried when Demykalon became marshal."

"What did he say?" Alastar was curious because he didn't recall Fhaen saying much of anything, except not to trust Demykalon.

"He said that Demykalon thought he was the rex, not Rex Ryen."

"Did he say anything else?"

"Not exactly, sir." Dareyn glanced around the anteroom, clearly uncomfortable. Finally, he added, "He said his cousin wouldn't have taken his stipend quite so early, except . . . But he didn't finish his sentence, and he never said what the reason was, even when I asked. He said it was better I didn't know."

Better Dareyn didn't know? Better for whom? "Do you think Maitre Fhaen knew he was not well before he told anyone?"

"Yes, sir. He didn't walk as fast, and he was out of breath if he walked more than a handful of steps. Maitre Obsolym had to know, too. He watched Maitre Fhaen like a sun eagle."

Alastar nodded. It all made sense. *Too much sense.* "Is there anything else?"

Dareyn worried his lips, tilted his head slightly, then said, "No, sir. Maitre Fhaen wasn't one for talking much. Not around me or anyone who wasn't a Maitre D'Structure."

"I appreciate what you do know, Dareyn. Thank you." Alastar paused. "Would you send word to have my horse ready?"

"Yes, sir."

Alastar returned to his study. As he sat down behind the desk, he thought about reading more in the last volume of Gauswn's journals, but recalled that the journals were all in the study at the Maitre's residence. Less than a quint later, Alastar rode across the east bridge, accompanied by two of the older seconds—Maercyl and Dhonaet—since Akoryt was using the more talented thirds who had finished their formal instruction. Elthyrd's factorage was less than a mille south on the East River Road, and actually on the river itself.

As he rode up to a small structure flanked by large two-story warehouses, Alastar saw just why the factorage was on the water, with the low barges tied to wharves, and men unloading and loading lengths of timber and planks, carrying them to and from the warehouses.

He dismounted and handed the gelding's reins to Maercyl. "I won't be too long." Then he walked into the small building, where he was met by Elthyrd himself.

"You're punctual. I'll say that, Maitre. Unlike some."

"This is quite a factorage. Do you handle all woods?" Seeing the amount of wood, Alastar could see why Elthyrd had dismissed the canvas side of his factoring as smaller.

"Everything. I have factorages in both Solis and Kephria. That's where the fine southern woods are landed. We get the best goldenwood of all . . ." Elthyrd smiled. "You didn't come to talk about woods." He gestured toward a doorway behind the long counter and to the right.

Alastar followed him into a spare study that held little more than a table desk, a small bookcase filled with what looked to be ledgers of some sort, and chairs—three in front of the desk and one behind it. Elthyrd did close the door before moving toward the desk, then turning and stopping.

"You're right. I didn't come to talk about woods, but the breadth of what you carry looks to be quite impressive. I came to talk about the imminent problems facing Solidar." Alastar extended the missive he had written earlier. "I put them in writing for you and so that, as you see fit, you can show my words to others."

"Best I sit down." Elthyrd dropped as much as sat into the chair behind the desk, making a vague gesture toward the chairs in front of it.

As Alastar seated himself, the factor broke the seal, took out the letter, and began to read. He frowned when he came to the end, but then seemed to reread parts of what Alastar had written. Finally, he looked up. "What do you want from me, or should I ask, from the council?"

"At the moment, nothing more than to be aware of what the situation is."

"Why?"

"Because everyone will try to recast the way things actually are after whatever is about to happen occurs. I'd like you and the other factors to see what the Collegium faces before that."

"Your words suggest more of a threat than a compromise."

Alastar shook his head. "We have absolutely no intention of acting if others reach a compromise, or even if they do not, so long as everyone strives to be reasonable."

"What's reasonable to me might not be to you."

"That's true, but if you decide to burn down L'Excelsis if you don't get your way, not that you would suggest such, I think most people would find that less than reasonable."

"That's a ridiculous example, but I see your point."

Alastar offered a sad smile. "Is it really ridiculous? Marshal Demykalon is testing new cannon. He made certain I witnessed those tests."

"You don't really think he'd actually fire them on anyone, do you?"

More likely than not. "I won't speculate on what the marshal will or will not do. I would say that firing cannon on anyone who disagrees with the rex would be less than reasonable . . . unless, of course, they used force first . . . but that would also be unreasonable."

"I'd say you don't have a favorable impression of

either the High Holders or the rex. Or the marshal, for that matter."

"Would you, if you were in my boots?"

"Probably not." Elthyrd offered a gruff chuckle. "I'm glad I'm not. When might you be doing more of those repairs?"

"When we can, as we can."

"Not much of a promise there."

"The only promise I can give is that we will do them."

"That's not perfect, but you've done two. That's better than your predecessor or the rex. What else?"

"I've told you what I came to tell you."

"I figured as much. For an imager, you're plainspoken." Elthyrd stood. "It will be interesting to see what happens."

Just hope it's interesting . . . and not worse. Alastar rose. "It will be." He inclined his head. "I appreciate your seeing me."

"We'll have to see how things turn out." The factor moved to the door and opened it.

Meaning that you think I've been an alarmist. That didn't bother Alastar. "We will, indeed."

In mere moments, Alastar was outside the factorage and mounting the gelding.

As the three imagers turned their mounts north on the East River Road, Dhonaet cleared his throat. "Maitre, sir, you weren't there long."

"We each said what we had to say. There wasn't any point to staying longer. Factor Elthyrd is very direct and appreciates brevity—unlike some, for whom brevity is mortal insult." Alastar couldn't help but see Maercyl's effort to hide a smile.

The return to Imagisle was quick and uneventful.

Only moments after Alastar returned to his study in the administration building, Dareyn rapped on the doorframe, since Alastar had left the door ajar, then stepped just inside the study. "There's a master stonemason here to see you, sir. He says his name is Gairock."

Master stonemason? Alastar frowned. *It has to be about the sewer repairs.* "Have him come in."

"As you wish, sir."

Alastar could definitely hear the disapproval in Dareyn's voice, but he just nodded.

Gairock was not a big man, more than a head shorter than Alastar, with a wiry build. His beard was mostly gray with a few remnants of brown, and he wore a scuffed brown leather jacket over a faded brown wool shirt. His heavy twill trousers were gray above battered brown boots.

Definitely a working stonemason. Alastar rose and gestured to the chairs. "Please sit down. What might I do for you?"

"Maitre . . . I'd not be one to go against the power of an imager . . ."

Alastar waited.

". . . I've heard tales that imagers made repairs to the sewers. I've gone to those places. I've seen the repairs."

"We have made repairs in two places. We made one repair because the stench was so great that it covered most of Imagisle. We made the second to placate the factors' council."

"Sir?"

"Not all imagers are powerful. Some cannot image even a small brick. Those who are powerful have wives and children who are not. Solidar is the only land where imagers are not hunted or slaves. We do our best not to upset those in power, as do the guilds, I would imagine."

"That is true . . ." Gairock's voice held a certain doubt.

"You are concerned that our repairs have taken work from the stonemasons?"

"There has been talk of that, Maitre."

"We may have to do another repair or two. Beyond

that, we have no intention of taking work from the stonemasons. We do reserve the right to work on our own dwellings and buildings here on Imagisle, just as any who have the skill may work on their own property."

"Times are hard, Maitre."

"Times are hard for the Collegium, too, master stonemason. The High Holders and the rex want the Collegium to do their bidding. Each has threatened us if we fail to support them."

"You let them threaten you?"

"They have only threatened," said Alastar. "If they act on those threats, then so will we. As Maitre of the Collegium, I never want it said that imagers threatened or acted against others in Solidar, except in their own defense." He smiled politely. "We will do what we can not to do more stonework beyond what I have described. I regret having to do those repairs, but they have been necessary because the rex would not pay the factors' council to make the repairs, and the High Holders are opposing the tariffs necessary to pay for such repairs and other needs. The guilds and the Collegium are caught between the High Holders and the rex."

"And you will do nothing?" Gairock appeared incredulous.

"We will not act first, master stonemason. That does not mean we will not act. If matters are not clear by the end of Feuillyt, come and see me again." Alastar stood, then added in as kindly a tone as he could manage, "The Collegium and I do understand, and we will do our best." That was as great a commitment as he was willing to make.

The stonemason rose and nodded courteously. "Thank you for seeing me, Maitre."

Once Gairock was well away, Alastar shook his head. It seemed as though, no matter what he tried to do, someone was unhappy. And for the moment . . . all he could do was wait.

Waiting was the hardest part, not only because he preferred to be the first to act, but because, while acting first would reduce the immediate damage, perhaps obviate it all, it would destroy the Collegium more certainly than would Ryen's wrath or Demykalon's cannon, assuming matters went that far. *Which they almost certainly will.*

Finally, he could stand it no more. He walked to the door. "Send word to have my horse ready."

"Yes, sir."

Alastar found himself pacing until Dareyn finally said, "Your horse is ready, sir. Will you need an escort?"

"No. I need to make a quick survey with regard to Imagisle. I hope to return in little more than a glass. I don't think Maitre Akoryt will be back here before then, but if he is, tell him where I've gone and that I'll let him know as soon as I can."

Alastar hurried from the administration building out to where a fresh-faced second held the reins to the gelding. He had to struggle to remember the student's name. "Thank you, Lannyt. I should be back in a glass or so."

The young imager inclined his head as he handed the reins over.

Alastar mounted quickly and urged the gelding onto the lane north along the center green. Once he was well away from the stable and past the cottages, he turned on a side lane that would lead to the Bridge of Desires, if indirectly, and raised first, a blurring concealment, and then a full one. He stayed close to the stone railing on the north side of the bridge, although he didn't sense anyone. Nor could he make out anyone on the point toward which he was headed. He had to be careful as he rode north on the West River Road, because there were coaches and carriages, and none of them could see him. That didn't mean that they couldn't run into him—or his shields—and that was the last thing he needed.

Just south of the Nord Bridge on the west side of the river was a rocky spur of land that jutted into the water, extending less than a hundred yards. As he neared it, Alastar caught a sense of an indistinct figure in a side lane across the West River Road. He smiled. *One of Akoryt's watchers.*

The army was making no secret of its presence, not with five mounted troopers, each with a rifle in a saddle sheath, posted to block the footpath that led from the road out to the point. The undergrowth on each side of the path had been cut back, and wagon tracks straddled the bare ground. The trees and bushes were high enough and thick enough on each side of even the widened path to conceal whatever was more than ten or fifteen yards from the road. With guards posted so close together, Alastar didn't see any way to determine what lay beyond the guards. If he took the cleared path, he'd run into one of the troopers. If he went through the bushes and brush—assuming he even could—the sound and the movement of branches and leaves would alert the troopers. All that suggested that Demykalon was up to little good. Alastar reined up some twenty yards short of the nearest trooper. While his concealment meant he wouldn't be seen, it didn't block sounds or smells.

Farther north an old man walked south, leading a mule that pulled a small cart filled with baskets of root vegetables. Closer to Alastar, a coach had stopped opposite the center trooper, and a man was addressing the trooper from the coach. The man was likely a factor from his voice.

". . . army troopers doing here?"

". . . spicers landing elveweed and curamyn here where they couldn't be seen. The rex ordered the marshal to look into it."

"They'd be stupid spicers to do that."

"I just know what I've been told, sir. The commander gives the orders."

Commander? That alone suggested that spicers were merely an excuse. No commander would be out on the riverbank looking for traces of spicers and smugglers, not to mention the fact that the factor was absolutely correct about such an unlikely place being used for smuggling.

The factor snorted, but motioned to his driver to move on.

". . . always said there were spicers in L'Excelsis . . ." muttered the old man as he neared Alastar. ". . . wouldn't be here though."

The cart passed within a few yards of Alastar. Once the old man was more than ten yards away, Alastar turned his mount back toward the Collegium. Once he was back, he left his mount at the stables, still saddled, and walked to the administration building. He'd hoped to have been able to do more largely undetected, but the locale and the picketing troopers made that unlikely.

All the things that Ryen, Demykalon, and Guerdyn had done were looking to make the situation a bloody mess. *That's what happens when everyone is convinced he or she is right.* He smiled wryly, knowing that he was one of those convinced he was right. *Except you are, just like everyone else believes he is.*

"Any messages?" Alastar asked Dareyn as he walked into the anteroom.

"No, sir, but Maitre Cyran was looking for you."

"Send someone to tell him I'm back."

Dareyn motioned to the second sitting on one of the anteroom chairs. "Maitre Cyran is in the armory. Run and tell him the Maitre is back."

The second hurried off, and Alastar walked into his study, thinking.

In a fraction of a quint, Cyran was striding into the Maitre's study. "You've been doing some scouting yourself, I'd wager."

"I have. I'll tell you in a moment. How did the repairs go?"

"We completed another hundred yards or so." Cyran sat down opposite Alastar. "We had to remove two more shops, but they were already empty. No one complained. All this road imaging is strengthening all of us, especially Shaelyt, Mhorys, and Narryn. Alyna's been having the thirds do some as well, mainly curbs and gutters around the drains. They're improving as well."

"That's good. What's not so good is what Demykalon is doing . . ." Alastar went on to describe what Akoryt had reported earlier and what he had found out himself. ". . . and that means that you'll likely find the same situation to the south. If they actually fire on the Collegium, you and your group need to destroy the guns and ammunition without risking any of the imagers."

"Concealments to get close; image red-hot iron into some of the ammunition? Something like that?"

"That will work, but you'll have to deal with sentries first. I'd try fine pepper and salt mist to the eyes first, but don't hesitate, and make sure that you're behind stone or earth when anyone images hot iron."

"I'll have them practice." Cyran paused. "Is Demykalon really that stupid?"

"He's not stupid at all. He's nowhere close. He'll claim he was only doing what was ordered by Ryen, or that his officers exceeded their orders. Or both. He'll likely even have documents to prove it. They'll take the blame . . . and Ryen will suffer. I'd be very surprised if Demykalon doesn't have even greater ambitions. He may even profess the need to replace the rex with a more effective and evenhanded ruler. After, of course, he has used the army and his new cannon to show how terrible Ryen is."

"And he'd be the more effective and evenhanded rex?" Cyran snorted.

"He would be if we let him be."

"How did Ryen let things get so far out of hand?"

"He really didn't," replied Alastar. "Maitre Fhaen and his predecessors did. They failed to support the rex where necessary and oppose him when required. They did not make it clear that the Collegium could and would oppose the worst abuses of power by the High Holders. They wanted the Collegium to be liked and funded by the rex without earning that support. That's not possible and never was. Power unused is ineffective or held in contempt. Power used is feared. Power abused is hated. The best those with power can do is to obtain respect for their wise use of it." He offered a crooked smile. "Right now, the best we may be able to gain is fearful respect." *If that . . . and only if most things you've planned work.*

"That's likely better than the alternative. I'd better get back and make preparations."

"Send Alyna here, if you would." Alastar stood.

"I can do that. I left her in charge of the group."

Alastar barely had time to take a breath after Cyran left before Akoryt hurried into the study. Alastar motioned for him to close the door, then, as soon as it was shut, asked, "What's happened, if anything?"

Akoryt replied first with a sardonic smile. "Enough to justify your concerns about the marshal. The army has moved two companies south and west of the Chateau D'Rex. They're split into squads in various places, but they're all within half a mille of the main entrance."

Alastar frowned. "There aren't any others posted around the chateau or any nearer?"

"No, sir."

"Has there been any change in the troopers posted south of Imagisle?"

"We haven't seen any. They do have mounted guards posted at the edge of the West River Road, in both the positions north and south of the Collegium. We haven't seen any more wagons moving."

Although Alastar continued discussing matters with Akoryt for nearly a quint, he didn't learn anything he had not already known or discovered.

Moments after Akoryt departed, Alyna knocked on the door and then stepped inside the study. "You wanted to see me?"

"I did. Please come in."

Alyna shut the door and walked toward the desk. Alastar just watched. He enjoyed those moments, but tried not to show that.

"You're looking concerned, Maitre," observed Alyna.

"In my position, wouldn't you?"

"I'm not in your position, and I'm very concerned. I took a look at the Chateau D'Rex. Ryen has guards posted everywhere."

"What about army troopers?"

"I didn't see any."

"Akoryt's scouts report that Demykalon has moved two companies near the Chateau D'Rex. Both of the army positions north and south of Imagisle have mounted guards to keep people from seeing what they're doing. They're claiming to be seeking smugglers and spicers."

"They couldn't tell a sun eagle from a spicer," said Alyna with a light laugh. "Neither could Demykalon."

The way the phrase came off her lips suggested familiarity with the phrase, a phrase Alastar had never heard before. "Sun eagle from a spicer?"

"It's a family expression."

Alastar wondered if that had been passed down from Vaelora and what else from Alyna's background might have come down from her. "You're as skeptical of Demykalon as I am."

"I might be more so."

"Why, might I ask?"

Alyna smiled wryly. "I'm good with numbers and measurements. You can't do that with character. So I tend to be skeptical based on people's actions. Anyone who gives a demonstration of what his cannon can do is not someone I'd trust as far as I could throw one of those cannon. If it's a boast, he's not to be trusted, and if it's a promise it's the kind you don't want to receive. Other than that, I couldn't tell you."

"Intuition?"

"Intuition is nothing more than the combination of knowledge, judgment, and feelings."

"Meaning?" asked Alastar almost, but not quite, playfully.

"Lack of knowledge and poor judgment will undermine the best feel one can have."

"Demykalon is knowledgeable and most likely has a good feel for people."

"Then his judgment is suspect."

Alastar raised his eyebrows.

"He thinks Ryen is a fool and that you will not act. That shows poor judgment. Ryen may not be the best rex. He may not exercise the best judgment, but he understands that the High Holders will bow only to power. In that, he is no fool."

"And what about you?" Not for the first time in dealing with Alyna, Alastar wished he had not offered his words.

"I'm a Maitre D'Structure through your understanding and judgment."

"And, most important, through your own abilities. I've also only seen good judgment and much knowledge."

Alyna dropped her glance for just an instant before looking directly into Alastar's eyes.

The directness of her study stunned him, yet he did not look away. He found himself smiling, and then saw that she was as well.

She laughed so softly and so briefly that the sound seemed to vanish more quickly than it had come. "Zaeryl hated that."

"Because he could not meet your gaze?"

She nodded.

"You are rather intense."

"As are you, Maitre." She paused. "I haven't eaten since breakfast . . ."

"Oh . . . I'm sorry." He stood. "You should go and get something. We'll be leaving the Collegium just before fourth glass. The others will be mustering at the stables at least two quints earlier."

Alyna rose with all the grace that he so admired. "I'll be there."

Once more, he just watched as she left the study. He couldn't help but wonder at the attraction she held for him. He couldn't define it, and it was far more than physical interest. *The intensity, the quiet directness, the intelligence, the ability, the range of understanding?* He laughed. *How many people have those traits, let alone an attractive woman?* Still, whatever might occur between them would have to wait until they dealt with Demykalon, Ryen, and Guerdyn. That might be a long time, given what had seemed a simple difference over tariffs had become.

At two quints past third glass, Alastar left his study and walked to the stables. All the members of his group were there—Alyna, Khaelis, Lhendyr, Warryk, and three thirds. All wore sabres, not that Alastar wanted the blades used, even his own, except as a last resort.

"We'll be riding out in about a quint. We'll be crossing the Bridge of Desires under a concealment. That means you'll all need to stay close. Are there any questions?"

"Sir?" ventured Khaelis. "You haven't said what we'll be doing."

"No . . . I haven't. There's a possibility that you may

have to do some imaging against those who intend to do harm to Imagisle."

"How will we know—?"

"If that is necessary, there won't be any doubt, and I'll be giving direct commands."

"How long will this take, sir?"

"I wish I could tell you. If we have to act, I'll begin with commands that will require less force, such as imaging salt into the eyes of troopers, or fine pepper."

Even as the three thirds nodded knowingly, Lhendyr and Khaelis exchanged puzzled glances.

The Maitre D'Aspect's question reminded Alastar that the skills he'd been having Cyran teach the student seconds and thirds obviously hadn't been taught to some of the older maitres when they'd been seconds and thirds. "If someone has salt in his eyes and is inhaling pepper, he'll be far less dangerous. You might want to practice imaging a cloud of fine pepper while we wait—away from the rest of us, please. Or a fine mist of water and salt. If we come up against a mounted force, I may command you to image away the girths and cinches securing their saddles. If required, you may have to use iron darts through the eyes to kill people. I hope that's not necessary, but it could be."

Then Khaelis asked, "Are we going to face army troopers?"

"If you face anyone, it will be troopers," admitted Alastar.

"What did we do—"

"It isn't what we did; it's what we didn't do." Alastar saw no point in shielding the junior maitres any longer. "We could not convince the High Council to agree to the rex's new tariffs, not without killing most of the Council. The rex has threatened to make the Collegium his enemy for not doing that."

"For not killing people?" asked Lhendyr incredulously.

"We may end up killing people anyway," replied Alastar, "but the Collegium cannot afford to be the one to begin the slaughter. If you have more questions about why, I'll be happy to answer them later."

"That's because too many people haven't seen what imagers can do in generations," added Alyna.

"And don't think that people should already know," added Alastar. "Most people don't look beyond what they have seen, and few believe anything they hear if it isn't in accord with what they wish to believe."

Alyna nodded. The three junior maitres exchanged glances. There were no more questions.

A quint later, two quints before fourth glass, Alastar led his small group out across the Bridge of Desires under a concealment. He did not want to risk waiting to leave Imagisle until the last moment. After crossing the bridge, carrying the same strong shields he always did, he turned north and rode several hundred yards, to a position from which he could see both the Bridge of Desires and the spur of land that held the army troopers and, most likely, their cannon. A block and a half farther north, he turned in to a wider lane flanked by a bistro and a bakery. There, he positioned the seven riders so that he could watch the bridge without being seen by someone riding down the West River Road. Only then did he drop the concealment.

A small boy whom Alastar had not noticed in the doorway of the bakery gaped as he took in the sudden appearance of the mounted imagers, then hurried back inside.

A quint passed, then another, before Lhendyr turned in the saddle and said something to Khaelis. Alastar had a good idea that the young Maitre D'Aspect was questioning why they were waiting for something that was obviously not going to happen.

"No patience," murmured Alyna.

"How long do you think Demykalon will wait?" asked Alastar.

"Another quint. Just to be careful."

"Do you think that I'm mistaken?"

"We can all be mistaken. I don't think you are. Demykalon wants to strike against the Collegium. It's only a question of when."

"And with what."

She nodded.

Less than a full quint later, a humming, not quite whistling, sound filled the air, followed by a splash in the River Aluse some twenty yards north of the Bridge of Desires.

Alastar managed to turn and see the last indication of the impact, white-tipped water being thrown south. Even as he glanced back upriver, a second whistling-humming sound was followed by others. Then came the explosions, seemingly unceasing, one after the other.

"Imagers!" snapped Alastar as he raised a concealment. "Follow me! You're under a concealment. Hold shields from here on." As he urged the gelding forward, he could see people hurrying out of the shops and the few dwellings between them on the west side of the road, some already staring at the shattered middle span of the Bridge of Desires.

At that moment, he could also see smoke coming from a point due west of the Bridge of Desires. *A totally hidden cannon emplacement?* He winced, but trying to change his plans now would only make things worse. He kept riding, hoping the third cannon emplacement wouldn't do too much damage before they could get back to it.

Covering the five hundred yards or so between the lane and the entrance to the spur of land seemed to take several quints, although Alastar doubted that even half a quint had passed before they were within yards of their goal. There were no longer just five mounted army troopers posted along the edge of the West River Road, but more like a company, half with blades unsheathed and at the ready, along with small round shields, and half with heavy rifles out, alternating rifles and blades.

So they can stop attacks at a distance and also deal with infighting.

"Khaelis, Warryk, and Lhendyr! Pepper across the troopers! As much and as fine as you can. Rein up! Remove girths and cinches. If they attack you, use iron darts to kill. Thirds! Stay with the other maitres! Blades out and ready! Alyna! Close on me! We're moving through."

While still holding the concealment, Alastar extended his own shields into a wedge anchored as evenly as possible to his saddle and the gelding and urged his mount forward toward the middle of the mounted troopers. As he charged through a narrow gap widened by his shields, whose impact pushed aside bewildered troopers, some of whom flailed at him futilely with their blades when they came inside the concealment, Alastar found his own eyes watering from the pepper, too fine to be pushed aside by shields. He sneezed, once, and then again . . . and again.

Once through the company of defenders, and past the last line of scrubby trees, Alastar could make out six cannon in an arc facing south with a slight angle eastward, directly at Imagisle. Two more fired and recoiled as Alastar reined up and ordered, "Halt!"

There was no shelter and no cover, just fifty yards of ground from which most brush had been removed. *Frig! All that rock, but none where we could use it.*

"At my command, hot iron into the ammunition. Then hold the strongest shields you can, Anchor them to the rock below and slant them at an angle to deflect shrapnel upward and over us. Ready! Image!"

The roar was deafening. Brilliance and blackness swept over them. The ground beneath them shuddered. When the sound of the initial explosion died away, Alastar still could not hear, for all the ringing in his ears. Nor could he see clearly, even after dropping the concealment, from the brightness of the explosion and the earlier impact of the pepper. The swirls of intermittent smoke made seeing even more difficult. Light-headed as he felt, Alastar immediately contracted his shields just to protect himself. That helped some. After several moments, he surveyed the area. All of the cannon carriages had suffered enough damage, with several having wheels on one side or another broken, that none appeared able to be used. As for the gun crews and any others . . .

Alastar swallowed as he made out bodies and parts of bodies. Then he straightened and looked to Alyna, who appeared unfazed, if with a serious expression on her face.

She extended a water bottle, saying something he could not hear, but he had no doubt it was to say it held lager or the like. "Thank you."

After taking a long swallow of the dark lager, Alastar looked south, and another puff of smoke reminded him of the third cannon emplacement. He took another swallow, then gestured.

Alyna frowned. "What?"

Alastar could barely make out the words, but replied, speaking as loudly as he could without shouting, "There's another cannon emplacement near the Bridge of Desires. I didn't see it before. We need to deal with it, you and I and a third. It's smaller. We need to see how the junior maitres are faring." He turned the gelding, took another swallow of lager, corked the bottle, and then extended it to Alyna.

She shook her head. "I have another."

Alastar slipped the bottle into one of his saddlebags. When he did, he saw more bodies, both of men and mounts, clearly those who had been behind the three imagers and to either side of their shields. Beyond the fallen, almost a score of troopers remained near the road, all of whom seemed to be wounded in some fashion.

Alastar turned the gelding and rode back toward the road, Alyna slightly to one side and back.

"Anyone else who moves gets the same!" declared Lhendyr, who had clearly taken charge, and positioned himself at the head of a wedge formed by the three junior maitres, with the thirds on each side.

"Lhendyr, you and the junior maitres finish up here. Take all the weapons and mounts from the troopers. They can fend for themselves. Lead the mounts you can find easily back down toward Imagisle. If anyone gives you trouble, do whatever's necessary." Alastar wished he didn't have to leave the surviving and wounded troopers to their own devices, but he didn't have the resources to deal with them, and the last thing he needed was army troopers on Imagisle. Then he added, "Alyna and I and Chervyt need to see what we can do about the other cannon emplacement."

"Yes, sir."

"Chervyt!" Alastar called out toward the thirds. "Close up and follow us!" Then he and Alyna circled around the wounded and captured troopers and headed south, with Chervyt hurrying to catch up. Turning to Alyna, now riding beside him, he said, "I can't believe I missed a cannon emplacement so close to Imagisle. It's almost as if . . . Frig!" He shook his head. "Desyrk! The little bastard! I'd wager he went to his brother, and he used a concealment to move cannon from the emplacement we just destroyed."

"He's probably still there, then," replied Alyna. "Neither Demykalon nor his brother would let him leave. They'd fear he was being used or that your discipline was a ruse."

Alastar saw another puff of smoke, then a second, followed by some time before there was a third and then a fourth puff. "Just two cannon, I'd guess."

"Just two?" Alyna's tone was sardonic, then changed to concern as she added, "Drink more of that lager."

"Yes, my lady." Alastar definitely wanted those words back.

"I'm not your lady . . . or anyone else's, Maitre." The words were not stinging, if firm, but somehow almost gentle while unyielding.

"My apologies. Your advice is good." Alastar extracted the water bottle and took one swallow and then another.

Alyna took out her second water bottle and did the same.

Alastar finished his bottle by the time they were within a block of where the two cannon continued to fire. He saw no sign of troopers anywhere. Smoke clouded the entire block, making it difficult to discern exactly where the cannon were concealed, and he reined the gelding to a slow walk, then a stop, pondering. The kind of explosion that he'd created on the point would likely cause damage to the adjoining dwellings and shops.

"Anyone nearby should have fled," suggested Alyna, almost as if he had spoken the words.

Alastar imaged hot iron needles—but nothing happened. Then he saw several of the iron needles glowing on the sidewalk in front of the shopfront from which another volley was fired. "He's holding shields . . ."

"How can he do that and have the cannon fire?" asked Alyna.

"He can't . . ." *Unless his shields are set so that the muzzles protrude.* Without knowing where the cannon were, Alastar couldn't very well image something down the barrel, and to move to where he could see that might well expose him to the cannon—and he doubted that even his shields could withstand that kind of impact. "We'll have to crush his shields. Rather . . . I'll have to do that, and when I signal, you image more hot iron needles."

"Can you . . . after all you did?"

"Desyrk can't be that strong after holding shields himself. Besides . . ." *What else can we do to stop the damage on Imagisle from getting worse? Every cannon shot destroys something or even may kill someone.* Alastar could only hope that his and Akoryt's preparations were minimizing the casualties. "Ready?"

"I'm ready when you are."

Alastar reached out with his shields until he encountered resistance, then began to press. For a moment, there was resistance to Alastar's efforts. Abruptly, that vanished—and then everything exploded around him, with the same violence as had occurred on the river point. He managed to hold his shields even as he and the gelding were thrust back yards, if not farther. The gelding stumbled, almost going to his knees before recovering.

"Alyna!" Alastar could not even hear his own voice for all the ringing and echoes in his ears. Dust and debris cascaded over and around his shields. He kept looking for Alyna, then took a deep breath as the dust cleared and he saw debris flow down and off her shields. After a moment, he could see that she appeared untouched. "Are you all right?"

"I'm fine. What about you?"

"A little tired. Other than that . . ." Alastar paused, then glanced around, looking for the third. "Chervyt!"

"Back here, sir."

Alastar glanced over his shoulder. "You're not injured, are you?"

"No, sir. I don't think I could raise a shield right now, though."

"You did when you needed it. Move back up the road a hundred yards or so."

"Yes, sir."

"We ought to do that also," suggested Alyna, pointing

to where the concealed cannon had been. Less than twenty yards ahead of them, low flames began to grow amid the wooden sections of the collapsed shops.

Still looking for signs of troopers or Desyrk, Alastar turned the gelding, moving more into the center of West River Road, empty of others, except the imagers. "Desyrk must have exploded everything in hopes of destroying us."

"I think that's what he did," replied Alyna. "I just don't think he was where it hurt him."

That, unfortunately, made sense. Desyrk wasn't the type for self-sacrifice, even seeking revenge.

"He can't have gone far," said Alastar.

"That may be," answered Alyna dryly. "But if he's holding a concealment, how do you suggest we find him?"

Alastar did not speak, but imaged powder-like dirt at a height of three yards, like a blanket, over the space in front of the ruined shops and north and south of that as well, then watched to see if it revealed anything. The dirt settled evenly, showing nothing. "Now, we'll head for the alley."

Moments later, the sound of hooves on stone, coming from the alley behind the silversmith's shop where Alastar had reined up, suggested someone departing in haste. Alastar shook his head. "There's no way to catch him now."

"You don't think that's a ruse?"

"Since when has he ever stood up directly to those he thinks are more powerful?"

"You don't think much of him."

"Not after the way he acted in dealing with Taurek and Bettaur. Do you?"

"I never did. He's another lazy pretty boy."

Alastar glanced at the burning remnants of the shop that had held the two cannon. While he likely could have imaged out the fire with water or sand, he wasn't about to waste the energy, not when he and Alyna would need to image-repair one of the bridges even to get to the Collegium. *And when there still might be other surprises.*

Alyna followed his gaze. "It might not spread too far."

"And it might, but at the moment, that's something the locals will have to take care of." Alastar felt callous saying that, but he didn't know how much more imaging might be required, and for the past weeks, if not years, no one in L'Excelsis or elsewhere in Solidar had exactly been helpful to the imagers. *But can you blame them?* He thought about extracting the water bottle from his saddlebag before he recalled that it was empty. Instead, he concentrated.

A rain of wet sand and water blanketed the flames. Even before the sandy rain stopped falling, Alastar's head was throbbing. He wished he had more lager. *You shouldn't have done that.* Except he remembered a small cot and a family no one had helped.

Alyna extended her water bottle. "I have some left. You need it more than I do."

Alastar didn't argue. "Thank you." He finished the lager in her bottle and returned it. "That helps." He thought his headache was throbbing slightly less. He hoped that wasn't wishful thinking.

"I'm glad you did that." Abruptly, she turned her head and gestured southward. "Here come Cyran and the others."

Alastar followed her gesture, then called, "Chervyt! Meet Maitre Cyran and tell him I'd like to have him join us here."

"Yes, sir." With that, the third urged his mount southward.

While Cyran, Taryn, and the junior maitres and thirds rode toward what remained of the Bridge of Desires, Alastar surveyed what he could see of Imagisle. A wall of thick gray smoke rose from the center of the Collegium, either from the administration building or from the dining hall, if not both. A thinner plume rose from somewhere along the green, most likely from one of the maitres' cottages.

Alastar was still taking in the obvious destruction when Alyna spoke.

"They were aiming at all the places you might be."

He thought about denying or downplaying that possibility before replying. "It does look that way, but taking out the Maitre won't bring down the Collegium." *Not now.*

"Perhaps not, but it would weaken it greatly."

"We have to make sure it's never in this position again."

"I'm sure Vaelora and Quaeryt felt the same way about the need to maintain the strength of the Collegium." Alyna's voice was dry.

"I stand reminded . . . and corrected," replied Alastar in an equally dry tone. "I do think we need to make some changes to the structure and procedures we use at the Collegium."

"Those will help."

"What you're saying is that it still depends on the imagers of the Collegium."

"Hasn't it always?"

Alastar offered an abrupt laugh. Then, in the fading late-afternoon light, he looked northward along the West River Road at the five imagers, leading a line of something less than twenty horses, heading south, some with bundles tied to saddles. He glanced south to see Chervyt easing his mount in beside Cyran. Then his eyes turned eastward toward Imagisle again. He hated to think how much damage Desyrk had created. *All because he didn't want to understand what was necessary and put his own pride above everything else.* His lips quirked into a lopsided smile. *Haven't we all done that . . . or been tempted to?*

When he turned his gaze south again, he had to frown. Less than a quarter mille south of the Bridge of Desires was a small open hill behind what looked to be a mill of some sort. The hill provided a perfect vantage point and would easily have held five or six cannon. *Why didn't Desyrk place his cannon there? Because it would have been too hard to get them there? Or he didn't see the possibilities?* Whatever the reason, Alastar was more than glad that the army hadn't taken advantage of the hill.

Cyran rode quickly toward Alastar and Alyna, then reined up and looked directly at Alastar.

"We silenced the battery to the north before they did much damage." Alastar turned in the saddle and pointed to the still smoldering shop, although the flames seemed to have gone out. "They had two cannon hidden there. We didn't see them until after we dealt with the battery on the point."

"Someone used a concealment to bring them in," added Alyna.

"Desyrk?" asked Cyran. "I wouldn't have put it past him, the little frigger."

"Most likely," answered Alastar, "but we never saw who it was. Whoever it was had strong enough shields to block red-hot iron needles until I crushed his shields. We heard him ride off down the alley. How did you do?"

"We lost two—shrapnel went through Mhorys's shields and concentrated rifle fire took out Nuasyn as well. There might have been some army survivors, but we didn't see any."

Alastar shook his head. He was sorry about the army deaths, and he hated to lose imagers, yet it could have been worse. Belatedly, he recalled that Nuasyn had been a student third.

"Nuasyn had practically begged to be included," Cyran added. "He had stronger shields than any of the thirds who've finished their instruction. That's why I agreed. I shouldn't have let him come." He shook his head. "We had some trouble even before we could get close to the guns. They'd filled the gaps in the wall with old masonry and stones, and when we imaged that out, the rest of the walls collapsed and we had to image away stones and rubble to get close enough to see the cannon. There were six of them. Nothing's left of the south bridge." He looked toward the damaged Bridge of Desires.

"We'll need to image repairs to that center span," Alastar said. "We'll all need to help with that."

"It might take a little time. We're pretty tired."

"We're all tired," said Alastar. "We'll do it as we can, but we need to get to the Collegium as soon as possible."

24

Even as tired as the master imagers were, by each imager repairing or replacing a section, or part of one, less than two quints passed before they had repaired the center span of the Bridge of Desires enough so that they could cross it and return to Imagisle.

Alastar did not attempt to assist, not after Alyna had looked at him and said, "Let the rest of us do it. You need to recover to do what we cannot." Then she had looked at Cyran and spoken exactly the same words. After that, she imaged the main support for the center arch.

This time, Alastar could see her sway slightly in the saddle and note that she had paled, despite the fading light immediately following sunset. He announced, "And that's enough imaging for you, Maitre Alyna."

She looked as if she might protest, then nodded. After that, Alastar, Cyran, and Alyna watched as the junior masters added supports and sections. Some of the thirds replaced the paving stones at the end.

Once Alyna and Cyran were convinced that the bridge repairs would hold, Alastar formed up the imagers in single file, just in case those repairs were not what they might have been. Then he rode over to Cyran.

"What is it?" asked the Maitre D'Esprit. "You have something in mind."

"We ought to post a couple of maitres on our side of the bridge . . . just in case."

"You really think Demykalon would send troops to Imagisle?"

"I don't think so, but I'm not convinced."

"What about one maitre, say Taryn, with two thirds? They could ride for help if they see anything?"

"That makes more sense." *Especially since Taryn doesn't have a wife and children to worry about.* "Thank you."

As Cyran turned his mount and headed toward Taryn, Alastar called out, "Glaesyn!" and waited until the older third eased his mount close to the gray gelding.

"Yes, sir?" replied the third, his voice slightly wary.

"Once we get across the bridge, you're to ride north to the park and find Maitre Akoryt or whoever is in charge and have him meet me near what's left of the administration building."

"Yes, sir."

Khaelis led the way to the bridge approach, followed by Alastar and Alyna, then the junior maitres, with Taryn and Cyran near the rear, followed by Coermyd and Akkard, leading the mounts bearing the bodies of Mhorys and Nuasyn. Behind them were two other thirds, leading the string of captured mounts.

Alastar and Alyna rode without speaking, and Alastar studied both the river and Imagisle as he neared the center of the bridge. He thought that the smoke from the area of the green had died away, but in the growing dimness of twilight, the flames from what looked to be both the administration building and the dining hall stood out, and the smoke there was thicker, although the light wind from the northwest looked to be carrying it over the river and across that part of L'Excelsis to the east of the River Aluse.

"Desyrk could have totally destroyed the bridge," Alyna said quietly, her words barely reaching Alastar.

He turned in the saddle and replied, "He had to know he wouldn't have that much time. He wanted to destroy as much of the Collegium as possible."

"He targeted your study. He wasn't as good on aiming at the Maitre's house. That's likely because his eyesight isn't that good and there aren't any tall and large landmarks near it."

"I can't imagine why he was after me." Alastar's tone was dryly sardonic.

"What will you do if you find him?"

"Blind him and put him before a hearing again."

"And if you can't blind him? Or capture him?"

"Whatever's necessary to make sure he's never again a danger to the Collegium or Solidar. He's likely wounded or killed at least some imagers or staff. I hope most of them followed the plan and got away."

"Some won't have listened."

"I think I mentioned that you're more skeptical than I am." *And that skepticism comes from the background of being from a High Holder's family and living for years in L'Excelsis.*

"I never disputed that, Maitre. In fact, I believe I was the one who suggested it."

"I believe you did." Alastar kept his voice light, then returned his attention to that part of Imagisle just beyond the bridge, but he did not see much damage except for where one shell's explosion had gouged out part of the shoulder to the eastern approach and several paving stones.

Once they crossed the bridge, Taryn and two thirds halted at the approach, and Glaesyn left the group, riding north toward the park. Alastar just hoped, again, that Akoryt had been able to evacuate everyone before the shelling had begun. As they reached the boulevard flanking the central green, he looked toward the Maitre's dwelling, where he could see that shutters had been ripped off the windows on the lower floor of the western end of the building, and several windows shattered. There were also several craters short of the porch, and to the west of the dwelling, but he didn't see any sign of fire.

Only one of the cottages appeared to have taken a shell, the third one, on the west side of the green, which Claeynd and his family occupied. On the other hand, even from the far end of the green Alastar could see that little remained of either the dining hall or the administration building, except smoke and flames and perhaps some sections of walls. He didn't see any sign of fire from either the anomen or the stables. *They weren't interested in upsetting the Nameless or hurting the horses.* For some reason, that thought amused him in a dark way.

He reined up well short of the flames still consuming the remnants of the administration building and the dining hall. Before him was utter destruction. Most of the walls of both structures had been reduced to piles of rubble. All that remained standing were some few sections of the stone walls, all of them showing damage. Although the acrid odor of burning wood and all sorts of other substances filled the air, the smoke was less than Alastar expected, most likely because the flames were subsiding and the light wind continued to carry the smoke eastward. The south end of the student quarters had collapsed, but nothing had caught fire there, it appeared. *Not yet, anyway.*

He saw no imagers and no one else. Since the fire did not appear to be spreading, he saw no point in trying to put it out, especially since most of the imagers, including himself, were tired, if not exhausted. He turned the gelding and addressed the imagers. "Those of you with families can seek them out. They should be in the north park. I may have to recall you; so please don't leave Imagisle, and don't have your families leave either. It won't likely be a good idea in any case. Matters will likely get worse off the isle, at least for a while."

"Worse?" asked Warryk. "How could anywhere else be worse?"

"We've removed the immediate threat to the Collegium. Rex Ryen has still named us his enemy. We can protect each other far more effectively here than you will be able to do on your own off Imagisle. The High Holders aren't exactly pleased with us, either."

"What did we do—"

"Warryk!" snapped Alyna. "If you weren't listening when the Maitre explained it, I will. For years, all the Collegium did was to take golds from the rex. Those golds came from the High Holders and the factors. The rex got nothing from those golds, and neither did the High Holders and factors. No one likes greedy beggars, especially if those beggars are imagers. If you don't understand that, then you deserve what's waiting for you across the river."

The ice in Alyna's voice chilled Alastar, and he wasn't even the target. Warryk seemed to shrivel in his saddle.

"I think the Maitre and Maitre Alyna have explained enough," added Cyran. "Those of you without families remain here. We have more than enough to do."

As the junior maitres sorted themselves out, Alastar turned to Alyna, who had drawn her mount up beside him. "You were quite effective. That's exactly why you're going to be in charge of rebuilding the Collegium."

"I am?"

"Do you know anyone else who's better qualified among the imagers? And after your very effective comments to Warryk, I don't think anyone's likely to question you."

"I'm an imager, not a builder."

"You're more of a builder than anyone else. If you can find someone else to design a new dining hall or a new administration building, that's fine. I'm going to be very involved in a few other matters." *Such as dealing with Ryen, Demykalon, Desyrk, and Guerdyn and some other High Holders.*

After a moment, she nodded. "I can see that."

At the sound of hooves, Alastar turned as Akoryt

rode up, alone, likely on Glaesyn's mount. Akoryt's face looked white in the uneven light cast by the few remaining flames consuming the last of the burnable parts of the two buildings largely leveled by the combination of shelling and fire.

"How bad was it?" Alastar braced himself for what Akoryt might report.

"It could have been worse," replied the Maitre D'Structure slowly. "Two seconds were killed because they disregarded instructions and went back to their quarters to get something. They were running by the administration building when the first shells hit. One other was wounded slightly. There are several other minor injuries, and two serious ones. Gaellen is doing his best with them. There are two student thirds missing. Seconda Thelia believes that they wanted something from your study. She overheard them talking about the founder's sabre. She came to tell me, but they'd vanished . . ."

The founder's sabre? Why would they want that? Or even to save it? With that thought, Alastar missed the next few words Akoryt uttered.

". . . of them—Johanyr, interestingly enough—is quite good with concealments. Or he was, if he was caught inside when the cannonballs hit the administration building."

Johanyr? "What about Taurek and Bettaur?"

"I couldn't see leaving them in the disciplinary cells, and there was no way to confine them effectively except chaining and blindfolding them. So I said that they were out on sufferance, and that if they behaved themselves they could remain out . . . and if they didn't, they'd face your judgment. So far, they've been very helpful—although they aren't talking to each other."

"That's the best you could have done. I certainly don't blame Taurek for not speaking to Bettaur. You're looking strained. What aren't you telling me?"

"Shabrena and some of the cooks and helpers left and then sneaked back. They told the others to remain, but that it was all foolishness, and they wanted to have dinner ready when everyone came back. I wasn't about to send people after them."

"How many? Do you know?"

"Four, I think. There were eleven in the kitchens. Seven are accounted for. Obsolym thinks one of the assistant gardeners didn't get the word, either. He was at the boathouse and went from there to do some work near the foot of the old east bridge. One of the shells hit the stonework too close to him. The others destroyed the bridge."

"Any other casualties?"

"I don't know of any others," replied Akoryt cautiously. "Obsolym might know of more. I haven't seen him in several quints."

"Do you know where he is?"

"He had the staff gathered more to the east side of the north park."

"I'll need to talk to him next," said Alastar. "You'll need to see about quarters. Everyone who has quarters that are intact can return to them. We'll have to make other arrangements for those whose quarters have been destroyed." He paused. "The student imagers without rooms can spend the night in Desyrk's cottage. There's no one there, and the cottage might as well serve some purpose. Make whatever accommodations you can. If necessary, some can sleep in the Maitre's dwelling."

"Yes, sir."

"If you have any better ideas or something I've overlooked, let me know."

Akoryt nodded.

"I mean it."

"I know, sir."

Once Akoryt turned his borrowed mount back toward the park to the north, Alastar motioned for Cyran and Alyna to ride closer and join him. "In a moment, I'm going to find Obsolym and see how he fared with the staff. I'll need Shaelyt and two solid thirds a glass before dawn tomorrow. Cyran, you'll be in charge of Imagisle while I'm otherwise occupied. Alyna will be in charge of rebuilding, starting tomorrow. Not tonight." Alastar turned to her. "First, use imaging to repair what can be safely restored. Don't worry about rebuilding the administration building or the dining hall—" He stopped as he saw the expression on her face.

"Unlike you, Maitre, the students do need to eat," Alyna said firmly.

"After they have shelter, then, but the administration building can definitely wait."

Both Cyran and Alyna nodded.

"Now, I need to see what Obsolym is doing. After that, I'll be back at the Maitre's dwelling. It's going to have to serve as the administration building for a while."

Obsolym, carrying a lantern, was right where Akoryt had said he would be. Beyond him, clustered around the benches by the walkway, were close to a hundred men, women, and children. Alastar could almost feel their scrutiny as he reined up short of the oldest maitre.

"Maitre Obsolym . . . how many staff people did we lose? How many were wounded or injured? Do you know?"

Obsolym did not immediately respond, but just looked up at the Maitre of the Collegium.

"Akoryt told me about the cooks and the gardener," prompted Alastar. "Were there any others?"

"None of this would have happened if you'd just done what the rex wanted," Obsolym said quietly.

"And then what?" replied Alastar. "After we assassinated the High Council and another score of High Holders, and that was what Ryen demanded, what other command would Ryen have made? And if we didn't comply with that, how long before this"—he gestured toward the south end of Imagisle—"happened anyway?"

Obsolym looked directly at Alastar . . . and then dropped his eyes. After a moment, he said, "I'm sorry, Maitre. I just never thought . . ."

"No one did." *Including you.* "That's been the problem."

"What will happen next?"

"It becomes our turn to straighten out the mess. You didn't think I let this happen just to make everyone feel sorry for the poor imagers?"

"No, sir."

Alastar could tell that the older maitre had his doubts. "Were there any other casualties?"

"I don't think so. Petros has the horses tethered or tied over by the boathouse. He said all the stableboys and the ostlers weren't hurt." Obsolym stopped, then ventured, "We saw all the flames . . ."

"The administration building was totally destroyed. So was the dining hall. There's damage to at least one of the cottages and a little to the Maitre's dwelling. The east bridge and the south bridge are gone. The Bridge of Desires lost much of the middle span, but we repaired it enough to return to Imagisle. We destroyed three army cannon emplacements. They had fourteen cannon firing on the Collegium. Oh . . . and we're fairly certain Desyrk used a concealment to help them place two of them, the ones that likely did most of the damage to the administration building and the dining hall."

"How can you be certain it was Desyrk?"

"When Maitre Alyna and I tried to deal with the last cannon emplacement, we ran into imager shields. That was either Desyrk or an imager we don't know about working for Marshal Demykalon. Given that Desyrk's brother is a subcommander or commander . . ."

"Subcommander," supplied Obsolym, his voice flat. "Chesyrk's a subcommander. Or he was."

Chesyrk? Where had he heard that name? Alastar knew someone had mentioned it, but he couldn't recall who . . . or when. But he didn't have time to try to recall it, not now. "You can have people return to their cottages or rooms. We were able to stop the shelling before the army got to dealing with most dwellings. One part of the student quarters, one imager cottage—Claeynd's, I think—and part of the Maitre's dwelling were damaged. There might be some damage we didn't see in the dark, but likely not much."

"Is that all, sir?"

"For now. There's not much else you or anyone else can do tonight except get people settled."

"Thank you, sir."

As Alastar rode back toward the stables, he thought over Obsolym's reaction, disbelief at what had happened, followed by despair and resignation. Had Obsolym believed that Alastar was unfair to Desyrk . . . or just that he could not believe that either Ryen or Demykalon would attack Imagisle? He wondered if he would ever understand the older imager or if their experiences were just too different. The other thing that had struck him was that Desyrk had referred to his brother as a commander. *Exaggeration . . . another aspect of his character.*

When Alastar returned to the stables and dismounted, he saw Chervyt standing in the shadows cast by one of the outside stable lanterns. "Are you all right?"

"I'm fine, sir. It's just . . . well . . . Nuasyn . . ."

"You were friends?"

"You might . . . Yes, we were friends."

Just from Chervyt's words, Alastar got the impression that the two had been more than friends, but he wasn't about to press. "I'm sorry. I didn't know that. Nuasyn, you know, persuaded Maitre Cyan to include him."

"Yes, sir. It's not his fault, or yours . . ." The third shook his head. "It's just . . ."

"Why did it have to be Nuasyn?" asked Alastar gently. *It's always someone.*

"Yes, sir."

"That's only a question the Nameless could answer." *And I've never heard answers from the Nameless.*

After a long silence, Chervyt spoke again. "Sir?"

"Yes?"

"Ah . . . why didn't you and the other maitres use concealments to hide the bridges or the Collegium?"

"That would have only delayed what happened. The army gunners would still have been able to range most of the buildings using maps. They wouldn't have been quite so accurate, but that would have meant more imagers and others might well have been killed or injured." All that was largely true enough, but certainly not the only reason Alastar had not used a concealment. "I thought we'd need all the strength we could muster to deal with the gunners and the troopers protecting them, and it turned out largely that way."

"Why were they attacking us? We didn't do anything to hurt them."

"The rex ordered them to attack us if we didn't attack the High Holders. We tried to work out something, but neither the rex nor the High Holders wanted to compromise."

"They killed imagers because we wouldn't kill High Holders?" Chervyt's voice rose in disbelief.

"It's a little more complicated than that, but that's what was at the bottom of it all."

"The rex really told you to kill High Holders?"

"He said that he wanted the High Council and the High Holders to accept larger tariffs, and that if it meant killing High Holders, then it was necessary, and that if I didn't succeed by this evening, then we would feel his wrath. I tried everything short of injuring or killing them. It wasn't enough."

"Nuasyn . . . the others . . . they died because you wouldn't kill people so he could have more golds?"

Alastar couldn't leave Chervyt with that impression, although it would have been easy enough to do so. "Not quite. The rex had already cut the golds he provided to the Collegium, and he doesn't have enough ships to stop smugglers or repair the roads. For years, the High Holders have opposed higher tariffs. But if we killed members of the Council at Ryen's behest, then all Solidar would be after the Collegium."

"It's . . . it's all so frigged . . ."

"Yes, it is, and we'll have to fix it if imagers are to be safe again." Alastar waited.

Chervyt did not speak for a time. Finally, he said, "Thank you, sir. I hope . . ." He shook his head. "Good night, sir."

"Good night, Chervyt."

Alastar began to walk toward the ruined and still smoldering administration building and then beyond it to the Maitre's house. The explanations he had offered over the day, he knew, would be only the first of many. He also knew that he and the other imagers had a long night ahead and more difficult days ahead. He just hoped that Akoryt and the others didn't discover more casualties.

25

In the grayness before dawn, Alastar, Cyran, and Alyna sat in the dim light of a single lamp, gathered around the desk in the study of the Maitre's dwelling.

"I don't like it," admitted Cyran, "but nothing else seems to have worked." He paused. "You will offer Ryen a last chance . . . even if he gave the orders, and it wasn't Demykalon's doing on his own?"

"I will," replied Alastar. *If only for everyone's peace of mind. Or your own, since you know he won't take it.*

"Do you think Guerdyn will be reasonable?"

"I doubt it, but I'll do my best to convince him. If he isn't, I'll see if we can reach Vaun." He eased back his chair and stood. "I need to meet Shaelyt and the thirds. You two keep everyone on Imagisle until this settles a bit. Have Akoryt see if he can determine what happened to those two imagers Seconda Thelia reported." *Trying to save—or steal—the founder's sabre?* He shook his head, then looked at Alyna. "Only work on those repairs that don't overstrain you and others."

She nodded as she and Cyran stood. The two followed Alastar to the front porch of the Maitre's dwelling. In the gloom beyond, Shaelyt, Belsior, and Neiryn stood waiting, holding their mounts. Neiryn also held the reins to Alastar's gelding.

"You will be careful?" murmured Alyna from where she stood almost at Alastar's elbow.

"As careful as I can be." *Although the greatest risks have already struck . . . you hope.* "I am taking two full water bottles of lager, along with everything else." He paused, then added, "Cyran . . . you might keep an eye out for Desyrk. I can't believe he'd show up, but I couldn't believe he'd direct cannon fire at the Collegium, either."

"He knew rifles might not work; that's why he used cannon," added Alyna.

"I've let it be known just what Desyrk did," said Cyran, "but another word of warning to the others can't hurt."

"Good." Alastar walked down the steps and took the gelding's reins from Neiryn. As he turned his mount, he could see the vague outline of the ruins of the administration building. *Can you ever justify the deaths and injuries?* He smiled with a wry bitterness. Justification would be easy. Living with the memories would likely be anything but easy. He still remembered the horror of Dyel and Mahara's deaths. *And you didn't cause them.*

Less than a quint later, accompanied by Shaelyt, Belsior, and Neiryn, Alastar rode out over the repaired but not completely rebuilt Bridge of Desires, nodding as they passed the stolid Secondus Maercyl, who stood watch there—just in case. In one of Alastar's saddlebags were several lengths of rope, which he hoped they would be able to use, as well as a considerable number of heavy cloth strips. In the other were the two water bottles filled with dark lager taken from the limited supply at the Maitre's dwelling.

"Where are we headed?" asked Shaelyt, riding beside Alastar. "You didn't say last night."

"It's better that no one heard. Our first stop will be the Chateau D'Rex. We'll ride up to the rear entry under a concealment. There's usually only one guard there. If there are more . . . we'll deal with them." Alastar hoped there weren't, because dealing with more than two would likely require lethal force.

"Isn't it a bit . . . early, sir?"

"It is, but that will make what needs to be done somewhat easier." Ryen was an extremely early riser, but

Alastar didn't want to reveal any more than necessary. He ignored Shaelyt's puzzled expression.

Once they crossed the bridge and turned north on the West River Road, Alastar studied the row of shops that had contained the one holding the cannon, but there was no trace of fire, although the two joining structures were definitely the worse for wear, with sagging walls and slanting roofs. Farther along, a few crafters and shopkeepers were up and out, sweeping or cleaning, as the four rode up the West River Road, but those out scarcely looked at the riders. *Likely more out of fear than disinterest.* When they neared the point, Alastar studied the area closely, but there were no signs of troopers. The blast had leveled enough of the trees and bushes that he could see that the disabled cannon had not yet been removed.

There were more shopkeepers out along the Boulevard D'Ouest by the time the four imagers reached the ring road north of the Chateau D'Rex. Alastar turned in the saddle. "Belsior, Neiryn, you're to hold shields until I tell you to release them. If you cannot hold them after a time, let go, and then resume when you can. You are not to say one word, during this time. The only exception is if Maitre Shaelyt is in danger."

"Yes, sir."

Alastar could see the question. "We have some unpleasant duties to undertake. They may be dangerous. That's all you have to know for now."

When they turned onto the ring road, heading south, Alastar raised a blurring concealment, then after they had ridden perhaps a hundred yards, shifted to a full concealment. At that point, he said, "We're under a concealment now. Make sure you don't run anyone down, because they won't see you." That warning was likely unnecessary, since the road was almost deserted except for a few farm carts most likely headed to the market square south of the Chateau D'Rex, a square Alastar thought was almost squalid and definitely unbecoming. *It really ought to be used for something more imposing. How can Ryen demand an imposing avenue, and then tolerate such a squalid square so close to his chateau?* But then Ryen was a mass of anger and contradictions.

Alastar did not see any army troopers near the chateau, nor were any guards stationed at the foot of the paved lane that led to the rear of the chateau. Two guards stood outside the closed iron-grille gates to the rear courtyard.

"A slow and quiet walk from here," said Alastar, turning in the saddle to address Belsior and Neiryn, before adding, to Shaelyt, "Clamp shields around the guard on your left when I say shields. Make sure they cover his mouth. We don't want him yelling. You'll have to hold him until he passes out. Then we'll tie them up, gag them, and blindfold them."

"What next, sir?"

"I'll see if I can get into the courtyard without being seen or heard. You keep anyone from seeing the three of you."

Neither guard moved as the four imagers rode up the paved lane toward the gate, not until Alastar was about fifteen yards from the nearest guard.

"Sammel? You hear horses?" The guard looked from side to side.

"Huh?" Sammel shook himself, as if he'd been half asleep.

"Horses . . . I said."

"Shields," Alastar said quietly, clamping his around the guard on the right, the one who had spoken. He immediately dismounted and handed the gelding's reins to Belsior, grabbed several lengths of rope from his saddlebags, as well as some cloth strips, handing some of each to Shaelyt before hurrying toward the unnamed guard. He stopped far enough back so that the concealment lay between him and the guard. He did not move until the man's eyes rolled, then held the shield several moments longer while he readied the rope. He began trussing the man before he released the shield. Even so, the guard was beginning to rouse himself by the time Alastar gagged and blindfolded him, then dragged him away from the gate and next to the wall.

He looked to Shaelyt, but the younger maitre had finished with Sammel not much after Alastar had blindfolded the first guard. Alastar walked away and motioned for Shaelyt to join him next to the gelding, then said in a low voice that would not carry beyond the other maitre, "Shaelyt, you'll need to conceal your presence once I enter the courtyard. I suspect a blurring concealment will suffice at this glass. But no one is to know we are here or have been—even if that means you have to kill someone. This is important for the safety of all imagers. Do you understand?" As he spoke, Alastar took two more lengths of rope from his saddlebags and wound them around his midsection under his riding jacket and stuffed several lengths of cloth inside his tunic.

"Yes, sir."

"Good. I'd tell you to wish me luck, but we can't depend on fortune. Wait over there under the chateau wall." Alastar turned and climbed the gate, comparatively low, at little more than two yards. He was glad for the heavy riding gloves. As he suspected, the rear courtyard held no guards, but a kitchen scull carried out something to one of the refuse barrels.

After she dumped it and headed back toward the kitchen door, another guard, standing outside the side door used by guards and servitors, called out, "You never stop to throw me a kiss, Cethana."

"Like you deserve one," snapped the woman.

"Every man deserves one now and again." The guard moved several paces from the door.

"Not at this Namer-early glass of the morning."

Taking advantage of the guard's distraction, Alastar slipped behind him, eased the door open and stepped inside, then flattened himself against the wall as another guard hurried down the narrow back hall and grabbed the door, opening it wider.

"Poelo! Don't leave the frigging door open! You want us both gutted!" The words were almost hissed.

The outer guard turned back. "I didn't open it."

"It was open . . ."

While the two argued in low voices, Alastar made his way to the grand staircase. He'd thought about taking the private back staircase, but it was so narrow that there was no way to avoid someone if he went that way. After he climbed the steps, he had to dodge a serving maid, carrying a tray back toward the kitchen, once he reached the upper hall, but the only person in the north corridor was the guard who was always posted outside Ryen's study. Again, he used shields to immobilize the guard.

When the study guard crumpled, Alastar trussed him quickly, gagged and blindfolded him with the strips of cloth he'd brought, and then opened the door and stepped into the study, dropping the concealment after closing the door and walking toward Ryen, seated at his desk and reading a sheet of something.

The rex's mouth opened, if only for an instant. Then he smiled. "I thought you might be here. I didn't expect you quite so early. Or so quietly."

"Imagisle is a mass of rubble." Alastar offered the exaggeration blandly. "I take it that was what you meant by bringing your wrath down on the Collegium."

"What else did you expect? You disobeyed my orders."

"Now . . . you're ordering the Collegium?"

"If I pay you, you'll take my orders."

"Even if they're unreasonable?"

"I'm the rex. I'm the one who decides what's reasonable and what's not."

Alastar nodded. "I see. Then I have one last question. Did you order Demykalon to fire on the Collegium with his cannon?"

"Of course. I don't make idle threats."

"And after that becomes known, to start destroying High Holder chateaux until they agree to your tariff terms?"

"What else? None of you seem willing to act unless forced."

"I'm glad to hear you confirm that."

"So you can make some threat you won't carry out, just like your predecessor."

"No. I don't make threats at all." With that, Alastar clamped full shields around the startled rex. "Neither you nor the High Council would see reason. The Collegium suffered, and there are too many dead imagers and staff. Enough is enough. One way or another, your successor will be more reasonable."

Alastar did not remove the shields until it was more than clear that Ryen would not take another breath.

On the way out, he used another concealment, and again clamped shields around the guard lying in the corridor until the man passed out once more. Then he untied him and removed the gag before making his way, still under concealment, to the grand staircase and then down and back to the rear entrance, waiting until the guard patrolling the lower hall moved out of sight, just so the man would not see the doors open. He still had to deal with the door guard, but that was easier. He just imaged a pair of coppers into the air several yards from the door and let them fall to the stones.

The outside guard looked around, then up, and quickly darted toward the coins. Alastar opened the door, stepped out, and closed it, then sidled away and along the walls until he reached the gate. He stopped, not seeing either Shaelyt or the thirds, then shook his head. He wouldn't, not with Shaelyt's concealment.

Even knowing where he'd told Shaelyt to be, he almost ran into the maitre's mount before he was inside the other's concealment.

To his credit, Shaelyt did not speak, but raised his eyebrows.

Alastar moved closer and explained. Then they shield-stunned the two gate guards and untied them, but left the gags and blindfolds in place before mounting and riding down the lane to the ring road. Alastar did not speak until they were well north of the chateau.

"We're still under a concealment, and we're headed northwest" was all he said.

"The army High Command?" murmured Shaelyt.

Alastar nodded.

By the time they turned off the ring road onto the north pike, the predawn gray had given way to the pale yellowish light that immediately preceded sunrise. When they neared the low walls that surrounded the army headquarters, the old gates were closed, and Alastar could see at least a squad of troopers mustered in the area behind them. The wall itself was brick, and clearly dated back to when the headquarters had been a private estate, most likely of a High Holder, since it was barely two yards high, if that.

He smiled. "I think we need a diversion, Maitre Shaelyt. I'd like you and the thirds to ride about a quarter mille west along the wall there. Under a concealment, of course. Then I'd like you to remove part of the wall and set fire to something just inside the wall. Make it flamboyant. Then head back down the pike and wait by the old warehouse just north of the ring road. Use a blurring shield if you can still manage it once you get there, or have the thirds alternate. I'll meet you there."

"Sir?"

"If I'm not there in two glasses, head back to Imagisle and inform Maitre Cyran and Maitre Alyna."

Alastar turned and rode eastward close to a third of a

mille, until he found a spot where several trees just inside the wall blocked the view of the wall from a good many of the buildings, especially the old chateau where Alastar suspected Demykalon had his study. The odds were that the marshal would be there. Even from Alastar's limited interaction with the marshal, he doubted that Demykalon would be the type to handle unpleasant duties in person, especially when he would be likely planning to lay the blame on someone else.

He looked back, then saw a column of fire. *Shaelyt did make it impressive.* With that, Alastar imaged away a part of the wall, a section just wide enough for him to ride through. Holding shields and a concealment, he did just that, then angled the gray across the grounds toward the old chateau. Since there was an empty hitching rail outside the chateau's main entrance, Alastar rode right up to it, dismounted, and then waited until the guard standing in the open entry portico looked the other way before moving away from the gelding and leaving it unconcealed. He moved up the stone steps quietly, then waited as the trooper saw the mount and moved forward to look more closely. Then he slipped behind the man and through the double doors. Once inside he continued into the main hall, where he paused to one side of the table desk where a squad leader sat, looking bored. He eased himself against the wall and watched for several moments, as first several rankers passed, and then an undercaptain, but no one spoke.

After a bit, he waited until a ranker hurried toward a side hall and followed the man, saying, "Pardon me," firmly but quietly, easing forward enough that the ranker was inside the concealment. He hoped to take advantage of the fact that imager grays and his visor cap were cut in the same style as the uniforms of army officers.

The man half-turned, looking surprised, but before he could utter a word, Alastar said, "I have an urgent message for the marshal, but I can't find his study. Is it in this wing?"

"No, sir. It's just off the small circular foyer on the other end." The ranker started to say more.

"Thank you," Alastar said quickly, preempting the ranker's words, and then stepped back quickly and to the man's blind side so that the ranker could not see him appear to vanish. The ranker looked from one side to the other, but Alastar kept moving back toward the main hall and then, as quietly as he could, circled behind the squad leader and into the west wing of the former chateau.

Less than thirty yards farther on, a fresh-faced undercaptain sat at another table desk outside a set of double doors.

Alastar paused, debating his next move. Then, as he heard footsteps, he saw the ranker he'd accosted a few moments before hurrying down the hallway. With a smile, Alastar eased along the wall until he was beside the study door . . . and waited.

The ranker stopped before the desk. "Sir, there was a courier with a message looking for the marshal, but I can't find him."

"There's been no one here. Did you check with the duty squad leader?"

"Yes, sir. He's seen no one."

Alastar stepped to the study door, easing it ajar and sliding inside, but leaving the door ajar. Then he flattened himself against the paneled wall as Demykalon looked up, then snapped, "Undercaptain! I said—"

Several moments passed before the undercaptain appeared in the partly open doorway.

"I'm sorry, sir. It must not have been latched."

"Make sure it is this time."

"Yes, sir." The junior officer took a quick look around the study as he closed the door.

The marshal shook his head, looked to the window,

and then back at the map spread on the desk in front of him.

Alastar waited until Demykalon was absorbed in the map before slowly making his way to a point less than two yards from the desk, where he saw that the map was one of L'Excelsis and the surrounding area.

The marshal looked up and frowned, his head going from side to side.

When Demykalon glanced toward the window, Alastar dropped the concealment. "Good morning, Marshal."

After the slightest of starts, Demykalon said, "No one announced you." His words were matter-of-fact. "I suppose I shouldn't be surprised. I've heard that imagers can conceal themselves."

"At the concealment, probably not. Nor should you be surprised at my being here. Not after you cannon-bombarded Imagisle last evening."

"Bombarded? They were only supposed to fire warning shots. Obviously Commander Chesyrk exceeded his orders." Demykalon shrugged. "That does happen when a man feels strongly that his brother has been wronged."

Chesyrk? A commander? Did Demykalon promote him to put him in charge of the attack on Imagisle? "That isn't what Ryen said. He said he ordered you to bombard Imagisle, then to be ready to bombard High Holder Guerdyn's own chateau."

"Bombard . . . fire upon . . . there is a difference. Chesyrk chose to interpret his orders with excessive enthusiasm."

"By the way, where is Chesyrk?"

Demykalon shrugged. "I thought you might know. He was with the northern cannon emplacement. But then, not everyone has returned . . . or will." The marshal smiled. "The damages you caused will have to come from the golds you or your successor receives for the Collegium. That doesn't include charges of murder, of course."

"Murder? Come now, your troopers opened fire on a civilian installation. Acting to stop an unprovoked attack is self-defense."

"Rather excessive self-defense."

"A number of troopers survived that clash," Alastar said evenly. "Possibly even the subcommander . . . commander." Alastar had his doubts about that, but he wanted to hear Demykalon's response. "Did you promote him to get him to handle that mission?"

"He was due for promotion." The marshal stood and moved to one side of the desk. "He's been due for a long time." The last words held a sardonic twist.

"Most convenient," observed Alastar, easing back slightly. "You assigned him so that you can claim that my treatment of his brother led him to exceed his orders."

"I was apparently right in that," replied the marshal. "I was also right in believing that the Collegium is a danger to the rex and all Solidar. Not even cannon apparently stopped you."

"Oh . . . you destroyed all too much of the Collegium," admitted Alastar. "I just wanted to make sure that it was your responsibility and doing. Why did you do it? Was it to weaken the Collegium? Or to show that Ryen was truly mad . . . and perhaps to pave the way for a more . . . reasonable lineage as rex?"

Demykalon smiled. "Wouldn't a more reasonable lineage be a greater blessing to Solidar than a mad rex? That's beside the point at the moment."

"Is it?" asked Alastar.

"However the order was interpreted by Commander Chesyrk, it was not my order, but that of the rex." Demykalon's hand dropped toward the hilt of his sabre.

Alastar didn't bother with more words. He clamped shields around Demykalon.

When the marshal was dead, Alastar released the shields, and eased the body to the floor. After that, he pulled the marshal's sabre from its scabbard and set it on the desk. He concentrated once more. The sabre vanished from the desk and reappeared thrust through Demykalon's chest . . . and more than a hand's span depth into the carpet and solid wood floor beneath.

Alastar did feel a flash of dizziness, but it passed almost immediately. Still . . . That suggested that he needed to be careful until his body had a chance to recover. He walked to the door of the study, raised a concealment, then quietly unlatched the door, slowly easing it open just a crack and peering through the crack at the undercaptain. The junior officer did not turn as Alastar opened the study door wider and slipped out, then closed and latched the door as quietly as he could. Even so, the latch clicked slightly.

The undercaptain turned immediately, half-rising, then settled back into his chair as he saw that the study door was closed. He paused, then again stood. Alastar moved farther from the door, keeping his back to the wall, as the junior officer walked over to the door and studied it, then turned and made his way back to his desk, where he reseated himself.

Alastar continued to move quietly and slowly away from the study, then back out of the old chateau. When he reached the steps outside and started down, he noticed that a ranker and an officer stood next to his gray gelding. He concentrated on making out their words as he made his way toward them, still holding his concealment.

"Whose mount is it?" demanded the rotund older captain.

"I don't know, sir. It's not—"

"Then take it to the stables, and let me know when you find out whose it is."

"Sir, begging your pardon . . ."

"Just do it, trooper! In the mood the marshal's in, you don't want to be explaining why some courier didn't stable his mount."

"Yes, sir. As you ordered, sir."

The captain stalked away. Once he had walked past the corner of the small building some ten yards away, Alastar moved closer to the clearly distraught trooper, expanding the concealment.

"You haven't happened to see another man in gray, have you?"

"No, sir." The junior squad leader was clearly flustered at the sudden appearance of the Maitre.

"Thank you. I wouldn't mention this to the captain, except to say that the courier claimed his mount right after he left. I was delivering an urgent message to the marshal." Alastar untied the gray gelding, mounted, and then rode away, glancing back at the bewildered ranker, who was looking from side to side, before continuing on his way back to the small gap he had earlier imaged in the low brick wall. As he'd suspected, it was so small that, so far, no one had even noticed it. At least, there were no troopers around.

He kept looking back, but he saw no signs of alarm or disturbance, although he had no doubts that, sooner or later, there would be anger and consternation in army headquarters. Then he reached back and took out one of the water bottles. He definitely needed some of the dark lager it held.

After riding several hundred yards farther and drinking almost half the lager in the water bottle, Alastar felt much better, and the light-headedness he'd felt began to recede. He couldn't help but think about why Demykalon had ordered Chesyrk to fire. *Was it really to make Ryen seem madder and more unreasonable? Or to weaken the Collegium? Or both?*

He had only ridden another block when he abruptly recalled where he had heard Chesyrk's name before—when Ryen had mentioned being briefed on the new cannon by Demykalon *and* Chesyrk. Yet Desyrk had insisted that his brother never accompanied the marshal to brief the rex.

Alastar was still mulling that over when he reached the old warehouse and rode toward Shaelyt and the two thirds. By then, he felt almost normal. *But you're likely not back to full strength, not after all the shields, concealments, and imaging all at once.* After a moment, a second thought came to him. *How did Maitre Quaeryt and the other founders manage all that they did?*

"Sir?" asked Shaelyt as Alastar reined up beside him.

"We have one more call to pay . . . or possibly two. We're headed for the Council Chateau. I'll need a few words with High Holder Guerdyn. Assuming he's there." Alastar turned the gelding toward the ring road, then added, "He won't wish to speak to me. So there's little point in sending a messenger to request a meeting."

Less than a glass passed on the ride from the warehouse around the top of the ring road, then east along the Boulevard D'Ouest, and north on the West River Road until they neared the walls around the Chateau D'Council.

"What do you need from us?" asked Shaelyt.

"For now, once we approach the grounds of the Council Chateau, you're to hold shields until we leave and I tell you to release them. If you cannot hold them after a time, release them, and then resume when you can."

"Yes, sir."

Alastar could see the unasked question on the faces of both Belsior and Neiryn. "I have some more possibly unpleasant duties to undertake. They may be dangerous, but it's unlikely you'll have to do more than hold your shields and wait."

The liveried guard at the gate looked up, but before he could speak, Alastar said, "I'm here to see High Holder Guerdyn."

"He's not expecting—"

"That doesn't matter. Open the gates."

The guard looked at Alastar and the three other mounted imagers, then offered a resigned expression. "Yes, sir."

Once the gates were open, as Alastar passed the guard, he said, "Thank you. Just leave the gates open. I'm sure we won't be very long."

"Yes, sir." The guard's voice was as resigned as his expression had been.

Within moments of Alastar's arrival at the front portico of the Council Chateau, the same footman who had greeted Alastar on every visit strode forth and announced, "High Holder Guerdyn is not receiving, Maitre."

"Then he is here?" said Alastar.

"Sir, all I can say is that he is not receiving."

Alastar dismounted and handed the gelding's reins to Neiryn, then walked up the steps to where the footman stood. "I will see him. You can attempt to stop me and regret it. Or you can stand aside."

"Sir . . . I beg you. You can do no worse to me than he will—"

Alastar clamped shields around the footman, watching closely, then released them when the man turned blue and his eyes rolled. He caught the falling figure and lowered him to the stone tiles at the top of the steps, then turned to Shaelyt and the two thirds. "If he wakes before I return, suggest to him that interrupting my meeting would be most unwise." With that, he raised a concealment, opened the right-hand door, and let himself in. He walked through the domed circular entry hall and through the archway on the right, making his way to the study door, which he opened, then closed after he entered. Only then did he drop the concealment.

"I told you I was not to be disturbed—" Guerdyn bolted from where he had been sitting at his desk and took a step toward Alastar before halting. "What are you doing here?"

"If I wish to see you, Guerdyn, I will. You should know that."

"That may be, but I do not have to talk to you." Guerdyn smiled.

"If you wish to test that, you may. I'd advise against it."

"You are serious, Maitre, I see."

"I'm very serious. Neither the High Council nor the rex appear willing to compromise on the matter of tariffs. Since neither of you will, I'll place a compromise on the table. Four coppers on a gold."

"Ryen will never accept that. Neither will the High Council."

"One way or another, the rex will accept it. One way or another, the High Council will."

"That sounds like a threat. I do not appreciate threats. Neither does the High Council."

"It's not a threat. It's a statement of fact, Guerdyn. You, or your successor as head of the High Council, will accept higher tariffs. Four coppers on the gold for the coming year. That will be adjusted, one way or another, next fall."

"You wouldn't dare." Guerdyn's smile was close to insolent. "You've already demonstrated that."

"That was before Marshal Demykalon attacked the Collegium with cannon." Alastar's smile in return was cold. "I don't threaten, and I don't make dares. Will you convince the High Council to accept four coppers?"

"No. They won't accept it, and I won't demean myself to insist on it. Nothing you can do will change my mind."

"I was afraid you'd say that." Alastar clamped shields around Guerdyn, then stood, waiting until the High Holder turned red, and then bluish. Only then did Alastar release the shields.

Guerdyn staggered, barely managing to put both hands on the desk to catch himself. His breath was ragged.

Alastar waited. "Four coppers or your death. And if you accept four coppers and back off, we will find you and kill you. That is not a threat, but a certain promise."

"You can threaten all you want. You wouldn't dare."

Alastar imaged stronger shields around Guerdyn. He held them for a long time. When he released them, the High Holder's body slumped over the desk, then slid to the floor. Holding shields, but nor raising a concealment, Alastar left the study, closing the door behind himself and walking to the main hall and then out to the portico.

The footman stood beside the doors, his eyes darting from the mounted imagers to Alastar, even as he shrank back against the wall without speaking.

Alastar nodded to him, without speaking, and walked to the gelding, taking back his mount's reins from Neiryn, and then mounting. Once in the saddle, he said, "We're heading south to the Nord Bridge, and then about a mille and a half north on the East River Road to High Holder Vaun's L'Excelsis chateau."

At roughly two quints past ninth glass, Alastar spied the brick wall set back some ten yards from the East River Road that surrounded Vaun's lands. As before, he had to wait for a man in workman's brown to reach the iron gates. The man looked as if he would open them, then stopped and asked, "Ah, sir . . . is the master expecting you?"

"He's not, but you really don't want to turn us away," replied Alastar.

The man studied the four only for an instant before he opened the gates, then nodded politely as they rode through, and immediately closed them. A footman in tan livery, trimmed in black, the same one that had received him previously, Alastar thought, hurried out the front door. He just looked at Alastar.

"I assume the High Holder is here," offered Alastar.

"He isn't expecting company, sir."

"The matter is urgent, and I think he will see me."

"Might I tell him . . . ?"

"Just tell him that Maitre Alastar is here. I'll wait in the entry hall." Alastar dismounted and followed the reluctant footman back into the entry hall, where he stopped and waited, if only for a few moments before the footman returned.

"He has a few moments, sir." The footman turned and led the way to the study door, stopping and gesturing to the open door. Once Alastar had entered, the footman closed the door.

Vaun turned from the window. He was wearing hose and shoes, but not a doublet, and a plain white shirt and a simple velvet tan jacket. His expression was bland, but Alastar could sense a certain irritation in the High Holder's movements.

"How is whatever you have in mind urgent enough to arrive without any notice and demand to see me?" Vaun did not gesture to any of the chairs or make a move toward them.

"I presented a compromise offer on next year's tariffs to High Holder Guerdyn. An increase of four coppers on a gold over the present tariff level. He refused to even consider it. I told him that the rex and the High Council would agree to it. He stated that he did not care whether the rex agreed or not. I suggested he should care. I even demonstrated why he should. He refused to consider the matter. Now, he doesn't have to worry." Alastar smiled coolly. "I thought you should know, and it might be best if you let Nacryon, Haebyn, and Moeryn know that."

"That is urgent?" Vaun didn't conceal the irritation in his voice.

"Since one of you will have to take over as head of the High Council, I thought you'd like to be the first to know."

To his credit, Vaun only nodded. "I see. What if whoever takes over refuses?"

"We will deal with his successor, and every other successor until the Council agrees."

Vaun frowned. "Why did you not do this earlier? What has changed?"

"Last night the army shelled Imagisle. Several buildings were destroyed. Some imagers and others were killed. Others were wounded. The attack was because we did not kill every member of the High Council to force agreement with Ryen's demands for higher tariffs."

Vaun's expression turned from concern to puzzlement. "Ryen ordered the shelling of Imagisle? I presume Demykalon did not act on his own initiative."

"Ryen did."

"Then why did you remove . . ." Vaun broke off his words. "Who is rex?"

"I assume Lorien is. Assuming he supports the compromise, he will remain so."

"Lorien . . ." Vaun nodded slowly. "How will Marshal Demykalon respond to this . . . change of circumstances?"

"The new marshal of the army will be the one to decide that."

"Don't you think . . . ?" Abruptly, Vaun shook his head. "You actually *planned* . . ."

"I gave all of you the chance to be reasonable," returned Alastar. "That opportunity is still open to you . . . and the other members of the High Council."

"There might be some question about your definition of reasonable." Vaun held up a hand as if to forestall any comment Alastar might make. "But I'm certainly not going to quibble. I doubt most of the other councilors will either."

"Except Haebyn?"

"He will not quibble, but he will never forget."

"Neither will I."

"I just might make that point," replied Vaun dryly.

"Once it is timely, say in a day or so, I will suggest that the High Council meet and agree to the terms you proposed, subject, of course, to the prior agreement of the rex."

"That would appear perfectly reasonable." Alastar inclined his head. "Unless there is some other matter we need to discuss, I will not intrude further upon you."

"I think this matter is quite enough for the present, Maitre Alastar."

"So do I, and I thank you." With another nod and a smile, Alastar turned, made his way to the study door, and from there to where Shaelyt and the thirds waited. He mounted quickly.

"Where are we headed now, sir?" asked Shaelyt.

"Back to the Chateau D'Rex to pay our respects to the rex."

Belsior and Neiryn exchanged glances.

"Rex Lorien," added Alastar. "He needs to know the terms for the new tariff schedule . . . and the reasons for them. He might also need a slight briefing on the situation." *And possibly more than that.* He turned his mount and started down the paved lane toward the East River Road.

26

When Alastar and the other three reached the main entrance to the Chateau D'Rex, it was two quints past the first glass of the afternoon, and Alastar had finished off the first water bottle filled with dark lager and most of the second. Five guards stood at the bottom of the white stone steps leading up to the main entry to the chateau—a good indication of consternation and disarray, since five guards weren't enough to stop any sort of attack and enough to reveal that there were problems. Alastar did not dismount when he reined up just short of the steps.

"Sir . . . the chateau is closed."

"Why? I'm here to see the rex."

"I can't say, sir. I'm sorry, sir. We're not to admit anyone."

"I'm not just anyone," Alastar said firmly.

"Sir . . . I can't make that decision."

"Who can?"

"Guard Captain Fonteau, sir."

"Then I suggest you find him . . . and quickly."

A guard hurried up the steps and in a few moments returned with an older guard, presumably Fonteau, who, upon seeing Alastar, looked very unhappy. "Sir . . ."

"I'm a very displeased master imager," Alastar said. "The army fired cannon on Imagisle last night. Imagers and others were killed. You don't want to make me even unhappier. You really don't."

The guard captain swallowed. "Sir . . . the family . . ."

"I'm not here to see the family. I'm here to see the rex."

"But . . . sir . . . Maitre Imager . . . the rex is dead."

Alastar paused. "Then it's even more important that I see Rex Lorien. He is all right, I trust?"

"Yes, sir, but . . ."

"The Collegium has been fired upon. Imagers are dead and buildings destroyed. Rex Ryen is dead . . . and you don't think matters aren't serious enough for me to see the new rex?" Alastar let his voice rise slightly in incredulity.

The guard captain sighed. "When you put it that way, sir . . . Perhaps you should join Submarshal, I mean Acting Marshal Petayn and Rex Lorien."

"Acting Marshal Petayn? Has Rex Lorien already removed Marshal Demykalon, not that he shouldn't have?"

"Marshal Demykalon was murdered."

"I cannot say I'm surprised . . . or even regretful, but under the circumstances, I think that meeting you mentioned is an excellent idea." Alastar dismounted, handed the gelding's reins to Belsior, then looked to Shaelyt. "I should be back in less than a glass. If I'm not, let Senior Imager Cyran know. He'll know exactly what to do to the chateau."

The guard captain swallowed.

Alastar turned to him. "Shall we go, Captain Fonteau?"

"Yes, sir."

Not surprisingly, the guard captain led Alastar to the same second-level study where the Maitre had left Ryen before dawn. The guard outside glanced from the captain to Alastar, then stepped aside. The captain opened the door, and announced, "Maitre Alastar of the Collegium."

Alastar stepped into the study, immediately seeing Lorien behind the desk. The new rex, more like ten years younger than Alastar, had the same lank black hair as his father, although his was cut shorter. His gray-blue eyes focused on Alastar. He did not wear any sign of mourning.

Alastar nodded, but did not smile. "Greetings, Rex Lorien."

"How did you get in here?" demanded Petayn, who sat across the broad desk from Lorien. Alastar had never met the submarshal, in fact, had never even heard of him in the time he had been in L'Excelsis. Petayn was smooth-faced, his sleek black hair graying at the temples.

"Through the main entrance."

"I'm surprised your entry was without bodies, although I did expect you far earlier."

"Given the death and destruction your cannon caused, you should be surprised that I am here at all."

"Death and destruction?" Lorien turned to Petayn. "You only mentioned warning shots."

Before Petayn could reply, Alastar did. "The cannon destroyed two of the three bridges and took out the middle span of the third. The administration building and the dining hall were totally destroyed by explosive shells that caused them to go up in flames despite their stone walls and slate roofs. Cottages and dwellings were also damaged. We still do not know the extent of the deaths and injuries." That was true, if misleading. "Had we not removed the cannon and the troopers manning them in less than a glass, the damage would have been far, far greater. If those were warning shots, Submarshal, I would not wish to witness an actual attack." With the briefest pause, Alastar went on. "And where might Marshal Demykalon be?"

"He's been murdered, and you doubtless had something to do with that. He was pinned to the floor with his own sabre stuck so deep into the floor and the stone beneath that we had to snap the blade to free his body."

"Rather an emphatic way to suggest that those who live by the blade might well die by it," said Lorien wryly.

That's not something his father would ever have said. Those few words gave Alastar some slight hope that working with the new rex might be easier than with his sire.

"Some might find that ironic, even amusing," declared Petayn. "But it was scarcely an honorable act. Imagers must not consider honor. They never have . . . at least."

"Honor?" Alastar raised his eyebrows. "You have a strange idea of honor. Firing on students and working men and women doesn't represent a concept of honor I've ever heard of."

"We were carrying out Rex Ryen's orders."

"Carrying out a dishonorable order makes it honorable?"

Petayn drew himself up stiffly. "Without order, there is chaos. We answer to the rex. If we questioned every order, the army would not work. Solidar would fall apart."

Alastar watched as Lorien's eyes focused on one man and then the other.

"I didn't suggest questioning every order—just the stupid or unwise ones. A *good* senior officer owes his superior not only obedience but the exercise of judgment."

"You seem to know a great deal about officers . . . for never having been one."

"No. I only know those things that are so obvious that you and Marshal Demykalon have long since forgotten them. Before I forget, have you recalled the cannon sent to destroy High Holder Guerdyn's chateau?"

"I don't believe you mentioned that, Submarshal," said Lorien, his voice every bit as cold as his sire's had been when irritated.

"I had not finished briefing you when the Maitre arrived," replied Petayn smoothly.

"The submarshal has informed me that you and your imagers destroyed almost a battalion of his men and damaged most of the new cannon. Is that an accurate assessment?" Lorien looked at Alastar, who remained standing.

"Most likely. It might have been less. We didn't bother to count or take prisoners. We needed to stop the attack before more students were killed."

Lorien looked at Petayn. "You will refrain from any more attacks on anyone until you have specific orders from me. Any troopers or working cannon outside of army posts will be returned to those posts immediately."

The submarshal appeared as if he wanted to protest, but then nodded. "Yes, sir."

"Given the army's position thus far," added Alastar, "the Collegium will support the rex's order as it can."

Petayn stiffened.

"You may go, Submarshal," said Lorien. "You need to promulgate and enforce that order."

"At your command, sir." Petayn stood easily, but Alastar sensed that Petayn was anything but pleased.

Once Petayn left, Alastar took the chair that the submarshal had not used, settling into it and looking directly at Lorien, deciding to let the rex say whatever he had in mind.

"There wasn't a mark on my father. The healer said that there was no sign of poison, but his face was contorted, as if he'd flown into a fit of rage. He was a difficult man." Lorien paused for several moments before continuing. "I have my own ideas about what has happened and why. I'd like yours, Maitre."

"I trust you know your father wished to raise tariffs on the High Holders and factors."

"He's been . . . he was angry about that for over a year. All this, it was just about tariffs?"

"The tariffs were also representative of his concerns about the diminishing power of the rex. When it became clear that the High Council would not accept an increase in tariffs of two parts in ten, a copper on a half silver, he insisted that the Collegium assassinate every member of the High Council. He said that if we did not change the Council's mind by fourth glass yesterday, the Collegium would feel his wrath. I proposed a compromise increase of four coppers on a gold. He refused. The High Council refused any increase. The cannon opened fire at about three quints past four yesterday. We stopped the cannon fire." Alastar hesitated. "There is one aspect to this that is not known. Last week, I removed a senior imager from his duties for lack of competence. Not in imaging, but in dealing with students. Desyrk deserted the Collegium and sought out his brother, one Commander Chesyrk. Marshal Demykalon placed Chesyrk in charge of the cannon that bombarded Imagisle. Desyrk used his skills to place two cannon far closer to the Collegium, and we did not detect them until considerably later. In the fighting Commander Chesyrk disappeared. He may have been killed. Former Maitre Desyrk escaped."

"That has to be your problem, Maitre."

"It is and will be, but I did not wish to conceal anything about the attack from you."

"Someone entered the chateau early this morning and may have even been in this study."

"I was. I told your father about the attack. He said we deserved it for not carrying out his orders. I suggested he accept the compromise. He refused. I told him that the Collegium would not pay for his stubbornness, and that one way or another he would accept the compromise increase. He flew into a rage. I did not attempt to save him from his own folly. Perhaps I should have, but I did not. I left and paid a visit to Marshal Demykalon. He said that he had ordered the destruction of the Collegium." Alastar shrugged. "That wasn't acceptable. After that, I visited High Holder Guerdyn. He also refused the compromise. I removed him and went to visit High Holder Vaun. We had an uncomfortable talk. He agreed that, if you would propose the compromise of four coppers on the gold, the High Council would likely accept. They will also accept modest increases, as necessary, in the future. What else would you like to know?"

Lorien looked at Alastar. Finally, he said, "I thought my sire was cold. You . . . Maitre . . ." He shook his head.

"What would you have had me do? Assassinate every High Council member and spark a rebellion? Destroy your chance for ruling? Turn Solidar back into warring states? Destroy the Collegium?" Alastar looked coldly at Lorien.

"What am I supposed to do now? Become your puppet?"

"No. You're supposed to become a reasonable rex. I could have worked out a compromise for your father. Over a number of years he could have gotten what he wanted. He just could not get it in a year. We've laid much of the groundwork for you. I really don't want your headaches. I have enough of my own. In addition to supporting you and making sure that the High Holders don't get out of hand, I've got to rebuild Imagisle and change the way imagers are trained. The Collegium has to be restructured so we don't need as much support from you. That will be to the benefit of both you and your successors and the Collegium and my successors. On top of that, I've got a renegade imager, and I'll have to keep an eye on Submarshal Petayn."

"Why should I trust you in the slightest?" asked Lorien.

"Because our interests coincide, and no one else's do. Without the Collegium, within years the marshal of the army would be rex. The Maitre of the Collegium can't be rex because the people, from High Holders all the way down to crafters, would revolt, not to mention the army. The High Holders want a weak rex who won't interfere with what they want. The factors want a rex who will keep the High Holders from strangling them and pirates from stealing their ships and cargoes, but they don't want to pay the tariffs necessary for that."

"I'm supposed to deal with all that?"

"With the support of the Collegium . . . yes."

"But you didn't support my father—"

"There's a difference between support and suicide, Lorien. A great deal. Your father wanted matters his way and no other way. What he wanted would have destroyed Solidar and him with it in a few years, if not sooner."

"It was sooner, much sooner."

"But Solidar is still here for you to rule. It wouldn't have been if the Collegium had followed his orders."

After another long silence, Lorien asked, "What would you advise I do about the army?"

"Make it smaller, much smaller, and increase the size of your navy. Other lands and pirates are a much bigger threat. You also might think about changing the patroller system so that the patrollers aren't beholden directly to the factors. If they report to a minister who reports to you, there's not as much need for an army within Solidar."

"Why not to you?" A hint of bitterness tinged the words of the new rex.

"For exactly the same reason that the Maitre of the Collegium cannot be a ruler. The first Maitre saw this, and the reasons and the problems have not changed."

Lorien started to speak, then stopped, and abruptly tilted his head and laughed sardonically. "That's why you could do nothing until Demykalon attacked you, isn't it?"

"We can only take drastic action"—*at least any action that can be attributed to imagers*—"in self-defense."

"And you let your students die?"

"I moved everyone out of the buildings and to places as safe as possible. We still had deaths and injuries—and several buildings totally destroyed, as well as two bridges. What would have been the reaction if we had acted first?"

Again, Lorien paused . . . then nodded slowly. "I had not thought of it in that fashion. For the time being, I think we should meet every day, perhaps at the fourth glass of the afternoon."

"I would agree to daily meetings. Why in the afternoon, though?"

"First, I do not think as well as I might in the morning. I need to think well in dealing with you. Second, we will know what has happened during the day, and I can prepare for the next day when I am closer to my best."

Alastar nodded.

"Maitre, I understand that there will be some times when these meetings may not be possible, but those times should be few."

"I would agree to that, as well." *And for now.* Alastar had no doubts that Lorien would wish to see him less and less over time.

"Then . . . until tomorrow at fourth glass . . . unless there is something else I should know."

"Not at present." Alastar inclined his head. "I will see you tomorrow." He offered a pleasant but not effusive smile before turning and leaving the study.

The guard captain was waiting for him outside in the corridor and accompanied him as Alastar walked to the grand staircase. Halfway down, he spoke. "Maitre, sir . . . might I ask if you can offer any explanations of why matters have turned out as they have and what we might need to prepare for here at the chateau?"

"I'm only one person involved in a complicated situation, Captain, but I will tell you what I can," *without undermining the chances for a more permanent resolution.* "Rex Ryen became so enraged at the refusal of the High Holders to accept his tariff terms, and only his, that he ordered the Collegium to assassinate the entire

High Council, if necessary, until they agreed. We refused when he would not attempt to reach a middle ground. He ordered the army to bombard Imagisle. We stopped the bombardment, but not before two buildings were destroyed and a number of people were killed and injured. After that, I met with the rex. He still refused to compromise and flew into a rage that killed him when I informed him that the Collegium would still not assassinate the entire High Council. He died of that rage. I then met with the marshal. He tried to pull a sabre on me. I used it to pin him to the floor of his study. I then rode and met with various members of the High Council. It appears as though the High Council and Rex Lorien may reach a compromise on increasing tariffs. As for the chateau here, I would maintain your guard and refuse entry to all army members except senior officers, and only one or two of those at a time. If you need assistance, send a messenger to the Collegium."

Surprisingly, at least to Alastar, the captain only nodded before saying, "I had guessed that something like that might have happened." He stopped at the bottom of the steps. "Rex Lorien is far more temperate than his sire . . . but he may not be as well informed as he might be."

"I will do my best to provide what I can. I trust you will do the same."

"The best that I can, sir."

"You sound as if you might have some difficulties," observed Alastar quietly.

The captain glanced around, then murmured, "Lady Asarya and young Ryentar . . . they're very different from Lorien."

"I've heard that Ryentar takes after his father. I know nothing of the Lady." That wasn't quite true, but Alastar wasn't certain how much to believe what Desyrk had said, not that the renegade imager had said much and his own single meeting with her had definitely left him wary. After a hesitation, he said, "Have you ever heard of a man named Desyrk?"

"I do not know anyone of that name, Maitre."

"But you've heard of him?"

Again . . . the captain glanced around before speaking. "I have overheard the name."

Alastar guessed. "He's been in the chateau, then?"

"That I do not know. I just heard the name."

"From whom?"

"I could not say. It was dark."

"A man or a woman?"

"It was murmured, whispered. It could have been either."

"Where in the chateau did you overhear this?"

The captain did not reply.

"Perhaps on the southeast circular staircase?" That was a guess on Alastar's part, but he wanted to confirm or eliminate the totally private staircase serving the private quarters of the rex and his wife.

The captain nodded. "That is truly all I know."

"Thank you. No one else will know." Even with the man's almost despairing look and the slightest emphasis on the word "know," Alastar wondered if he was telling Alastar all that he knew, but it seemed clear that the captain was not about to say more. The fact that Lorien had shown no reaction to the mention of Desyrk's name was also interesting.

The two walked without speaking to the entry doors, where the captain halted. Alastar stepped out into the gray afternoon, a dampish wind blowing into his face. Even from the top of the stone steps down to the paved entry road, Alastar could see Shaelyt's relief when the junior master caught sight of him. As he walked down the adamantine white stone steps that were too high and steep for a regial chateau, he noticed that only two guards remained on the steps, each at a side at the top.

"Sir?" asked Shaelyt as Alastar approached.

Alastar managed not to smile when he saw the junior master's inquiring look. He took the gelding's reins from Belsior and mounted before replying, "Rex Lorien was quite civil. Submarshal Petayn was less so. We're headed back to the Collegium. I need to meet with all the maitres."

"Not just the senior maitres?"

"No. All of you."

Once they were on the ring road, Alastar kept his eyes out for trouble, but he saw nothing out of the ordinary, just people walking, some riders, wagons, and a coach or two. *As if nothing had happened.* And for most people, almost all people in Solidar, Alastar realized, nothing had really changed.

He also couldn't help but overhear a few fragments of the murmured conversation between Neiryn and Belsior.

". . . should have known better . . ."

". . . an old-time Maitre . . ."

". . . about time . . ."

Alastar just wished it hadn't been up to him to act like an old-time Maitre. There was always a price to pay for exercising power, but he didn't want to think about that at the moment. *Even if you'll regret it later?* He was far more concerned to find that Desyrk had been in the Chateau D'Rex, and likely on more than one occasion if his name had been mentioned even once. *But why? And who had allowed or invited him there? Ryen?* Alastar shook his head. He could think of only one or possibly two possibilities, and both seemed totally improbable, especially given Ryen's temper and outbursts.

The guard captain had clearly wanted Alastar to know about Desyrk, or his name, and that raised the question of why. If the captain had been telling the truth, and he did not know more about Desyrk . . . then why had he been afraid? And if afraid, then why had he even admitted hearing Desyrk's name? He was no closer to having an answer when he reached the Collegium stables than he had been when he had left the chateau, but no sooner had he dismounted than Cyran appeared, a worried expression on his face.

"How did it go?"

"Largely as planned. Can you gather all the maitres possible, including the Maitres D'Aspect, and bring them to the Maitre's dwelling. I'd like to tell everyone at once so that there's as little misunderstanding as possible." There would always be some misunderstanding. That was something Alastar had learned young.

"How successful?"

Alastar shrugged, not wanting to say too much in public yet. "Rex Lorien and the High Council look to be on the way to a compromise. Acting Marshal Petayn is very displeased, but has agreed to return all army squads and cannon to headquarters."

A smile, both wry and of relief, appeared on the senior imager's face. "That's better than I'd hoped."

"All the maitres need to hear what happened, most of it, anyway . . . and Dareyn." Alastar dismounted and led the gelding toward the stable boy, to whom he said, "Take good care of him. He's been a long ways today."

"Yes, sir."

"I'll gather the maitres," said Cyran. "Alyna's likely already there. We've been doing what repairs we can. We've managed everything small. That leaves the administration building, the dining hall, and the bridges . . . not to mention some craters here and there. Akoryt's worked with Dareyn to salvage what little survived the fire."

"Good. I'll see you shortly." Alastar turned and began to walk. He could still smell the acrid odor of burned wood. The smell got stronger until he reached the ruins of the two buildings, then persisted, if less strongly, as he neared his dwelling. Alyna was indeed standing on the front porch, as if she had been waiting for him. He stopped short of the steps, taking in her worried expression. "Is something wrong?"

"Are you all right?"

"Physically. It's been a long day. Cyran's gathering all the maitres so that I can tell everyone at once."

She nodded. "That's good. Everyone's been worried. I worried . . . too."

Alastar had the feeling she'd meant to say more, but had tempered her words.

"Thank you. I appreciate your worry and concerns."

Alyna looked away, just slightly. "Before everyone gets here, I'd like you to look at the side wall. I've repaired the shutters and replaced the glass as well as I could." She smiled, although Alastar could see the darkness under her eyes. Then she walked down the steps and moved to his left toward the west end of the house, stopping short of a small crater beneath the stone wall, where it appeared an explosion had ripped away the ground almost a yard deep, revealing the large gray stone foundation blocks.

From what he could see, the outside wall showed no damage whatsoever. "It's as though it was never struck."

"There wasn't any damage at all, except to the shutters and the windows." Alyna pointed to the crater. "From that, there shouldn't have been much of this end of the dwelling remaining."

Alastar frowned. He wasn't thinking as clearly as he should be. After a moment, he realized what she was suggesting. "You think the dwelling was imaged into being in the same way the Chateau D'Rex was?"

"Not the same way, but by the same imagers. It's almost four hundred years old. Does it look it? I've never really studied the walls here before." She smiled wryly. "I don't imagine anyone comes here and just looks at that wall. Are the stones worn or chipped or scratched? Why weren't windows on the other sides of the house shattered?"

"They imaged it to stand forever," mused Alastar. "I wonder why. Nothing else here was imaged that solid." He studied the windows and their casements. "I can't tell what you did and what you didn't." Then he looked to her. "You didn't have to do that."

"Cyran and I decided it was necessary. Where else is there for people to meet and for you to work? Besides, the damage was small . . . as I said." After the slightest hesitation, she added, "You need to eat. Your eyes are pinkish. There are cold meats and cheese in the kitchen."

"Pinkish?"

"I've noticed that's the way they look when you need to eat or drink."

What else has she noticed. "With all the imaging you've done, you need to eat as well. We'll need to hurry. It won't be that long before the others arrive."

"They can wait a few moments for you to eat, if necessary."

That might have been, but Alastar *was* hungry. Once they reached the kitchen, where the sideboard held a platter with meat and cheese, with a warm loaf of bread nearby, he was ready to tear into the food when he noticed Jienna standing near the rear door, grinning.

"It's about time you ate, Maitre."

"Thank you."

"Thank Maitre Alyna, too. I've been cooking all day. Most went to the students." Jienna smiled again. "Now . . . eat. Both of you. There's lager in the pitcher."

Alastar had just finished the last chunk of bread when Cyran walked into the kitchen.

"Everyone's here."

"Have them come into the dining room. It will be crowded, but . . . I think they'll all fit." Alastar took a last swallow of lager. He had to admit that he felt much better. He looked at Alyna. "Are my eyes still pinkish?"

"A little, but it's fading."

"How did you come to notice that?"

"I told you. I've been watching." Her smile contained a definite element of amusement before she moved through the open door to the serving pantry and the dining room beyond.

Alastar followed.

It was several quints past fourth glass before the remaining maitres all sat crowded around the dining room table. From one end, Alastar looked down the table, realizing that he'd never actually sat at the table. Cyran was to his right, Alyna to his left. Then came Obsolym and Akoryt, Taryn and Gaellen, followed by Claeynd, Khaelis, Tiranya, Shaelyt, Lhendyr, Narryn, Petros, and Warryk. Dareyn stood by the door.

Alastar cleared his throat and began. "I've just returned from the Chateau D'Rex. Rex Ryen died of a rage early this morning, and Lorien is now rex. After the death of Marshal Demykalon, Submarshal Petayn has become acting marshal, and I also met with him briefly. Rex Lorien has ordered the army to return and remain on its posts. Earlier I met with High Holder Vaun, who is now the acting head of the High Council. It now appears likely that the High Council and the rex will reach a compromise on the tariff level for next year. That leaves us with the problem of rebuilding the Collegium and restructuring how we operate so that, in the future, we will not be so reliant on the generosity of the rex. And unfortunately, we also have to find Desyrk and deal with him—"

"What do you intend?" asked Obsolym warily.

"Given what he has done, what would you suggest?" countered Alastar.

"You did humiliate him . . ."

"I removed him from duties for lack of competence. I did not discipline him otherwise." *Although you were thinking about it.* "He was the one who left Imagisle and helped direct cannon fire against the Collegium—"

"He did that?" asked Taryn, a note of astonishment in his voice.

"He did. I'm sorry. I forgot to mention that to everyone. Maitre Alyna was there as well. I told Maitre Cyran and a few others about that last night. The last two days have been long."

"It seems to me, junior as I might be," interjected Akoryt, "that the only question is whether we blind him or kill him."

"If we can capture him, we'll have a hearing and decide," declared Alastar.

"Can we trust Submarshal Petayn?" asked Akoryt.

"What happened to Marshal Demykalon?" asked Obsolym almost at the same time.

"Marshal Demykalon ordered the cannon attack on Imagisle. Let's just say that he didn't survive the recoil. Submarshal Petayn was not pleased, but said that he would obey Rex Lorien's order. I suspect he will . . . for now."

"What about High Holder Guerdyn?" asked Alyna. "He declared he would never accept higher tariffs."

"He told me the same thing," replied Alastar. "He won't have to worry about that now. His reaction to my insisting on a compromise led to a seizure. I didn't bother trying to save him." Alastar wasn't about to admit directly what he'd done. People could and would speculate, but Guerdyn's death was better left somewhat murky.

"You killed him?" asked Obsolym.

"There's not a mark on his body and not a trace of poison in it, either. We'll leave it at that."

Obsolym swallowed.

Alastar turned to Akoryt. "Do you have any better idea of how many were killed, how many injured, and the extent of their injuries?"

"Yes, sir. Eleven deaths, so far. Six imagers and students, four cooks, a gardener. Two of them were Johanyr and Klovyl. We found their bodies—what was left of them—in the ruins of the administration building. Gaellen says that there are almost a score with minor injuries, one with serious wounds, and two with broken bones. The most serious is a prime who took stone splinters. Gaellen isn't sure he'll make it. The other two are Shannyr and Kaylet." Akoryt's expression turned rueful with the second name. "Kaylet broke both wrists when he tripped walking on the river wall in the dark."

"Who is the prime?"

"Nyell. He's only been here since late Agostas."

Alastar recalled the name, but couldn't connect it with a face. "What about Shannyr?"

"A broken collarbone, Gaellen says."

"Was he with Johanyr and Klovyl?"

"Probably. He was near the administration building."

Another problem? Or a fatal solution? Alastar would have to look into that. "Is there anything else I should know?"

"I can't think of anything right now, sir."

"Are there any more questions about what has happened?"

The dining room was silent.

"That's all I had to tell you. If Maitres Cyran, Alyna, Akoryt, and Petros would remain . . . and Dareyn . . . we need to talk briefly about repairs and rebuilding."

Once the other maitres had left, Alastar looked around the table. "What should I know about what's happened here while I was gone?"

"The student quarters weren't badly damaged, except for one corner of two rooms," Akoryt began, "but we'll have to make arrangements for them to be fed."

"You can use the kitchen in Desyrk's cottage for some of them. Clear out the main room and put tables there," said Alastar. "Some of them can be fed here. Jienna said she had already. If one of the other cooks can assist her, that will help. You'll have to alternate which students eat when in both places."

"We'll assign them times," replied Akoryt.

"Good. What else is of immediate concern?"

"The strong room was not badly damaged, but it would not be wise to leave what is there . . ." Dareyn looked to Alastar.

"What's valuable can be put in the small strong room here. You'll need to be here as well. If you'd see what you can work out with Arhgen. He may have to create another set of ledgers as well, unless he had any at his quarters."

"Yes, sir."

"Is there anything else anyone has that Dareyn should know?"

"Can anyone help with making up rosters and lists of students?" asked Akoryt.

"Ah . . ." Alastar interjected. "I do have a listing here in the study. It's just a list with a sentence or two about students, staff, and maitres. I had Dareyn put that together when I became Maitre so that I could learn something about everyone. That might help."

"Greatly," admitted the red-haired maitre.

"Is there anything else we should consider?" Alastar looked to Dareyn.

"Everyone is usually paid on the last day of the month, sir."

"I'll need you to work with Arhgen to come up with a temporary pay ledger, then."

Dareyn nodded.

Dealing with various other administrative questions took another quint before Alastar excused Dareyn and turned to the remaining maitres. "Is there anything anyone wants to say that they didn't wish to say with everyone here?"

"Obsolym's going to make trouble," suggested Cyran.

"I hope you're wrong," said Alastar, "but he's having a hard time understanding the problems we face."

"He's always been good at ignoring them. Speaking of problems, what about Desyrk?"

Alastar shrugged. "He'll likely make more trouble, but he could be anywhere, and since he's good at concealment, we'll just have to be on our guard."

"I don't like it," murmured Petros. "Always was a lazy dandy."

"No one mentioned that before," said Alastar, giving a quick glance to Alyna in trying to convey that he knew she had.

Alyna offered a faint knowing expression, while the other three exchanged glances. Then Petros gave an embarrassed smile. "He's been like that for so long that I guess we just . . . well . . . assumed."

"Try to assume I know nothing except what's happened in the last two months," said Alastar dryly. "I take it he's been known to have lady friends beyond his wife."

"He's been gone some nights over the past few years, but no one knows where. I don't think he's done that since you've been here," added Petros.

"And Maitre Fhaen let him? Did Fhaen even know?"

"When I asked him," said Cyran, "he said that so long as Desyrk did his job, what he did in his free time was his own business if it didn't hurt or cost the Collegium."

"He used concealments a great deal," added Akoryt. "Once he crossed the bridge, he just vanished."

And his wife put up with it? But then Alastar realized that she well might have feared Desyrk's anger if she'd tried to leave . . . or maybe she had nowhere to go. "Can anyone else add anything that might help find him?" When no one spoke, he said, "Then we'll get on with seeing who can do what and when with the rebuilding. When you have time, Alyna, would you be able to draw up plans for a new administration building? While we're at it, we might as well rebuild with a structure suited to what we need now, with a proper library and a lower-level strong room large enough to hold records as well as golds. Maybe we ought to think about building a separate wing for instruction with small studies for maitres as well. Everyone think about it, and give your suggestions to Alyna."

"I can do plans. I think I should do some rough plans and sketches first and have the other maitres look at them . . ."

As she went on to explain Alastar listened and watched. The watching was more pleasant. After she finished, he discussed with the others what they could do. Less than two quints later, the meeting was over.

When they all rose from the table, Alastar cleared his throat. "I'd like to have a brief meeting at seventh glass tomorrow morning."

"We'll be here," replied Cyran cheerfully. "Where else would we want to be at the moment?"

When the others began to head for the front door, Alastar motioned to Alyna. "If you have a moment . . . I mean . . . unless you and Tiranya . . ."

"I'm certain Tiranya won't even notice." Alyna smiled. "We share a cottage. We're not partners."

That thought had not even occurred to Alastar. "The chairs in the salon are more comfortable."

"That would be good." They ended up sitting in two green velvet armchairs angled toward each other, with a small circular table between them. Although it was approaching sunset, Alastar did not light any of the lamps.

"What did you have in mind?" Alyna asked.

Just getting to know you better. "Talking. Learning more about you. You're part Pharsi. Have you ever had one of those . . . flashes of farsight?"

For just an instant, Alyna was totally still. "Why do you ask?"

Her words were pleasant, but Alastar sensed a wariness behind them. "Because Vaelora did, and it seemed to run in her family." The last phrase was a bit of a guess on his part, but from what he'd read in Gauswn's journal entries, there was a certain implication. *Or is that just your inference?*

"That's an . . . interesting observation. Why do you think I might have it?"

"Because it's clear the talent for imaging runs strongly in your blood. The farsight might as well."

"You are persistent."

"I've been reading the journals of the first chorister of the Collegium. He mentions that Vaelora had that talent. He also mentions that she said it was far less useful than people supposed, that it only allowed one to prepare somewhat. She must have been quite a woman."

"I imagine she was."

"Just as you are."

Alyna looked directly at Alastar. In the waning light, her black eyes seemed almost to see through him. "What do you want from me?" Her words were quiet but firm.

"Right now, the chance to know you better."

"That cuts both ways. You already know far more about me than I do of you."

"What would you like to know?"

"To begin with, anything you'd care to share." Her smile was warm, if reserved.

"I'm in my thirty-eighth year. I've been married and widowed. I have no children. I was born to a factor's clerk. He lost his position when the factor died. My father went to work on the docks . . . and doing other things. His leg was injured, and he could barely walk. No one would give him work. He became a beggar. My mother went to work as a scull at an inn. Then my father was run down by a drunken son of a shahib—that's what they call the old High Holders, the ones whose lands date back before the unification. The son was more upset that his horse had to be put down than that he'd killed a man. The death gold helped, but it didn't last that long. Ma . . . my mother was never the same after that. She found out that I was an imager, because I could image coppers. Sometimes, those were all we had, and . . ." Alastar stopped for a moment. He didn't like remembering those times. "Well . . . then she got consumption and insisted I go to the Collegium. Maitre Voltyn—he was in charge then—he let her spend the last year at the Collegium instead of giving her the two golds. He wanted to do both, but she wouldn't have it. Until the night she died, she insisted I do my best." He offered a shrug. "I've tried. After that, I was a student imager, and then a full one . . . nothing that much different from other maitres."

"More than you think, I'd say. How old were you when you first imaged coppers?"

"Six, I think."

"That's young."

"I had no idea about it. I just knew we needed the coppers."

"And you weren't caught?"

"I practiced for what I thought was a very long time." He managed a soft laugh. "Maybe two weeks or so. That's a very long time when you're that age."

Alyna nodded. "Then . . . you were an only child?"

"No . . . I had a younger brother and sister—Dyel and Mahara. They died of the red flux a year or so before I went to the Collegium at Westisle."

"You didn't have it?"

"I did, but I was fortunate."

"I wouldn't call your early years all that fortunate."

"In one way, they were. I was loved." *And appreciated.* "That counts for a great deal."

Alyna was silent, and Alastar wondered if she had actually been loved, but he wasn't about to ask that question.

"You were widowed . . ." The way Alyna said the words was clearly to give Alastar a choice of whether he wanted to speak of that.

"I was. We weren't married all that long, not as marriages should go . . ." Alastar paused, wondering how much he should say. "We were both Maitres D'Aspect then . . . Thealia . . . she was two years older. I was flattered . . ."

"What was she like?"

"She was tall and slender, almost swan-like. Silver-blond hair. Her eyes were gray."

"Was she beautiful?" asked Alyna quietly.

Not in the way you are. "I can't answer that fairly . . . or honestly. Sometimes, I thought she was. She was good-looking. Everyone said I was fortunate."

"Are you trying to please me?" Alyna's voice was even.

"I'd like to . . . but no, I'm not. When you first love someone, or think you do, it colors what you see. And when you're young, when it's first love, you see what you want to. As you get older, you see things differently. I know more about you, right now, than I ever did before Thealia and I were married."

"You sound like you weren't that happy even then."

"I thought I was. It was only after she died . . . years after . . . that I began to see things differently."

"You don't think that you've made yourself see them that way?"

Alastar offered a wry smile. "That's always a danger . . . for anyone, but I don't think so." He paused. "I'm not saying she wasn't attractive or that she secretly disliked me, or that she married me just because she thought I was the best catch." *Although there was some of that.* "She did want to be admired and loved, and I did both."

"What happened?"

"Something that I should have seen. Something that I've already seen here."

"That doesn't tell me much," observed Alyna, a touch of humor in the way she spoke the words.

"It was becoming clear that I'd be a Maitre D'Structure before long. Zhelan had just become Maitre of the Westisle Collegium. There's an understanding that, in order to be considered, you have to undertake certain assignments that require more than . . . normal imaging. Mine was to rebuild the stone piers in the west harbor. The west harbor is some five milles from the main harbor. I left early that morning. Sometime after I left, without telling anyone, Thealia went out to the east harbor and re-imaged the stone piers in the old east harbor . . . and dredged some of the channel as well. She was certainly capable of it, except for one thing." Alastar glanced at Alyna.

Her face was impassive.

"I didn't know she was pregnant. She must have known. She didn't tell anyone. She came back. She told Maitre Zhelan, then went to our cottage to rest. She never woke up."

Alyna did not speak for several moments. "But . . . didn't she know?"

"Limitations were for everyone else. She always said that women imagers couldn't ask for favors. She was right. She should have been a Maitre D'Structure before that."

Alyna's face tightened.

Alastar could almost see her thoughts and spoke quickly. "I didn't insist on making you a Maitre D'Structure to redress the past. I didn't do it out of guilt." *Or not too much.* "I didn't have the power to insist she have what she deserved. You have the abilities and skills of a Maitre D'Structure. Every senior maitre here knows and admits that. I didn't present you with something undeserved. And I did it . . . well, frankly, I did it, if you must know, because I never wanted to be like Zhelan or, as it turns out, like Maitre Fhaen. That might not be the noblest of motives, but it's the way it is."

"You did it for your mother, too, I think."

Those words stopped Alastar cold. For several moments, he was speechless.

"She never got what she deserved, either, did she?"

"No," he finally admitted.

Her smile was gentle and warm. "You're not at all like Fhaen. I don't think you could be." The smile faded. "How did you feel after she died?"

"Numb. I couldn't believe it. Not then. Later . . . I understood. Isn't life often like that, understanding too late?" He gave a soft laugh. "Perhaps that happens more often for young men." At that, Alastar glanced around the now almost dark salon, then imaged flame into the wick of the nearest lamp. He stood and walked to the wall sconce, where he adjusted the flame, then turned back to face Alyna. "I didn't mean to . . ."

"I'm glad you did. I don't believe in secrets, not if I want to trust someone." After a pause, she said, "You haven't told many people, have you?"

"Not since it happened. You're the only one, really."

"Thank you."

For what? For telling you about thoughtless love, stupidity, and blindness?

Almost as if he had uttered his thoughts, Alyna stood and moved toward Alastar, stopping a yard away before she went on. "In a High Hold, nothing is quite what it seems. Words have two meanings. At times, they can have more. For a girl, or a woman, it is dangerous to reveal who you are. It is more dangerous to share confidences or dreams."

"That can be true anywhere."

"It can. I'm glad you trust me." She took his hand and squeezed it. Then she let go, not abruptly, but almost as if she did not wish to.

"You trusted me first," he pointed out, "for which I'm glad."

"So am I." She smiled, this time, almost sadly. "We need to talk like this more often . . . if you're willing."

Alastar understood all too well. “I would like that.”

“So would I.” After another pause, she said, “I think I’d better go now.”

Without saying more, Alastar walked to the front door with her, then out onto the porch. They stopped at the top of the steps.

“In the morning,” he said.

“I’ll be here.” She smiled, an expression both warm and worried, Alastar thought, before turning and heading down the steps and south toward her cottage.

He stood on the porch and watched as she disappeared into the deepening twilight.

27

On Vendrei morning, even before sunrise, a chattering against the windows roused Alastar. He was half glad to be roused, given that the rattling dragged him from a dream in which he was riding through a darkness so deep that he could see nothing, searching for something absolutely essential—and he had no idea what that might be. He swung his legs over the side of the bed, then stood and walked to the window, where he saw small white pellets bouncing off the glass. *Large sleet . . . or small hail.* That was all the Collegium needed—bad weather even before they could begin to organize the rebuilding.

By the time he had decided he'd had more than enough exercise in the past few days, didn't need a run, especially over sleet or icy walks, and washed, shaved, and dressed, the hail-like sleet had stopped, leaving a thin blanket of white on the ground and grass, and the stone roads and walks wet, but not icy. He walked down the staircase to the main floor, where already Akoryt stood in the entry hall foyer, although it was barely sixth glass.

"The first students should be here in a few moments. Some are already nearing the walk. You could eat in the study . . ."

"I can eat with the students." Alastar grinned. "It might keep them quieter than usual."

"It might. For some."

"It will be fine."

Akoryt nodded, if dubiously.

Alastar smiled in return and made his way to the

dining room, where he sat down at the head of the table and was immediately served by a second whose face he recognized, but whose name he could not recall. On his platter were cheesed scrambled eggs and ham strips, plus a small loaf of bread. A large mug of tea followed.

As he began to eat, two seconds entered the dining room. Recognizing one of the seconds as he took a place near the end of the table, Alastar asked, "How is your arm, Dylert?"

Dylert looked up, clearly surprised, then replied, "It's much better, sir. There's only a light dressing. That's just because the new skin is tender, Maitre Gaellen says."

Alastar smiled. "And you haven't been doing any more imaging in the bushes?"

"No, sir."

The student imagers who next seated themselves at the table were Arion and Taurek. Alastar definitely hadn't expected to see the two together.

Nor had either expected to see Alastar, because both were silent for an instant before Arion said, "Good morning, Maitre. Thank you for hosting us."

"Yes, sir," added Taurek.

"You're both welcome."

Alastar continued eating, but tried to listen to the low conversation between Arion and Taurek, even though he could only catch fragments.

". . . manners . . . good as golds . . . better sometimes . . ."

". . . don't deserve the respect . . ."

". . . not just . . . respect . . . makes life more pleasant . . ."

Alastar almost nodded, but caught himself.

Another secondus—Borlan—hurried in, nodding immediately to Alastar. "Maitre."

After Alastar finished eating and downing the last drops of tea from the mug, he slipped from the table and returned to the front hall, hoping that Akoryt was still somewhere near, and saw the younger maitre standing on the porch talking to two girls. One was Linzya, but Alastar did not recognize the other, a slender sandy blonde who looked very composed. There was something about her . . . but he couldn't quite place it, and he was still musing when the two entered the hall foyer.

"Good morning," he offered, "the dining room is to your left."

"Good morning, Maitre," replied the blonde, politely and clearly, inclining her head respectfully. "Thank you. We appreciate your sharing your house with us."

"We really do, sir," added Linzya.

"You're more than welcome."

Once the two passed him, Alastar went out to the porch.

"Sir?" asked Akoryt.

"I didn't recall the blond student . . ."

"That was Thelia."

At that moment, Alastar realized why the student he'd somehow never met seemed familiar, and the similarity of names chilled him. *Thank the Nameless she's not any more like her . . .* "The very competent daughter of Factoria Kathila?"

Akoryt nodded.

"I also noticed that Taurek came with Arion. Your doing?"

"I did ask Arion—he's a good and thoughtful sort—if he'd mind taking Taurek under his wing, so to speak, in terms of teaching him how to recognize what people aren't saying. It seems to be working, but we'll see."

What Alastar saw was that Akoryt was far better at dealing with students than Desyrk could ever have hoped to be. "From what little I've seen, it's already helping." *And it will certainly keep Taurek out of trouble for now, especially if Bettaur sees Taurek with Arion.*

"We can all meet in the study. That way we won't force out the last students to eat."

Akoryt nodded.

"I'll see you then." Alastar reentered the house and walked to the study. There he settled behind the desk, thinking. He still worried about Petayn and the army, and he didn't like the idea of Desyrk running loose, especially when his brother Chesyrk had commanded the cannon firing on Imagisle. Desyrk clearly possessed an outsized sense of self-worth and an equally outproportioned feeling of being unjustly wronged. All that meant trouble. *Then there's Lorien, his wife . . . and his mother, and who knows what she'll tell him.* Alastar wondered if Lorien was even that close to her, but he couldn't count on the two of them not being close.

He was still pondering when Dareyn knocked on the study door. "Sir . . . the other maitres are all here. I've taken the liberty of borrowing a chair from the dining room."

Alastar stood as Alyna, Cyran, Akoryt, and Petros entered and as Dareyn slipped in behind them, added the chair he carried to the three before the desk, then left.

"Are there any more problems?" asked Alastar once everyone was seated. "Besides the ones we've already discussed?"

"What if Desyrk tries to sneak back here and cause trouble?" asked Petros. "How would we even know he was here?"

"We could image a fine layer of dust across part of the Bridge of Desires and have seconds and thirds just watch," said Alyna. "He'll leave footprints or stir up the dust."

"That will work . . . if we don't have a wind," said Cyran.

"Farther beyond the dust, image a fine layer of heavy dark sand. A light wind or a brisk breeze won't move that," added Akoryt.

"A goose might help," suggested Petros, "or a hound that can smell."

Alastar laughed. "See what you can work out. But don't spend too much time on it. Desyrk may not even try to reach the Collegium. He might feel more comfortable attacking those of us who leave Imagisle."

"That's more likely," said Akoryt.

"Do any of you know anything about either Lady Asarya or Lady Chelia?" Alastar found himself looking at Alyna, suspecting she might know something.

She raised her eyebrows. "I've heard it said that Lady Asarya is a forceful personality and that she and Ryen did not share quarters after Lord Ryentar was born. Other than that . . ."

"Lady Chelia?"

"She is the youngest daughter of High Holder Ryel, the elder. She's apparently unlike the rest of her family in that she is both retiring . . . and openly less forceful."

"Wasn't Ryel head of the High Council?" Alastar recalled that Vaun had mentioned something about that.

"Her father was indeed. He was the father of the present High Holder. Chelia is the youngest sister of Ryel the younger. There was a bit of a scandal about that because Ryel the elder wanted Lorien to marry Khanara, the older daughter. Lorien wisely insisted on Chelia. There was supposedly some talk about Chelia marrying Ryentar, but Lady Asarya was said to oppose that strongly."

Alastar nodded. He wanted to follow up on that later with Alyna, but he merely said, "Thank you. Is there anything else we all should know?" He thought he saw a twinkle in Alyna's eyes at his wording.

She merely said, "Lady Chelia is quiet and faultlessly polite when she's in public . . . and likely so in private, but that I would not know."

"Can anyone else add anything?"

The other three maitres shook their heads.

"Petros . . . where can we store foodstuffs and supplies, once we purchase more?"

"The small supply shed by the stables has some space, and we could use one of the tack rooms . . ."

For the next glass, Alastar and the others went over the accommodations necessary at the Collegium as a result of the destruction of the dining hall and the administration building.

When they finished, Alyna let the other three maitres precede her out of the study, then paused by the door and said in a low voice, "Chelia is sweet . . . or she was when we were young. She's very sharp in a quiet way, and I've heard that she and Lady Asarya are on polite but not warm terms."

"Lorien listens to her?"

"I don't know. He should, but he needs to be careful. Lady Asarya has always wanted her way. She even went hunting alone, even before she took separate quarters in the Chateau D'Rex. That is, with just her personal guards at the hunting park that was hers."

"Hers?"

"Her father—High Holder Delcoeur—insisted on it, although the lodge and grounds were part of her dowry. Ryen agreed."

"You mentioned that Lady Asarya opposed Chelia marrying Ryentar, but not Lorien. That seems odd. If Chelia wasn't suited to the younger son . . ."

"That was just a rumor. I don't know more than that. It happened well after I became a maitre, and I actually . . ." Alyna offered a rueful face. "I overheard Smarthyl and Fhaen talking. They were arguing in whispers. I didn't dare stay long."

"Why didn't Ryen . . . do something?"

"Asarya was a cousin to Smarthyl. He was almost senior imager."

Smarthyl? Where had he seen that name? Alastar knew he should know, but he'd really been at Imagisle for such a short time that he didn't remember all the names instantly. To make matters worse, the more he learned, the more interrelated everything seemed to become. *Except it always was. You just didn't know it.* "Fhaen didn't like Smarthyl?"

"No. That was another reason why he named Cyran senior imager."

Alastar had wondered about Cyran's comparatively young age, but he'd assumed that Cyran had been named because he was the only Maitre D'Esprit. *But maybe he was* . . . "Smarthyl was only a Maitre D'Structure?"

Alyna nodded. "That was how . . ."

"And why he had to request that either Zhelan or I become Maitre here when he realized he was dying?"

"He had no choice. No one would have listened to Cyran because of his age."

"And Fhaen even worried about me."

"You were already a Maitre D'Image. That was something that Ryen couldn't argue with," Alyna said. "Much as he would have liked."

"How did Maitre Zhelan feel about being Maitre in Westisle when it became clear you were a Maitre D'Image and he was only a Maitre D'Esprit?"

"I deferred to his experience, and he deferred to my ability." Alastar kept his tone dry. "What else could we do?"

After Alyna left, Dareyn appeared at the study door. "There's a message here for you. A courier in brown delivered it. Said there was no need for a response." He extended the envelope.

Alastar took it. He did not recognize the seal, or the yellow and brown sealing wax. After a moment he took his belt knife and slit the envelope, leaving the seal untouched, and extracted the single sheet within. He began to read.

Maitre Alastar—

I have just received word of the unsettling events in L'Excelsis. If what news I have received is correct, Rex Ryen died of a seizure. So did High Holder Guerdyn, while you dispatched Marshal Demykalon. Of most concern to me is the report that Demykalon turned cannon on Imagisle and killed and wounded a number of people, including students. Considering the efforts you have made to work out a compromise on the tariff issue, it is clear that the late rex, and his errant marshal, exceeded the bounds of law and the strictures of the Nameless.

In this regard, I offer my condolences and my support in achieving the sort of compromise you have sought from the beginning.

With kindest regards,

The signature was simply "Moeryn."

Had the brief letter come from Vaun or the other members of the High Council, Alastar would have regarded its contents as entirely political. While Moeryn doubtless had some political interests, from the beginning he had seemed warmer and more open. *Because he listens to his wife? Or because she is worth listening to and he does? Or just because he's more practical?*

Alastar suspected it was the latter, with small touches of the others.

"Sir?" prompted Dareyn, still standing just outside the study door.

"It's from High Holder Moeryn, offering his condolences and his support for a compromise over the tariff issue."

"Little late for that, if you ask me, sir."

"He wasn't the problem. He was somewhat supportive from the beginning." Alastar refolded the single sheet and slipped it back into the envelope. "Dareyn, I should know this, but it's slipped my mind. Maitre Smarthyl?"

The second nodded. "We don't hear much from him now. He went to Mont D'Image to take over there, after Maitre Cythan died. Said he was glad to go. He came from up there anyway, somewhere northwest of Asseroiles."

Alastar could have smacked the side of his own head. He'd seen the name on the seasonal report, but with all the papers and all the new names, he'd been unable to place where he'd seen it. "Thank you. I knew I'd read his name somewhere."

"Don't hear much from him these days, just his reports."

"He and Maitre Fhaen were never close, were they?"

"I wouldn't know, sir. They were right polite to each other."

"Manners are always useful," Alastar temporized.

After a moment of silence, Dareyn spoke again. "Sir . . . if you have the key to the strong room here . . . Arhgen and I will be moving things from the old strong room."

"I'll bring it out in a moment."

"I'll be at the table here, sir."

Alastar waited until the door was closed, then went to the desk and slid open a small panel underneath, and from the small compartment extracted a single brass key before replacing the panel. Then he brought the key out to his assistant. "Here you go."

"Thank you, sir. Secondus Fherrat will be sitting out here while I'm gone."

"Thank you."

Alastar went back into the study, but did not sit down, instead walked over to the windows, where he looked south toward the ruins of the administrative building. While the sleet had begun to melt, the sky remained a hazy gray. He thought about walking around Imagisle, but nothing had changed since the day before, and a walk would do little. *Your time would be better spent drafting recommendations for Lorien . . . and the rationale behind each.* He also knew he needed to meet with Elthyrd before long, but such a meeting wouldn't be that useful until he had a better feel for Lorien. Then there was the question of how to deal with Petayn and the army.

"First things first," he told himself as he walked back to the desk. Even as he seated himself, he wondered what else he was overlooking.

28

Alastar reined up at the base of the main entry steps to the Chateau D'Rex half a quint before fourth glass. He dismounted and handed the gelding's reins to Coermyd, accompanied by Akkard. "I have no idea how long this will take. Perhaps a glass, but it could be shorter."

"We'll be here, sir."

A single guard escorted Alastar up the outside steps, across the spacious entry hall, and up the grand staircase to the upper level and back along the north corridor to the rex's study. As soon as he entered the chamber and removed his visor cap, Alastar noted the changes. The massive black oak desk was gone, replaced by a smaller goldenwood table desk. A small circular conference table, also of goldenwood, with four chairs, had also been added.

Lorien rose from behind the table desk and walked to the table, standing behind the chair closest to the east end of the study. Alastar took the chair to Lorien's right, not the one across from him. He didn't want to suggest any form of confrontation.

As he seated himself, Lorien said, "Now that we have had the family memorial for Father . . . I've been thinking."

Alastar nodded for the rex to continue, even as he wondered about whether there would be a public memorial.

"How much can I trust you?"

"More than you can trust most others, including those closest to you, except for your lady."

"Oh? Why might that be?"

"Because I've heard that she is intelligent, and what befalls you will befall her, what triumphs you have will benefit her."

"What of you, Maitre?"

"The Collegium has already suffered losses, both in lives and buildings. We were forced to act in self-defense. It would be best if we did not have to act again anytime soon. The High Holders may respect us, but they know their interests differ from ours. The same is true of the factors. Most senior officers of the army would just as soon wipe out all imagers."

"Because, perhaps, you are the only force that holds them in check?" Lorien brushed back his errant lock of black hair in a gesture all too reminiscent of his late sire.

"That and the fact that they know the army is too large and the navy too small, and that the Collegium will push to redress that balance." Alastar was not unaware that Lorien did not address why the only member of his family he should trust was Chelia. He hoped that meant a certain understanding of the dangers of younger brothers and forceful mothers. "Part of your father's difficulties lay in the excessive size of the army and the pay of too many senior officers."

"What of the Collegium? Is not it a drain?"

Alastar laughed, but softly. "At most, the Collegium in all its branches has totaled perhaps five hundred people. What it requires is less than a single battalion of troopers and officers. Just in L'Excelsis, Acting Marshal Petayn has three regiments—fifteen battalions. He has five others spread across Solidar."

Lorien frowned. "He's only supposed to have six in all."

"The late Marshal Demykalon told me most firmly there were eight." Alastar shrugged. "Even if there are only six, that amounts to thirty battalions, and I sincerely doubt Solidar needs more than four regiments. It needs warships and vessels to protect its trading vessels against raiders and pirates far more than those two—or four—unnecessary regiments."

"Why exactly do your interests support mine? I don't think you really answered that."

"We can support you at far less expense than can your army. We also cannot afford to rule, unlike whoever might be marshal. Neither the High Holders nor the factors would allow that. Nor would the people. But none of them really cares that much who is rex, so long as it is not an imager and so long as their tariffs are not excessive and their liberties not too constrained."

"You haven't said much about loyalty."

"Our loyalty is to the rex of Solidar. Loyalty beyond that, to an individual ruler, must be earned."

"I can see you don't believe in flattery, Maitre."

"Wouldn't you trust me less if I attempted it?"

Lorien actually smiled, if but for a moment. "What my father did was scarcely to your liking, but was he not correct about the problems of financing Solidar?"

"He was correct that something needed to be done. He was also correct about the fact that the High Holders did not wish him to rule effectively. What he was not correct about was how to proceed to gain the revenues he needed and how best to strengthen Solidar."

"Gracious of you to admit he was right about something."

"Not gracious. Accurate," replied Alastar quietly. "What your father did, Lorien, was not working. You need to decide on what will work and follow that course."

The rex brushed back his hair again and said, "Before we even talk about what you think I should do, do me the courtesy of telling me what my father did that did not or would not work. With specifics, if you would."

"Your father maintained too large an army, especially with too many regiments close to L'Excelsis. Having a peacetime army with close to eight thousand men less than three milles from the Chateau D'Rex is a veiled threat. Those regiments are too far from anywhere that a foreign enemy might attack. Paying all those officers and men required far too many golds and left him without enough for more important tasks, such as rebuilding roads, improving port facilities, building warships designed to deal with the pirates of the Southern Gulf, or even foreign warships that might threaten Solidaran trading vessels. Then there is the matter of building more ships of the right construction to deal with the various threats on the sea and in the shallower waters off the coasts of Solidar."

"You did mention that already. What else?"

"Your sire was openly contemptuous of the High Holders and the larger factors, some of whom may be wealthier than the smaller High Holders, and made no effort at all to work out differences—"

"The High Holders made no effort and were contemptuous of him, and he was rex."

"It would have been wiser to make the efforts first, perhaps even to reduce the size of the army and to engage in some small road building and port improvements while pointing out that he could not do more without higher tariffs. The factors would understand some of that. After doing that, if using some form of force became necessary, the factors and the people would be more likely to excuse that use of force. At present, you won't face that problem."

"A mixed blessing, that, as much from the Namer as the Nameless."

"Your father also ignored my suggestion that the civic patrols in all the larger cities should be at least partly paid by the rex and that their chief—or at least those chiefs in major cities—report to a minister of justice, as should all justicers, including the High Justicers."

"Why might that be advisable? Would not many feel my thumb was on the scales of justice?"

"They might, but it would allow you to replace those whose interest is in lining their wallets, and that is of greater concern to the factors . . . and matters little one way or the other to most High Holders, since they retain the right to do justice on their own lands."

"Since you have managed to put the High Holders in their place, it seems to me that dealing with the army . . ." Lorien looked almost guilelessly at Alastar. "What would you suggest? In specifics, please."

"Over time, the eight army regiments should be reduced to four, and no more than two battalions should be posted at headquarters. The others should be posted at or near major ports. As part of the reduction in force, one or even two of the regiments here should be dispatched to Lucayl with the mission to patrol the shore and to root out all pirate enclaves there. The regiment remaining here should be allowed to shrink to two or three battalions by not replacing troopers or officers as their terms of service end or as officers reach the age for stipends. Some of those leaving will need to be replaced, but new replacements should be kept to a minimum. Also move one of the regiments from Estisle to Solis as well. If you're paying them, they should be doing something. As for ships, you'll need to meet with the sea marshal to work that out, because he'll likely want large and expensive ships of the line and little more. You'll need some of those, but the immediate need is for smaller vessels of shallow draft—"

"How as an imager are you qualified to make that judgment?"

"I grew up almost on the docks of Westisle. My father worked for a factor, and all imagers trained at Westisle, as I was, learn about merchanters and trade."

Lorien's lips quirked. "I do believe that you should be at any meeting with the sea marshal, Maitre . . . and at many other meetings for a time, if you understand what I mean."

"As a veiled suggestion that various people should be . . . reasonable, you mean."

"Not so veiled, I think. Solidar does not need any more . . . unrest." Lorien paused. "You had earlier mentioned an imager who had assisted, if that is the proper word, Marshal Demykalon in the attack on Imagisle. Have you had any fortune in locating him?"

"No, and it's likely we won't, not unless someone provides information to us. Outside of wearing imager grays, if he still is, he looks much the same as anyone else, just like a merchanter or a small factor. He is well-spoken and moderately good-looking . . . actually very good-looking." Alastar wasn't about to mention concealment shields.

"What might he look like?"

"He's got a languid and charming manner. Brown hair with a natural wave to it, a little longer than is fashionable, except for younger High Holders. He's about your height. His eyes . . . sometimes they're hazel and sometimes brown."

Lorien nodded. "I see your point. Many men would fit that description."

Alastar wondered whether Lorien knew that Desyrk had been in the chateau . . . or that someone in the chateau had mentioned his name. "You've never heard his name come up?"

"Not until you mentioned it. Why do you ask?"

"As I might have mentioned earlier, his brother was a subcommander who used to accompany Marshal Ghalyn to brief your sire. He was later promoted to commander. There is always the possibility his name might have been mentioned."

"Not around me."

"If you hear anything . . ."

"I will certainly let you know, Maitre." Lorien smiled politely. "I will be summoning Acting Marshal Petayn and Sea Marshal Wilkorn to a meeting on Lundi . . .

and I'll let you know when to be here for that. Until tomorrow at fourth glass." Lorien stood.

"Until then," agreed Alastar as he rose.

Again, a guard accompanied him from the study back to the entry steps of the chateau.

As Alastar rode down the drive from the chateau's entry, he glanced to the east to take in the beginning of the uncompleted Avenue D'Rex. *You'll need to work out finishing that once you put the Collegium back together.* After a moment, he had a second thought. *A few more golds of compensation might make it easier . . . if you can persuade Lorien.*

When Alastar returned to the Maitre's dwelling three quints later, he found Iskhar waiting for him in the hall foyer and motioned for the chorister to accompany him to the study. Alastar didn't bother to sit down before asking, "What can I do for you?"

"I hesitate to bother you, Maitre, but I need to complete the arrangements for the services for those who died . . . in the attack."

That was something that Alastar had overlooked. *Because you really don't want to deal with the deaths you caused?* "I appreciate that, Iskhar. What do you need from me?"

"I thought . . . I know you are not fond of speaking to large groups, but . . ."

Alastar understood all too well. How, as Maitre, could he not offer appreciation for the lives of those who had died for the Collegium? *Especially since you can't even acknowledge the true nature of their sacrifice.* "You must understand. I have not done much speaking, unlike the founder, who was apparently a chorister or the closest to that possible."

"You have been reading Gauswn's journals?"

"They do help me get to sleep. They also provide a certain perspective." Alastar smiled wryly. "If Chorister Gauswn was correct, Maitre Quaeryt was the greatest imager, perhaps the greatest figure in the history of Solidar, and today no one knows anything about him. Even here in the Collegium, most only know him as the founder."

"Do you believe what he wrote?"

"Do you?" countered Alastar.

"It must be so. I cannot believe it is otherwise." Iskhar smiled sadly. "I do not know if I would like to have known a man that powerful . . . I am more than happy to be a chorister. I would not wish to be in your boots, Maitre, or any Maitre's, for that matter."

"Sometimes, I wonder what I'm doing in them, Iskhar." After a moment, Alastar asked, "When will the services be? On Solayi afternoon?"

"I'd thought so. At the first glass of the afternoon."

"Will you be holding services for all those who were killed?"

"It appears that way, Maitre. Shabrena was widowed years ago, and the other three cooks had no family. The gardener came from . . . one of the taudis as a boy. He was an orphan." Iskhar cleared his throat. "When you have a moment, you might also want to reassure Mhorys's widow about the future."

"The fact that so long as she doesn't remarry someone outside the Collegium she and her children can live here."

"That's never been made an official rule, but . . ."

"It's come up so seldom that it's never been necessary. I'll talk to her this evening." Alastar paused, realizing that none of the other imagers who were killed had been married, because all had been students. The other aspect of the deaths was that, as evidenced by the examples of the cooks and the gardener, so many of those who worked and lived on Imagisle had come out of circumstances far worse than had Alastar himself. "You and your predecessor . . ."

"I beg your pardon, sir?"

"I was just thinking that many of those who work here were found and recommended by you and your predecessor."

"That is true—but only if they were of worthy character. Some we tried to help were not, but they soon left of their own will."

Because they realized it was too dangerous to be a thief or worse among so many imagers, no doubt. "If you need anything else, let me know."

The chorister nodded.

Alastar walked him to the door of the dwelling and stood on the porch until Iskhar was on the stone walk toward the anomen. Then he turned and walked back to the study. He knew little about Mhorys except that he had been one of the older Maitres D'Aspect, most likely close to Alastar's age. He'd been pleasant and hardworking. Alastar knew even less about Mhorys's wife, except that she was not an imager, and that the couple had two children, both daughters.

He rummaged through the papers in the cabinet behind the desk until he found the roster he'd asked for and made notes in when he'd first come to Imagisle. He remembered jotting down something about most of the maitres. He smiled in relief when he saw that he'd noted that Mhorys's wife was Carmina. He hadn't written down the daughters' names, however, just the letters "2-Ds."

There's still time before the evening meal. With that thought, he hurried from the study, pausing at the small table Dareyn was using. "I need to visit Mhorys's wife. I may not be back before you leave. If not, I'll see you in the morning. Oh . . . and one other thing. I never found out the names of the three cooks or assistants besides Shabrena who were killed. If you could find out?" Alastar was embarrassed that he didn't know and had to ask.

"Yes, sir."

Mhorys's cottage was the one next to that of Claeynd. As he passed Claeynd's door, Alastar slowed his steps and studied the dwelling, but so far as he could tell, Claeynd or Alyna or other imagers had managed to repair the damage, the only visible sign being a smoothed area of dirt, rather than what had been a side yard garden before the cannon shell had struck. Alastar nodded and continued to the stone walk leading up to the door, draped in green and black. He knocked firmly, but not excessively, and waited.

The woman who opened the door was red-haired, with bright blue eyes, eyes that were bloodshot. Her face was pale enough that her few freckles stood out, although Alastar could see that she was attractive, or would have been had she obviously not been so distraught.

"Matriana Carmina," offered Alastar, employing the seldom-used formal term for the non-imaging wife of an imager.

Carmina's eyes widened as she saw Alastar standing on the front step of the modest cottage. "Maitre . . ."

"I just came to express my sorrow at your loss."

Carmina said nothing, just looked, almost blankly, at Alastar. She did not invite him inside.

Since Alastar was not about to press, he went on, "I did not know your husband well, because I have been here such a short time, but he was hardworking and even-tempered, and as good a man and imager as any Maitre could wish. It was a tragedy that he died too young."

"A tragedy . . . a polite term . . . for such . . ." Her words came slowly.

"I'm sorry," Alastar said. "I wish my words could offer more comfort."

Abruptly, Carmina's eyes cleared and focused on Alastar. "What will we do? I know no one . . ."

"That is one trouble you will not have. You will

receive his stipend and retain the use of the cottage for now, and for as long as necessary."

"Necessary? Who determines that?"

"I should have said so long as you do not remarry, even if you live to a great age. If anything should befall you before your daughters are of age, they will be taken care of and educated here." Alastar paused. "Even if they do not turn out to be imagers."

Carmina looked at Alastar unbelievingly.

"It has always been that way," he replied. "It's just that so few maitres or imagers with both a wife and children have died recently that people forget."

Her eyes brightened. She shook her head. "That . . . well . . . it's some comfort, especially for Mhora and Charlina, Mhora not showing any sign of being an imager."

"And Charlina being too young?"

"She's but six."

"You'll all be taken care of," Alastar said, wanting to emphasize that. "There will be a memorial service on Solayi." He paused. "At the first glass of the afternoon."

Carmina nodded, but did not speak.

Finally, Alastar said, "I won't trouble you more. I wanted you to know I understand your sorrow."

"How would you?" Her words were bitter.

Alastar resisted the urge to explain. "I am more sorrowed than I can say." *And you have every right to be angry at me.* He nodded and stepped back.

Suddenly, her face softened, if slightly. "I'm sorry, Maitre. You're trying to help. I'm just angry."

"I understand that, too," Alastar said, knowing his words were even more true than what he had expressed.

"I'll be there. At the services." She stepped back and closed the door.

Alastar turned and walked slowly back to the Maitre's house, knowing that he also needed to visit the two injured imagers as well. *But that can wait until tomorrow.*

He still needed to go over the ledger that Arhgen had left him to see how much in golds the Collegium had and to figure out what was necessary, because sooner or later, he was going to have to ask Lorien for more. He took a deep breath and kept walking.

Despite having had a long day, with a suspicion that he had not come anywhere close to doing all that he needed to do, eighth glass arrived, finding Alastar in his study, tired but scarcely sleepy. Because he wanted to clear his mind of the events of the day, especially of the brief visit with Carmina D'Mhorys, if but for a time, he reached for the last volume of Chorister Gauswn's journals and began to read.

Pages later, he came across another revealing passage, so different from the almost mundane accounts of the chorister that it was almost as if winter had descended upon the study.

> I once asked Maitre Quaeryt how he had accomplished the imaging that defeated the Bovarians. He demurred. I asked him several more times, over the first years at the Collegium. Finally, many years later, when it was clear to us both that he and Vaelora did not have too many years left, he said that how he accomplished what he did was better forgotten, that three times in the history of Solidar was quite enough . . .

Three times? Alastar had no idea what the first time had been. After several moments, he continued reading.

> . . . I asked if he feared that someone else would discover how he had done what he had. He laughed. It was a bitter laugh. He said the cost of that knowledge had been so high that it was unlikely that anyone could ever muster the price again, even if they knew how he had done what he did. He told me never to ask again.

The darkness in his eyes and the iron in his voice convinced me. I never did.

Hints . . . why just a few hints over all these years and pages of journals?

Alastar slowly closed the volume, then rose, and imaged out the single lamp in the study before heading for his bedchamber.

29

After a brief meeting with the senior maitres on Samedi morning, during which they discussed details of the rebuilding and other adjustments necessary to keep the Collegium functioning, Alastar set out for the infirmary to check on the imagers who had been injured during the cannon attack.

He had only taken a few steps inside the infirmary when Gaellen hurried up. "Good morning, Maitre. You're here to see about the three young imagers?"

"And whoever else is here and injured."

"The wounds of the Collegium workers were either fatal or minor, and the minor ones are all in their cottages or quarters."

"How is Nyell? Akoryt said he took stone splinters."

"I think he might be all right, if his wounds don't fester. I imaged the splinters I could see out of him. That's dangerous, but less so than cutting into him. They weren't as deep as I thought."

"And you imaged clear spirits into the deeper wounds?"

"As soon as I could. We'll see in another day or two."

"What about the two who were injured by doing what they shouldn't have been?"

"Kaylet and Shannyr? They should be fine."

"After I finish talking with you, I thought I'd pay my respects to the three of them, although I suspect Kaylet and Shannyr might not be exceptionally pleased to see me."

Gaellen grinned. "Some young men will be young men, even when cannon shells are falling around them."

Except Shannyr hadn't been doing that, and Alastar wanted to know what he had been doing and why, but not until he'd seen the other two. "If you'd lead the way."

Gaellen walked down the hallway to the second door and opened it slowly. Nyell was lying on his side, propped into that position with folded blankets, seemingly dozing, except he was moaning softly.

Alastar looked to Gaellen.

"Most of the splinters hit on one side of his back and buttocks. Lying on his back is more painful." Gaellen spoke softly.

Deciding not to wake the injured imager, Alastar eased back from the doorway.

Gaellen eased the door almost all the way closed. "I'll tell him you came to see him."

"Thank you. Which door is Kaylet's?"

"The next one on the left. Shannyr's at the end. Do you need me?"

Alastar shook his head, then made his way to the next chamber. As soon as he stepped inside the room and saw Kaylet, he had a hard time not offering a knowing smile as he saw the thin-faced young secondus with too-long floppy brown hair. Both wrists were in heavy braces, and Kaylet wore a woeful expression that changed into concern as he saw the Maitre.

"Sir?"

"I heard you broke your wrists," said Alastar. "Both of them."

"Yes, sir."

"How did it happen? That's rather difficult to do, I would think, both of them at once, that is."

"Didn't Maitre Akoryt—" Kaylet broke off with a momentary look of hope in his eyes, that faded almost as soon as it appeared, followed by the same mournful expression that Alastar had seen initially.

"He did. I'd like to hear what you have to say."

"Yes, sir." Kaylet paused, as if considering how much to say.

"All of it, if you please," said Alastar.

"Yes, sir," said Kaylet, his voice despairing. "Maitre Claeynd—he was in charge—took us to the north park. That was after Maitre Akoryt sent word for all of us to leave the Collegium buildings. Nothing happened. We just stood there and looked at each other. Maitre Claeynd's wife was with us. She's a third herself, you know? . . ."

That was something Alastar knew, but hadn't recalled until Kaylet mentioned it.

". . . she had their children with her. One of them was crying. She was sick, I guess. Orlana—she's always trying to be so good—she was playing with their little boy, but he . . . well he was getting bored . . ." Kaylet paused. "Sir . . . ?"

"Go on."

"Like I said, the boy was getting bored. So I made some faces. He got bored of that after a little while. So I did a handstand and made faces upside down."

Alastar had a feeling he knew where the story would end, but he just nodded.

"Well . . . then I jumped up on the river wall and did another handstand." At Alastar's glance, he added quickly, "The wall's more than a yard wide on top, sir. I used to do handstands on the wire."

"You came from a carnival family?"

Kaylet swallowed. "Ah . . . yes, sir."

"That's not in your records."

"No, sir. People think less of carnival people than they do of Pharsi. My father also thought Maitre Fhaen might not give him the two golds if he knew that."

Even Fhaen wouldn't have stooped that low. "So how did you fall?"

"I was going to do a backflip into a handstand . . .

except my feet slipped when I started, and I tried to get my hands down to keep from hitting my head . . . I don't know what happened."

Alastar was afraid he did. "Who was in the group watching you? The other imagers?"

"Konan was there. Orlana—I told you about her—and Borlan, Marraet . . . there were others. And Seliora, she was there. She was trying to get away from Bettaur. He thinks every girl . . ." Kaylet stopped. "I'm sorry, sir. I shouldn't have . . . Anyway, Kierstia—the maitre's wife, she bound my wrists until Maitre Gaellen could do something because the cannon shells started hitting the Collegium right after I slipped and fell."

"Was the stone slippery?"

"I looked before I started. It didn't seem to be."

"I see." Alastar managed a serious expression. "You know, Kaylet, even with your experience, walking on the river wall isn't the safest thing to do, and doing flips is less so." After a pause, he added, "Even if you were trying to impress Seliora."

Kaylet flushed . . . and swallowed. "Sir . . . I wasn't hurting anyone . . ."

"No . . . except yourself. I hope it was worth it. Did Seliora come to see you?"

"Yes, sir." Kaylet grinned.

Alastar couldn't help but like the young man. "By the way, did you tell anyone here you came from a carnival family?"

"Not until now, sir."

"Best you keep it that way, at least until you become a maitre."

"Yes, sir."

"Now, try and take better care of yourself, young man." With a smile, one he didn't totally feel, Alastar turned and left the chamber, making his way to the next door.

Shannyr's right arm was in a sling, one bound to his

body. He glanced up as Alastar entered the sickroom, and if Kaylet's expression had been mournful, then Shannyr's was more like terror-struck as he beheld the Collegium Maitre.

"We need to talk, Shannyr."

"Yes, sir." The two words seemed to tremble.

"Tell me why you, Johanyr, and Klovyl were trying to get into the administration building in the middle of the cannon attack."

"Sir, I don't know—"

"Spare me the lie, Shannyr." Alastar's voice was cold.

"It was Bettaur, sir."

That scarcely surprised Alastar. "Bettaur? He wasn't even with you."

Shannyr did not comment.

"Go on and explain," added Alastar.

"No, sir. He couldn't be, not with Maitre Akoryt and Tertia Kierstia watching him like sun eagles. But he said that it would show you and the other maitres that we meant well if we rescued the founder's sabre from the administration building."

Why would Bettaur say that? The only reason Alastar could come up with was that Bettaur wanted the three dead . . . or injured and out of the way. *But why?*

"Did Bettaur tell you this? Personally?"

"No, sir. He told Johanyr. Johanyr said we'd have to hurry."

"Did Johanyr say anything else?"

"No, sir. Just that Bettaur wouldn't like it if we didn't save the founder's sabre."

"Did he say why?"

"No, sir."

"How did you get out when Johanyr and Klovyl didn't?"

"Johanyr said I wasn't tall enough and that I needed to stay outside in case anyone came along."

Was Johanyr even after the founder's sabre? Was going into the administration building Johanyr's idea, or Bettaur's? "Didn't you all know that it was dangerous?"

"Johanyr said that no one could hit the administration building from across the river, even if they tried."

Alastar managed not to shake his head. "I'm not sure I understand. If the army cannon couldn't hit the building, then why did anyone need to go and rescue the sabre?"

"That's what Johanyr said."

"Has Bettaur come to see you?"

"No, sir. I don't imagine he could."

"Do you want him to come?"

Shannyr looked down.

"Bettaur can be rather nasty when things don't go his way, I take it?"

Alastar waited.

"Couldn't you just send me to Westisle, sir?"

"You're not going anywhere until you're better," replied Alastar.

"Yes, sir." Both Shannyr's words and posture reflected complete dejection.

"We'll talk later." That was a fact, not a promise, because one way or another, Alastar would be talking to the injured third again, and likely much more than once.

After leaving Shannyr's sickroom, Alastar headed back toward the entry, looking for Gaellen, but the Maitre D'Aspect was already standing outside his study, as if waiting.

"What do you think, Maitre?"

"It appears as though both Kaylet and Shannyr will recover. How long do you plan to keep Kaylet here?"

"He's fine, except for the fractures. It's just that he can't do much of anything. If he had a family, someone to . . . do everything . . ."

"Just let me know when you think he can leave."

Gaellen frowned. "That will be several weeks, I'd judge."

"Oh . . . and Tertius Bettaur is not to see either Kaylet or Shannyr. I doubt that he'll try, but if he does, don't let him near them."

"More trouble? Hasn't Bettaur done enough? Why would he—"

"I don't know that it's Bettaur, but I'd feel a great deal better if he doesn't see either until I get to what's behind a few events."

"I can do that. Do you mind if I just say that because of the nature of their injuries no one is to see anyone without my permission or yours?"

"That would be fine. Thank you."

From the infirmary, Alastar returned to the Maitre's dwelling, hoping that Akoryt might be there, but the Maitre D'Structure was not, although Dareyn was seated behind the small table desk in the hall outside Alastar's personal study.

"I put those names on your desk, sir . . . and something about each of them. Thought that might help."

"Thank you very, very much." Alastar meant that. "Do you know where Maitre Akoryt might be, Dareyn?"

"He left word that he'd be at the stables helping Maitre Petros."

"That's where I'm headed. I'll be back after that."

As Alastar walked back south on the west walk, the one that would take him past the ruins of the administration building, he wished that he'd talked to Bettaur about his background, rather than deciding to wait until the third completed his detention. *But how could you have known what else would happen?* Except there was the old saying about not putting things off . . . *And you shouldn't have.*

Even before Alastar reached the stables, a third carrying a bucket of grain saw him and hurried into the stables.

In moments, Akoryt emerged and stepped forward to meet Alastar. "You've got a determined stride there, Maitre."

"Where's Bettaur?"

"He's in the tack room. Petros has him cleaning saddles and riding gear. You did say that he needed special disciplinary assignments."

"I did, but I need to talk to him. Some more things have come up."

"Do you think he was behind the three trying to get the founder's sabre?"

"I just talked to Shannyr. He says that Johanyr said Bettaur was, that Bettaur said they'd all be in better standing if they rescued it. But . . ."

"It could have been Johanyr's idea, and he was using Bettaur," finished Akoryt.

"Or not," added Alastar.

"Did Shannyr give a reason?"

"He said that Johanyr said that if they saved the sabre they'd be in better standing."

"That doesn't make sense."

"In more ways than one."

"Do you want me to come with you?" asked Akoryt.

"I think not. Not this time."

Alastar could see a certain relief in Akoryt's eyes before he made his way into the stables and to the tack room.

Bettaur turned from the saddle he was cleaning, then inclined his head. "Maitre." He smiled pleasantly.

"I was going over the rosters of student imagers, Bettaur. All your record says is that you entered the Collegium six years ago, in Finitas of 383 After Lydor."

"Not quite six years ago, Maitre."

"Close enough. Tell me about your background."

"I was an orphan. That's what they told me."

"Who told you?"

"My guardians."

"Who were?"

"Elsevier D'Tuuryl and his lady."

"A wealthy landowner of Tuuryl and his wife?"

"They were. They died in the gray plague that ravaged the lands west of L'Excelsis the year after I came to the Collegium."

"Do you know who your true parents were?"

"No, sir." Bettaur shrugged apologetically. "I doubt I was truly an orphan."

"Oh?"

"In the year or so before I came to the Collegium, I noticed that at times, a messenger in a dark cloak visited Holder Elsevier, and thereafter I usually was paid a visit by the local tailor." Bettaur smiled ironically. "I have no idea from where the messenger came, and Elsevier and Alysetta refused to speak of anything about my past, except to say that I had been well-loved. They were very kind and gentle, especially Alysetta."

With those words, Bettaur's voice wavered slightly, but Alastar had no idea whether the waver was real or feigned.

"Did they have any other children?"

"No. She said that I was the only child she would ever have."

"Did she use that phrase?"

"She did. I wondered, just as you are, Maitre, but that was all she ever said."

Alastar nodded. "Who brought you here? Your guardians?"

"No, sir. Maitre Fhaen came in a coach. The Collegium coach. That was after I imaged a comb for Alysetta."

"Did they tell you that you were coming to the Collegium?"

"Not until Maitre Fhaen arrived."

Stranger and stranger. Alastar offered several more questions, the answers to which shed no more light on

Bettaur's past, then asked, "When did you last talk to Johanyr?"

"I didn't speak to him since before the detention meeting. Maitre Akoryt released me from the detention cell only a glass before the cannon began to fire, and I was with him or Tertia Kierstia all the time until after the bombardment ended."

"That was with the group of student imagers that included Orlana, Borlan, Marraet . . . oh, and Kaylet and Seliora?"

"I think there were others."

"But not Johanyr, Klovyl, or Shannyr?"

"No, sir." Bettaur's voice was firm.

"Thank you. I'm trying to find out why Johanyr and Klovyl were in the administration building when it was hit by cannon fire. Do you have any idea why that might be?"

"I couldn't tell you, sir. I certainly wouldn't have wanted to be anywhere near where the cannonballs were striking."

"Thank you. We may talk later." Alastar turned and left the tack room.

Akoryt was waiting outside the stables. "Did he say anything?"

"He said he hadn't talked to Johanyr since before he was locked up. Or any of the others. Shannyr certainly didn't talk to him."

Akoryt shook his head. "I'm very glad not to be in your boots, Maitre."

Alastar smiled ruefully. "I'll be back at the Maitre's house if you need me."

As Alastar walked back along the east side of the central green, he glanced across to the far side as he passed the doorway with the green and black mourning drape. Like so many good imagers, Mhorys had been the quiet type. *Is that trait from innate character or from experience?* Alastar shrugged. There was no way, not really, of knowing.

When he reached the hallway outside his study, he asked, "Dareyn . . . are there any messages?"

"Just one. Rex Lorien would appreciate your presence at third glass, rather than at fourth glass. Oh, and Maitre Alyna will be back shortly. She wanted a word with you."

"Good. I need to talk to her about several things. Just have her come in."

"Yes, sir. How are the injured students?"

"Nyell seems to be holding his own. Maitre Gaellen is cautiously optimistic. Both Shannyr and Kaylet will recover. They'll be in the infirmary for a time though."

"Maitre Obsolym wanted to know."

"You can certainly tell him that . . . and anyone else who asks."

Once Alastar was in his study, he did not sit down, but walked slowly around the room, thinking. Something nagged at him, but he couldn't quite place it. He was still pondering when the door opened and Alyna entered.

She smiled cheerfully, and Alastar felt better. He also immediately realized that it had been a long time, if ever, that someone's smile had done that.

"You've been busy this morning, Dareyn says."

"I've been busy finding more puzzles and problems." Alastar gestured to the chairs in front of the desk, standing beside one and waiting until Alyna took one before seating himself. "Tell me what you know about the founder's sabre, if you would."

"The founder's sabre?" Alyna smiled again. "There's a story that Erion, the great hunter, the god of the lesser moon, and the consort of the daughter of Artiema, bestowed the sabre on Maitre Quaeryt, and that the sabre has great powers. When wielded by the right imager, no one can prevail against the wielder."

Alastar shook his head. "Quaeryt was such a powerful imager that I doubt he ever needed to use his sabre. That's if the sabre that was mounted on the wall of the study was even his. Was there any proof of that?"

"I have no idea. Obsolym might know, if anyone does. What about those journals you've been reading?"

Abruptly, Alastar recalled one of the passages he had read. "There was a reference to a blade of Erion that had saved Quaeryt, but Gauswn wrote that it had been returned to Khel. There was no mention of it ever being Quaeryt's weapon."

"That's most likely where the legend came from." After a pause, she asked, "Why did you want to know about the founder's sabre? Because of Johanyr and Klovyl? Do you think Johanyr or Bettaur thought they could use the blade against you?"

"I don't know what to think. I talked to Shannyr and Bettaur earlier . . ." Alastar went on to recount what he had learned, and not learned, from each. When he finished, he asked, "What do you think?"

"Bettaur's very careful of his words, isn't he?"

"Very much so."

"He said he didn't *talk* to any of them."

Alastar laughed. "So . . . how do we find out if he sent a note?"

"Let me see what I can do, dear Maitre."

"You think Bettaur charmed one of the few young women student imagers?"

"That's more likely."

"I don't think it will be Seliora."

"Oh?"

"That's something else you should know. Kaylet's injury wasn't exactly an accident . . ." Alastar explained what he had learned from the former acrobat.

"You think that Bettaur was stupid enough to image oil or something on the stone?"

"More likely on Kaylet's shoes. And he's not stupid,

except in so far as arrogance makes one stupid. If what Kaylet said about not revealing his past is correct, Bettaur wouldn't have known that Kaylet wouldn't have slipped by accident. But that arrogance . . ." Alastar broke off his words and said instead, "I have to wonder from the wrong side of which High Holder's family blanket Bettaur comes . . ."

"You almost said that such arrogance is typical of High Holders, didn't you?" asked Alyna gently.

"Not quite. I was going to say that it runs strongly in High Holder males." He looked directly into Alyna's black eyes. "I really was."

"I was giving you just a little jab." But she did smile. "You think his supposed foster mother was in fact his real mother?"

"She could have been. I'm also cynical enough to believe that she and her husband may not have died from the gray plague. Most of those who died were either very young or very old."

"Poison? Or do you suspect something else?"

"I don't know, except there is little information on Bettaur, his guardians are dead, and Maitre Fhaen brought him to the Collegium. Both Bettaur and Dareyn agree on that."

"Do you think that Maitre Fhaen told Desyrk not to be hard on Bettaur?" asked Alyna. "And that's why he got away with so much with Taurek?"

Alastar thought over what he recalled of his conversation with Desyrk about the problems between the two. "Desyrk did start to say something about Maitre Fhaen, but he broke it off and said that Fhaen had told him to remember that student imagers were just boys."

"That doesn't sound like Fhaen at all."

"So we're left with the fact that Bettaur's the bastard child of someone powerful, that Fhaen knew something about it, and that someone was powerful enough that

Fhaen probably hinted to Desyrk that it would be best if Bettaur didn't have too many problems."

"You don't think . . . Ryen?"

"Everything fits that possibility except for the fact that Bettaur doesn't have a single, solitary feature resembling either Ryen or Lorien. That makes it unlikely, if not impossible."

"You're probably right about that." After a moment, Alyna went on, "You're going to the Chateau D'Rex every day now, aren't you?"

"It looks as though that's the way it will be."

"You need to be careful."

"I always carry shields."

"They're not proof against everything."

"Falling off the grand staircase? Or poison? Perhaps, I shouldn't eat or drink anything there." Alastar's words were half humorous.

"For as long as Lorien is rex."

"What do you suggest?"

"Just . . . be careful, especially off Imagisle."

"And not on it?"

"Poisons are very complex, most of them. I don't think there's an imager who could image poison into something without creating such an awful taste or smell that you'd be warned." Alyna smiled. "Have you ever tried to image wine or lager?"

"No. Redberry juice when I was a junior imager at Westisle. It tasted . . . well . . . awful." Alastar grimaced at the memory.

"You'd likely do better now, because you know more, and it might even be barely drinkable, but poisons . . . no."

"Are poisons part of the education of a lady in a High Holder's family?" he inquired dryly.

"No. I overheard more than I was supposed to. I was, as my father put it, 'prone to excessive curiosity.' That was another reason why he was happy, I think, that I turned out to be an imager."

"What about your sister?"

"Loryna wouldn't think of it, and, even if she did, she wouldn't likely tell me anything. That's because she wouldn't want me to think less of her. There are certain . . . ingredients that one can put in certain dishes that create odors or colors if some poisons are used. Those are usually the fast-acting ones." Alyna shrugged. "But since no High Holder wants a poisoning traced to his table . . ."

"No one uses fast-acting poisons?"

"Except at other High Holders' functions. Usually ones with many attendees . . . or small functions where the poisoner is not actually present."

Alastar found it hard to imagine living in a society that engaged in that kind of rat and terrier game, but he didn't doubt that it existed. "That makes me even happier that I'm an imager . . . even at present."

"I think most of the maitres who have considered the matter are glad you're here right now."

"I'm thankful you're also here." *For many reasons.*

"You're being kind."

"I'm being accurate. I'm not exactly noted for kindness, especially at the moment."

"The greatest kindness is to do what is necessary and painful when no one else will."

"If the act is correct . . . and that's not always easy to know. I'm still wondering about what I've been doing these past few days." He paused. "Have any of the other maitres offered suggestions or requests about the new buildings?"

"Akoryt was the first. So did Petros and Taryn . . . and Cyran—he's afraid of being too forward." She smiled sadly. "He'll always be a good senior imager, if the Maitre is good, but . . ."

"Would you ever want to be—"

"No. Neither senior imager, nor Maitre. Solidar isn't ready for a woman Maitre, and I'd rather not be senior imager."

"You're too strong-willed, behind that quiet and reserved exterior, to be subservient, or appear to be, directly to the will of another. You also don't like to ask for what you deserve."

"Zaeryl sent me another letter . . ."

"You're changing the subject."

"I am."

Alastar smiled. "What did he say?"

"Not to trust Guerdyn—that was indirectly stated in a veiled way . . ."

For a moment Alastar wondered why Zaerlyn would say that about a dead man, except he realized that Rivages was days away, even for a fast courier.

". . . He also said that he'd heard good words about you from some of the High Holders in the south. That's about as close to praise as anyone gets from him."

"You come from a demanding family."

"All families are, I think, in one way or another."

Far from the first time, Alastar was again struck by her insight. "I enjoy being with you, talking with you," he said quietly.

"I know. I enjoy it also."

"But? There's a hint of reservation there."

"I don't like to do things halfway. So far as the Collegium is concerned, that's sometimes necessary." She looked at Alastar directly and intently once more.

"I understand. I don't, either."

"For now . . . then?"

"For now." *But only for now.*

"Still friends?"

Alastar laughed, gently. "Never just friends, but I'll behave."

"You always have, dear Maitre. That's one of your many endearing traits."

Alastar wasn't about to ask what his less endearing traits might be.

Alyna rose from the chair. "I have things to do, and so do you."

"Until later, then, whenever that is."

"Until later."

Alastar walked her to the front porch then watched as she walked briskly through the chill afternoon toward the cottage she shared with Tiranya.

Then he returned to his study.

Given Lorien's peremptory request, Alastar was almost tempted to arrive at the chateau a few moments late, but since he'd derive no advantage from doing so and might pay in some fashion later, he resisted the urge . . . and reined up promptly at the entry steps a quint before the glass struck. Another guard, one he had not seen before, ushered him upstairs to Lorien's study, where the new rex was standing by the small conference table.

"How are you and the other imagers coming on rebuilding your Collegium?" asked Lorien as he seated himself.

Alastar sat and set his cap on the side of the table before replying. "We've finished all the repairs to buildings that were damaged. We haven't begun on rebuilding the dining hall or the administration building." Seeing a certain glint in Lorien's eyes, Alastar asked, "Why?"

"Are you going to leave that avenue unfinished?"

"We hadn't thought to, but we won't be able to finish it until we can rebuild some of the Collegium."

"I trust that will not take an excessively long time."

"We will be as expeditious as possible."

Lorien nodded. "Lady Asarya and I thought that it might be appropriate to name it in honor of my sire."

"L'Avenue D'Rex Ryen?"

"It was his idea."

"We will complete it. You and Lady Asarya can choose the name you feel appropriate."

"Good. Have you heard anything from the High Holders?"

"Not yet, but it will likely take several days before we should press. If I don't hear anything by Meredi, I'll meet with Vaun. You'll need to put your proposal in writing, an increase of four coppers on the gold above the existing tariff levels, with the possibility of smaller increases in the years after next year."

"Smaller?" Lorien's eyebrows rose.

"Smaller. If you establish the right to annual increases . . ."

Abruptly, Lorien smiled. "Of course." The smile vanished. "But this coming year, how will we manage?"

"By reducing expenses by the army and by looking at other places where the golds have not been wisely spent. In the end, you will come out better."

"Speaking of the army . . ." Lorien drew out the words before continuing, "Instead of our fourth-glass meeting on Lundi, I'd appreciate your being here at first glass for the meeting with Acting Marshal Petayn and Sea Marshal Wilkorn . . . for those discussions on the future of the army and the navy that you recommended."

"I will be here."

"Excellent. There are a few other things we should discuss. First, there is the question of my father's memorial service . . ."

Alastar almost groaned. He should have thought about that. "Perhaps on Lundi or Mardi?"

"That's too soon to arrange it properly. We have already had the private services, but a public memorial at the Anomen D'Rex next Samedi would be most appropriate, don't you think?"

The less pomp and formality the better. Alastar wasn't about to say that, not directly. "You'd like to leave the best possible memory of your father, I take it. I would suggest subdued formality. That is, of course, only a suggestion. You and your mother and brother need to decide what is appropriate."

"Subdued formality . . ." mused Lorien.

Alastar could tell the afternoon would not end soon, and certainly not soon enough for him.

30

Going over the details of what Lorien proposed for his father's public memorial took another two glasses, and more details than Alastar had thought were necessary, many of which, it was clear, were the result of Lady Asarya's "suggestions." Once he left the Chateau D'Rex, Alastar rode back along the route of the Avenue D'Rex Ryen, noting just how far the imagers had gotten, which was almost a third of the total distance, and how well and with what care to details that Alyna and the others had finished the paving, sidewalks, drains, and gutters on that section. He also noted that already some of the damaged or truncated shops were being replaced with new or refurbished establishments of a far more commercial nature than the apothecaries they replaced. He had the feeling that the apothecaries of the former lane were not faring so badly, and some likely had received additional golds for their property.

When he reached the Maitre's dwelling, the dining room was filled with hungry pupils, unsurprisingly, since all imagers were effectively barred from leaving Imagisle. He waited until only a few students remained in the dining room before joining them, eating quickly, and then retiring to his study. Once there, he began work on the homily he would have to deliver on Solayi for those who died in the cannon attack. That was anything but easy, since he didn't know that much about most of the victims, and, in the case of Johanyr and Klovyl, much of what he did know was not anything suitable for a memorial service. At the same time, he could not slight any of those who died, and he discovered that finding suitable words was extraordinarily difficult.

Well after eighth glass that evening, when Alastar had finally worked out an acceptable homily, and when Jienna and the other cook had long since left for the night, Alastar took three crystal beakers from the pantry that held glassware and platters and carried them carefully into his study, where he set them on the desk and picked up the small lamp that he had imaged into light. Carrying the lamp, he returned to the kitchen, where he opened the door that concealed the narrow steps, then picked up an empty pitcher and made his way down to the cellar. There, he drew a half pitcher of lager from the small keg, then returned to the kitchen, setting down the pitcher in order to close the cellar door, before taking the lamp and pitcher back to his study.

He imaged out the small lamp, leaving the larger one in the wall bracket overlooking the desk still lit, and sat down. He poured half a beaker of lager and sipped it, concentrating on how it tasted before setting the beaker down beside the other two, so that all three were in a row. Then he looked at the first empty beaker and concentrated on imaging the exact same amount of lager into it. Almost instantly, the beaker was half full.

Alastar studied the two beakers, but as far as he could tell, there was the same amount of lager in each.

"So far, so good," he murmured.

Then he lifted the second beaker and took the tiniest sip of the liquid in it. While the smell was like lager, if a poor variety, at the first taste, he winced. Only by the greatest stretch of imagination could it be called lager, although it tasted drinkable, and he had tasted worse, but not in a very long time. Still, it would do for his purposes.

He set the two beakers directly in front of him, the

one with real lager on the right, and the one with imaged lager on the left, then concentrated again. He *thought* he saw the slightest movement of the liquids in both beakers, although he couldn't be sure. He reached for the goblet on the right. It smelled like the imaged lager. He sipped. It was the imaged lager. He set down that beaker and tasted the one on the left. It was the real lager, although it tasted a shade off.

He poured real lager into the other empty beaker, and lifted it, as if in a toast, and then attempted to image out the real lager and replace it with imaged lager. Liquid spilled over his hand.

He set the beaker down, imaged away the liquid, then refilled the beaker and tried again, with the same result.

"Hmmm . . ."

He set the beaker back on the desk, wiped his hands on the handkerchief he almost never used, then imaged the liquid from the beaker, and poured fresh lager into it. This time, he left the beaker on the desktop and image-replaced the lager. Not a drop of liquid moved.

He went through another attempt with the toasting motion, only to get liquid on his hands, even though he did not image until he held the beaker still.

He set down the beaker and wiped his hands once more, thinking. *Your hand must move imperceptibly, even though you think it's not.* At least, he knew what was possible and what was not, in case certain circumstances arose.

He imaged away all the liquid in the three beakers, picked them up, and took them to the kitchen, then came back for the pitcher and carried it to the kitchen. He thought about trying to wash the three, and decided against it. When he returned to the study, he glanced at the third volume of Chorister Gauswn's journals, then shook his head.

You're tired enough that you won't remember much, and you might miss something. With that thought, he imaged out the study lamp and made his way to the stairs and up to his bedchamber.

31

On Solayi morning, after an early breakfast before most of the student imagers straggled in, Alastar went back over his homily for the memorial services, and then spent almost three glasses working on various possibilities for reducing the costs incurred by the rex, including the number of army regiments. All those costs were estimates, because he had no solid numbers whatsoever, only the base pay rates for troopers and officers and the figures on what various goods and materials cost the Collegium. At the same time, he doubted that either Lorien or Petayn knew even that much, at least from what he'd observed. Add to that the lack of a minister for the army, since the marshal of the army functioned as such. *Not a good system for knowing costs.* That led to a proposal for restructuring the government to increase accountability. *Which is where you should have begun.*

When he set aside those papers and walked from the study, he found Alyna sitting at Dareyn's table in the hallway.

She immediately stood. "I thought I might accompany you to the services, if you don't mind." Her words were almost shy.

"I'd like that. Very much."

With his words came her smile, the one that likely was not special to anyone else, but which somehow warmed him. "I worried . . ."

"You don't have to worry." That was the last thing Alastar wanted.

"You mean that, don't you?"

"Yes."

"Thank you." Before Alastar could reply, she said, "We had better set out, if you don't want to hurry. It's already two quints before two."

"Then we will." Alastar moved to the front door, opening it for her. He'd debated whether to wear an overcoat or heavier jacket, but although the day was gray, there was no wind, and he knew the anomen was likely to be close with as many people as would be there. When they neared the ancient but polished brass-bound double doors of the anomen, it was still a quint before the chimes would strike.

Standing on one side of the stone walkway just outside the door was Chervyt, while on the other side were Lhendyr and a woman who had to be his wife, along with Carmina, and her two daughters. Alastar struggled for a moment to recall their names. *Charlina and Mhora.*

"You talk to Carmina first," murmured Alyna. "I'll talk to Chervyt until you can."

"Thank you." Alastar's words were even more subdued than Alyna's as he stepped toward Carmina.

"Maitre . . . I did appreciate your coming to see me. I wasn't at my best." Carmina met Alastar's eyes and offered a sad smile.

"Matriana . . . no one would be at her best after suffering such a loss. If there is anything else I can do, now or in the future, please don't hesitate to let me know." He glanced to Charlina, a solid red-haired little girl with dark blue eyes that Alastar would have called knowing, and then to Mhora, older, perhaps ten or eleven, and more slender. "That goes for you two young women as well." His eyes went back to Carmina. With a nod toward Charlina, he said, "Most likely. I'll be inquiring from time to time as to how things are going."

"You're most kind, Maitre."

Hardly, not when your husband paid the price for all

of us. "I'd rather not have to have thanks for what I can do. I'd rather that I were talking to you both."

"So would I, but we do what we must," Carmina returned.

Alastar turned slightly toward Lhendyr and his wife. "Thank you for standing by Carmina as well."

"The least we could do, sir. The least."

"You and Mhorys always provided an excellent example for the younger maitres, and I have appreciated that and always will." Alastar offered a warm smile before easing away toward Chervyt.

". . . think the Maitre has some words." Alyna slipped away, back toward Carmina, as Alastar stopped before Chervyt.

"I'm sorry, Chervyt, both for you and for Nuasyn. I wouldn't know, but I think it must be particularly hard to lose such a close friend, when there are so few you can truly be close to."

Chervyt's eyes brightened, and he swallowed before he spoke. "Thank you, sir. I . . . I don't know what to say . . . it's like . . . everything . . ."

"Perhaps like a certain brightness has left your life?"

Chervyt nodded.

"Having such a brightness is a blessing, but the loss makes things seem darker for a time . . . but only for a time. If you need to talk, I'll listen. If you'd rather not, know that I'll understand."

"Thank you, sir."

Alastar turned back toward the door of the anomen to find Alyna at his elbow. "We'll need to be at the front on one side."

She nodded.

"How is Carmina, do you think? I tried to be concerned without being false."

"She'll be fine."

"I worry about the little one. I have the feeling that

she sees and understands too much too young . . . and that she'll likely be an imager."

"Would you like me to occasionally visit her?"

"If you could without upsetting Carmina."

"I can manage that."

Once inside the anomen, Alastar and Alyna made their way to the front and to the left side, not that such was difficult, despite the fact that the nave was already crowded, because everyone immediately moved aside, a deference that Alastar found vaguely disconcerting.

Shortly after the chime of the glass died away, Chorister Iskhar stepped out from the pulpit and stood in the middle of the sacristy dais. "We are gathered here together this afternoon in the spirit of the Nameless, in affirmation of the quest for goodness and mercy in all that we do, and in celebration of the lives of those brought to a close by the senseless violence against the Collegium. We are here to remember Mhorys, Nuasyn, Klovyl, Johanyr, Shabrena, Ellya, Vierli, Jeena, and Albyrt, to give thanks for their lives, for their loves, and for their sacrifice."

The opening hymn was "The Glory of the Nameless." Alastar sang in a low voice, glancing at Alyna, who remained standing beside him. He couldn't help but note that she sang far better than he did, despite her earlier statement that she was a poor singer. Then came the confession. Alastar had always wondered how effective the confession was, despite the claim by choristers that, without confession, there could be no understanding and no healing.

"We do not name You, for naming is presumptuous, and we would not presume upon the creator of all that was, is, and will be. We do not pray to You, nor ask boons or blessings from You, for requesting such asks You to favor us over others who are also your creations. Rather we confess that we always risk the sins of pride and presumption and that the very names we bear symbolize those sins, for we too often strive to arrogate our names and ourselves above others, to insist that our petty plans and arid achievements have meaning beyond those whom we love or over whom we have influence and power. Let us never forget that we are less than nothing against your Nameless magnificence and that all that we are and all that we may become is a gift to be cherished and treasured, and that we must also respect and cherish the gifts of others, in celebration of You who cannot be named or known, only respected and worshipped."

"In peace and harmony," came the response.

After that came the charge from Iskhar. "Life is a gift from the Nameless, for from the glory of the Nameless do we come; through the glory of the Nameless do we live, and to that glory do we return. Our lives can only reflect and enhance that glory, as did that of all those whom we honor, whom we remember, and who will live forever in our hearts and in the glory of the Nameless."

Another hymn followed—"In the Footsteps of the Nameless."

"When we walk the narrow way of what is always right,
when we follow all the precepts that foil the Namer's blight . . ."

Alastar had some doubt about following the footsteps of the Nameless, since it seemed to him that following anything blindly more likely led to trouble than to glory, but that wasn't a point he was about to make.

Then Iskhar said, "Now we will hear from Maitre Alastar."

Alastar realized that, with Iskhar's words, Alyna had glanced warmly at him, and that surprised him enough that he did not step forward for several moments. He walked purposefully, but not hurriedly, and stepped up on the dais. When he turned and looked out across the anomen, completely filled, both with imagers and their families, but also with so many of those who worked and lived on Imagisle, far more than he realized, he could see more than a few green-and-black mourning scarves worn by the women.

He paused, not wanting to hurry, then gently and quietly cleared his throat before beginning. "Nine members of the Collegium died this past week. Mhorys, Nuasyn, Klovyl, Johanyr, Shabrena, Ellya, Vierli, Jeena, and Albyrt. All were valued; all left those who cared for them, and for whom they cared; all worked in their own ways to make the Collegium, and thus, all Terahnar, a better place. Yet for all that shared purpose, each was an individual and differed from anyone else. What I will say about each is only a fraction of what could be said and far, far less than what each and every one of us should recall." Alastar paused again.

"Mhorys was a hardworking, good-tempered Maitre D'Aspect who died protecting all that he held dear, just as he had lived supporting and protecting all that he held to be of worth and value . . ." From there, Alastar went through each of the other eight. When he finished with Albyrt, he said, "One was an imager, three were student imagers, four were cooks and assistants, and one was a gardener. Each offered what they were and what they did to make Imagisle a better place. The very least we can do is to give thanks for their lives, their loves, and their sacrifices." *You, especially.*

Alastar had to swallow. He stood there for several moments, just taking in those in the anomen. More than a few people were weeping, including Carmina. He hoped that the tears would be a beginning of healing. *But do you ever fully heal?*

He stepped down from the dais and rejoined Alyna.

Chorister Iskhar stepped forward to the pulpit once

again. "At this time, we wear black and green, black for the dark uncertainties of life, and green for its triumph, manifested every year in the coming of spring. So is it that, like nature, we come from the dark of winter and uncertainty into life which unfolds in uncertainty, alternating between black and green, and in the end return to the life and glory of the Nameless. In that spirit, let us offer thanks for the spirits and the lives of those who died for us," intoned Iskhar, "and let us remember them as each was, not merely as a name, but as a living breathing individual whose spirit touched many and in ways only the Nameless can fully fathom. Let us set aside the gloom of mourning, and from this day forth, recall the glory of their lives and the warmth and joy they have left with us . . ."

Warmth and joy? Alastar had his doubts, even as he could sense that some of the women had let the mourning scarves slip from their hair.

Then came the traditional closing hymn—"For the Glory."

> *"For the glory, for the life,*
> *for the beauty and the strife,*
> *for all that is and ever shall be,*
> *all together, through forever,*
> *in eternal Nameless glory . . ."*

As the last words of the closing hymn echoed through the anomen, Alastar straightened. "We need to speak to Iskhar."

"You do," said Alyna, with a warm but mischievous tone. "I'll be close."

Alastar moved toward the chorister, who stepped down from the dais to meet him. "A good service, Iskhar."

"A better appreciation of those it honored, I think."

Alastar laughed softly. "Now that we've congratulated each other, do you think it helped those who suffered and those who worry about what might happen in the days to come?" What he couldn't ask was why he'd been forced to sacrifice nine lives for the sake of the others.

"Recognizing the worth of those who die always helps. It never helps enough."

With that, Alastar could agree. "Thank you. I'll see you again this evening."

"You need two services today, Maitre?"

"Two might help." Alastar managed a rueful smile before turning and rejoining Alyna.

By the time the two reached the doors of the anomen only a few people remained, none of whom Alastar immediately recognized, and none of whom even paid him more than a passing glance. He did pick up a few fragments of conversations.

". . . leastwise . . . sounded like he meant it . . ."

". . . supposed to . . . part of being Maitre . . ."

". . . don't understand . . . army killed Albyrt . . . and . . . does nothing . . ."

Did nothing? Alastar managed not to smile bitterly. More than a hundred troopers dead, possibly even two hundred or more, a dead rex, a dead High Holder, and a dead marshal, and he'd done nothing?

"You spoke well," said Alyna once they were walking toward the Maitre's dwelling.

"I tried to say what was necessary."

"Without saying too much," she added.

He shook his head. "I tried to mitigate the damage—and, if people had listened, just listened, there would likely only have been three deaths, instead of nine. Almost no one's thinking about how many people died elsewhere."

"Does that bother you?"

"People are like that. But yes, it bothers me. It bothers me that so few understand that the Collegium has done so little over the past few years—"

"You're being kind. It's been longer than that here in

L'Excelsis. You mentioned what imagers do in Westisle, but until you had us repair the sewers, I can't think of a single thing the Collegium did outside Imagisle."

"We'll have to do more. Oh . . . I forgot to mention that Rex Lorien wants us to finish the avenue after we rebuild the Collegium . . . and that he's having a public memorial service for his father next Samedi."

"That's necessary, but I'd be surprised to see many tears."

"Will there be that many people there?"

"High Holders won't attend, except for any who are ministers, and factors who sell to the Chateau D'Rex will attend . . . and many others." A rueful smile crossed her lips.

"There's a reason for that, I take it?"

"The family will strew coppers and silvers in his memory."

"I wonder if that was why Lorien asked . . ."

"About the new avenue?" she said. "I wouldn't be surprised. I imagine he said he wanted it done, and you said it would be after the rebuilding."

"It did go something like that," admitted Alastar. "Have you discovered anything about Bettaur?"

"I haven't had an opportunity to talk to Seliora yet, not in a way that would be conducive to finding out what . . ." Alyna shook her head. "It's not that. It's that I'd rather not bring up the questions when Orlana, Linzya, or Dorya are around, and if I ask Seliora for a moment, the other girls will be on her to find out what I wanted."

"Because some of them are sweet on Bettaur?"

"How about all of them except Seliora," replied Alyna.

"That's another problem, then."

"From what I can tell, he's been on his best behavior with all of them . . . or almost best behavior. He can be witty and charming."

"I'm well aware of that. It's part of what's gotten him

in trouble." Alastar frowned. "Has Tiranya had trouble because she insisted on Bettaur behaving?"

"No. She handled it so quietly that it's created another problem."

"Oh?" That seemed like the safest response to Alastar.

"The way he smiles at her makes the girls a little jealous of her."

Everything about that young man is trouble.

"I'm hoping to talk to Seliora this afternoon. She'd know if Bettaur passed a note. I think she would. I'm not sure the other girls would admit it."

"If necessary, I could talk to them," Alastar suggested.

"That might be best as a last resort." Alyna offered the smile that was slightly mischievous.

Alastar couldn't help but smile back.

"If you wouldn't mind . . ." ventured Alyna.

"Just walking you to your cottage?"

She nodded.

"I would mind, but I'll forgo the pleasure of your company for the greater good."

"And I will forgo the pleasure of your company for the same reason."

While Alyna's voice was cheerful and pleasant, there was something . . . something left unsaid. "Did I offend you?"

Alyna stopped. "You listen to what's not said, don't you? That's rare, especially in a man."

"You mean, especially in a Maitre Imager?"

She smiled. "Not bad."

Alastar tried to figure out exactly how his words had put her off. Without an immediate rational thought in mind, he went with his gut feeling. "I didn't mean to be condescending in saying I'd forgo the pleasure of your company, as if it were only my feelings that counted. I don't know if that's exactly the way to say it . . ."

"I'm glad you listen," she said softly. "I can't tell you

what that means." The smile returned. "I was telling the truth when I said I'd forgo the pleasure of your company, because I've never enjoyed talking and being with anyone the way I do with you."

"I've come to look forward to seeing you and talking with you. I've never had that before, especially not with a woman."

Alyna frowned.

"It wasn't the same with Thealia. I had so much yet to learn. I was afraid to reveal what I didn't know, as are many young men." He smiled wryly. "There was so much I didn't know, and so much more that I didn't even know that I didn't know."

"Is that all?"

"No. You're an equal. You quietly insist on that, and in some matters, you're definitely more knowledgeable."

"Most men don't like that."

"That may be. That is their loss." He stopped short of the steps to her cottage and looked at her again, taking in her dark eyes and perfect skin, and slight quizzical look.

"Men and women imagers becoming close, truly close, is like hedgehogs," she murmured.

He took her hand, neither large nor small, and bent and kissed it, before releasing it and stepping back. "Then we must be very careful."

"I will see you tomorrow." With a last smile, an expression somewhere between warm and enigmatic, she turned and entered the cottage.

As Alastar walked back to the Maitre's house, he kept thinking about hedgehogs . . . and being careful, wondering where the line was between being too careful and too headstrong, and whether he would be able to recognize where it lay.

Not having an answer, or one with which he was satisfied, he tried to read some more in Gauswn's journals, but his eyes kept drifting toward the windows. After half a glass in which he read and reread the same page several times and still did not remember what he had read, he decided to put aside the volume and make a list of all the problems he needed to address in the coming weeks, with a second listing of those that needed to be resolved over the coming year.

Slightly before seventh glass, Alastar once more stood in the anomen, thinking far more about what awaited him in the days ahead than truly about the service. Yet, whether he liked it or not, among other duties, his was also to set an example, and from what he'd seen of Johanyr and Bettaur, who definitely remained a problem, more than just a handful of student imagers needed some ethical guidance. *Not that those who do will likely take in what Iskhar has to say, let alone make those guidelines part of their behavior.*

Alastar forced himself to concentrate on what the chorister had to say as he began his homily with the traditional, "Good evening, and it is a good evening."

"Good evening," came the chorused reply, although Alastar's response was barely murmured.

"All evenings are good evenings under the Nameless," Iskhar went on, "even in times that are less than good. Earlier today, we held a memorial service for those who died either in the attack on the Collegium or in defending the Collegium against that attack. I have heard some ask why the Nameless could allow such an attack. That is not the right question. The Nameless grants us freedom of action. With that freedom, we choose to do good or evil. We also have the freedom to respond to the good or evil actions of others. To ask why the Nameless permits an evil action is to avoid understanding that we are the ones who either act to do evil or fail to act to prevent it. The imagers of the Collegium acted to stop worse evil, because failure to stop the cannon bombardment would have resulted in the deaths of many more. Yet to stop evil, they killed far more troopers than we lost. That is the conundrum we always face in responding to evil. The response is necessary, but it is so often as costly as the evil to which it responds. Would it not be far better to find ways to head off or transform that evil than to wait and then respond . . ."

As Iskhar went on to talk about transformation, Alastar could not help but wonder if anything short of what he had done would have been adequate to change the course of the seemingly inevitable confrontation between the rex and the High Holders. *But that confrontation was only inevitable because past Maitres had refused to act as the founder had designed the Collegium to act.*

The question wasn't whether Alastar could return the Collegium to its proper role. That was a necessity, if imagers were to survive as other than fugitives in Solidar. *The question is just how high the price will be . . . and for how long it must be paid.*

32

Just after seventh glass on Lundi morning, another gray day that matched Alastar's mood when he thought about meeting with Lorien and Petayn later in the day, the remaining senior maitres—Cyran, Obsolym, Taryn, Akoryt, and Alyna—sat around Alastar's desk in his study.

"Has anyone heard anything about Desyrk?" asked Alastar.

There were headshakes around the table.

"Are there any problems that we haven't already talked about?"

"Petros worries about storage space," said Cyran. "He's got winter fodder coming in. We took that space for food supplies because of the loss of the cellars and bins in the dining hall."

"Can you make space in the armory?"

"Some." Cyran's reply was reluctant. "That will make it hard to get to some weapons."

"Outside of the sabres, have we used anything else there in years?" asked Alastar dryly.

"Well . . . no, sir."

"Then do what you can." Alastar turned to Akoryt. "Is there enough space in the anomen to hold some instructionals there?"

"Most of them. We can work around the others."

"Some of you may not have heard," Alastar went on, "but Rex Lorien does want the avenue finished. I've persuaded him that more construction will have to wait until after we rebuild the administration building and dining hall. He's not pleased, but he understands. He also wants me to meet with the acting marshal and the sea marshal this afternoon."

"What about the tariff problem?" asked Taryn.

"The rex is supposed to be drafting a proposal to present to the High Council. He hasn't heard from them, nor have I. I didn't expect them to respond immediately."

"They'll do whatever you suggested," said Obsolym. "Next year might be different."

"We'll have to make sure it doesn't come up again." Alastar paused. "Is there anything else? If not . . ." He turned to Alyna. "The new administration building?"

"I've talked to all the maitres." Alyna offered a wry expression. "There were a number of suggestions. All of them were good. One or two may not be possible. Everyone agreed that the studies for all the maitres should be on the same hallway and that should be a different corridor from the instructional rooms. If we don't want the building to sprawl onto the green, I'd suggest it be two stories with the studies on the upper level . . ."

Alastar nodded as she began to present what had been suggested.

More than a glass later, after Cyran, Taryn, and Obsolym had left, Alastar remained in the study with Alyna and Akoryt. After closing the study door, he turned to Akoryt. "From what I've seen and what you've reported, it appears that Taurek is doing well. We may have more problems with Bettaur . . ." Alastar went on to explain about what he had learned, then looked to Alyna.

"I did finally get a few words with Seliora. She's certain that Orlana passed something to Johanyr, but she has no idea what it might have been. Both Orlana and Dorya would likely do anything he asked, so long as it appeared reasonable to them."

"Reasonable to them?" Akoryt frowned. "How far might that stretch?"

"They'd pass a note, especially if it appeared innocuous. Bettaur also was very convincing in telling Orlana and Dorya how misunderstood his acts were, and how everything was blown out of proportion, that no one could ever have accused him of so much as laying a finger on Taurek."

"All of which is true," commented Alastar. "But in order to protect those involved, none of the maitres would tell what actually happened, and certainly the four involved with setting up Taurek wouldn't reveal what they did." He paused. "We should think about having open meetings, perhaps even formal hearings, in cases like this."

"Do you think that's wise?" asked Akoryt.

"Having kept the proceedings quiet certainly has made the situation worse," Alyna said.

"There's a balance here," mused Alastar. "We need to think about what kinds of student problems should be resolved quietly and which should be handled in full open hearings with students and imagers present."

"That would be quite a change," observed Akoryt.

"It might make the maitres more cognizant of the fact that how they handle matters could come up in public," replied Alastar, "but that's a blade that cuts both ways. If we do change things, we'll need to be very careful."

"So what do we do with Bettaur now?" asked Akoryt.

"Keep a very close eye and tight rein on him." *What else can we do, given that the detention cells were in the administration building?* "And don't trust him any farther than you can throw a horse."

"Thank you," replied Akoryt solemnly, a solemnness more effective than sarcasm.

Once Akoryt had left, Alastar walked from the study to the front porch with Alyna, but as he stood there, he realized that with the gray skies and the bitter wind out of the northeast, the air felt more like winter than fall, although true winter was still more than a month away.

"About Seliora . . . she's part Pharsi, isn't she?" Even as he asked the question, Alastar wondered what exactly being Pharsi meant. Certainly, Alyna was part Pharsi, given that she was a descendant of Vaelora.

"Are you suggesting something?"

"No. Just wondering. We use names, and sometimes . . . I'm not even sure what those names mean."

"'Seliora' means something like 'the daughter of Artiema,' except it comes from a Pharsi word meaning the greater moon."

"You're more literal than I meant. I was actually wondering if names convey a meaning beyond meaning. Are you Pharsi because one of your ancestors was Vaelora? Am I because my great-grandmother came from Sandeol?"

"You never said anything about that."

"I guess I didn't," he admitted almost sheepishly.

"Every time I talk with you, there's something new." She smiled. "I'm freezing, and I need to get ready for my mathematics instructional."

"Then I won't keep you." Alastar stayed on the porch and watched her stride toward the anomen. He didn't even mind the cold.

After dealing with Dareyn and Arhgen and determining what supplies were immediately necessary for the Collegium—and how to pay for them—Alastar made certain he was at the Chateau D'Rex more than a quint before first glass. Since he had to wait outside in the wind with Glaesyn and Belsior, he was glad he'd worn his heavy gray riding jacket and gloves.

"Didn't the first Maitre turn the stone of the chateau white?" asked Glaesyn.

"That's what has been said," replied Alastar cautiously. "I'd tend to believe that because the white stone of the exterior is so hard that a blade won't scratch it, and the blade will break before the stone will show even a trace of a scratch."

"Could you do that, sir?" Belsior looked intently at Alastar.

"For a small section of wall . . . I think. I've done it for a stone chest . . . once." Alastar regretted saying that and immediately went on. "According to some records, Maitre Quaeryt said it was unlikely that anyone could ever again muster the price to do what he did."

"What was that price?"

"We don't know exactly. It's said that he personally killed over a hundred thousand men in the Wars of Consolidation, but I don't see how that was possible."

"A hundred thousand?"

"That number appears in several histories." Alastar turned. A squad of troopers was riding up the entry lane, doubtless escorting Acting Marshal Petayn and Sea Marshal Wilkorn. "Excuse me, but it's time for an entrance." He dismounted and handed the gelding's reins to Belsior, then walked up the steps to the main doors to the chateau.

The guard there glanced at the oncoming group, then back at Alastar, then swallowed. "Ah . . . perhaps you should go up and announce yourself, sir."

"Thank you." Alastar inclined his head politely, then made his way inside the chateau, up the grand staircase, and back to the study.

The guard at the study door stiffened slightly as Alastar approached, then rapped, and announced, "Maitre Alastar, sir."

"Have him come in."

Lorien rose from behind the goldenwood table desk.

Before the rex could speak, Alastar asked, because he wanted to bring up the subject before the others arrived, "How are you coming on your tariff proposal for the High Council?"

"I hope to have that ready by Meredi. Have you seen the marshals?"

"They were approaching when I entered the chateau."

"You didn't wait for them, I see. Interesting."

"I thought it might be better if I were here first."

"Better for you. Is it better for me?"

"I would think so, because it implies that I am united in purpose with you."

"Unfortunately, you're likely correct." Lorien glanced toward the window and the gray skies to the north. "How much do you distrust the marshals?"

"I trust them to react to anything that would threaten or reduce their power."

"Are you any different, Maitre?"

"In that respect, no. The difference is that I'm fighting for a very small group of people whose very lives will be threatened if I fail. The marshals are fighting for personal power and glory. They could take stipends and live comfortably for the rest of their lives if they do not agree with what you or I might propose. As shown by Demykalon's acts, any great failure on the part of the Maitre of the Collegium could result in the death of many if not most imagers."

"Your acts killed hundreds. Theirs only killed, what, a score."

"But a score is one part in five of all imagers in Solidar. A hundred troopers lost is one trooper out of every seventy-five just here in L'Excelsis. It's not only the total number, but the impact, both on the imagers . . . and on your future."

"I might beg to differ . . ." Lorien broke off his words as the duty guard announced, "Acting Marshal Petayn and Sea Marshal Wilkorn."

The smooth-faced Petayn was the first to enter, his graying black hair perfectly in place, and wearing the silver starbursts of a full marshal, rather than the gold of a submarshal. Behind him was another marshal, most likely the sea marshal. While Petayn was of average height, perhaps a digit or two shorter than Alastar, Wilkorn was a broad-shouldered, hefty figure close to half a head taller than the Maitre.

"Your Grace," offered Petayn, inclining his head.

Wilkorn merely nodded.

Lorien gestured to the small conference table. Alastar took the seat to Lorien's left, and Petayn to his right, leaving Wilkorn in the seat facing Lorien.

"I trust you had no difficulties in returning your forces to headquarters, Marshal," offered Lorien as an opening statement.

"They are all where they should be, sir."

Lorien raised his eyebrows.

"On post at headquarters. Even those who died as a result of the perhaps excessive reaction of the imagers to warning shots fired at Imagisle."

"In less than half a glass," said Alastar quietly, "the cannon killed or wounded more than a score, largely students, cooks, and others who posed no threat to anyone, damaged four structures, and destroyed two completely. You will pardon me if I express a certain doubt that those were warning shots."

"I share that doubt," added Lorien, "but the late Marshal Demykalon has paid for those excesses, and the purpose of this meeting is to discuss the future of the army and the navy of Solidar. At present, as I recall, Marshal Petayn, you have some eight regiments of troopers, three of which are posted at headquarters. And you, Marshal Wilkorn, have a fleet of twelve ships. According to the orders issued by Ryen, Rex Regis, and his predecessors, the size of the army was to be fixed at six regiments. The size of the fleet was set at twelve ships, with periodic replacements as necessary. Are there any questions about those orders?" Lorien looked to Petayn, then Wilkorn.

"No, sir," replied Petayn, then the sea marshal.

"Why might you have eight regiments instead of six, and why three in L'Excelsis, instead of two?"

"I have no idea, sir," replied Petayn. "Those decisions were made by Marshal Demykalon, and I was not privy to them."

Alastar very much had his doubts about that, but said nothing.

"You will, then, over the next year, reduce the number of regiments to six. You will also reduce the number of officers correspondingly. Six of the standard size, and not outsized regiments. You will provide a monthly report of your progress to me. Should you disregard this order, which I will provide in writing, it will be regarded as treason, and you will be punished accordingly. Is that clear?"

"Very clear." Petayn's voice was pleasant, almost as if he had expected such an order.

Perhaps he had, reflected Alastar. Because Lorien had already informed him? Or someone else had?

"That brings us to the question of the piracy taking place in the Southern Gulf. Maitre Alastar and the factors of Solidar have proposed some measures to deal with the pirates, including building smaller armed vessels and relocating one or more regiments to patrol the shores in those areas where the pirates appeared to have based themselves. I would like to hear your thoughts on the matter. You first, Marshal Petayn."

"I have no objection to relocating some forces to pursue the pirates, but that will require some additional funding . . ."

"I am most certain you can find a way to accomplish the tasks within current funding, perhaps by a rapid reduction in force and certain other economies. I look forward to seeing your proposal and trust it will include the movement of more than a regiment from L'Excelsis to, shall we say, the vicinity of Lucayl." Lorien smiled politely and looked to Wilkorn.

The sea marshal did not look at the rex, but at Alastar. After a moment, he cleared his throat and squared his shoulders. "I understand you are proposing that Rex Lorien's priority in naval vessels should be small shallow-water gunboats, little more than armed schooners or sloops. That won't help us in the slightest in dealing with the Ferrans, or even the Jariolans. They aren't building shallow-draft vessels—"

"Ferrum doesn't have a large shallow expanse of water bordering its largest port," countered Alastar, "the way Solidar does with the waters surrounding the shipping channels to Solis. Ferrum isn't losing ships and cargoes every year to pirates."

"You don't need ships. Deal with the pirates from the shore side, the way Rex Lorien has suggested," said Wilkorn.

"I'm glad to hear that you see the wisdom in that," said Alastar warmly. "If two of the three regiments posted here in L'Excelsis were transferred to Lucayl and perhaps Thuyl and elsewhere around the Southern Gulf, together with a few gunboats, you might be able to reduce or eliminate the pirates, and that would increase factor support of the expansion of the navy . . ."

"You keep talking about shallow-water gunboats," declared Wilkorn. "We don't even have enough true warships. Both the Ferrans and the Jariolans have fleets far larger than ours, and Emperor Josef V of Ferrum has commissioned three new ships of the line. They're already under construction. Gunboats must wait."

Alastar sighed. Loudly. "Even if Rex Lorien had the funds to build a flotilla of what you call true warships, which at the moment he does not, it would take years to construct all the ships you need. In those years, our merchants and traders will lose ships to pirates every year. Each ship that is lost means tariffs that are not paid. At the very least, a handful of small gunboats able to patrol the shallow waters of the Southern Gulf will result in more tariffs, possibly enough to greatly defer the cost of their construction. At present, there would be little such gain from your warships, Sea Marshal." As Alastar saw the big man's face begin to redden, he held up a hand to forestall an outburst. "Over time, you are undoubtedly correct that Solidar needs more new warships, particularly those armed with the newer cannon developed during the time of Marshal Demykalon. But since funds are limited, it is prudent to develop the best plans for those warships over the next year and to begin to construct them in, say, the middle of the following year."

"The middle of the *following* year?"

"Unless you and Marshal Petayn can find funding out of that which remains in the army coffers. Then it might be possible to commence construction earlier."

Wilkorn looked to Petayn.

The acting marshal shrugged. "I have not had the opportunity to study the master ledgers in enough detail to see where economies might be made. If we could have a few days to conduct such a review and provide our recommendations?"

"That would seem reasonable. Next Lundi at this same time." Lorien turned to Alastar. "I'd also appreciate a similar report on the financial state of the Collegium." Then he stood. As the marshals rose and began to leave, he added in a low voice to Alastar, "Fourth glass tomorrow. As usual."

By the time that Alastar was riding away from the Chateau D'Rex with the two thirds, he had definite feelings that, regardless of what Petayn had promised, nothing was going to happen quickly . . . and not at all, if Petayn could manage it. Not only that, but he also had the feeling that the entire meeting had been a charade, conducted almost solely for his benefit. Nor had anyone mentioned the two regiments of naval marines. All that left him with another thought, that Lorien was far more devious than his sire had been. Alastar also wasn't happy with Lorien's delay in preparing the tariff message. Stating what the tariff levels would be for the coming year was hardly difficult, although checking receipts after the fact would be time-consuming.

Alastar could see stalling a decision on reducing the size of the army, as well as what ships to build and when to build them. *But what does Lorien gain by stalling the tariff announcement? Is Petayn pressing him to raise tariffs by more to avoid reducing the size of the army?* That was the simplest and most likely explanation, but Alastar had come to understand that, in L'Excelsis, the simplest and most sensible reason was seldom the answer to a question.

He was still mulling over those questions when he entered the Maitre's dwelling and made his way toward the study. Dareyn immediately rose from his small table and handed a sealed letter to Alastar. "It's from High Holder Vaun. That's what the dispatch rider said."

The tan wax of the seal tended to confirm that, and Alastar took his belt knife and slit open the envelope. He began to read. The text was simple.

> *Maitre—*
> *The High Council will be meeting on Mardi, 31 Feuillyt, the first glass of the afternoon at the Chateau D'Council. Your presence would be welcome, since the matter will affect both the High Holders and the Collegium.*
> *I trust I will be seeing you.*

The signature and seal were those of Vaun.

Trust I will be seeing you? Alastar snorted. *As if you could afford not to be there after all that has happened.*

"There's also another letter, sir. From Factor Elthyrd." Dareyn smiled apologetically.

Elthyrd's letter was shorter than Vaun's and more to

the point, asking if Alastar could oblige him by meeting him at his factorage at Alastar's convenience sometime Meredi morning.

Alastar immediately wrote a reply agreeing to meet Elthyrd at eighth glass, even as he wondered precisely what the head factor had in mind. *Information about tariffs? Or Lorien? The last of the sewer repairs?* Alastar shook his head. It could be any of those . . . or something else entirely. After signing the missive and giving it to Dareyn for dispatch, Alastar returned to his desk and sat down, his mind returning to Lorien and Petayn.

33

After the morning meeting of senior imagers on Mardi, Alyna remained in the study and laid several sheets of paper on Alastar's desk. "These are rough sketches of the administration building that include the more feasible suggestions of the various maitres."

"More feasible? Such as the location of studies for the maitres?"

"Also a small grand hall, one that can be used for an imager justicing hall. You'd suggested something along those lines."

Alastar managed not to smile. He'd only suggested open disciplinary meetings, but Alyna, he suspected, had taken that idea a step further. *But it's a good idea, and likely overdue.* "What else?"

"Separate vaults in the lower level for golds and important records and artifacts."

"Such as the founder's sabre?"

"Petros's men did find it, you know. There's not much left but the blade and tang."

"So much for its indestructibility."

"The indestructible blade . . . wasn't that the one that went back to Khel?"

"I have my doubts about its indestructibility as well."

"You? After telling the thirds about the indestructibility of the walls of the Chateau D'Rex?"

Alastar wondered how she'd heard about that, but did not press. Instead, he said, "Tell me about the plans and why you located things where you did."

Almost a glass later, he straightened and stretched out his back. He hadn't even realized that it had gotten cramped. "I can't believe what you've done. These are only rough plans?"

"Very rough. I'll have to work out the foundation and wall thicknesses, how the windows will be supported, and where they'll be placed so that the light inside is good while the windows are symmetrical, both from inside and outside . . ."

When she finished, she asked, "Do you have any questions? That's what you always say."

"I'm too overwhelmed to have questions," he replied. "I do have some other concerns. I'm worried about what's happening between Lorien and Petayn." He went on and explained the previous day's meeting with Lorien and the marshals, as well as his feelings afterward.

"You don't usually overstate things," she finally said. "Petayn sounds distracted. Could he be having troubles of his own?"

"Other senior officers who believe they're better qualified to be marshal?" Alastar pursed his lips for a moment. "Wilkorn is next senior, but I didn't sense any friction between the two. It was as if they were talking about two separate problems. If Petayn has difficulties, I can't believe they're with Wilkorn. I don't even know who the other senior officers are. I didn't exactly think I'd have to worry about the officers in the High Command when I became Maitre." At the look on Alyna's face, he added, "I know. I should have, because everything affects the Collegium, but I was under the misimpression that I might actually have a little time to work out the problems. I had no idea Fhaen was as ill as he was."

Alyna raised her eyebrows.

"Oh, as soon as I got here, I knew, but by then . . . well . . . it was clear that Obsolym and Desyrk didn't want me; no one thought Cyran was experienced enough; and no one had talked to Akoryt or Taryn . . . or any of the Maitres D'Aspect. With so many things left undone, it seemed like all my time was spent trying to discover what needed to be done and how . . . and then Ryen started in on the tariff matter."

Alyna gathered the papers she'd spread on the desk and rolled them up swiftly, then tied them in deft movements with a red velvet cord. "What do you *feel* will happen next?"

"That somehow everything will go back the way it was, and I'll have to do more of what I didn't want to do . . . and be even harsher."

"That sounds about right. Even after all that's happened, they're all likely thinking that you wouldn't dare do more." At Alastar's expression, she added, "Yes, I am even more cynical than you, dear Maitre. Ryen was furious at being balked by the High Holders, and they were doubtless outraged that he dared to demand more from them. Petayn and the army officers are likely furious and chagrined at the damage a handful of imagers wrought. If Petayn cannot find a way to best you, in some fashion, he may not survive as marshal." She paused. "I need to go. I have an instructional in little more than a quint."

"I'll walk you out."

After following Alyna, Alastar paused outside the study. "Dareyn . . . do you know where Maitre Akoryt is?"

"I believe he's in the anomen. Something about organizing instructionals."

"Thank you. That's where I'll be. I'll be back well before I have to leave to meet with the High Council." He turned back to Alyna. "I'll go with you as far as we're going the same way."

She nodded, but did not say more until they were alone on the porch, when she offered the smile with the hint of mischief. "Although we're both headed to the anomen, I hope your words only apply to the walk this morning."

Alastar almost missed the first step of those descending from the porch.

Alyna reached out and grasped his arm. "I didn't mean to unsettle you that much."

Her smile had turned to concern.

"You definitely caught me off-guard."

"That doesn't happen very often." Her voice was warmly amused.

More with you. He wasn't about to voice that. "My thoughts were elsewhere." Even as he said that, he wished he could take back the words. "I mean . . . I don't know what I mean."

She laughed softly. "No one would believe you said those words."

"I can't believe I did," he admitted ruefully. "I probably shouldn't make it a habit."

"Not in public, perhaps. In private, it's . . . I like it." Her words were low. She flushed. "Now I'm the one off-guard."

"As you just said . . . in private . . . or just when the two of us are without others around, it's allowed."

Neither said anything for several steps.

"You're not what I expected in a Maitre," she finally said.

"That makes us even. You're definitely not what I expected in the daughter of a High Holder, but then it's clear your holding isn't like most, either."

"And?" Alyna spoke the single word humorously.

"I'm very glad of it."

When Alyna and Alastar entered the anomen, he could see Akoryt standing several yards away, talking to Iskhar. Alastar turned to Alyna. "I'll see you later."

"I do hope so." Her words were cheerfully pleasant. She turned toward the side corridor.

That left Alastar wondering as he waited for Akoryt to finish his conversation with the chorister. Before long, Iskhar nodded a last time to Akoryt and then turned and headed toward the back of the anomen, presumably to his own study.

Akoryt turned and walked over to Alastar. "You're obviously looking for me, Maitre. What can I do for you?"

"I've been thinking over my meeting with Rex Lorien and the reactions of Acting Marshal Petayn. I have the feeling that the marshal may have less than honorable activities in mind. Can you deploy thirds who can handle concealments so that they can get close enough to see anything unusual on or around the High Command headquarters? There will be some preparations for Rex Ryen's memorial services on Samedi, but I'd like them to look beyond that."

"I might have to use a few seconds, and they and some of the thirds would miss instructionals."

"We'll have to make those up later." *The last thing we need is to be unprepared if Petayn has something else in mind.* "Also . . . perhaps some more conventional patrols along the East and West River Roads."

"We can do that."

After more discussions with Akoryt, Alastar returned to the Maitre's dwelling, where he then spent time with Arhgen planning the Collegium's immediately forthcoming expenditures.

A little less than a quint past noon, he was in the saddle once more, riding the gray gelding northward on the West River Road, accompanied by Neiryn and Coermyd.

"Sir . . . do you think there will be more fighting," asked Coermyd deferentially.

"I hope not, but that's not up to me or anyone in the Collegium. That depends on the rex and the High Holders." *And the senior army officers.*

"After all they did?"

"The rex hasn't seen the damage. He only knows his

father died. One High Holder is dead. We're the ones whose people were killed and whose buildings were destroyed."

"Lots of troopers died," offered Coermyd.

"You're right. That has some of the army officers concerned, but none of them seems to consider that they died because they were trying to kill us when we hadn't done a thing to them."

"It doesn't make sense, sir."

It makes too much sense, given the way people want power. But Alastar wasn't about to try to explain that, not while riding, anyway.

When they reached the Chateau D'Council, the thirds waited outside in the chill air, while a very nervous footman—the one who had always met Alastar—avoided looking at Alastar as he escorted the Maitre to the receiving study. Little appeared to have changed except that instead of the four armchairs being set around a low table, the low table had been replaced by a circular table and another wooden armchair had been placed at the table. Alastar suspected the circular table was older and perhaps somewhat worn, because it was covered with a maroon linen cloth. The four High Holders rose from the original armchairs, leaving little doubt for whom the wooden chair was intended.

"Might I ask the purpose of this meeting?" Alastar looked to Vaun.

The one who responded was not Vaun, but Haebyn. "I thought the remaining members of the High Council needed to hear exactly where matters stand and to discuss what we should do, especially before we are faced with another unreasonable demand from the new rex."

Unfortunately, Alastar could well understand what Haebyn had in mind. He smiled coldly. "Where matters stand is that the rex and the High Council will come to an agreement on tariffs. Rex Lorien has ordered Submarshal and Acting Marshal Petayn to recall all army units to their bases and not to make any more attacks on High Holders or the Collegium."

"There have been no attacks on High Holders," declared Nacryon.

Moeryn smiled faintly and knowingly, and Alastar wondered just what the High Holder from Khelgror knew.

"Army cannon and troopers were in position to bombard High Holder Guerdyn's chateau when they were recalled. His personal chateau, not the Chateau D'Council here." Alastar snorted. "The Collegium has had enough of destruction and squabbling. Rex Ryen refused to desist in his unreasonable demands. That was because the tariff issue was only a pretext for him to bring a series of attacks on the High Council and the High Holders, as well as against the Collegium." Alastar could see puzzled expressions on the faces of Haebyn and Nacryon. "Rex Lorien has agreed to be more reasonable."

"Then . . . there will be no increases in tariffs?" Haebyn began to smile.

Alastar understood that Vaun was going to take the easy way, the political way, and make Alastar lay out the terms. "There will be tariff increases." Alastar looked squarely at Haebyn. "I'm not asking the High Council to consider an increase in tariffs. The Collegium and I have had enough of this bickering over coppers. Rex Lorien will publish a tariff increasing the tariffs by four coppers on a gold for the coming year, and announce the possibility of smaller increases in the following years."

"That's opening the gates to continual increases," protested Nacryon.

"You cannot possibly expect the High Council to agree . . . ?" Haebyn's tone was somewhere between dismissive and snide.

"Then, one by one, beginning with you, every remaining High Holder on the Council will die, until the Council agrees."

"That is a strong promise. You cannot—"

Alastar clamped shields around Haebyn, then continued as the High Holder began to turn red. "Marshal Demykalon is gone. Rex Ryen is gone. High Holder Guerdyn is gone. A half a battalion of troopers are gone. Do you really believe that we cannot remove enough of you that any of this High Council will remain?"

Haebyn flushed even more, unable to speak. Nacryon swallowed and glanced from Haebyn to Vaun, then to Alastar. Moeryn nodded.

After several moments of silence, Alastar released the shields.

Haebyn offered an explosive exhalation and then began to gasp for breath, staggering and putting his hands on the table to steady himself.

"Are you sure that Rex Lorien will agree?" asked Vaun mildly.

"Rex Lorien has declared that he will have a proposal ready later this week. He has also asked Acting Marshal Petayn for a plan to reduce the number of army regiments, and to transfer some to locations along the Southern Gulf in order to reduce piracy by eliminating shore bases for piracy." Alastar wasn't about to mention the naval marines, because they would be needed far more than land troopers. "Sea Marshal Wilkorn has been asked to provide a plan to build some smaller craft to deal with the pirates and for a longer-term increase of larger vessels to combat the larger ships of Jariola and Ferrum. Depending on the actions of the High Council and the High Holders, there may be an even greater shift in time."

"And if they go back on their word?" asked Vaun.

"Then the Collegium will be forced to deal with them once again."

"Why is the Collegium insisting on this so . . . forcefully?" Vaun's voice remained level.

"Because it appears that no one else wishes to reach an agreement. The Collegium does not wish to suffer any more injury and insult. Imagisle is a mass of rubble. Many young imagers are wounded. Some may not live. You have suffered comparatively little. These terms are indeed a bargain for you. If you do not wish to accept that bargain, we will be more than happy to increase the price."

"That's not a bargain," declared Haebyn. "You're imposing your will on others."

"Absolutely. But both you and Rex Ryen wished to impose your wills on each other and Solidar suffered. So did the Collegium. We're insisting on compromise. We're not even asking for anything more."

"This is absurd," declared Nacryon. "We have no choice."

"Oh . . . yes, you do. The same one that Rex Ryen or Marshal Demykalon had. It is a choice. A few coppers more on each gold, and the rest of your life to enjoy most of those golds."

"It is a choice," observed Vaun. "Not terribly appealing . . ."

"You have a choice," pointed out Alastar. "So did Ryen. The student imagers who were killed had none. Nor did the cooks who died preparing dinner, nor . . . a great number of innocents." Alastar offered another cold smile. "I won't ask for your decision. The Collegium will act—or not—based on what it is. Good day."

A small pistol appeared in Haebyn's hand, firing as it appeared.

The unexpected impact on Alastar's shields forced him back, even as the small iron ball rebounded from those shields.

"Dear me." Alastar drew out the words, then imaged a long knife through each of Haebyn's boots and deep into the carpet and tile floor beneath, pinning Haebyn in place.

The High Holder screamed, if but for an instant.

Nacryon stood there, his mouth open.

Even Vaun swallowed. The faintest smile crossed Moeryn's face, but was gone so quickly that Alastar doubted any of the other High Holders had even seen it.

"I won't be nearly so generous if any of you should be so foolish as to attempt any further violence upon any member of the Collegium." With that, Alastar turned and walked from the study, strengthening his shields more as he did.

The footman, who had obviously been watching surreptitiously, scurried ahead of Alastar and hurried to the entry hall, where he quickly opened the door.

As he rode from the Chateau D'Council, Alastar still found himself amazed that Haebyn would have been so stupid as to use a pistol, especially given how unreliable they supposedly were. *Except even Demykalon had said the single-shot weapons were reliable, and Haebyn's was probably forged specially with great attention to detail and likely cost more than an imager maitre's stipend for an entire year.* But had the High Holder been stupid or just unable to believe that anyone could force him to compromise? *You may indeed be unable to make him agree.* If so, Solidar would suffer no great loss at his absence.

By the time Alastar returned to the Collegium and answered questions from Dareyn and Arhgen, then checked with Akoryt about whether his scouts had discovered anything—and they had not, not yet—it was time for him to leave for his meeting with Rex Lorien.

Again, Coermyd and Neiryn accompanied him. They had little to say on the ride, and Alastar had less, trying to think about all the possible stratagems Lorien might possibly be trying . . . and what he could do in each case.

When Alastar did walk into the rex's study, Lorien turned from the window where he stood and said pleasantly, "We need to go down to the treasury strong room, Maitre."

Alastar followed the young rex from the study to a narrow circular staircase that descended two levels, presumably, he thought, to the lowest level. A few steps down the corridor, they stopped outside an iron gate, with two guards. Lorien produced a set of keys and opened both locks. The antechamber within held a second locked door, which Lorien opened as well. The chamber beyond held twelve ironbound chests, each with a ledger chained to it. In turn, Lorien unlocked each of the eleven and lifted the lids.

"A simple system," the rex declared. "A chest for each month's revenues, and two for what might be left at the end of the previous year, and a ledger to record what is received and what is disbursed. I'd like you to look into each chest."

Alastar began with the chest labeled IANUS. It was empty. So were those for the next five months. The chest for Agostas was roughly a quarter full, holding, Alastar estimated by mentally comparing it to the chests at the Collegium, two thousand golds. The chest for Erntyn held possibly twice that. The chests for Feuillyt and Finitas were, expectedly to Alastar, empty. Of the last two chests, each four times as large as any of the others, one was empty, and the other perhaps half full. Still, given the size of the previous year's chests, there had to be somewhere more than fifteen thousand golds remaining in the treasury.

"The chest for Feuillyt there." Lorien gestured. "It should be filled by now. And the carryover chests should have half again what they do."

"The Feuillyt chest is empty because your father didn't work things out with the High Holders."

"According to Minister Salucar, in previous years, until three years ago, half of those chests held golds even before the year's tariffs were collected."

"The crops have been bad all over Solidar this year."

"Tariffs were too low to provide reserves, and now . . ." Lorien's face turned even more somber. "We'll go back to the study. You need to see something else before we speak more."

Once the two had climbed the staircase and stood in the study, Lorien pointed to the ledger on the desk. "That's Salucar's master ledger. I assume there's something similar at the Collegium?"

"There is. There's a copy near my desk all the time. There was, at least, until the cannon fire set the administration building aflame and the fire destroyed it and most of the records."

"Go ahead," Lorien said. "Read the last few pages. Read any pages you wish for that matter."

Alastar studied the entries on the last pages, then flipped to the front of the ledger and read several pages there, comparing a number of entries.

"What do you think now, Maitre?"

"Do you happen to have a master ledger from several years ago?"

Lorien frowned, then said, "From two years ago." He walked to the small cabinet against the wall, behind the desk and toward the window, opened it, and took out another ledger, which he handed to Alastar.

Although he was conscious of Lorien's impatience and scrutiny, Alastar forced himself to check several of the entries for 387 A.L. before setting the older ledger beside the first. He had been initially stunned by the amount of golds in the chests in Lorien's treasury strong room—fifteen thousand or even close to twenty thousand golds—until he had gone over the ledgers and realized that the total amounted to less than a season's expenditures from all the rex's accounts.

The costs for running the Collegium were more than

a hundred golds a week, and the Collegium was roughly the size of a battalion of troopers. Even given that troopers were paid considerably less, on average, than imagers and the Collegium workers, the army alone would require over a hundred thousand golds a year, just in pay, and the weekly disbursements for pay for the army confirmed that. *Roughly ten thousand a month . . . and Lorien has only some twenty thousand or so left, with doubtless lower tariffs coming in.* And that didn't even count everything else.

Once again, that brought home to Alastar that the one thing the late Ryen hadn't been unreasonable—or mad—about was the need for higher tariffs. *Or a much smaller army . . . if not both.*

"Well . . . Maitre?" demanded Lorien.

"As I've said all along, both to your father and you, you need both higher tariffs and a smaller army."

"Marshal Petayn thinks the army is too small, as it is."

"There's a small problem with the marshal's figures," Alastar said. "Two years ago, the army pay disbursements were running fifteen hundred golds a week. They're now costing you a little over two thousand. Pay for the army alone is up one part in five. That doesn't include food. While your father and you have been struggling to make ends meet, and not repairing roads and sewers, and the like, the army is costing you an additional twenty-five thousand golds a year for two more regiments than ordered—regiments that aren't even being used."

"I'm not sure I believe you."

Alastar shrugged. "Those are the numbers from your master ledger. Petayn and Demykalon both admitted that they have two more army regiments than ordered . . . and that doesn't include the two regiments of naval marines. I still agree with the need for higher tariffs, but not at the levels your father proposed. Cut out those extra regiments, say, back to four or five regiments, and in time you'll have an additional thirty to fifty thousand more golds to pay for other needs . . . and that's without the additional funds from higher tariffs."

"I'll have to think about that."

Alastar was perfectly willing to let Lorien think it over. That was a start in cutting back a bloated and unnecessary army. "The High Council requested I meet with them yesterday."

"What did they have to say?"

"They're waiting for your formal declaration of next year's tariffs. I said that I'd recommended an increase of four coppers on the gold, with likely smaller increases in years to come to make up, as necessary, past deficits."

"Recommended? Dictated, as I recall."

"They'll most likely accept four coppers and future increases."

"You haven't left me much choice."

"If you insist on more, you'll likely have a High Holder rebellion on your hands, a great number of unhappy factors, and a very unhappy Collegium." What Alastar didn't need to say was that, whatever happened, the senior officers of the army were going to be less than pleased. While he had wanted to bring up the matter of rescinding Ryen's reduction in the monthly stipend received by the Collegium, it was clear that doing so would be singularly inappropriate and unwise at the moment.

"What other less than pleasing news do you have?"

"Besides the fact that the Collegium still has two buildings in ruins, that we can't immediately get to finishing the new avenue, that the sewer repairs we promised to the factors' council will be delayed, and that Petayn will violently oppose, if he has not already, cuts to the numbers of army regiments . . . and that the longer you delay in proposing the new tariff schedule, the longer before you'll receive this year's tariffs."

"That's quite enough for today, Maitre. I will see you tomorrow at fourth glass." Lorien's voice was firm, just short of being curt.

Alastar couldn't blame him, but men who were rulers did inherit the sins of their fathers. "Then, tomorrow at fourth glass." He inclined his head and walked from the study, all too conscious of Lorien's eyes on his back.

Belatedly, as Alastar rode back toward the Collegium, he realized something else he'd totally overlooked. Why hadn't Ryen—and now Lorien—placed at least some of the golds with the larger merchant bankers or even the relatively new Banque D'Excelsis . . . so that he could earn some interest? None of them could afford to default, not without losing everything; so the risk wouldn't have been that great. *Or didn't anyone think of that?* Except Salucar certainly should have thought of that possibility. Or had he, and had Ryen refused to consider the possibility?

Either way, Alastar wasn't going to bring that up, at least not for a while. *Even if it is another sign of shortsightedness.*

34

Eighth glass on Meredi morning found Alastar stepping into the small study at Elthyrd's wood factorage.

"Well, Maitre Alastar, you were more accurate than I was. I did not think that old Dafou was that mad." Elthyrd reseated himself and gestured for Alastar to sit down in one of the chairs before the stark goldenwood table desk.

"More arrogant than mad, I fear, and partly with just cause, but ordering cannon to fire upon innocent students was not forgivable, either for Demykalon or Ryen."

"Do you really think that all this will change anything for long?"

"That will depend on whether the High Council and Rex Lorien can work out the tariff agreement . . . and how far Lorien is willing to go with the army."

"The army? What does that have to do with it?"

"A great deal, unfortunately, since Demykalon and his predecessor increased its size by two full regiments, four, if you include the two regiments of naval marines. That amounts to more than fifty thousand golds just for troopers and officers."

"Fifty thousand?"

Alastar nodded. "Marshal Petayn seems to be trying to convince the rex not to reduce the size of the army. If Lorien does not, I doubt that he will have enough golds to get through the next year."

"You're saying that if young Lorien does, he'll have trouble with the army."

"I wouldn't say that."

"It's the same thing." Elthyrd shook his head. "How soon will Rex Lorien begin building more warships to fight the pirates?"

"That is the rex's decision, but I cannot imagine it would be before next year," replied Alastar cautiously.

"Next year? I lost two shares when the *Pride of Thuyl* went down last month, and another share in Agostas when the Southern Gulf pirates captured and converted the *Chevan.*" The factor's voice rose as he continued. "No one is doing anything. The Sea Marshal claims his warships can't go into the shallow waters north of Lucayl."

"Wasn't the *Chevan* retaken?"

"If you can call it that. The *Rex Clayar* turned her into kindling and towed the wreck back to Solis. The pirates had already off-loaded the cargo. You tell me that it will be two years before . . ." Elthyrd shook his head.

"The higher tariffs don't take effect until next year. Also, the sea marshal needs to have a shallow-water warship designed, one that will go where the pirates are."

"That kind of ship is much less costly to build."

"I'm sure it is, but the rex is short of golds, and Marshal Petayn doesn't want to reduce the army, as I mentioned, and Sea Marshal Wilkorn is more concerned about the Ferran and Jariolan fleets than pirates."

"Petayn doesn't need all those troopers at headquarters. They're useless. You and you imagers already proved that."

"If Rex Lorien *immediately* reduces the number of regiments near L'Excelsis, by half, which is what is necessary, at a minimum, you'll have over three thousand, possibly up to five thousand footloose troopers and junior officers, plus some unnecessary field-grade and senior officers. If they're released without stipends or some recompense, that might result in a bit of local brigandage . . . and great unrest on the part of the remaining troopers, who will worry that they'll get the same treatment."

"So what was the point of all this, if nothing is saved and no new ships are built?"

"Saving golds and building ships over time . . . unless you want to pay higher tariffs this year," replied Alastar. "You could, of course, ask for a meeting with Rex Lorien and bring up those questions to him personally."

"Baah! He'll say less than you have, and he won't say it as plainly. What *is* he doing?"

"He has declared that he will have a proposal ready later this week," Alastar continued, knowing that, while Lorien had promised it by the end of the day, such was unlikely. "He has also asked Acting Marshal Petayn for a plan to reduce the number of army regiments and to transfer some to locations along the Southern Gulf in order to reduce piracy by eliminating shore bases for piracy. Sea Marshal Wilkorn has been asked to provide a plan for building some smaller craft to deal with the pirates and for a longer-term increase of larger vessels to combat the larger ships of Jariola and Ferrum. Depending on the actions of the High Council and the High Holders, there may be an even greater shift in time."

"Back to doing nothing at all," Elthyrd growled. "Much as you and I don't always see eye-to-eye, at least I know what you'll do and what you won't, and when. You keep your word. There wouldn't have been any hope of any improvement without you, and don't you think I don't know it." He paused and looked at Alastar. "What will you do if they don't act?"

"What I can," replied Alastar.

"Ha! From any other man, that would mean nothing." The factor shook his head. "Words! From one man, they mean nothing. From another, they mean everything that they say. From a woman, they definitely mean something, but the Namer knows what half the time." Abruptly, he looked at Alastar. "You're not married, are you?"

"I'm a widower. My wife died years ago."

"You're missing the greatest trials and the greatest joys in life, Maitre, and I don't know whether to envy you or pity you. It's probably better you're not married at the moment." Elthyrd paused. "Don't ask me to explain that. You'll find out soon enough, if another worthy woman enters your life. If one doesn't, it won't matter. Is there anything else we need to talk about now?"

"Not at the moment."

"Good. I promised I'd inspect a shipment of goldenwood and dark mahogany. Won't pay unless it's up to standards." The factor rose from behind the desk. "I'll walk you out."

Alastar stood, and the two walked out into a clear but cold and windy morning. Alastar didn't hesitate to put on his gray leather gloves once he left the factor. He also made certain his cap was firmly seated on his head. Dhonaet and Maercyl immediately mounted and led the gray gelding to Alastar, then followed him after he mounted and turned south on the East River Road. With the old east bridge still not replaced, Alastar had to ride to the Sud Bridge over the Aluse and then north on the West River Road to the repaired Bridge of Desires in order to return to the Collegium. For the time being, Alastar was more than happy to have but one bridge to Imagisle. Besides which, he'd been thinking about replacing the old east bridge with a wider and more functional bridge. From a symbolic point of view that would be even more necessary once the Avenue D'Rex was completed, because Alastar wanted to build more support for the Collegium with the factors of L'Excelsis and because he wanted the people to feel that the Collegium was linked to the city as well as to the rex.

Once back on Imagisle, he immediately sought out Akoryt, finding him in the anomen.

"Have your scouts noticed anything unusual at army headquarters?"

"No, sir. Not a thing. Except that they're polishing the brass on a pair of fancy wagons."

"That's for the memorial service on Samedi, something I'll have to attend as well. I'll need two pair of seconds and thirds in their best grays, boots polished and all that. They'll need to be ready around first glass. The service begins at second glass."

"Two pair?"

"One to take care of the horses and a second to escort me into the Anomen D'Rex. They'll need to carry shields."

Akoryt offered a concerned look.

"It's called keeping up appearances, which, after the last few weeks, we need to do."

"Yes, sir. I'll make sure they're ready."

"I assume both Bettaur and Taurek are behaving."

"Having Arion mentor Taurek is working well. Bettaur will likely continue to behave as long as he knows everyone is watching him."

"Somehow I'm not surprised."

After discussing more details about the patrols of the river roads, Alastar returned to the Maitre's dwelling, where he found Alyna.

"Have you been waiting long?" He gestured for her to come into the study with him.

"No. I had Tiranya send word with one of the primes when you finished with Akoryt. I wanted to talk to you about when you wanted us to start on the rebuilding, but I can't stay long."

With that information, Alastar remained standing

beside his desk. "When will you have your calculations done for the foundations of the administration building and the dining hall?"

"I did the dining hall first. Those are done. Tomorrow sometime for the administration building."

"Once they're done . . . would you feel like supervising the imaging?"

"That is rather gently put . . ."

"I'd appreciate . . ." Then Alastar laughed. "I apologize. Maitre D'Structure Alyna, you are in charge of designing and rebuilding those two buildings. You have the authority to enlist any maitres you need to get the task done. The only exception is if Cyran or I need them for the defense of Imagisle."

Alyna inclined her head, but Alastar caught the hint of the mischievous smile. "Thank you, sir. We'll begin on Vendrei, unless it rains or snows."

"Good." He paused. "Have you learned any more about Bettaur?"

"He's been trying to convince Orlana and Dorya that his being disciplined was just a misunderstanding, and that he really had Taurek's best interests at heart."

"He probably half-believes that himself. That kind always does. Have you said anything?"

"I didn't have to. Both Tiranya and Seliora made it clear that if the two of them believed what Bettaur said, they'd likely end up like Shannyr, if not Johanyr."

"That's going to make Bettaur angrier."

"Tiranya told them to be pleasant to him, but not to believe a word."

"That may make it worse, not that she didn't do the right thing. Sometimes I think the Bettaurs of the world cause as much evil and misery as the out-and-out villains, and so many of them get away with it for so long before the reckoning comes due."

"Most like him, especially the pretty boys, except

that's redundant, have the same reaction—that it's a misunderstanding and so unfair."

Alastar couldn't help but smile at the gentle irony in her voice, but another thought occurred to him. "What about the girls who are seconds—Thelia, Linzya . . . and the others?"

"Thelia saw through him as soon as she arrived, and Linzya listens to her. I'll make sure Tiranya spreads the word to Paemyna and Mauryna." Alyna paused. "And now, if you'll excuse me, I need to get back to the anomen in time for my mathematics instructional."

"I won't keep you." Again, as soon as Alastar said the words, he wished he hadn't phrased them quite that way, but he managed to smile pleasantly, without flushing, he hoped.

After she left, he closed the study door and shook his head. Never had he made so many unintended double entendres with anyone . . . and the way he'd almost dealt with Alyna over the rebuilding . . . it wasn't quite the same thing, but it reminded him of what Elthyrd said. "*It's probably better you're not married at the moment.*" Why? Because he'd try to protect her too much, and she'd resent it? *Except you haven't even asked her . . . and if you do . . .* She'd as much as said that she wasn't interested until he managed to get the Collegium back on sound footings, or at a minimum to where she wasn't second in his thoughts and feelings. *At least, that's what you think she meant.*

The remainder of the morning and the early afternoon he dealt with as many of the small details of being Maitre that he'd put aside as he could before he finally hurried to the stables where the gelding and the two seconds—Maercyl and Dhonaet, again—waited for him. They arrived at the Chateau D'Rex a quint before fourth glass, and Alastar made his way up the steps and was escorted up the grand staircase to the rex's study.

Lorien was once more standing by the window, looking out to the north.

Alastar had to admit that the wall of clouds in the distance did look ominous, and he hoped that he and Lorien could finish early enough that he wouldn't have to ride through a downpour to get back to the Collegium.

The young rex turned abruptly. "Have you any news, Maitre?"

"We'll begin rebuilding the buildings that were destroyed later this week. I met this morning with Factor Elthyrd, the head of the factors' council of L'Excelsis. The factors are hopeful that there will not be any delay in constructing vessels to deal with the pirates plaguing the Southern Gulf. I told the good factor that you had issued instructions to Sea Marshal Wilkorn to prepare plans for the future of the navy to deal with both the pirates and the future threat of Jariolan and Ferran warships."

"He thinks we can build ships overnight, I'd wager. Did he complain that we were not acting quickly enough?"

"I pointed out that you needed increased tariffs if you were going to be able to pay for those ships. Speaking of that, how is your declaration establishing next year's tariffs coming?"

"I'm still working on it. Here . . . let me read it to you." Lorien turned back to the desk and picked up a single piece of paper. He cleared his throat and, lifting the sheet, began, almost as if he were announcing a proclamation, "Whereas the great land of Solidar is blessed with fertile lands and great industry, and whereas it is the duty of the Rex to provide those amenities and services to support and encourage productive use of all resources, especially those services provided by the army and the navy, the highways, the justicers and courts, and the Rex's post couriers, the costs of such provisions having risen for years without adjustments, it is hereby decreed that the tariff for the coming year, the year 390 after the establishment of L'Excelsis as the capital of all Solidar, shall be increased by four coppers for each gold currently due under the existing tallage, as registered in the records of the Ministry of Finance in L'Excelsis. The same rate of increase shall apply to all tariffs paid on goods imported into Solidar at all ports, and upon all sales or transfers of lands or other properties . . ."

Lorien stopped and coughed to clear his throat. "I don't know as I'm pleased with the wording . . ."

"Isn't that the wording suggested by Minister Salucar?"

"It doesn't sound right . . . all those 'whereas' phrases, you know?"

"How else would you phrase it? If you begin with 'because,' it almost sounds whining . . . 'Because the great land of Solidar is blessed . . . and because it is the duty of the Rex . . .' Doesn't that sound like you resent having to do those things which it is your duty to do?"

"What about 'since'?" Lorien looked at the paper and began again, "Since the great land of Solidar is blessed with fertile lands and great industry, and since it is the duty of the Rex to provide those amenities . . ." He stopped and shook his head. "That sounds almost simpering. I hate sounding simpering, and over a trifling increase of four coppers on a gold, I definitely do not wish to sound simpering."

"You could just go with 'whereas.' It, at least, sounds regial."

"I need something that sounds regial without sounding pompous."

"Take out the use of 'whereas.' Just start with a statement. 'The great land of Solidar is blessed with fertile lands and great industry, and it is the duty of the Rex to provide . . .' Then you could say, 'Therefore, since the costs . . .' "

"No . . . that's not the right tone, and there's still a simpering 'since,' and 'because' isn't any better. 'Because' sounds like a fishwife."

Although Alastar doubted that Lorien had ever been within a mille of a fishwife, he just said, "Then stay with 'whereas'; hold your nose, so to speak, and put out the declaration of tariffs. The numbers are clear enough, and getting it out will bring in your tariffs sooner."

"That may be, but I'm the one that will have to live with what I write, not you . . . I don't want to go down as the great meaningless pontificator or the rex who sounded like a fishwife."

"Begging your pardon, Lorien, but no one is ever going to look at any tariff declaration of any rex as an indication of his skill or lack of skill with words. The words that people will remember will be those where people might actually listen, for example, what you will say at your father's memorial service."

"Yes . . . I do have to work on that. Maybe . . . yes, I'll put this aside until I finish the appreciation."

Alastar was definitely beginning to wonder what game Lorien was playing at. The young rex couldn't be that scattered, and there was no reek of lager or stronger spirits about him. Or was he stalling on the tariff issue?

"I take it that Marshal Petayn has again conveyed his concern that the tariff increase that the High Holders will accept is insufficient to maintain his oversized and underutilized army?"

"I would appreciate it, Maitre, if you would not presume about what others may or may not have said to me, or what their concerns may be."

"He's already said that twice, if not more, in my presence. I'm not presuming when I state a position he himself has stated so directly. You and your father need additional revenues. I have arranged for additional revenues. The Collegium has paid dearly for that arrangement. Your father paid dearly for not being able to accept any arrangement."

"You have made that very clear, Maitre. But I have to live with whatever arrangement is made."

"If you make the mistakes your father made, that life will not be pleasant, and it may not be all that long, given the unrest among the High Holders and within the army."

"And the Collegium? Is that a veiled threat?"

"Stating what is obvious, Lorien, is neither veiled nor a threat. It is the situation you face. The longer you put off issuing an acceptable tariff schedule, the more the High Holders will feel that you are indecisive or trying to scheme for higher tariffs. In addition, the longer before you receive this year's tariffs. None of those conditions will improve your position as rex."

"And what of the army, which is oversized and rather close? And not very pleased with your disposal of Marshal Demykalon."

"You will either control the army, or it will control you."

"That is easy enough for you to say, Maitre, but I am not an imager."

"No, you are not. But, provided you act sensibly, you have the Collegium behind you, and the Collegium would far rather have you ruling Solidar than either the army or the High Council."

"I find it interesting that you profess no interest in ruling."

"I also profess no interest in seeing all but a handful of imagers killed or fleeing and forced into hiding, and that, as I have told you, is what would come of any imager attempting to rule. Worse would occur, if somewhat later, should an imager actually come to rule."

"You believe that?"

"It is what has happened in every land on Terahnar except Solidar."

Lorien shook his head. "Enough! I must consider. We will discuss this further tomorrow."

Alastar could tell that, for whatever reason, Lorien was not about to issue the tariff proclamation immediately, and that he felt Alastar could not force the issue. *And you can't, because if another rex dies in his study with you present, that will have the same effect as would the Collegium attacking directly.* He simply nodded. "Until tomorrow."

"Good." Lorien did not look at Alastar, but turned toward the window. "Until then."

Alastar did not say more, but slipped out of the study. *Who's gotten to him . . . and with what?* Alastar's immediate reaction was that Petayn had offered a veiled threat . . . or perhaps one not even veiled. *That's what you've been trying to avoid.* Unfortunately, there were other possibilities as well, less likely but still possible.

Alastar had just reached the bottom of the grand staircase when Lady Asarya appeared. "We meet again."

"You have certainly managed to meet me once more." Alastar made his voice light.

"You had a rather pensive expression. Worry doesn't become you, Maitre." Lady Asarya smiled, a pleasant expression that offered warmth and made Alastar again realize that she was still a quite attractive woman. She wore garments tailored in what Alastar perceived as her usual style—tunic, trousers, and boots—but the tunic and trousers were green trimmed in black—mourning colors. The boots were black. "Have you a moment?"

"For you . . . of course."

"Then we should go to the salon—mine. This way . . ."

Alastar could think of several reasons for that, but merely nodded as he moved to walk beside her toward the south corridor. After a moment, he added, "I'm sorry for your loss."

Asarya smiled politely. "The black and green are for

propriety, not loss. There's little point in hypocrisy, is there? Ryen and I hadn't been remotely close for more than twenty years. Appearances are necessary. That is all. What's important is that my son has a better future, thanks to certain imagers from the Collegium, and that the High Holders are brought into line."

"And your sons? How do they feel?"

"They have lost their father. How would you expect them to feel?"

"I have no expectations, Lady. Some sons are grief-struck at the loss of a parent. Some are relieved. Some are greatly saddened and carry on. I would not presume to guess. Just as I would not presume to guess at the reasons why you have managed to encounter me more than is likely to have happened by mere happenstance."

"Never disregard happenstance, Maitre. Nor chance. Nor what appears to be chance and is not. You are right. Not all of our meetings have been happenstance. I did want to meet with the Maitre who has done so much to keep outright rebellion from happening."

Alastar didn't believe a word. "You could have managed that earlier."

"No. That would not have been possible. Ryen would have been furious. It was bad enough that my cousin is an imager."

Alastar managed a frown. "I've been over the records of all the imagers here at Imagisle . . ."

"You obviously did not look far enough." She smiled. "Smarthyl."

"Smarthyl? The senior imager at Mont D'Image? He's a cousin of yours? I've looked at his record too, but there's no mention of that."

"He is a friend of the archivist . . ."

"Of Maitre Obsolym?"

"I believe that's his name. I've never paid that much attention to the Collegium since Smarthyl left. It didn't seem . . ."

"Relevant?"

"I believe you said that, Maitre, not me."

"Only after your hinting."

"That's a woman's prerogative, I believe."

"Among others."

"What is new that I should know?"

"Lorien appears to be stalling over the wording of his tariff proclamation." Alastar delivered the words evenly.

"He can be deliberate when there is no choice, or when nothing is at stake."

"That's not the kindest thing to say about your son."

"I lost my illusions long ago, Maitre. Even about my sons. Lorien cultivates the impression of deliberation because he is . . . less than decisive. Ryentar, on the other hand, will stick to a course once he starts upon it, even when it is proved to him that such a course is absolute folly . . . or worse. Lorien appears cold, but is too tender for his own good. Ryentar projects warmth, so much so that everyone likes him, yet deep within him is a cold emptiness and, if he feels wronged, an unquenchable anger." Asarya shrugged.

Asarya's words called up what Obsolym had said about Ryentar—that he was more like his father. Yet . . .

Asarya stopped short of the open doorway ahead. "I'd prefer we not talk about either for a time."

"As you wish."

She gestured for him to enter.

Alastar smiled and said, "I could not precede you, Lady."

Echoing his own words, she replied, "As you wish," and entered the salon, where a young blond woman, also wearing the green and black of mourning, immediately rose from one of the cushioned armchairs.

"Have you met Lady Chelia, Maitre?"

"I've not had that honor, or that privilege." Alastar inclined his head to the statuesque beauty—not only tall and well-proportioned, if fully figured, but slightly square-chinned with a slight dimple, a straight nose, a fair but not pale complexion, blond hair, and brilliant blue eyes. In an instant, Alastar *knew* he had seen those eyes, and someone very similar in appearance. *Bettaur!* He managed not to stiffen as the realization struck him.

"It is my pleasure, Maitre." Chelia's voice was warm, yet reserved. She glanced to Asarya. "You didn't warn me that such a distinguished personage was coming."

"I didn't know if he would. I asked, and he was kind enough to indulge me."

More like wariness, rather than kindness. "How could I refuse?"

"Rather easily, I think, if you wished," replied Asarya pleasantly.

"Not easily, with all your charm, certainly not wisely." Alastar turned toward Chelia. "And I would have lost the opportunity to meet this lovely young lady."

"You sound like Ryentar," offered Chelia.

"I doubt it. He offers warmth all the time. I only have words."

"Both can deceive," observed Chelia. "Words are more honest in their deception, because lies can be discovered through truth."

"And false warmth cannot?" asked Alastar not quite playfully.

"Usually the damage is greater before discovery occurs," returned Chelia.

Without saying a negative word, Chelia had suggested that she did not have the highest opinion of Ryentar . . . or so it seemed. *But why would she even hint at that in front of Asarya?*

"I feel that words offer a wider range for deception and devastation," said Asarya. "That is one of a number of areas where Chelia and I do not see matters in exactly the same light."

Another charade? Yet when Alastar looked at Chelia and caught what he thought was a quickly concealed expression of surprise, he had the feeling that the younger woman had been caught unaware as well. "I would have to agree with you, Lady Asarya, at least in part, in that the use of words can engender far greater damage and destruction in the world of the physical. But the use or misuse of feelings can blight a life forever, and perhaps continue beyond one generation, while the words that can create the circumstances to kill an individual often end their destruction with that death."

"Often . . ." mused Asarya. "You are very careful with your words, Maitre. That suggests you are also quite skilled in their use."

"Not so skilled as I would like. My words failed to convince many about the need to compromise on the issue of tariffs." Mentioning the tariff issue was a dangerous gambit, but Alastar wanted to see Asarya's reaction.

"What happened subsequently suggests that it is wise to heed your words, Maitre."

"Not because they were my words, Lady, but because there was truth in what I spoke."

"Truth, Maitre . . . or power?"

Alastar laughed softly. "You give one pause, Lady."

"I notice you did not answer."

"Because you offered a choice between alternatives, neither of which applied fully or completely accurately." Alastar could see and feel Chelia's eyes following the conversation, shifting from him to Asarya and back again, although she maintained an expression of vague amusement, much as one might in observing a fight between two beasts, with neither of which she was even faintly enamored. "The truth one finds in words lies more in one's own convictions than in the accuracy of what those words convey."

"You mean to say," said Chelia sweetly, "that we wish to hear the words that support our beliefs? How original."

"No, it's rather a threadbare observation, for all its accuracy. I tried, and obviously failed, to convey the idea more elegantly." Alastar offered a self-deprecating laugh. "Elegance, I should remember, is often complicit in deception."

"You see," observed Asarya, "the maitre is indeed most skilled with words . . . among other things."

"As are you, Lady."

Asarya smiled. "I do not believe that Lady Chelia and I should detain you longer, Maitre, Your exposition was, however, truly fascinating."

"Only because of your inspiration, Lady." Alastar smiled and inclined his head. "Good day, Ladies."

"A pleasant evening to you, Maitre."

Alastar continued to smile before turning and leaving the salon. He had hoped Asarya would let him have the last word. The fact that she had worried him even more than the fact that she had clearly used him as a counter of some sort in dealing with Chelia . . . and he had no idea why or what Asarya had in mind . . . only that he doubted it was anywhere close to being for his benefit or that of the Collegium.

When he started down the outside steps, he saw Maercyl and Dhonaet immediately mount and then ride forward, leading the gray gelding to meet him.

"We need to get moving," Alastar said, after mounting and looking to the northwest and the wall of clouds that looked to be roughly over the grounds of the army headquarters.

"Yes, sir," replied Maercyl.

Even in the short time it took the three to reach the Boulevard D'Ouest, scattered droplets began to fall. When they reached the West River Road and headed south, the droplets were a steady downpour, and when Alastar finally started across the Bridge of Desires, it was like riding through a wall of water. Needless to say, just as he dismounted outside the stables, after a last blast of water and wind, the rain ended.

Alastar, thoroughly soaked, let the stable boys groom the gelding and began to walk toward the Maitre's dwelling, his thoughts on the webs within webs that seemed to permeate everything in L'Excelsis.

35

The first thing Alastar did after breakfast on Jeudi morning was to summon Akoryt. While he waited, he kept trying to puzzle out his meeting with Asarya and Chelia. Clearly, Asarya had managed to use the conversation, if one could call it that, to position Alastar as a powerful man who well might be, or in fact was, a danger to Lorien. Why was another question, since Alastar had a vested interest in Lorien's success. Yet Asarya had seemed relatively evenhanded in discussing her sons' faults, but had that merely been to set up matters so that she could then portray Alastar as dangerous to Lorien? That seemed most likely, but that still left the question of why? So Lorien and Chelia would try some indirect way of removing Alastar? Then there was something about Lady Chelia . . . but it wasn't only her resemblance to Bettaur, which suggested, along with other hints, that their fathers might well be the same man—which definitely fit with what Alastar had discovered. There was something else beyond that tickling Alastar's mind . . . he just couldn't place it.

He still couldn't place it when Akoryt entered the study. Alastar pushed that puzzle aside and said, "If you'd close the door."

"Yes, sir." Akoryt did just that, then asked, "Have I—"

"Nothing like that. I didn't mean to be peremptory in sending a message for you to come here. For most matters, I would have sought you out. For this . . . I did not wish us to be overheard. I'm going to need you to have some more scouting done. I have more concerns about the army. Rex Lorien initially agreed to reduce the size of the army and to issue the new tariff schedule. Now, several days later, he's put off doing either, despite the fact that the High Holders have agreed to the proposed tariff schedule. Both Marshal Petayn and Sea Marshal Wilkorn oppose reductions in force, and another meeting has been scheduled for next Lundi to discuss the matter further."

Akoryt frowned.

"After our last . . . encounter with the army, you can see why I might be somewhat concerned."

"Sir . . . we did inflict considerable damage . . ."

"That was because we used their own powder against them. Even so, we lost two imagers out of something like fifteen. What if they attacked Imagisle with hundreds, if not thousands, of troopers? How many would we then lose?"

"But they would lose far, far more."

"They have over seven thousand troopers just here in L'Excelsis, and it appears as if the Collegium is the only force capable of keeping the marshals from getting their way."

"What about the High Holders?"

"They're spread out all across Solidar, and I doubt any have a guard force of even a hundred."

"Do you really think . . . ?"

"I could be wrong. I hope I'm wrong. But if I'm right, and we're not prepared . . ."

"I see your point, sir. I'll get right on it."

Less than a quint after Akoryt had left, Dareyn appeared at the study door with Arhgen.

"Sir? Do you know if Rex Lorien has rescinded the reduction in the monthly stipend for the Collegium?"

Another thing you forgot to ask about. Except it wasn't that Alastar had so much forgotten as not wanted to bring up at the times he had met with Lorien. "At the moment, it appears that the reduction remains in force. That's likely to remain so at least until the matter of the

High Holders' tariffs is resolved. Hopefully, that will be accomplished before the end of the month, but whether that happens remains to be seen."

"Then you wish to avoid unnecessary purchases?" asked Arhgen.

"That's correct, but some purchases still may have to be made. If Petros doesn't purchase winter fodder now, then we may not be able to obtain any at any price by mid-Finitas. If you have questions . . ." Alastar almost laughed. That was clearly why Arhgen was at the door. "Come on in, and we'll go over what everyone tells you is absolutely necessary, and we'll see what really has to be purchased now and what purchases can be put off."

In the end, going over what Arhgen had questions about and working out how much of what could be purchased and when took almost two glasses. Then Alastar went to find Obsolym. The elder Maitre D'Structure was in a smallish room in the anomen finishing up a basic instructional for primes. Alastar waited until they all left before approaching Obsolym.

"Yes, Maitre?"

"Some things have come up. Once more, I need your knowledge and insight. Was Desyrk in charge of instructionals and student discipline before Maitre Smarthyl left for Mont D'Image?"

"No, sir. Smarthyl was. He thought he would be senior maitre, but then Maitre Cyran demonstrated all the abilities of a Maitre D'Esprit. Maitre Fhaen suggested that Smarthyl might be happier to take over the senior imager position—that's the head position there, you know?"

Alastar forbore observing that he'd known that for many years, only nodding. "When was that? Do you recall?"

"A little over five years ago. It might have been longer."

"That was about the time when Bettaur came to the Collegium, wasn't it?"

"Around that time. I couldn't be sure." Obsolym tilted his head. "No . . . Bettaur came just after Smarthyl left. I remember that, because Desyrk should have been the one to settle incoming students, but Maitre Fhaen and Desyrk did it together. Maitre Fhaen said that there were certain students who needed to be eased into the Collegium, and he wanted Desyrk to know how and when to do that, and Bettaur was the first one of those."

"Tertius Arion arrived after Bettaur, then?"

"Several months later, as I recall."

Alastar nodded. "Thank you."

"Might I ask why you wanted to know, sir?"

"I just wondered how close Bettaur might have been to Maitre Desyrk, and if he was, how that might have happened."

"I wouldn't say that they were close, but once Bettaur was settled, I don't think Maitre Fhaen ever asked about him." Obsolym raised his eyebrows, suggesting that Alastar hadn't really answered the question.

"I'm trying to figure out who Desyrk might be seeking support from, besides his family, and since he seemed to bend over backward for Bettaur, I was just thinking . . ." Alastar shrugged.

"But Bettaur's parents are dead."

Alastar shook his head. "His mother and his guardian are dead, but it doesn't matter because from what Bettaur and you have said, Desyrk wouldn't seek out Bettaur's father."

"If you already knew . . ."

"After the way you've seen how Bettaur twists the truth, would you trust his unsupported word?" asked Alastar sardonically.

Obsolym offered a rueful smile. "I fear I see your point."

"Thank you. I won't keep you longer."

As he walked back toward the Maitre's dwelling, Alastar couldn't help thinking about the situation. Lady

Asarya was a cousin to Smarthyl and linked in some way to Ryel the elder, who had been Lady Chelia's father and most likely Bettaur's as well. Desyrk had accompanied Marshal Ghalyn to the Chateau D'Rex, and someone had whispered his name in presumably a less than casual way. Yet Smarthyl had left L'Excelsis more than five years earlier to go to Mont D'Image on the seemingly flimsiest of reasons. Why?

Does it even matter?

Alastar had the feeling that all those entangled relationships had a definite bearing on his own difficulties, but, again, he didn't know enough to sort out how or why. He set aside those questions once he reached his study . . . and the master ledger he needed to study again.

Slightly after first glass, Dareyn rapped on the door. "I have a message from the rex." He held an envelope.

Alastar rose and crossed the room to take it. "Does he expect a response?"

"I don't think so. The courier just delivered it and left."

Alastar frowned, then took his belt knife and slit the envelope. He scanned the few sentences with the precise signature of the rex immediately below it.

> *In view of matters, and because I have not completed my draft of the tariff proclamation, I have postponed this afternoon's meeting until tomorrow afternoon at fourth glass . . .*

Alastar couldn't say he was totally surprised with the first sentence.

> *You will doubtless be pleased to know that Marshal Petayn has sent a missive confirming that he is immediately moving more than a regiment to Lucayl as you recommended. The first units are already moving south.*

That was all. Alastar looked to Dareyn. "I need to find Maitre Akoryt. Did he say where he was going?"

"No, sir."

"I'll try the anomen and then the stables. If he shows up here in the meantime, have him wait for me."

"Yes, sir."

Alastar did manage to find Akoryt, if leaving the stables.

"Maitre . . . I was coming to tell you that I have the thirds in position to see, as well as they can, what is happening at army headquarters."

"You'll likely have to make some adjustments. I've just received word from Rex Lorien that he has been informed that Marshal Petayn is immediately relocating a regiment south and east to Solis."

Akoryt frowned. "If all they're doing is moving a regiment to the south . . ."

"You can't prepare to move an entire regiment in three days. That means they're up to something else. Since the best route to Solis is by the river roads, and since the best road south, at least as far as Caluse, is the West River Road, no one will think much of them traveling that way . . . but that means they can be very close to Imagisle. I want to know how many troopers are leaving headquarters, and where they are at all times. I also want to know what the troopers remaining at headquarters are doing."

"Do you think they'll really attack Imagisle?"

"I have no idea what they have in mind," temporized Alastar, "but the last thing we need is to be surprised."

"Yes, sir. I'll make the adjustments."

When Alastar returned to the Maitre's dwelling, Alyna was waiting . . . in the study.

She rose from one of the chairs in front of the desk as he entered. "Dareyn said it was all right if I waited here."

"Perfectly all right." Alastar smiled.

"I've finished the plans. I don't see any reason why we can't start on the foundation for the dining hall or the administration building tomorrow."

"The dining hall first, I think," Alastar replied. "You can start, as you can, tomorrow, but we have another problem. Just a small one," he said ironically. He went on to explain, everything from the meetings to Lorien's stalling, Petayn's regimental "relocation" and even the memorial services. When he finished, he asked, "Do you think I'm overreacting?"

"You may not be taking the threat seriously enough."

"Go on."

"What if the threat isn't against the Collegium at all? What if Petayn is playing Lorien? Or both of you? Think about who will be at the memorial services on Samedi."

"Lorien, Chelia, Lady Asarya, Ryentar . . ."

". . . and you. What happens if something goes wrong . . . or if the army takes the chateau while you're all at the services and then bombards the anomen?"

"There would be quite a few people killed. Their cannon aren't that accurate."

"Who were you thinking of accompanying you? Two or three thirds."

"Probably two. Akoryt has most of them scouting what the troopers are doing."

"You need to take more than seconds or thirds to the service. Shaelyt and I could accompany you."

Alastar shook his head. "We don't know what Petayn will do. I'd feel more comfortable with you and Cyran here." He paused and said in a lower voice, "Cyran will listen to you, and the others will listen to him."

"Shaelyt won't be enough to support you."

"I'll take Taryn as well, then."

"That's good. He has solid shields." She paused. "Do you still think we should start building tomorrow?"

"I doubt very much is going to happen the day before

memorial services. I don't think you should do any building on Samedi, though. Tell everyone you'll need to measure and check the foundations . . . or something like that."

Alyna smiled. "That's not a bad idea, although I'll have to stake the foundation lines today. Otherwise, they won't be anywhere close to true."

While she spoke, Alastar was very much aware just how close she was . . . and how much he wanted to reach out and draw her into his arms—and far more than that.

Suddenly, she wasn't talking, and neither was he. They just stood there looking at each other.

Then she smiled and said softly. "Not yet. Not now." She stepped back, just a half step, before adding, "We'll start at seventh glass tomorrow morning." Blushing, she went on, "Imaging the foundations of the dining hall."

Alastar managed not to grin, although he found himself smiling. "I thought I was the only one who had words come out inadvertently."

Alyna shook her head ruefully. "You make care very difficult, Maitre dear."

"You make me forget I'm Maitre."

"That isn't good. Not now."

"I know." *But it's hard not to think about how much she means . . . after not caring for so long.*

"So do I." She smiled again. "I'll see you tomorrow. You are having a meeting of senior maitres in the morning, aren't you?"

"Yes. Everyone should know what's happening."

"And what might happen."

"That, too."

"I need to go."

Alastar almost reached for her hand, but instead gestured toward the study door. "I'll walk out with you."

"I'd like that." She actually took his hand.

Alastar could feel that her hand was trembling, and he squeezed gently. "So would I."

When they passed Dareyn, Alastar had the feeling that the elder secondus looked away. Once outside on the front porch, he glanced to the west. "Looks like rain coming in."

"It does." After a brief pause, she added, "I hope we never have to resort to talking about the weather, except when it matters. Not to come up with words when we have nothing to say."

"I'll remember that," said Alastar with a smile.

"That would be good." She stepped away, then offered a last smile before turning and heading down the steps and along the paved lane toward her cottage.

He watched until she was out of sight.

"Maitre Alyna smiles more these days," said Dareyn when Alastar walked back to the study.

Alastar almost said, "So do I," instead replying, "I don't have any way to compare."

"Trust me, sir. She looks happier since you became Maitre, especially the last few weeks."

"I understand she and Maitre Fhaen were barely cordial."

"Like winter between them, but most of the maitres seem happier since you took over. Most of the imagers, in fact."

"Even with all the troubles?"

"All times have troubles, sir. It's not the troubles, but how you face them."

"That's true, but I'm afraid we're not finished with facing them."

"You'll find a way, sir."

Alastar certainly hoped so.

36

For the next several glasses Alastar busied himself with various small tasks that had languished, while he pondered on just what Lorien had in mind, on what exactly Petayn had planned, and while he waited for Akoryt to return with any news about the army. It was less than a quint before sixth glass, just after Alastar had hurriedly eaten some supper with a tableful of thirds, by the time Akoryt returned to the Maitre's dwelling.

Belatedly, Alastar imaged two lamps into light as he ushered the red-haired Maitre D'Structure into the study, then sat behind the desk. He leaned forward. "What have you discovered so far?"

"Not much. There's definitely a regiment readying to move out. They've got supply wagons and cannon lined up—"

"How many cannon?" interrupted Alastar.

"Not that many. Five, from what Akkard reported."

"Are they the new ones, like the ones that fired on the Collegium?"

"They look the same."

"What about supply wagons?"

"There were five of those, too."

"Spare mounts?"

"Not that Akkard saw, but they looked to be leaving tomorrow. There wouldn't be much reason to load the wagons if they weren't leaving."

Alastar reached for the message that Lorien had sent, reading the lines once more, and going over the words, especially the ones saying, "the first units are already moving south." He looked up. "They didn't see any sign of companies moving out of headquarters, then?"

"No, sir. Not unless they moved out before first or second glass."

Alastar frowned. "And there have been no troopers on the West River Road?"

"No, sir. Why?"

"I told you about the message from the rex. He reported that Marshal Petayn said that units were already moving south."

"We haven't seen any sign of that."

"I believe you. The only question is whether the rex or Petayn is lying . . . and if either is . . . why?"

"I gathered that you recommended strongly that the army send troopers to the Southern Gulf. Maybe he wants to shade things so that you won't get upset."

Alastar didn't immediately recall saying anything about his recommendations to Akoryt, but he might have . . . or Akoryt might have learned that from Cyran. "That's possible, but he said that Petayn wrote that . . . and if the units haven't left, then that's a double lie . . . and one Lorien knows I'd likely discover."

"Maybe Petayn thought the units would be ready sooner than they were . . . or he exaggerated to keep Rex Lorien from getting upset. Or maybe he'd promised to have them on their way by today."

"Those are all possibilities. The discrepancy bothers me." Alastar offered a shrug of both frustration and resignation. "All I can say is that the thirds and whatever seconds you're using need to keep their eyes out for army companies that may not be where they should be." Alastar almost laughed at his own words. "Except how can anyone tell where they should be? In any case, have someone follow that regiment tomorrow . . . and send word if companies split off."

"We can do that, sir. We may have to cancel more instructionals."

"Go ahead. For the moment, this is far more important."

Akoryt nodded.

"Has anyone seen any signs of Desyrk?"

"No. I wouldn't expect to, would you?"

"We can hope," replied Alastar dryly.

"Is there anything else?"

"Not for tonight. Go home while you can."

"Yes, sir."

After Akoryt departed, Alastar remained in the study, thinking, but that didn't last long because there was a loud knocking. When Alastar reached the door of the residence, he found Cyran standing on the porch. He motioned the senior imager inside, and the two went to the study, where Alastar again settled behind the desk. "You're here later than is your custom." *Much later.*

"I saw Akoryt leaving after seventh glass," said the senior maitre blandly.

"And you wondered what else was happening because that's late for him to be reporting something unless it's important?" Alastar offered a grin he didn't really feel.

"I thought I might be helpful."

"You will be. I'll be telling the senior maitres all about it in the morning, but there's no reason you shouldn't know now." Alastar cleared his throat.

"Is there a problem with the rex?"

"You mean another problem? Yes, and there's likely one with Petayn and the army as well." Alastar went on to explain, waiting for Cyran's reaction when he finished.

"It doesn't seem to me that the rex would lie about what Petayn wrote him," said Cyran slowly. "It also doesn't seem that likely that Petayn would lie in writing to the rex."

"Then, if Petayn is telling the truth, where are those companies that already left headquarters? Akoryt's scouts haven't seen any sign of them, and it appears as though a regiment is preparing to depart tomorrow."

"What if Petayn didn't write the message to the rex?" asked Cyran.

"I don't see that. Every message has to have the marshal's seal. Lorien would know that, and I can't see anyone stealing the seal and forging his signature just to say that a regiment is departing earlier than anticipated." Alastar worried his lips. "I have to believe that Petayn moved those troopers somewhere that Lorien might discover and wanted to mislead the rex."

"Somewhere south of the chateau . . . or near it?"

"That's my worry, and there's so much woodland there—the hunting park and other lands—that there's no way to tell. We don't have enough imagers to scout the entire area."

"Do you think he's mad enough to try to become rex?"

"It's possible. It's also possible that he has something else in mind."

"Another attack on Imagisle?"

"That's also possible. That's why I don't want too many imagers away from here. Shaelyt and Taryn will go with me and four seconds and thirds to the memorial services for Rex Ryen. Everyone else will remain on Imagisle, just in case, with you in charge and Alyna and Akoryt assisting you. Whatever might happen, the first time we're likely to find out is on Samedi afternoon."

Although the two talked for another quint, at the end, Alastar found they had merely rehashed what they'd discussed, and he finally said, "This isn't getting us anywhere. You need to go home and get some rest."

"Some rest? After this? You know how to ruin a man's sleep, you know?"

"If it makes you feel any better, it's not helping my sleep, either."

Once he saw Cyran to the door and returned to the

study, he sat behind the desk. He wasn't in the slightest sleepy, and he had no intention of going up to bed to toss and turn.

Finally, he turned to Gauswn's journals. He opened the third and final leather-bound book to the last entry about Quaeryt, marked with a black ribbon, and reread it slowly.

The memorial for Quaeryt and Vaelora was yesterday . . .

The same questions he'd had the first time he'd read the passage came to mind. *They died at the same time? Or were they murdered?* To Alastar, a double murder, especially of that couple and at the Collegium, seemed totally unlikely, since there was no mention of that anywhere in any history, and he was certain that there would have been. *Yet . . . dying at the same time . . . ?* After a time, he continued to read.

> . . . The entire Collegium was still. Across the river, it was as though nothing had happened. Rex Clayar did declare mourning for the Chateau D'Rex . . . I cannot help but deplore the fact that the magnitude of what they accomplished has already been largely forgotten, or attributed to others, even by those within the Collegium. That was their wish . . .

Their wish? They wanted their accomplishments forgotten?

> . . . Yet, as Maitre Quaeryt once said to me, the evidence of history suggests that such is the fate of any lost one who is a son of Erion, that the greater the deeds, the less remembered he will be . . . that only those who attempted great deeds and failed are remembered.

Elsior—he is now Maitre, if reluctantly—echoed that thought this morning before the memorial. He said that Maitre Quaeryt and Lady Vaelora had been and would always be the greatest figures in the history of Solidar, and the most forgotten, because, had anyone besides a handful of imagers known, they would not have succeeded.

And that was it. The last forty pages did not mention anything about Quaeryt or Vaelora, and very little about Elsior.

After he closed the last volume of the journal, Alastar sat in the study for a long time.

If what Gauswn wrote happened to be correct, and it most likely was largely so, with any misrepresentation more likely through omission than commission, then it appeared as though Quaeryt and Vaelora had put into practice the idea that achieving the impossible was in fact possible . . . if one didn't care who claimed the accomplishment. That was in fact a total rejection of Naming in any fashion, yet Gauswn had also noted, from what he had said and observed, that Quaeryt doubted the very existence of the Nameless. For a man, especially the greatest imager who ever lived, to reject all glory without even the support of the tenets of the Nameless . . . that made Alastar feel very small indeed.

37

Alastar met with the senior imagers promptly at seventh glass on Vendrei morning and briefed them on the situation, but not on the speculations he had shared with Alyna and Cyran, also informing Taryn that he and Shaelyt would be accompanying him to the memorial services on Samedi.

"That sounds like Marshal Petayn has ideas about who should rule Solidar," said Obsolym. "He always did have grandiose ideas."

"I thought you didn't know him," said Alastar.

"I don't. Desyrk said something like that. I thought it came from his brother, and he was likely to know."

"Has anyone else heard anything about Petayn?" asked Alastar.

The others shook their heads.

"So that's the situation. Akoryt's men will let us know where the troopers are and where they're headed once they leave headquarters. So far they haven't come across any other companies of troopers, but I'm inclined to believe that there are others somewhere west or south of the Chateau D'Rex."

"You're basing that on the letter from the rex," said Obsolym. "Can you trust either Lorien or Marshal Petayn?"

"Only to act in what they perceive as their own interests," replied Alastar. "But it wouldn't be in either's interest to lie about what Petayn reportedly wrote to Lorien."

"Unless they've decided to work together," Obsolym pointed out.

"That's also possible, but can any of you see any reason for them to lie about when the troopers began to leave headquarters?"

"To keep you off-balance?" suggested Taryn.

"That's possible," said Akoryt, "but it would put either Lorien or Petayn in a dangerous position unless the Maitre is killed and the Collegium greatly weakened. That's quite a risk for no real advantage."

"What if they're both telling the truth?" asked Alyna. "That means there are more troopers out there that Petayn has misled the rex about, and that Petayn is acting against the rex and doesn't think we'll be able to stop what he has planned."

"It's impossible to say for certain," Alastar said, "but that strikes me as the most likely. It's probably connected with the memorial services tomorrow. We may have to change our plans. That will depend on what Akoryt's scouts report. I'll let you all know as we learn more." Alastar didn't want to say more at the moment. "If that's all . . . you can get on with your day."

As he stood, he smiled. "And building the foundations for the new dining hall."

Alyna lagged behind the others in leaving, and Alastar walked out to the front porch of the residence with her, where, once the others were out of earshot, she turned to him. "Petayn knows what imagers can do."

"You're suggesting that either what he plans has nothing at all to do with us . . . or everything, and it's going to require massive force on his part?"

"What will become of the Collegium if you're gone and so are most of the senior masters?"

"It's unlikely that anything he can do will take out you, me, and Cyran."

"He doesn't have to do that. All he has to do is remove you. You've pointed out that Maitre Zhelan won't come to L'Excelsis. Even if he does, he won't be as strong, and he's much older. That would leave Cyran, sooner or later.

Cyran's not a leader. The Collegium in L'Excelsis will become even weaker. It may never recover. It certainly could not remove Petayn . . . and even if it did, who would accept any rex that we suggested?"

"You wouldn't allow that."

"Solidar won't accept a woman Maitre . . . or a woman senior imager if Cyran is Maitre." Alyna looked directly at Alastar. "Whatever happens tomorrow . . . you have to survive . . . and in good health. If Taryn and Shaelyt have to sacrifice themselves to save you, let them."

"It might be nice to let them make that decision themselves."

"They already have. We talked it over last night."

Somehow that didn't surprise Alastar. "Did they agree, or did you persuade them?"

"I let them persuade me," Alyna replied sweetly.

Alastar managed not to wince. In some ways, dealing with Lorien and Petayn might be easier than dealing with Alyna. "That's definitely the most effective form of persuasion."

"I thought so."

"That means I have to find a way to resolve matters without hazarding any of us."

"That would be best." She paused. "But if you can't, your responsibility is to the Collegium, not to Taryn or Shaelyt."

"I think you've made that clear." He smiled, guilelessly, he hoped. "By the way, I would appreciate it, in the event there is another attack on Imagisle, that you remain close to Cyran and recall that the chief duty of the Collegium strategist and builder is to survive in order to provide future strategy and buildings." In turn, he paused. "If that doesn't persuade you, you might consider that I would be enormously offended if I go to all the trouble of surviving and you aren't here for me to tell you that you worried too much. I want to be very clear on that."

Alyna moistened her lips before speaking. She managed a smile, if briefly. "As one hedgehog to another, I don't want there to be another Maitre here in my life . . . and I intend to live a long time."

"I don't want another builder in my life." This time he reached out and took her hands, gently, but firmly. "And in two long lives."

They stood there for long moments.

Finally, Alyna said, "I'd better go."

He nodded, then watched as she walked swiftly toward the ruins of the dining hall. He shivered slightly in the chill morning air, a definite sign that winter might indeed come early, although it was technically a month away. *Less than a month after tomorrow.*

After he returned to his study, Alastar shook his head. He'd definitely been outmaneuvered. He'd known, but hadn't fully considered, that Taryn was the only senior maitre, besides Alyna, without a family, and that Shaelyt had no family either.

The question was exactly what Petayn had in mind. Alastar found it hard to believe that the acting marshal would attack either Lorien or especially the Collegium a second time. Yet the signs pointed to some form of attack. Would Petayn loose cannon on the Anomen D'Rex during the services? Or somehow seal it off and set fire to the interior? But that would take too long and might not be certain, especially since Petayn knew that Alastar would be there. *Unless he used some incendiary oils. Antiagon Fire!* Demykalon had said that the army had the formula and methodology . . . and they had Desyrk. *You don't know that's what he'll do . . .*

Alastar went over what he recalled of the arrangements for the memorial service, thinking about who would be where. Petayn and Alastar would be at the front on the left. Alastar would have Taryn and Shaelyt, and presumably Petayn would have another officer, an aide at the very least. Lorien and Chelia, as well as

Lady Asarya and Ryentar, would be on the front on the right, with a squad of Chateau guards. But if Petayn was going to be there . . .

He shook his head. That didn't make sense, but he couldn't dismiss the feeling that something was very wrong. The very thought of Antiagon Fire in the Anomen D'Rex . . . and the other aspect of that was that, since imagers were known to be the only means by which Antiagon Fire could be created . . . if anything happened to Lorien and his family . . . What was the best defense against Antiagon Fire? Imager shields, of course, or sand or earth could smother it. Water was worse than useless.

Each piece by itself made sense, but together? *What are you missing?*

He considered other possibilities, but could come up with nothing. Finally, he turned to other matters. Although he continued to deal with those over the next two glasses, Alastar was still turning over ways to deal with the possibilities involved in an attack by the army when Akoryt arrived in his study just before first glass.

Once the tired-looking Maitre D'Structure had seated himself, Alastar asked, "What news do you have?"

Akoryt offered a sour smile. "The regiment did not leave army headquarters until after ninth glass this morning. They did not take the Boulevard D'Ouest to the West River Road. Instead, they are moving west toward the road bordering Poignard Hill. I'd guess they'll take that south until it reaches the West River Road, and then take the south river road—that's what it becomes—to Caluse and on from there on to Nordeau. The old road is still the best one all the way to Villerive."

Alastar nodded, although he definitely had his doubts. "Just keep watching them. Have any of your scouts seen any sign of other army companies?"

"Not so far, sir."

"Could you find a trustworthy but older second to

ride over to the Anomen D'Rex to see what may be happening there? That's where the memorial services for Rex Ryen will be held tomorrow. I'd like to know if there are any army troopers near there."

"I can manage that, sir."

"Thank you."

Once Akoryt left, Alastar decided to walk to the dining hall . . . or what would become the new dining hall. When he neared the construction/imaging site, he raised a concealment, since he wanted to see the progress without being seen himself. He had to say that he was pleasantly surprised. Although the plans had shown the foundation, he hadn't expected exactly what he saw. On the east side, the foundation wall was already complete, a long line of apparently seamless gray stone. Half the north foundation wall had been imaged into place, and stone footings outlined the footprint of the remainder of the building. Since the cellar level would be stone-floored, there would be considerable dry storage space, and there would be several meeting rooms on the main level, in addition to a wide hallway, the dining hall proper, and the kitchens and main-level food and dish pantries.

With a nod, Alastar turned and made his way back to the residence . . . and his small study.

He had only been there for a quint or so when Dareyn appeared at the door, holding up an envelope. "There's another message from the Chateau D'Rex, sir."

"And the courier didn't stay for a reply, I take it?" Alastar rose, walked to the doorway, and took the envelope.

"No, sir."

"He's canceling the afternoon meeting, then."

"Again, sir?"

"We'll see." Alastar used his knife to slit open the envelope, then extracted the letter, half-turning and tossing the envelope onto the desk as he began to read.

Maitre Alastar—

With all the preparations for the memorial service and a number of unforeseen events, I have not been able to complete the work on the tariff proposal.

I look forward to seeing you at the memorial service, and at a more formal meeting at the Chateau on Lundi at fourth glass.

The signature and seal were that of Lorien.

Alastar wondered just how many more times Lorien intended to put off meeting. Or was the latest missive just a ruse to keep Alastar from thinking about what else Lorien, or Lorien and Petayn, had in mind?

Should you ride to the chateau and bully your way in?

He shook his head. That would solve nothing. If Lorien was going to make a mess of matters, after all that he'd seen, nothing short of force would change his mind, and using more force against the rex with no obvious reason would endanger the Collegium with no real benefit. *Except that Lorien's willfulness—or indecisiveness—or whatever else motivates him is likely to endanger us all anyway.*

Two quints later, Dareyn brought in another envelope, this one sealed in tan wax with the seal that Alastar now recognized as that of High Holder Vaun. He suspected he knew the general contents of it as well, but opened it and began to read.

Maitre Alastar—

When you met with the High Council this past Mardi, you suggested that a new tariff proclamation would be forthcoming from Rex Lorien in the near future. The implication was that it would be a matter of days. Several days have passed, and we have heard nothing from either you or the rex.

Might we inquire as to when we will see such a pro-

posal, that is, if the rex has informed you of what he plans and when he will make the announcement?

With kindest regards,

The signature and seal were those of Vaun, as the acting head of the High Council.

An inquiry so soon after his meeting with the four High Holders suggested that several if not all of them were more than a little concerned.

Should you answer? How? Alastar shrugged, then sat down and began to compose a reply. Almost a glass later, and after several discarded versions, he read over what he had written a last time before he signed and sealed it.

Councilor Vaun—

I last met with Rex Lorien on the matter of the tariff proclamation and its contents on Meredi afternoon. At that time, he expressed some dissatisfaction with the draft provided by Minister Salucar and with my suggestions for revising that draft. He did not express reservations over the tariff level previously discussed, but about the wording of the document. He subsequently canceled further meetings this week, saying that he did not wish to deal with the matter until after the memorial services for his sire on Samedi. He has set our next meeting for Lundi afternoon.

Under the circumstances, I trust you can understand why I have been reluctant to press him until after the services have been conducted, but I am confident that matters will be resolved shortly.

How they'll be resolved is another matter.

After signing and sealing the reply, he gave it to Dareyn to arrange for an imager courier to take it to the Chateau D'Council.

Then, at a little after third glass, with no word from

Akoryt, not that Alastar expected any until much later, he decided to go and see how Alyna and her team of imagers had done in creating the foundations for the new dining hall, since from what he could make out from the front porch, they appeared to have finished for the day.

He was a good hundred yards away when he saw Alyna walking toward him. They met near the south end of the green on the edge of which the imager cottages were situated, not all that far from the one she shared with Tiranya.

"You didn't come by earlier," she said with a smile.

"I did. I used a concealment. I didn't want to distract anyone. That was when you'd finished the east foundation wall and half of the north wall. How did it go?"

"The foundation is complete. We're all tired. It would have been easier and more accurate, if I had better surveying equipment. We had to redo some parts of the footings several times."

"I'm sorry . . ." Alastar didn't know what else to say. He hadn't even thought about surveying equipment.

"You don't have to be sorry. I never even mentioned it to you. It just became obvious . . . well, more obvious, today."

"Would better equipment help for the administration building?"

"It would help, but it's not necessary. You don't need to worry about telescope diopters and things like that. Not now."

Alastar still didn't even know what a telescope diopter was. "We'll talk about that later." He paused. "Where is your equipment?"

"Warryk took it back to the cottage while I was inspecting the last wall. Now," she said with a wan smile. "If you don't mind, dear Maitre . . ."

Belatedly, Alastar realized that she was pale and that

there was a tiredness in her eyes and frame. "You need some food and rest. I can get something—"

"Tiranya sent word she has an early supper ready. Then I'm going to collapse into bed."

"I'll see you in the morning at the seniors' meeting. No work on the dining hall tomorrow. None."

"I already let them all know that." She reached out and touched his hand with hers.

Even in that brief instant, Alastar could feel how cold her hand was, far colder than it should have been, given that she was wearing a heavy gray jacket over her grays. "You need food and to get warm. I'll walk with you."

"It's not that far," she protested.

"Even so . . ." He took her arm.

He would have enjoyed the fraction of a quint it took to get to her cottage far more if he hadn't been worrying that she had overextended herself in imaging.

Tiranya opened the door even before they reached the steps. "Good. I'm glad you brought her back, Maitre. Warryk said she'd overdone things. Again."

"I'm fine," Alyna said indignantly.

"You'll be better after you eat and rest," replied Alastar, releasing her arm. "I'll see you in the morning."

"Until then." Alyna smiled, but the expression faded as she turned to enter the cottage.

From the doorway, Tiranya mouthed, "Thank you."

Alastar smiled and nodded in return.

The walk back to the Maitre's residence was longer than the walk out had been . . . and colder, colder than it should have been, even with the light north wind.

Akoryt didn't arrive at the Maitre's residence until a quint before sixth glass. He appeared even more tired and worn as he dropped into one of the chairs before Alastar's desk. He said nothing for a moment. "There haven't been any army troopers near the Anomen D'Rex today, except for the pair stationed at the main doors . . .

unless the half score of workmen were troopers in workmen's clothes."

"What were they doing?"

"Wyckal said that they were mostly cleaning and sweeping the square. A small wagon was there when he arrived to watch, but one of the workmen drove it off, then came back to pick up the workers at fourth glass."

"That could mean anything."

"It could." Akoryt paused, then added, "The regiment that departed from headquarters this morning has stopped at Lake Shaelyt."

"Lake Shaelyt?" Alastar hadn't even known there was a lake by that name. "The same name as the maitre?"

Akoryt nodded. "He was likely named after the lake. It was named after an officer who died in the Wars of Consolidation. That's what I heard. It's about five milles south of the Chateau D'Rex, maybe a little less."

"Just five milles? In a day?"

"They did leave late, and it's almost ten milles from headquarters."

"But only about four, perhaps less, from Imagisle. Have someone watch them all the time. If they turn and head back north, either along the West River Road or the . . . Poignard Hill road, we'll need to know immediately."

"I thought so. I've already arranged for that."

"Excellent." Alastar shook his head. "I can't believe Petayn would do something like this."

"What if it's something different, sir?"

"I can't think of what that might be . . . and that worries me." *And it means you're missing something. But what?* "Do you have any thoughts on that?"

"Could the sea marshal be behind all this?"

"Anything's possible, but Wilkorn? Under what the rex proposed, he'd be getting a bigger navy, if not one so large as he'd prefer, nor as quickly as he'd like. Even so, I can't see him doing something like this . . . or Petayn listening to him. As for the other officers, I don't even know any of the other commanders."

"Wasn't Desyrk's brother a commander?"

"That's right. Demykalon promoted him to commander, but that would make him the most junior commander in any of the regiments. Wilkorn and several others would outrank him. That's if he survived, and we don't know that he did. Demykalon didn't seem to know, and Petayn never mentioned him. But then, there's no reason that he would," mused Alastar. *And a number he might not.*

"Will Marshal Petayn be at the memorial service, sir?"

"He's supposed to be there, standing almost beside me."

"Then . . . whatever might happen won't be then, but . . ."

"You'd start to worry as soon as the service ends and the rex is on his way back to the Chateau D'Rex?"

"Yes, sir."

"So would I." Alastar corrected himself. "So will I." After a moment, he added, "You need to go get something to eat. Try to get some sleep tonight. One way or another, tomorrow's likely to be a very long day." He stood.

So did Akoryt. "Yes, sir. Seventh glass tomorrow?"

"Seventh glass," affirmed Alastar.

After Akoryt left, Alastar turned toward the window, looking out into the deep twilight that was almost night. He couldn't help but worry about Alyna, although he felt she was in good hands with Tiranya, but . . .

She tries to do too much. He laughed softly, sardonically. *And you don't?*

38

Obsolym was the last one to arrive for the senior maitres' meeting on Samedi morning, and he stepped into the Maitre's study a good half a quint before seventh glass, then took the last seat left in the study, one of those Dareyn had brought in earlier.

"Now that we're all here," began Alastar, "I'd like to brief you on what we know. First, there won't be any imaging work done on the dining hall today. Second, the army has conducted some rather . . . unusual maneuvers. The marshal reported to the rex that troopers left headquarters on Jeudi, but Akoryt and his thirds could find no trace of them. A regiment left headquarters yesterday and traveled by the Poignard Hill road south to the West River Road less than three milles south of here, where they spent the night. The rex has postponed his daily meetings with me until, for now, at least, until next Lundi. He also is stalling on issuing a proclamation dealing with tariffs, a delay about which the High Council has expressed some concern."

"Lorien doesn't sound any better than Dafou," suggested Taryn.

"From what I've seen so far," replied Alastar, "he doesn't like to decide difficult things quickly. He also seems partial to the army, and that worries me." *More than a little.*

"You seem to be suggesting that the regiment south of here might be used against the Collegium," offered Obsolym. "Do you really think that's possible?"

"Anything is possible," replied Alastar.

"You aren't suggesting attacking them, are you?" pressed Obsolym.

"That's the last thing we need to do. It's one thing to defend ourselves and the students, it's another to destroy thousands—assuming we could even do that—before anything happens. We've talked about that before."

"Why would they do that after what you did to them before?" Obsolym seemed truly curious.

Wasn't he here when I brought this up before? Alastar thought back, then realized that while he'd thought over the question Obsolym had raised time and time again, he'd never actually discussed it with any of the senior maitres except Akoryt. "We used their own powder against them. What would happen if a regiment, more than two thousand troopers in all, invaded Imagisle all at once? We have fifteen maitres at the moment and a handful of thirds who could defend themselves with shields for a time, and kill a few troopers. Those are odds of over a hundred to one. It's been almost four hundred years since imagers were trained to kill large numbers of troopers, and only a handful of them were successful at that. If the stories are correct, only Quaeryt could dispatch hundreds or thousands. I'm certain Marshal Petayn knows those figures as well, and he might very well feel that the loss of even several thousand troopers might well be worth the cost to break the Collegium."

"He couldn't kill every one of us," said Obsolym.

"Probably not," admitted Alastar, "but even if every maitre escaped . . . then what? The most we could do at that point would be to wreak revenge on those who planned and ordered the attack . . . and that would only weaken Solidar and make imagers truly hated."

"You sound like we're doomed," snapped Obsolym.

Alastar shook his head. "We're not. But what our survival will require—if there is such an attack—is that every single trooper who sets foot on Imagisle, or tries to, is immediately killed, whether with an imaged iron dart or stones imaged into his chest, or anything else. If there is such an attack, there can be absolutely no mercy—unless a trooper is so badly wounded he can't move and it would be a waste of effort to kill him. We need to show that any such attack will be suicidal for any attacker." His voice was cold as he finished.

"No mercy?" Not totally surprisingly, that was Cyran.

"When we've already been bombarded by cannon, with no thought about children and students?" countered Alastar. "I'm talking about killing only troopers who are attacking us. They're willing to kill anyone."

"What about everyone else?" asked Akoryt.

"If there is an attack and any troopers actually reach Imagisle, put all the students who aren't able to defend themselves in here, with enough thirds who can hold shields over windows and doors."

"When do you think an attack might come, if it does?" asked Alyna.

"Sometime immediately after first glass, about the time that there's likely to be an attack on the Anomen D'Rex."

"Marshal Petayn wouldn't do that . . . would he?" asked Obsolym.

"I would hope not, but something is going to happen, and I'd prefer that the Collegium be prepared for the worst," replied Alastar. "If I'm wrong, then we do nothing, and no one off Imagisle is the wiser. If I'm right, and we're not prepared, there will be all too many dead junior imagers and students. I have no intention of having the Collegium act first. If Petayn does act, however, we need to strike back hard enough and fiercely enough that no one will attempt another attack on the Collegium. Ever."

"He couldn't be that unwise . . ." Obsolym shook his head.

"What exactly has the Collegium done in centuries to make him think otherwise?"

The question hung in the air for long moments.

"That no one has an answer to the Maitre's question is reply enough," said Akoryt dryly.

"Given that," said Alastar, "if there is an attack, the troopers will arrive either over the Bridge of Desires or by barge or boat. Cyran, don't be afraid to destroy the middle span of the bridge again. That will require them to use boats or attempt to bridge the gap. Either way, that will spread them out so that they don't arrive in a mass . . ."

For the next glass, Alastar and the senior maitres discussed the ways to defend Imagisle. Then he dismissed them to make their preparations, preparations he hoped would not be necessary and feared would be.

At two quints past ninth glass, Akoryt returned to the study and took a seat opposite Alastar. "From what the thirds report, there are four mounted companies forming up at headquarters. They're all in dress uniforms, and each company has a fancy wagon with four horses. The horses are hitched with parade harnesses."

"Four horses?" asked Alastar. *And almost a full battalion. For a memorial service?*

"Yes, sir."

"Are the wagons the kind that troopers sit on?"

"The scouts say that they're more like parade wagons, fancy high-sided and enclosed. With lots of brasswork."

"And enough space inside to conceal anything . . . except cannon. They couldn't take the weight."

"Oh, there's one coach, too."

"You're sure about that?"

"That's what they say."

Alastar frowned. That suggested that Petayn—or some senior officer—intended to be there. *To command the operation in person?* "What else?"

"They're all carrying both rifles and sabres."

Rifles for a ceremonial duty? "You're sure about the rifles?"

"Yes, sir."

Alastar and Akoryt went over the details of what the thirds had seen for more than a quint, but Alastar learned little more than Akoryt had reported in the first few moments, and Akoryt, already looking tired, once more departed.

At two quints before noon, Alastar set out for the stables, carrying two water bottles filled with dark lager. Once there, he had a few more words with Cyran, then mounted up. Riding with him over the Bridge of Desires on the way to the Anomen D'Rex were Taryn, Shaelyt, and two thirds and a second—Chervyt, Glaesyn, and Maercyl, just enough to hold their mounts in readiness. Alastar was carrying full shields, as he had been almost every moment since he'd arrived in L'Excelsis.

Once the six reined up in front of the anomen, a good two quints before first glass, Alastar gathered everyone together. "Chervyt, you're in command of your group. I want you three to wait over there in the lane opposite the middle of the east side of the anomen. If anything happens, raise a concealment, hold your shields . . . and wait. Wait," emphasized Alastar. "I need to know that you'll be here. If you go looking for us, we'll never meet up. And if something does happen, and we're not back in half a glass, Chervyt, you and Glaesyn wait. Maercyl, you ride back to the Collegium and see if you can report. If they're in trouble, stay near Imagisle, but don't hazard yourself. Is that clear? All three of you?"

"Yes, sir."

Alastar dismounted, followed by the other two masters, and the three walked toward the main entrance of the anomen.

The chateau guard captain, whose name Alastar could not remember and who wore a dress uniform of green and gold, hurried forward and motioned to the imagers. "Maitre, sir. If you'd come with me and wait by the side door. You're supposed to enter after the marshal and before Rex Lorien and Lady Chelia."

"What about Lady Asarya?"

The captain did not meet Alastar's eyes for a moment, then said, "She has a violent flux. Nothing stays in her stomach. So does Lord Ryentar."

"Oh?"

"I . . . well . . . I heard her retching, sir. She also left word that she wasn't about to make an appearance when she was so ill. Not for a man who had nothing to do with her for twenty years."

Alastar wondered who had conveyed such words, although he could understand the sentiment. "Who might have conveyed . . ."

"Maryssa, her personal maid. We've known each other . . . for years."

That made sense, but Asarya's absence bothered him. So did Ryentar's. *Now . . . if Lorien doesn't appear . . .* Still, he nodded.

The captain cleared his throat, then paused. "Ah . . . this way, sir."

Alastar and the other two turned and followed the captain. Alastar finally remembered the guard captain's name—Fonteau.

Once they reached the side door, Alastar smiled pleasantly and asked, "How are your preparations going, Captain Fonteau?"

Fonteau glanced around and, seeing only the two chateau guards posted by the side door and the imagers, replied, "I didn't expect quite so many . . . mourners so early."

"It's not every day that a rex dies," Alastar pointed out gently.

"If you'll excuse me for a moment, Maitre?"

"Do what you need to do, Captain."

Once Fonteau hurried back toward the main entrance to the anomen, Alastar looked to Shaelyt and Taryn. He said nothing, but raised his eyebrows.

"I like this less and less, sir," murmured Taryn.

"As do I. Keep your shields at all times, especially once we're in the anomen."

Little more than a quint passed while Alastar, Taryn, and Shaelyt stood there, well away from the small side door with the two chateau guards wearing dress uniforms of gold and green.

From where he stood, Alastar surveyed the area, watching as the mounted troopers rode up the street from the south—making a far less impressive approach than they would have, Alastar had to admit, once the Avenue D'Rex Ryen was completed. Behind the first mounted flag-bearers, one with the regial ensign, one with the flag of Solidar, both flanking the trooper bearing the green and black flag of mourning, came a military coach, behind which rode another mourning flag-bearer followed by a company of troopers. The mass of the troopers conveyed a definite majesty and pomp, stretching back almost as far as Alastar could see. Before that long, the coach stopped at the main entrance to the anomen, and three officers stepped out.

The third was definitely Petayn, wearing the full dress uniform of a marshal. Alastar did not recognize either of the other two. Rather than walking along the side of the anomen and joining Alastar, the three continued directly into the anomen. The fact that Petayn and another commander were in fact physically present bothered Alastar . . . more than a little, because it meant he had no idea of exactly what might happen, especially since he couldn't imagine anything violent happening with Petayn present.

Maybe it is all just a coincidence . . . that a regiment is departing and the troopers are here because Lorien wanted more pomp and majesty.

A fraction of a quint later, the guard captain appeared. "Maitre, you and the other masters can enter now. Your space is marked by the brass stands and the gray velvet rope." He gestured toward the side door.

Alastar let Shaelyt precede him, and Taryn follow as they stepped through the door and then into a side hall where they turned left and made their way toward the archway opening into the nave just short of the sacristy.

When the guard captain had mentioned the rope stands, Alastar had imagined slender brass posts with wide circular bases. The supposed stands were more like cylinders a good hand in diameter and slightly taller than waist high. There were four, two against the anomen wall, and two set out slightly more than two yards. The space reserved for Alastar as Maitre was the foremost on the left side, as Lorien had earlier indicated. Beside his space was another space, set off with the same heavy stands, connected by green velvet rope, in which stood Petayn, a commander Alastar had never seen before, and a captain he also did not know.

Across the anomen from them was a larger—and still empty—space enclosed by stands linked by a green and gold rope. Another set of stands, linked by a black rope, ran from the edge of the army's "enclosure" on the side farthest from the sacristy across the nave to the back edge of the regial enclosure. The space behind the black rope was largely filled all the way to the back of the anomen.

For a moment, given Ryen's definite lack of popularity, Alastar wondered why there were so many people there—until he recalled that coins would be scattered and thrown after the service was concluded, and those coins would not be just coppers, but also included some golds and quite a few silvers. Then, there were also the merchants and crafters who serviced the Chateau D'Rex, who likely did not ever wish to let it be known that they had not been present.

As he entered the area roped off in gray, Alastar turned to Petayn. "Good afternoon, Marshal. Your troopers offer an imposing presence."

"I would hope so, Maitre. Any rex deserves that last gesture of respect." Petayn's smile was pleasant, but little more, and his voice barely cordial.

Gesture of respect? "It's too bad that it's come to gestures, but that's often what happens when one insists on having it all his way . . . or not at all."

"You do seem to understand that, Maitre." Petayn half-turned, indicating he preferred to not continue the conversation.

Alastar did not press, but studied the sacristy. As in all anomens, it was bare except for the sole pulpit, and there were no decorations on the walls. Presumably there were some benches along the side walls of the nave for the elderly and infirm, but the numbers of those in the nave kept Alastar from seeing whether that was so.

The brass rope stands bothered Alastar. While he understood the necessity of reserving some places, they seemed unduly clunky. *But they have to be heavy to anchor the velvet ropes.*

He reached out and lifted the rope separating him from the open space that stretched across the nave to the empty rope-enclosed area where Lorien and Chelia were supposed to stand. *If they even show up.* Yet Alastar couldn't imagine that the rex wouldn't appear, not when he had been so directly involved in planning the service. He lifted the rope again. It wasn't that heavy.

Then he heard a horn fanfare. It took him only an instant to realize that it announced Lorien's arrival. A fraction of a quint later, Lorien and Chelia emerged from the side hall opposite where Alastar stood, at the front of the nave, accompanied by a pair of chateau guards in the dress uniforms. Lorien wore a dark green tunic and trousers trimmed in black, as did Chelia, although the severity of the colors tended to wash her out. *Or is that because she's also been fighting a flux?* Looking at Chelia across the anomen, Alastar once more had the feeling that she reminded him of someone else besides Bettaur, but who it was he still couldn't place.

Just as the bell of the anomen chimed the first glass, Chorister Dumont stepped out onto the dais and positioned himself in the middle. Although Alastar had never seen or met the chorister, a tall and slender man with shimmering black hair, Lorien had informed him who would be conducting the service. Dumont's voice was deep and resonant as he offered the invocation. "We are gathered here together this afternoon in the spirit of the Nameless, in affirmation of the quest for goodness and mercy in all that we do, and in celebration of the life of Ryen D'Rex, and in memory of his service to the land of Solidar."

The opening hymn was traditional—"The Glory of the Nameless." Alastar did not sing, but merely mouthed the words, even as he continued to study the anomen, as discreetly as he could. Neither Shaelyt nor Taryn sang all that loudly, either, he noticed. Then came the confession.

"We do not name You, for naming is presumptuous . . ." As Dumont's voice carried to every corner of the anomen, Alastar barely murmured the words, still trying to catch sight of anything that might give him a clue to what might happen. He *knew* something would, but how could Petayn possibly control anything powerful enough to deal with Lorien and Alastar and still survive?

". . . celebration of You who cannot be named or known, only respected and worshipped," concluded Dumont.

"In peace and harmony," responded the audience. Alastar didn't think of most of them as mourners or worshippers.

Next came the charge from Dumont. "Life is a gift from the Nameless, for from the glory of the Nameless do we come . . ." Another hymn followed, one not traditional, but used at Lorien's insistence—"In Vain A Crown of Gold."

"All words of praise will die as spoken
As night precedes the dawn unwoken . . .
To claim in vain a crown of gold,
Belies the truth the Nameless told . . ."

Only a fraction of the congregation, if it could be termed such, Alastar thought wryly, knew the words, much less the melody, and he still wondered why Lorien had insisted on the song. While it was true that Ryen had never paraded his riches, he had certainly exercised his power and been more than a little angered—to say the least—when he had been thwarted.

Then Dumont announced, "Now we will hear from Rex Lorien . . ."

Alastar felt/sensed something, almost like imager shields pressing on him.

The instant the pressure ended, yellow-green flames exploded around the army officers and metal fragments or shrapnel impacted his shields . . .

Metal? The only metal inside the anomen was that in the heavy brass rope stands!

"Shields! Follow me . . ." Even before he uttered the words, Alastar raised a second set of shields around Lorien and Chelia, barely instants before Alastar felt the quick and light pressure and the regial couple was also surrounded by the yellow-green flames.

By that time, Alastar was already halfway across the nave, but even with his shields, he was rocked back by the force of the explosion, and then pushed forward by explosions behind him, most like from those brass rope holders. As he caught his balance, Alastar glanced back toward the east side of the nave . . . and swallowed hard. Already three officers were half-blackened masses of yellow-green flames, and the would-be mourners were screaming, yelling, and scrambling toward the main doors at the north end of the anomen.

When he neared Lorien and Chelia, both unable to move much because of the shield around them, Alastar melded his personal shields with the one he'd thrown around them. "We need to get you two out of here safely." With that, he raised a larger concealment, just large enough so that Taryn and Shaelyt could see him and the regial couple, and then said, "Stay right beside me."

Lorien looked blankly at Alastar, who immediately took the rex's arm. "This way! Now!" Keeping a concealment around a clearly stunned Lorien and Chelia, who appeared far more angry than dazed, Alastar led the group into the west hall off the nave, then out through the side door, and around the south end of the anomen.

Behind them the screaming seemed to fade slightly as the five crossed the modest street that would have been a grander avenue had the imagers finished the work on the Avenue D'Rex Ryen.

"Chervyt!" snapped Alastar as he neared the narrow lane where the three other imagers were supposed to be.

"Over here, sir!" The concealment around the more junior imagers vanished.

"Glaesyn, you and Maercyl need to double up so that the rex and his lady can share a mount." Alastar turned toward the rex, not quite so dazed-looking as he had been initially. "Lorien, you and your lady will have to ride double."

"Share?" Lorien sounded aghast.

"If the past quint hasn't convinced you that you need every imager I have with me, what will?" Alastar belatedly expanded the concealment so the entire group was within its scope.

"Our coach is just over there."

"So is Desyrk, the renegade imager who almost succeeded in getting you killed, and so is a battalion of troopers whose loyalties are very much in doubt at this moment."

"Dear . . ." murmured Chelia, so softly that Alastar could not hear the remainder of what she said.

"I suppose that's for the best," conceded the irritated rex. "Where are you taking us?"

"Back to Imagisle."

"Imagisle?" demanded Lorien.

"You and Lady Chelia were targeted with explosives and Antiagon Fire. So were we, and so was Marshal Petayn. Petayn and the other commander are dead. So is the captain who was with them. There are other army companies around. Your guards are certainly loyal to you, but if the army attacks the chateau, they won't stand a chance. The imagers are the only ones likely to be able to protect you." The way matters had developed, Alastar wasn't even sure of that, but it wasn't the moment to suggest that. *Not yet.*

"But . . . my mother, my brother?"

"They weren't the targets. You were. Besides," Alastar said coldly, "if the army intended to attack the chateau, it already has." He wasn't about to offer other possibilities.

"But—"

"No 'but's!" snapped Alastar. "I've done what you wanted, and this is the mess you've created. We're doing it my way this time." *And the only way I can be even halfway certain of protecting Imagisle and you is to keep you close.* Except he wasn't about to utter those words.

Lorien started to open his mouth, when Chelia actually reached out and covered it, saying, "Don't make things worse. Mount up. Or should I mount first?"

As Alastar looked at her, he almost froze. *The Namer and sowshit!* Now he knew what had been nagging at him. *No wonder . . .* Alastar recalled what Lady Asarya had said . . . words that had a meaning different from the way Alastar had taken them . . . *What's important is that my son has a better future, thanks to certain imagers from the Collegium.* So many things made so much more sense. "Mount up, now." Those were the only words he could manage for a moment. Shaking his head, he turned toward Shaelyt. "You lead the way. I'm carrying a concealment, but you may have to use shields to push people or riders aside."

"Yes, sir."

"We'll take the route that the avenue will take, as close as possible. That will be faster than going north to the Boulevard D'Ouest."

No one said a thing.

Alastar looked to Lorien. "You and your lady ride beside me."

Lorien glared at Alastar, but nodded, more than a little reluctantly.

"Head out, Shaelyt. South for a block before we move back to the avenue route."

"Yes, sir."

After urging the gelding forward, Alastar took out one of the water bottles and drank the dark lager, slowly, while they rode along the street to the east of the Anomen D'Rex, which held people, wagons, and riders, if not so many that the imagers had much difficulty in avoiding them. While he rode, Alastar continued to take small swallows of the lager and thought over what had happened, recalling that he had felt the imaging pressure in the anomen before each of the explosions. From his experience, that meant whoever had been imaging the Antiagon Fire into exploding had to have been very close. *But why?* He almost shook his head. Because Desyrk didn't see that well from a distance. *Can you use that to find him?* He'd just have to see. His lips quirked at the inadvertent pun.

As they neared the river Alastar could hear the sound of cannon, not the continuous booming of an entire battery, but distinct reports in close but not rapid succession. He took a last swallow of lager, corked the water bottle, and slipped it back into one of his saddlebags, looking at Lorien and Chelia. Neither returned his glance.

Shaelyt turned in the saddle. "Sir?"

"I hear. We'll have to see what we can do."

"What is it?" demanded Lorien, lifting his head.

"Cannon. The army is apparently attacking Imagisle again."

"I ordered them to avoid Imagisle," Lorien declared.

"I'm certain you did," Alastar said, although he wasn't all that sure he believed his own words. "Someone didn't follow those orders, it appears."

Within half a quint, Alastar had reached a point on the modest street that led to the Bridge of Desires from where he could see that the middle section of the Bridge of Desires was missing, cleanly severed, suggesting that Cyran, Alyna, or one of the senior maitres had removed it. He could also make out troopers crouched behind hastily thrown up earthworks beside the causeway from the West River Road to the bridge proper. Every so often one of them would raise his head enough to fire a rifle toward Imagisle, presumably toward an imager.

For several moments, Alastar wondered why the troopers were firing so infrequently, until he watched one of them attempt to fire, then convulse and slump. He couldn't see the exact cause, but given that little more than the rifle barrel and the man's head had appeared above the earthworks, it was likely that the trooper had been killed by a small iron dart or the equivalent. A boat bobbed in the waters of the River Aluse, slowly moving downstream with the current, with two bodies slumped in the middle of the craft.

While the army troopers were being held at bay, the

cannon continued to fire, each shell wreaking some sort of destruction on the Collegium. After riding another hundred yards, Alastar reined up some yards back of the small square created by where the West River Road, the street he had followed, and the approach road to the bridge causeway all converged. Concealment or no concealment, he didn't want to get too close to the troopers until he could get a better idea of what had happened and how he could see what he, Taryn, and Shaelyt could do.

This time, the army cannon, four of them, were positioned on the small hill behind the mill, the same hill that Alastar had noted after the first attack. The smoke that surrounded them indicated that they had been firing for some time. Alastar's lips quirked. Desyrk hadn't put the cannon there the first time because he couldn't have sighted or directed them. He'd used the bridge as a guide. *That means, if Desyrk has returned here, he won't be with the cannon. Of course, he could be anywhere else.*

Still, Alastar had the feeling that, if Desyrk didn't happen to be near Imagisle, he would be before long. He turned in the saddle and motioned Taryn forward.

Before the Maitre D'Structure could move forward, Lorien spoke. "There are hundreds of troopers there. How could this happen?"

"A regiment or more," returned Alastar. "We'll worry about how it happened after we put an end to it." *If we can . . . somehow.* He looked to Taryn, who had eased his mount around Lorien and Chelia. "I'd like you to take out the cannon. Hot iron needles, the way we did before. Do you think you can do that?"

Taryn looked at Alastar. "Yes, sir . . . provided you don't send Shaelyt off to do something else."

Alastar couldn't help but smile, if briefly. He knew from where that had come. "I'll keep him close at all times."

Taryn nodded. "Be careful, sir." Then he eased his mount forward. After a few steps, both the maitre and his mount vanished.

"He disappeared," said Lorien. "Just disappeared."

"It's a concealment. That's why it's been so hard to find our renegade imager. He's also good with concealments."

"That's why . . ." Lorien shut his mouth abruptly.

Unhappily, Alastar suspected he knew the general tenor of what the rex might have said, but he only replied, "Exactly."

Lorien couldn't conceal a certain surprise.

Alastar motioned for Glaesyn and Chervyt to move forward. "You two need to maintain a concealment and shields here. Can you handle that?"

"Yes, sir," Chervyt immediately replied.

Alastar looked at Lorien, then Chelia. "If you try to leave, it could mean your life. The officers leading these regiments"—he gestured toward the bridge—"are the ones behind the attempted assassination at the anomen. I'd strongly advise against leaving or doing anything foolish."

"We'll stay," declared Chelia, looking to Lorien and adding, "Won't we?"

"We'll stay." Lorien's voice was sullenly resigned.

"Shaelyt, we need to move forward."

The younger maitre nodded and urged his mount forward, and the two moved out across the western end of the small square toward the Bridge of Desires. Alastar kept studying the troopers and the bridge. There was suddenly something different there—a plank span having appeared to connect the end spans. Almost immediately, the timber span dropped into the river, as if cut loose at both ends.

Alyna! She was the only imager with that precise a control, especially at a distance. *At a distance* . . . Abruptly, what should have been obvious struck Alastar—Desyrk had to be somewhere close, most likely somewhere almost directly in front of Alastar and Shaelyt.

"Rein up," murmured Alastar, waiting only a moment until Shaelyt did before he imaged a blanket of dust over the troopers behind the earthworks on the south side of the causeway. For just an instant the dust formed a bubble, and in that instant, Alastar imaged an iron dart at it, one traveling as fast as a rifle bullet. Shards of metal sprayed everywhere, a few even slamming back into Alastar's shields, but Desyrk's shields held.

Before Desyrk could retaliate with something similar, Alastar clamped a second set of shields around Desyrk's shields, trying to collapse them. In the meantime, the cannon continued to fire, and troopers popped up and down, aiming at Imagisle.

No matter how hard he tried, though, Alastar could not break Desyrk's shields, even though he was less than fifty yards from the renegade imager. He could feel beads of sweat forming on his forehead.

Another round of cannon fire echoed from the south.

Alastar had to do something . . . something. But what? *How can you even hurt him if you can't break his shields?*

Suddenly . . . he *knew.* "Shaelyt, you're going to have to shield us both. Ready?"

"Yes, sir."

"Now!" Alastar dropped his own shields, both sets, and concentrated on imaging out a huge chunk of ground a good twenty yards on each side of where he knew Desyrk's shields were. Imaging it out and directly above where it had been—a good fifteen yards higher. A dark mass appeared low in the air less than fifty yards from the two imagers . . . then plummeted into the chasm that had appeared simultaneously, all happening so quickly that Alastar did not even hear screams.

At that instant, he convulsed, struck by darkness

deeper than night . . . and a chill that turned his bones to ice.

The *Namer's sowshit!* . . .

Alastar's head was splitting . . . and when he opened his eyes, the light burned them. He squinted. He found he was still in the saddle, if partly supported by Shaelyt, who had moved his mount so that the two horses were as close as they could be.

"I'm all right . . ." managed Alastar, slowly straightening up. *You think.* "Did I get him?"

"Yes, sir . . . ah . . . and a little bit more."

Alastar's head was slowly spinning, enough that he couldn't make out more than blurred images around him. At least, that was the way it felt. "The cannon?"

"They're gone . . ."

Alastar reached back gingerly for one of the water bottles, but it slipped from his hand, dropped to the pavement, and shattered. "You'd better get the other one. I'm . . . shaky."

Without a word Shaelyt extracted the other water bottle, uncorked it, and handed it to Alastar, who took it in both hands before slowly drinking. He lowered it slightly and peered out toward the river. Everything looked white . . . and his breath was a white fog. The air was bitter cold, but then for a moment, a gust of warmer air washed over him, warmer only by comparison. "What happened?"

"You . . . you imaged a chunk out of the riverbank and then dropped it on Desyrk and all the troopers around him. The river flowed into the hole—"

"What about—" Alastar broke off what he was about to ask. There wasn't really a river wall on the west side of the Aluse, only on the east side and, of course, all the way around Imagisle.

"The river covered everything. Then there was a big bubble that sort of popped, and more water flooded in, except the air was so cold it burned, and everything for almost a quarter mille on each side froze. It was cold enough around us, but there . . ." Shaelyt shook his head. "It froze the troopers, too. Then Taryn blew up the cannon."

"How is he?"

"He's with the rex and the thirds."

Alastar took another long swallow of the watered dark lager. The spinning feeling in his head had begun to diminish. "How long before I recovered?"

"Less than a quint, sir."

"Thank you. What about the other troopers?"

"Ah . . . sir . . . between you and Taryn . . . and the imagers on the isle, there weren't very many left."

"You mean that the ones who survived tried to flee and they got picked off?"

"Not all of them. Maybe half of them. Fifty or sixty escaped. That's a guess."

Out of over two thousand. Alastar looked toward the Bridge of Desires. Outside of the missing middle span, it appeared fine. The only problem was that now that ice covered what was likely a muddy marsh, if not worse, between the end of the square that was also the West River Road and the causeway leading to the bridge.

Even as Alastar watched, the white ice in front of him began to crack and shift. He took another swallow of the watered lager and slowly turned in the saddle. Some twenty yards behind him were Taryn, the three junior imagers, and Lorien and Chelia. He looked back toward the river and the bridge.

More of the ice was cracking.

"We'll have to rebuild a bridge somewhere, or the causeway here, even to get back to Imagisle."

"I think they've already started, sir," said Shaelyt, pointing to the Bridge of Desires, where the middle span had already been replaced.

"Then we'll wait for them to come to us." That was fine with Alastar. He couldn't have imaged a soiled copper.

"What about the rex and his lady?"

"They can wait, too. They'll be safer on Imagisle for now. At least, until we can sort out what happened at the Chateau D'Rex and with the army." Alastar took another swallow of lager. Much as he hated to admit it, there definitely were times to wait.

39

More than three glasses passed before Alyna, Cyran, and the imagers on Imagisle were able to image away mud and water and not only rebuild the causeway, but create a solid stone foundation beneath it. At that point Alastar was more than tired of avoiding answering Lorien's questions, partly because he had no answers to many of them and partly because he didn't want to reply to some of those for which he thought he might have answers. One answer he did have was who had been in command of the regiment, verified to be Chesyrk, who had clearly not died earlier, and whose body had been found frozen solid just south of the crater created by Alastar's imaging. Two captive troopers had also claimed that Chesyrk had led the attack.

Once the bridge and causeway were verified to be solid, Maercyl led the way, with Alastar and Lorien and Chelia riding side by side over the span and onto Imagisle.

There were craters in the ground here and there, and one in the shoulder of the road. When they neared the Maitre's house, he could see more craters, but no apparent damage, not even to the shutters of glass. Farther south, however, a number of the cottages had suffered some damage, as well as the infirmary, and he could see a haze of smoke from where the stables were. *Or used to be.* He could only hope that too many people had not been wounded or killed. The anomen looked to be untouched.

Alastar did not stop until they reached the Maitre's

dwelling. When he reined up, he turned to Lorien. "You and your lady will share the guest quarters on the second level. You will be quite safe there. In perhaps a glass, we will have dinner." He looked to Dareyn, who stood on the steps to the front porch, with Alyna and Akoryt waiting on the porch slightly to the side. "Please escort the rex and his lady to the larger guest quarters."

"Yes, sir." Dareyn waited until the pair had dismounted. "This way, Your Graces."

Alastar dismounted after the regial pair. His legs were a trace shaky, but he managed not to stagger when his boots hit the stone pavement. He looked up to Alyna. "I'm very glad to see you." He would have liked to say more, but not with so many people around.

"Are you all right?"

"I am now, so long as I don't do much imaging for a while." Alastar took the steps and stood beside her.

She looked to Taryn and then to Shaelyt.

"He seems to be, maitre," answered Shaelyt.

"Shaelyt kept me from falling off my horse," Alastar admitted.

"What about Desyrk? Do you know?" asked Akoryt.

"Chesyrk was in command of the regiment, and Desyrk was with him. They're both dead. Let's go into the study, where I can sit down, and I'll tell you all about it. There's a lot to tell. Taryn, Shaelyt, you need to come, too." He offered a plaintive smile to Alyna. "And maybe we all could have a lager or two?"

She shook her head. "I'm certain that no one will deny the Maitre his wish, even if it isn't his last." Her smile was forced, and almost under her breath, she added, "Thank the Nameless."

After everyone was settled in some fashion in the study, Alastar took several swallows from the beaker of dark lager that Jienna brought in on a tray. While she was serving the others, he belatedly wondered if he shouldn't have suggested the dining room. Once Jienna left the study, he began, "I should have realized that the clunky brass rope holders in the anomen were big for a reason." He paused as he could see the puzzlement on several faces. "I'll explain . . ." And he did, telling almost everything from the time he, Taryn, and Shaelyt entered the anomen until they rode back across the re-imaged Bridge of Desires. "Now, Taryn, if you would tell about how you took out the cannon."

Taryn flushed slightly. "It really wasn't that difficult. I just used a concealment to get close enough. I reined up behind one of the mill walls and then kept imaging red-hot iron darts until things started exploding. I waited until there was nothing else to explode. There weren't any troopers to stop me, or not many after that, and they couldn't see me anyway. Then I rode back and helped the thirds make sure that the rex and his lady stayed safe. When you all finished repairing the bridge and the causeway, we rode over it."

"I'm certain it wasn't that easy or uneventful," said Alastar.

"Ahhh . . ." ventured Dareyn from the door. "I didn't want to interrupt, but Maitre Khaelis has been waiting to deliver a message."

"Besides," added Khaelis as he moved toward Alastar, "I wanted to hear what happened. We only saw what happened near the bridge." He handed the envelope to the Maitre. "An army trooper delivered this. He rode up under both a parley ensign and a white flag of surrender. He was shaking in his boots by the time he reached the bridge. He said that it's from Acting Marshal Wilkorn to whoever's in charge. He's waiting outside for a reply. Maitre Cyran didn't give him much choice."

"Good thought by Cyran. That way we don't have to send one of our imagers out there." Alastar opened the envelope, sealed in green wax, but with no imprint, and began to read aloud.

"Maitre Alastar—

"I trust and hope you will be the one reading this. If not, I offer condolences to your successor. You are doubtless aware of the explosions of Antiagon Fire at the anomen. Marshal Petayn, Commander Sacheur, and Major Allain all perished. There were no remains found of either any imagers, nor of Rex Lorien or Lady Chelia, and I can only hope that all are safe and well and in the custody of the Collegium.

It appears that Commander Chesyrk, aided by his brother Maitre Desyrk, and perhaps others, attempted to remove at a stroke the leadership of the Collegium, the rex and his lady, and Marshal Petayn and Commander Sacheur, the most senior commander remaining at headquarters besides Chesyrk himself, not to mention attempting to also remove me and Vice-Marshal Vallaun. From reports received by the few survivors, it appears unlikely that either of the brothers was successful in taking Imagisle. The Chateau D'Rex is undamaged and was never occupied by army forces.

I would have attempted to meet with you in person, but at the moment, I am recovering from the effects of a slightly mistimed explosion. Vice-Marshal Vallaun was not so fortunate, and I find myself as the senior officer in headquarters, and most likely in either the army or navy, if currently restrained in mobility. I can now assure you that the army and navy will follow to the letter and the spirit any plans put forth by the lawful rex of Solidar, be it Rex Lorien, or, if he has not survived, the regent for Rex Charyn . . ."

"Frig!" muttered Alastar.

"What—" began Akoryt.

"Wait," commanded Alastar, "I'll explain in a moment." *If not totally.* He cleared his throat and continued.

> *"All army companies, or their survivors, have been recalled to headquarters and confined to the post, pending an investigation of the circumstances that led to the events at the Anomen D'Rex and the second unprovoked and unwarranted attack on Imagisle and the Collegium . . ."*

"He really doesn't want you angry at him," murmured Alyna.

> *". . . with the possible exception of scattered survivors or any troopers in your custody.*
>
> *I remain at your service and that of the rightful rex of Solidar."*

After a moment, Alastar added, "Wilkorn signed it as the Acting Marshal of the Army."

"He's emphasizing the 'rightful rex' of Solidar a great deal," observed Alyna.

"I did notice that," replied Alastar. "I'll need to write a reply immediately, but before I do, we need to discuss what we do next. I think a number of maitres should accompany me to the Chateau D'Rex tomorrow morning, along with Rex Lorien and Lady Chelia, and put matters to rights."

"What about . . ." began Akoryt, before saying, "Oh . . . if Marshal Wilkorn . . . but how do we know?"

"I can start by talking to the messenger," said Alastar dryly. "Just Alyna with me, if you please. We'll be back shortly."

The two left the study.

Out in the front hall stood a young but broad-shouldered and muscular trooper. He swallowed as

Alastar and Alyna walked toward him, and as Alyna said, "This is Maitre Alastar."

"I will have a reply for you to take back to Marshal Wilkorn very shortly. Did you see him personally?"

"Yes, sir. He insisted on it. He said you would want to know that he had written the letter himself."

"How badly was he wounded?"

"He has some burns and a broken leg and arm, the surgeon said. He was thrown into a wall."

"When did that happen? Do you know?"

"It was sometime before noon at a staff meeting. That's what he—the marshal, I mean—that's what he told me."

Alastar nodded. *Desyrk . . . a concealment and more Antiagon Fire . . . and then a quick ride to the Anomen D'Rex.* "Marshal Wilkorn is the senior marshal and in command?"

"Yes, sir."

"Do you know what happened to the battalion that escorted Marshal Petayn to the Anomen D'Rex?"

"That was Major Allain's battalion, sir. They returned to headquarters. They didn't get there until a glass before I left."

"Do you know if there are other companies or battalions that are not at headquarters?"

"Tenth Battalion was posted around the Chateau D'Rex, but they were returning to headquarters when I left. That's all I know, sir."

"Is there anything else I should know?" Alastar looked hard at the trooper.

"Ah . . . yes, sir. Marshal Wilkorn said to tell you that small gunboats for use against pirates was a very good idea." The trooper looked vaguely puzzled as he delivered the message.

Alastar smiled. "Thank you. It won't be too long before you're on your way." He paused. "You didn't ride the whole way alone, did you?"

"No, sir. My squad is waiting for me on the other side of the river."

"Good."

Alastar nodded, then turned. He and Alyna walked back to the study.

Akoryt and Taryn looked askance at Alastar.

"It appears that the message is accurate, especially given the personal word entrusted to the messenger. Even if there are some matters still undisclosed, we'll need to deal with matters at the chateau tomorrow. Akoryt, Taryn, if you'd convey what happened here to Maitre Cyran. We'll need some guards on the bridge this evening, and some here at the house, just to make certain Rex Lorien is safe and remains here. Tell Maitre Cyran that I'd like to see him here after he's made arrangements with which he's satisfied."

"Yes, sir."

"Shaelyt, would you please convey the same information to the other junior masters?"

"Yes, sir."

Alastar smiled warmly at the Maitre D'Aspect. "And thank you. More than I can convey for being there to support me, both with imaging and your presence, when I desperately needed both."

"Sir . . . I was only . . ."

"Not only. Matters could have gone very badly without you. I know that, and so should you." Alastar cleared his throat. He'd been talking too much. "Now . . . Maitre Alyna and I need to talk over things in order to clear up matters with Rex Lorien and Lady Chelia."

In moments, Alyna and Alastar were alone in the study.

"You did a magnificent job of keeping the troopers at bay," Alastar said. "Did anyone get hurt?"

"Not from the rifles. Only a handful were hurt from the cannon fire. But the cottages and the stables . . . even some of the sheds—there's not that much left. Except for the imagers who could image across the river, Akoryt had everyone up in the north part of the isle. I don't think many of the troopers wanted to expose themselves. Not after what happened to the first ones."

"I imagine you were particularly deadly."

"I did as much damage as I could, as quickly as possible. I didn't want them to get the idea that if they all fired at once they could cause more damage."

Alastar frowned. "Just where were you?"

"On the first span of the bridge, of course. I did use a concealment. I could see better from there, and it took less effort."

He winced.

"Good," she said gently.

Alastar knew exactly what she meant. At least, he hadn't protested vocally. "How long had they been attacking when we arrived?"

"The scouts warned us that the troopers were moving north on the West River Road at about a quint before first glass. The first shells hit just after the bell rang the glass."

"You'd been fighting more than a glass and a half when we arrived, then?"

She nodded.

Alastar looked down at her. "I'm so glad you're all right. I can't tell you . . ." He swallowed.

"You just have, dear Maitre."

He reached out and drew her to him.

After a time, she eased back, if seemingly reluctantly. "You do have a rex upstairs, you know?"

"Should we go up . . . or request their presence down here?"

"Upstairs, I would venture. You've probably ordered him around enough today."

Alastar smiled at the wry tone in her voice. He was about to tell her to lead the way, when he realized she hadn't the faintest idea of the upstairs.

"Then we had best mollify him . . . and explain some things of . . . interest."

The two walked from the study out to where Dareyn waited. There, Alastar said, "Dareyn . . . will you see if Jienna and the cooks can come up with a meal for four before too long? I don't think the rex and his wife have eaten for some time. I know we haven't."

"Yes, sir. I . . . I already did, except I said it might be as few as four or as many as eight."

"Excellent. Then Maitre Cyran can join us if he wishes when he arrives." He turned to Alyna. "This way . . ."

The stairs were wide enough that they walked up side by side. Alastar liked that, very much.

At the door to the guest quarters, he knocked.

"Yes?" answered Chelia.

"Might we enter? It's Maitres Alastar and Alyna."

"You might as well." There was heavy resignation in Lorien's tone of voice.

As Alastar opened the door, Lorien rose from one of the two armchairs in the sitting room that adjoined the small bedchamber. After a moment, so did the blond Chelia.

Since there were only two armchairs in the sitting room and a single settee, and since Alastar intended to be as brief as possible, he didn't bother to sit or to suggest that anyone else should. "I just received a missive from Marshal Wilkorn. He is the sole surviving senior officer in L'Excelsis, and he has gathered all troopers, except for scattered survivors, back to headquarters and pledges complete and unconditional obedience to the lawful rex of Solidar. The Chateau D'Rex appears unharmed, unlike the Anomen D'Rex. Tomorrow morning, you and Chelia will ride with us back to the Chateau D'Rex where we will straighten out certain problems."

Chelia paled. "You can't mean . . ."

Lorien looked puzzled—again.

Alastar understood exactly what Chelia meant . . . and it also confirmed that she either knew or suspected what Alastar did. "No, Charyn is most likely perfectly safe." *For now.* He looked at Lorien. "You are going to write a grant of lands, good lands, perhaps one of your best properties, but one of those farthest from L'Excelsis. You are going to grant them to your brother and to his heirs in perpetuity as a High Holding, with the sole condition that he has been disinherited of any right of succession, for reasons too obvious to be named, and that he is never ever to set foot in L'Excelsis again, nor to approach the city or the Chateau D'Rex on pain of death. We will tell him that, if you do not enforce that, the Collegium will. Further he will depart tomorrow, and your mother, the Lady Asarya, will accompany him."

"I don't understand," said Lorien.

"I believe Lady Chelia can enlighten you." Alastar looked to Chelia. "Or would you prefer that I do?"

"It might be best if you did." Chelia's voice was both sad and wary.

"I will attempt to explain this in a roundabout way. Why did your mother object to the idea of your marrying Khanara and Ryentar's marrying Chelia?"

"She never explained. She just said that it was impossible. She and Father almost came to blows over it."

"High Holder Ryel never pushed Ryentar's marrying Chelia, did he? It was your father's idea, wasn't it?"

"How did you know that?"

"Because it's the only thing that makes sense," said Alastar dryly. "Your mother said it was impossible for a very real reason, something along the lines of incest."

Lorien looked at Chelia, and a horrified expression crossed his face. "You can't . . . it isn't . . ."

"I'm afraid it is," said Alastar. "And that ties in to why your brother and mother were so conveniently ill earlier today."

"I can't believe . . ." Lorien's face stiffened. "Maybe . . . I can at that." He looked to Chelia. "Why didn't you say anything?"

"I didn't know. I only suspected . . . and by the time I did . . . Father was dead, and I wasn't about to ask your mother."

"I suppose not." Lorien's shoulders dropped. "But . . . why . . . were they . . . pretending to be sick."

"I can't prove all of it, but the renegade imager, Desyrk, he had some ties to your mother, after Chelia's father died. Desyrk wanted to destroy the Collegium and make his brother marshal of the armies. Your mother wanted Ryentar to be rex, not you."

"Ryentar always has been her favorite."

"We need to go to the chateau tonight!" declared Chelia.

"I'm sorry, Lady," said Alyna. "That is not possible. Almost every imager is exhausted, and nothing will happen to your son tonight."

"Nor would anything happen for some time," added Alastar. "Ryentar would wish to be loved as a good and successful regent. Otherwise, the Collegium, the marshal, and the High Council would look askance at how he obtained power."

"I don't like it," declared Chelia. "If anything happens . . ."

"I don't like it, either," admitted Alastar, "but Maitre Alyna happens to be correct. I'm afraid saving ourselves, saving you, destroying an army, and keeping Imagisle from being totally destroyed is about all we could accomplish today." He couldn't keep a hint of sarcasm out of his voice.

"He's likely right," offered Lorien.

"I don't have to like it. And I warned you about her . . ."

Alastar wouldn't have wanted to receive the look she gave her husband. In hopes of deflecting some of that, he went on, "By the way, you will also promulgate a tariff proclamation that the Collegium will draft and you will sign, along the lines we discussed earlier. Marshal Wilkorn has agreed to the reductions in the army and the changes we discussed for the navy."

"I don't have much choice, do I?"

"None." Alastar inclined his head. "Dinner will be ready shortly. Until then."

He and Alyna made their way from the sitting room. Alyna closed the door quietly, and neither spoke until they were back in the study.

"How could Ryen not have known?" Alyna frowned. "He must have. That was why they had separate quarters."

"It's also, I suspect, why Smarthyl went to Mont D'Image."

"But . . ." Alyna nodded. "Of course. If Ryen harmed her, he'd still find out, but he was far enough away that it would be difficult for Ryen to remove him . . . and if he did, Fhaen would have known."

"That's also why Fhaen waited so long to send for me. Ryen wasn't stupid. Prone to rage, perhaps, but not stupid. He knew. But he could get back at her by pressing a wedding between Ryentar and Chelia. Ryel—the elder—couldn't object. Not publicly."

"From what Zaeryl said," added Alyna, "he likely would have laughed if all of it had come out. He enjoyed women. Apparently, most of them enjoyed him."

"Including Asarya."

"Given Ryen, can you blame her?"

Alastar shook his head. "She was foolish to dally with Desyrk, though." He frowned. "Were Smarthyl and Desyrk at all close?"

"I never saw any sign of it. It doesn't mean that they weren't. Both were very private people."

"As I found out with Desyrk."

Alyna looked intently at him. "You're exhausted."

"So are you."

"Then we ought to get on with dinner . . . And then get to . . . get some sleep."

"We should." Alastar didn't comment on her quick change of phrase. He didn't even smile. *Except inside.*

Later, after a quiet and less than comfortable dinner of lamb chops glazed in apple mint and cheesed potatoes and fried apples, most likely the best meal that Jienna and the other cook could get together on short notice, Lorien and Chelia retired to the guest quarters.

Alyna and Alastar stood on the front porch.

"I need to be going," she finally said, "and you need some sleep."

"So do you." Once more he gently wrapped his arms around her and held her.

Her arms went around him almost before he finished embracing her.

After a time, she looked up. "We aren't getting any sleep this way . . ."

"No . . . we aren't. We'll have to do something about that . . . soon."

"Oh?"

"Yes," he said. "We do, right after we clean up this mess. That is, if you'll accept my proposal."

She smiled mischievously. "I don't believe you made one."

"I'm making it now."

"I accept, dear Maitre."

"Then I'll walk you to your cottage."

"You wouldn't have if I'd refused?"

"No . . . I would have carried you and dropped you on your doorstep."

"That almost would have been worth it . . . except you're too tired and you would have dropped me earlier." She took his hand.

They walked down the steps together.

40

Alastar was up early on Solayi—the first day of Finitas, the last month of the year. When he entered the study, he couldn't help but wonder if the date meant anything in the grander scheme of the world and the Nameless . . . or just happened to be coincidental. Given that he had his doubts about the Nameless, he decided it was merely coincidence. *Still* . . . He shook his head and sat down at the desk and began to write, first, the draft of Lorien's tariff proclamation, knowing full well that Lorien would not have even tried. When he finished that and had barely begun on the general draft of the declaration about Ryentar, the study door opened.

Jienna stood there. "Are the rex and his lady supposed to eat without you?"

"I'll be right there." Alastar set aside the pen and immediately rose, following Jienna to the dining room, where three places had been set, with the empty position at the head of the table, and Lorien on the right, Chelia on the left. Neither rose as Alastar entered and seated himself.

"I apologize. I did not realize you were awake. I was working on the two drafts I mentioned yesterday so that we could leave as early as possible." He looked to Chelia, who had dark circles under her eyes. "I know you would like to return as soon as possible, but the declaration dealing with Ryentar and Asarya needs to be signed and sealed as soon as practicable after we reach the chateau. I'll also need to have Marshal Wilkorn detail a company of troopers to accompany them to whichever holding you designate." Alastar's eyes went to Lorien. "Have you chosen?"

"There's an older, but quite expansive holding with lands in Montagne." Lorien gave a sour smile. "Is that far enough away to suit you?"

"That should do. You'll have to rename it."

"We should give him some reminder. What about High Holder Regial?"

Alastar refrained from smiling. "That would be satisfactory."

At that moment, Jienna and one of the primes arrived with platters for the three, lightly browned egg toast, ham strips, and fried apples on the side, with a small loaf of bread for each.

"You'll have to do with lager this morning, Your Graces," Jienna announced. "It's what we have, and we're lucky to have that, no thanks to the army and their Namer-fired cannon."

Alastar couldn't quite hold the smile he felt at hearing Jienna's humorously tart words.

Chelia actually did smile. "This looks wonderful . . . and I never did thank you for dinner last night."

"Yes," added Lorien. "Dinner was excellent."

As soon as Jienna left, Chelia looked to Alastar. "It won't be too long, will it?"

"No. I have no desire to prolong anything, and the sooner this is all cleaned up, the better." *Especially the part with your half brother.* "But we do have to finish eating and one draft before we can depart. I would advise eating, because it may be a long day, certainly a long morning." With that, Alastar took a swallow of lager, and then poured berry syrup over the egg toast before handing the pitcher to Chelia.

After eating, Alastar and Lorien retired to the study, where, once Alastar arranged for the mustering of the imager group to escort Lorien and Chelia, he finished drafting the declaration of partial disinheriting for Ryentar, after considering—and modifying slightly—Lorien's suggestions.

When they finished, Lorien looked at Alastar. "You realize that Mother will be your lifelong enemy."

"I would suggest that you tell her that such a course would be unwise . . . and possibly fatal. You might point out what we know, and what we have already done. If . . . if nothing untoward occurs, then the Collegium will live and let live. Otherwise . . ."

"You're more ruthless than Petayn or even my father."

"No. I'm only ruthless when imagers and the Collegium are threatened. Otherwise I'm for moderation and practical solutions. Keep that in mind. I tried to resolve matters without violence, until your father ordered the attack on the Collegium. Now . . . we need to go. There's little sense in having your wife worry any longer than necessary." *And every reason to deal with Asarya and Ryentar before matters worsen again.* Alastar rolled up both sets of papers and tied them up, then walked out of the study. Belatedly, Lorien followed, almost bumping into Chelia, who had clearly been waiting outside in the hall, most likely impatiently.

Alyna was standing outside on the porch, as were the others, along with mounts for her, Alastar, Lorien, and Chelia. Already mounted were Taryn, and four Maitres D'Aspect—Shaelyt, Warryk, Claeynd, and Lhendyr, as well as Maercyl, Akkard, and Belsior, the comparatively large number of imagers because, although Alastar doubted that they would find significant—or any—armed resistance at the Chateau D'Rex, there was definitely the possibility of other difficulties. Alastar noted that the two craters beside the drive had been filled in. He smiled at Alyna and gestured. "Your doing?"

"I had Belsior and Akkard do it for exercise and practice."

"The seconds and thirds are going to get a great deal

of exercise and practice in the month ahead . . . as will everyone. I hope we didn't keep you waiting, but we had to finish drafting the document for Ryentar."

"I thought it might be something like that." She smiled warmly.

Alastar wanted to hold her, but only took her hand for a moment, before gesturing toward the mounts, then pulled on his riding gloves and walked to the gray gelding, patting him on the shoulder and saying, "You've seen a lot lately, fellow," before placing the bound papers in one of the saddlebags and then mounting.

By the time everyone was mounted, it was nearing eighth glass, and the anomen bell chimed as Belsior led the way over the Bridge of Desires, followed by Alastar and Alyna, riding side by side, and then Lorien and Chelia, followed closely by Shaelyt and Taryn, and then the other maitres, with Maercyl and Akkard in the rear.

Alastar himself felt perfectly fine, even carrying full shields, as if the massive imaging he'd done the day before had actually strengthened him. He looked ahead to the causeway on the west side of the River Aluse, more like a wide wall rising out of a muddy swamp, at least for the thirty yards between the bridge and the square from which he had imaged destruction onto Desyrk and the ill-fated regiment.

He knew from experience that heavy imaging created frost and sometimes ice, but he'd never attempted such a large single imaging before, and the results had shaken him, although he'd been so exhausted the night before that he hadn't had a chance to think that much about it. Now . . . seeing the devastation, he couldn't help but think about the entries in Gauswn's journals. *You and Taryn destroyed close to two thousand troopers and turned a good chunk of the riverbank into a muddy swamp . . . and that was nothing . . .*

"You're looking very serious," observed Alyna quietly.

"I was thinking about the first Maitre. If the histories are correct, he killed close to a hundred thousand men in three separate battles. That's fifty times what happened here yesterday . . . and without Shaelyt I'd have hit the stones of the square, if I hadn't been frozen solid myself . . ."

"I told you . . ."

"I tried not to do too much, but I couldn't let Desyrk escape." Alastar snorted, then said more quietly, "Quaeryt must have frozen half of L'Excelsis—well, it was called Variana then." With those words, he wondered why there hadn't been a winter effect at Liantiago . . . or had there been and no one mentioned it for other reasons?

"Be thankful you don't have to bear that burden, dear."

"Rebuilding the Collegium will be burden enough." He turned and grinned at her. "More measuring and surveying for you."

"That's not a burden. Not too much, anyway, although . . ."

"I know. You need better equipment."

"I can manage. The last thing the Collegium needs to spend golds on is surveying equipment."

Alastar couldn't argue with that, much as he would have liked to.

Once imagers neared the West River Road and the local shopkeepers and those outside saw the riders, almost all fled into the shops. *Not all that surprising, given the events of the past month.*

While bystanders along the way did not flee once the riders headed north and then west on the Boulevard D'Ouest, everyone cleared the road as they approached. *Word has definitely spread.* He turned to Alyna. "When we get to the chateau, assuming there aren't other problems, I'd appreciate it if you would accompany Shaelyt and Chelia to find young Charyn."

"I think that's a very good idea. Once we make sure

he's safe, I'd like to leave Shaelyt there with him and Chelia . . . just in case."

"We'll most likely be in the rex's study on the upper level on the east side of the north corridor. There will probably be a guard outside."

Alyna nodded, but Alastar didn't miss the hint of an amused smile.

As Alastar turned the gray gelding onto the ring road north of the Chateau D'Rex, some two quints later, he turned in the saddle. "Lorien, Chelia, in just a moment, Shaelyt, right behind you, will place a partial concealment and a shield around you. I don't expect trouble, but it won't hurt to be careful." Alastar had other reasons as well, especially since he wanted to find out some things before revealing the presence of the rex and his lady.

"I can understand that." Lorien's voice was still less than pleased, and slightly sour.

Alastar couldn't blame him. "Shaelyt?"

"Yes, sir."

"Go ahead with the shields and a blurring concealment, just around the two of them."

In moments, Alastar could make out only that two riders followed him. "Good!" He turned his attention back to the ring road, not that he needed to worry because, at the sight of the imagers, pedestrians, riders, and even wagons continued to hurry away from the group headed south toward the Chateau D'Rex.

When Alastar and Alyna reined up at the foot of the white stone steps leading up to the main entrance of the chateau, Guard Captain Fonteau appeared almost immediately and hurried down the steps. He wore the same resigned expression he had exhibited the first time Alastar had met him.

"Regent Ryentar has matters well in hand, sir."

"I'm sure he does," replied Alastar sardonically. "How is young Charyn?"

"He's fine, sir. I just saw him a quint ago."

Alastar could almost feel the relief from Chelia, although he did not look back. "That's good. Very good, especially for Ryentar."

Fonteau offered a puzzled look.

"Didn't you notice?" Alastar gestured. "If you'd remove the partial concealment, Maitre Shaelyt."

Fonteau gaped.

"We took the liberty of rescuing Rex Lorien and Lady Chelia from the fires and explosions at the Anomen D'Rex. They would have been very upset if anything had happened to Charyn . . . and I cannot tell you how displeased the Collegium would be if anything had happened to him."

"No, sir. He's fine."

"Good. You will escort Lady Chelia, Maitre Alyna, and Maitre Shaelyt to the heir. Immediately. I assume that Ryentar is in the rex's study."

"He was a quint or so ago."

"And Lady Asarya?"

"I believe she is in her chambers or her salon."

Alastar nodded and dismounted, as did Alyna, then turned. "Shaelyt, you'll accompany Maitre Alyna. Taryn and Warryk, you'll be with me. Lhendyr, you're in charge out here. You and Claeynd are to keep things peaceful. No army troopers are to approach. I don't expect any, but if they do, use whatever is necessary, and send word to me. If Lady Asarya attempts to leave, restrain her with shields. Rex Lorien and I will likely be in his study." Alastar extracted the papers from the saddlebag, continuing to survey the steps and the area around the front of the chateau.

As soon as Alyna, Shaelyt, and Chelia departed with Fonteau, Alastar let Lorien lead the way up the outside steps, then up the grand staircase and to the rex's study. The chateau guard posted outside the study stared as Lorien approached.

"Sir! We thought . . ."

"I'm quite well," said Lorien coolly.

"Taryn, you and Warryk are to keep this hallway secure. Use whatever imaging is necessary."

"Yes, sir."

Alastar then opened the study door and let Lorien enter first.

Ryentar's face showed a startled expression for less than an instant before he rose from the desk. "Well . . . brother, it's good to see you're alive and well." Ryentar offered the warm and welcoming smile that Alastar found so incredibly genuine . . . and thus all the more deceptive. If Ryel the elder had been that effective, Alastar could definitely see how he had charmed so many people.

Lorien snorted. "Save the smiles for others. I've seen enough of them."

"I've been so worried about you, and you're treating me like I was one of *them*."

"Which 'them' might you be referring to?" asked Alastar. "Those who tried to assassinate your brother so that you could become regent and eventually rex? Or those who made two unsuccessful attempts at destroying the Collegium? Or perhaps those who murdered most of the senior army commanders? Except . . . they're all the same."

"I don't know what you're talking about." Ryentar's face bore a look of total confusion.

Alastar didn't trust that expression, either. *That's the difficulty with those who are good actors. In the end, you can't trust anything.* "It doesn't matter if you do, High Holder Regial," declared Alastar.

"High Holder Regial? What do you mean?"

"Move away from the desk," Alastar ordered. "The rex needs to sign and seal something." He handed the bound papers to Lorien.

"You don't order me—"

Ryentar's words were the first hint of anger Alastar had heard from the genial-appearing soon-to-be-disinherited second son.

Alastar did not speak, but placed shields loosely around Ryentar and used them to move him away from the desk to the window.

"You can't . . ." Ryentar's words died away as he looked at Lorien.

"I could have you executed," said Lorien coldly. "You can thank Maitre Alastar for a less fatal solution."

The genial expression immediately reappeared on Ryentar's face. "What might that be?"

"You're getting the grand estate in Montagne, along with the lands in perpetuity for you and any heirs you may have, and the title of High Holder Regial. If you ever approach within a hundred milles of L'Excelsis, your life and your estate is forfeit."

"That means you can't ever be on the High Council, unlike your father," added Alastar.

"My father . . ." Ryentar looked from Lorien to Alastar and back again. Then he shook his head and smiled. "I suppose that will have to do."

"Your mother will be accompanying you as well, with the same provisos," added Alastar. *And she won't be nearly so pleased.* Not that Alastar believed for a moment that Ryentar was at all pleased.

Ryentar maintained a pleasant, almost jovial smile, as Lorien settled himself behind the desk and unrolled the two sheets, setting one aside and smoothing the other.

"Your seal is in the drawer on the right," offered Ryentar helpfully.

"Thank you." The sarcasm in Lorien's voice was unmistakable as he opened the drawer and extracted the seal.

Alastar imaged a flame at the tip of the candle wick under the small brazier that held the sealing wax. Lorien had to wait more than several moments before the green wax melted. Then he stirred it with the spoon before lifting the spoon and deftly depositing the circle of wax on the heavy paper. Then he raised the seal, turned it, and breathed on it before making the impression.

"There. Your grant of lands with the conditions. You'll get the original after the chateau scrivener makes copies."

"You're most kind, brother."

"I'm not. Maitre Alastar is. Don't forget that, either."

"I suppose that wouldn't be wise."

The study door opened, and Taryn said, "Lady Asarya insists on seeing the rex, Maitre."

"Then escort her in," said Alastar. "She certainly deserves it." He didn't keep the heavy irony from his last words.

"Lorien! What are you doing?" demanded Asarya, looking at Alastar and then at Ryentar.

"Exiling me to Montagne," said Ryentar. "As High Holder Regial, no less. I believe you are to accompany me, according to Maitre Alastar."

Asarya turned back to face Alastar. "You wouldn't do that to a grieving widow, would you?"

"I might have, were you grieving for Ryel the elder or even for poor deluded Desyrk, or the thousands of dead troopers, or officers and dead imagers, but since your grief doesn't extend to them, but only yourself."

"Desyrk?" questioned Lorien.

"Another of your mother's conquests," replied Alastar, adding, "You'll also need to request a company from Marshal Wilkorn to escort them both to Montagne."

"I'm about to draft that right now," replied Lorien.

"You wouldn't . . . I cannot believe that my own son . . ." Asarya's words were quiet.

"Your older and less-favored son. The one you conspired to replace." Lorien's words were cold. He picked up the pen.

"Why not? You look like your father. You act like your father. You'll end up as worthless as he did."

Lorien paled and his jaw set. "For that—"

"No," said Alastar. "That's exactly what she wants. The last thing she desires is a long life hundreds of milles from L'Excelsis, thinking of how close she came. If you execute her, deserved as it may be, that will soil your name more than hers. Right now, all the blood is on the hands of the Collegium. It's best to leave it there."

Asarya's eyes turned cold as she looked at Alastar. "You think I'll stay there in a hill country holding?"

"If you want to live. Frankly, I'd just as soon you attempted to leave, or to escape on your way there. That would make matters *so* much easier. Both for Rex Lorien and for the Collegium."

"Perhaps I won't give you that satisfaction."

"That's your choice, Lady Asarya," replied Alastar.

Asarya smiled and turned to Lorien. "You know . . . in the long run, now it doesn't matter at all."

Lorien looked puzzled for a moment.

Even Alastar was . . . until he realized what she meant. "In that respect, you're perfectly correct, Lady Asarya, but it also points out that some means to an end are acceptable, ethically and to the Nameless . . . and some are not." He looked to Taryn. "Escort her back to her quarters, and have Warryk guard and shield the door until a detachment of troopers arrives." *Or until we can make other suitable arrangements.*

As Asarya and Taryn left the study, Ryentar was not quite smirking, until Alastar glanced at him. The smirk vanished.

"You'll also be under guard," Alastar said.

"I didn't expect any less," replied Ryentar. "Under guard until I reach my gilded prison."

Alastar thought of pointing out that Ryentar had no idea how privileged he was, but realized that any words like that would mean nothing to him.

The door opened, and Alyna stepped into the study, her eyes sweeping the room before centering on Alastar. "Everything's settled with Charyn."

"Good."

"And here?"

"Lady Asarya just left. High Holder Regial will be leaving shortly for protective custody."

Alyna's eyes turned to Ryentar. "You know, I've never trusted pretty boys. You've given me another reason why."

Alastar smiled faintly.

41

In the end, between making various arrangements and then waiting for Wilkorn's troopers to arrive, Alastar and Alyna, and all the others from Imagisle, did not return to the Collegium until well after fourth glass. By the time Alastar and Alyna had turned over their mounts to the stable boys outside a shed roughly imaged into existence by Petros and his seconds and thirds and walked back to the Maitre's residence, the sky had darkened, the wind had picked up, and fat droplets of rain were splatting on the paving stones of the walk leading up to the porch. The two hurried up onto the covered porch.

"It's been quite a day," mused Alastar as he paused, not really wanting to go inside and explain everything, although, he realized after a moment, it was Solayi afternoon, almost evening, and Dareyn was most likely not there. In fact, for both Dareyn's sake and his own, he hoped the dutiful second was not. He turned to look back toward the anomen and along the green.

"Quite a month," said Alyna, taking his hand, but standing beside him and looking south along the occasionally still-cratered green, bordered by the cottages of married imagers, some of which had already been at least partly image-repaired. "I'd say it would be one never to be forgotten, but people always forget."

"Unless it's special to them."

"Oh?"

"It's been special to me, but not just . . ." He shook his head. "You know what I mean."

"I might, but I like to hear it."

"You've made it special."

"So have you."

Neither spoke for several moments as the rain began to fall more heavily, pattering on the porch roof and on the steps and stone walk.

"You're still thinking about Lorien and Chelia, aren't you?" asked Alyna.

"I am," Alastar admitted. "In some ways, Lady Asarya was successful, in spite of everything."

"You mean because Lorien married Ryel's daughter, Charyn's bloodline includes Ryel as well as Lorien's mother and father? Does that bother you?"

Alastar laughed softly. "Not that much. No matter how worthy the end, some means of achieving it will destroy its worth."

"That's why you had to let Ryen and Demykalon and Petayn attack the Collegium."

He nodded. "I still don't like the fact that it had to go that way, but I couldn't find another solution, not in time. Another question that puzzled me was why Asarya was working with Desyrk. I can understand why Desyrk wanted me dead. I can even understand why Asarya did, but was Desyrk the only way she could find of removing me and Lorien?"

"Dear . . . who else besides Desyrk would be foolish enough, and egotistical enough, to think he could prevail against you?"

"He and Asarya very well might have. Without all the information you provided I wouldn't have known where to look and what to look for."

"You're kind."

Alastar laughed and shook his head. "As I told you once, I'm not that kind. I try to be as fair as possible."

"You're kinder than you let on, if with an imaged iron fist behind the velvet glove. You could have had both Ryentar and Asarya executed. And Bettaur, too." Her voice turned more serious. "He's Ryel's son, too, isn't he?"

"How did you know?" Alastar paused. "I don't know for certain, but he looks so much like both Chelia and Ryentar . . ."

"After I saw them both, I decided he couldn't not be. It also explains a few things."

"Such as Fhaen's excessive protectiveness?" Alastar shook his head. "The elder Ryel must have been quite a charmer."

"Power and charm make most men extremely attractive to most women. I prefer fairness and power." She smiled. "You're also handsome in a way that doesn't remind me of pretty boys."

"I'm glad that—"

She turned to him. "You've also been kind enough to let me decide when. That's now. The other explanations can wait." She put both arms around his neck and drew him to her.

42

On Lundi morning, some two quints before seventh glass, Alastar stood outside on the porch of the Maitre's residence, waiting for Alyna, Akoryt, and Bettaur and Taurek. *Just another detail to straighten out before you brief all the maitres.* The early morning definitely felt like winter was around the corner, especially with the wet raw cold that resulted from the rain of the night before and the bitter northwest wind. He could have waited inside, but he would have paced back and forth. Besides, he could watch Alyna for longer.

After dealing with Bettaur and Taurek, he'd have to conduct a meeting for all the Collegium maitres, since he had opened the seniors' meeting to all maitres so that he could brief them all in detail on what had happened both on Solayi and earlier. While Akoryt and Cyran knew most of that, even they didn't know everything, and some of the more junior maitres knew very little except what they'd seen in the two attacks on Imagisle. Alastar also wanted everyone to hear all the facts at the same time, not that each wouldn't take away a different impression. He just hoped those impressions would not be too different.

He smiled as he saw four figures walking up the stone walk on the west side of the green, one of them markedly smaller than the other three. He was still smiling when Alyna reached the steps of the residence.

"You look happy this morning," she said with a smile.

"So do you." Alastar nodded to Akoryt and the two thirds, then gestured toward the front door. "We'll meet in the study."

Once everyone was inside the study, with the door firmly closed, Alastar turned to the two thirds. "Because of the attacks on the Collegium and the obvious fact that the detention cells have been effectively destroyed, neither of you served your full time in detention. Waiting until the new administration building is complete and then requiring completion of that time seems rather ludicrous at this point. It would also be a waste of your talents. Therefore, you will serve in another fashion, and successful completion of that service will result in your restoration to full tertius status and privileges." Alastar turned to Bettaur. "With one exception in your case."

He paused, then resumed, "*Any* failure during that service will result in an immediate hearing before me to determine your fitness to ever become a full imager." Alastar looked at Taurek. "Failure for you includes, far from exclusively, I might add, use of imaging against others, although personal protection shields are allowed and encouraged, or any use of physical force against others. Do you understand?"

"Yes, sir."

Alastar turned to Bettaur. "I am very much aware of your tendency and past acts in manipulating others for personal gain and to injure others, either through words, personal charm, notes, and various forms of misrepresentation, not to mention covert use of imaging. And even the use of oil on the shoes of other student imagers." Alastar paused as he watched the young man try to conceal his surprise, then said, "Unlike in the past, everyone will be watching you. If you attempt any of those, any of them, you will also face me in a hearing—and that could happen any time until you are qualified as a maitre. In that sense, you are on probation until you are deemed worthy to be a maitre. Do you understand?"

"Yes, sir." Bettaur's voice was subdued.

"You both will work at imaging every day under the

direct supervision of Maitre Alyna, or in her absence, the direction of Maitre Akoryt or any maitre I may designate. If any maitre has the slightest difficulty with either of you . . . and that includes notes, plots, schemes, or rumors, you will face a hearing." Alastar smiled coolly and looked straight at Bettaur. "You did see what happened to Maitre Desyrk, I believe."

Bettaur swallowed. "Yes, sir."

"Good." Alastar turned to Akoryt. "Would you like to add anything?"

"I think you've covered everything."

Alastar looked to Alyna.

"Yes, I would." She turned her black eyes on Bettaur. "You have great personal charm, and you could be a good imager. In fact, you could become one of the more important imagers in the Collegium in time. That is, if you work for everyone's good. Or . . . you could also turn out exactly like Desyrk—except you wouldn't live that long, because I detest spoiled pretty boys who rely on charm and manipulation rather than work to develop their skills and talents." Her voice was like ice as she finished.

Bettaur actually paled.

So did Taurek, Alastar noticed.

The study was silent for several moments before Alastar spoke. "Have we made matters clear enough?"

"Yes, sir . . . and Maitre Alyna," Bettaur said quickly.

"Yes, sir," said Taurek almost simultaneously.

"Good," said Alastar. "You will wait here for Maitre Alyna during the maitres' meeting in the dining room. You will begin by assisting her in the rebuilding of the Collegium, which will likely leave you exhausted enough that the temptation for any sort of mischief should be greatly reduced. You will also follow her instructions in all matters dealing with imaging and the Collegium."

"Yes, sir."

Once Alastar closed the study door and stood in the hallway with Alyna and Akoryt, he added, "I would appreciate it if they were required to image to the point of exhaustion, and that such imaging require perfection."

"Those were already my thoughts," replied Alyna.

Akoryt nodded. "Bettaur will still bear watching. I'll talk to all the maitres about it."

"That would be good," said Alastar.

"If you'll excuse me for a bit—until the meeting?" asked the red-haired maitre.

"Of course." Alastar refrained from smiling, although he appreciated Akoryt's sensitivity.

As Akoryt headed for the front door and the porch, Alastar did smile . . . at Alyna. "I'm glad we share the same views." After a pause, he asked, "Do you think we got the point across?"

"If we didn't, they will deserve what they will get."

"Now . . . for the maitres."

"In a quint." She offered a mischievous smile. "Might I prevail upon you for a quick tour of the upstairs?"

"I'd be delighted."

They returned to the front hall just before the anomen bell chimed seventh glass, and entered the dining room behind Gaellen, who turned his head as he entered. "I'm sorry, sir, but I had to redo the splints on Kaylet's wrists. It took longer . . ."

"Today . . . we have a little time," Alastar replied cheerfully.

Once all the maitres were seated around the table, Alastar stood so that all of them could hear him. "I felt that all of you should know the complete story of what has happened over the last several weeks . . . or as complete a story as I've been able to piece together. Some of what I'll tell you has an element of supposition. It has to, because those who could tell us are dead. There were several factors that combined to create the mess we have just survived. First, Ryen felt as though he had been played by Maitre Fhaen and the Collegium, and that he had been handing golds over to us with no value in return for years. As prone to anger as he may have been, as I've said earlier, he was absolutely right about that. But he was so angry and impatient that he was unwilling to give us any time at all to remedy that problem. He told me bluntly that Fhaen had advised him badly, and that he would not take the same advice from me. The High Council refused to accept the possibility that tariffs needed to increase. It also felt that the Collegium would do nothing, since it had done nothing to show its power in well over a hundred years.

"Then there was Lady Asarya. She was angry with Ryen, and for reasons we do not need to discuss, favored her younger son over the elder, perhaps because Lorien resembles his father as well as for other reasons.

"Add to this distasteful brew Marshal Demykalon, who felt, with some justification, that Solidar was not being governed as wisely as it could be. He felt that, if he could destroy or even weaken the Collegium, then he could eventually use his position as marshal to either rule through Ryen or Lorien or supplant them entirely. In his anger and fury, Ryen tasked Demykalon with using enough cannon fire to force the Collegium to assassinate enough of the High Council to get his unrealistically high tariffs accepted. Demykalon agreed to this order because he thought he could weaken the Collegium, although he knew the High Council would never accept a tariff increase of one copper on a half silver. No one could accept a raise of one part in five in a single year. But I believe, from what he said, that he thought he could work out an arrangement with the High Council to become rex with a token increase in tariffs. He had already increased the number of regiments in the army above that set forth in the charter. In pursuit of his own ambitions, he promoted Chesyrk to commander and gave him the orders to bombard the

Collegium. It can't have been by chance that he assigned the one senior officer in the entire army who he was certain would carry out those orders, because Desyrk had fled to him with tales of his demotion and my supposedly unfair treatment of him.

"I had no idea that Desyrk knew Lady Asarya, or that she had such hatred for her husband and her elder son, but with Ryen and Demykalon dead, she saw her opportunity. I doubt we'll ever know all the details, but she clearly enlisted Chesyrk and Desyrk. Desyrk was furious at me and the Collegium, and Chesyrk felt that he'd been passed over and marginalized by both Demykalon and Petayn. Chesyrk had been a favorite of Marshal Ghalyn, who often took him to the chateau to brief Rex Ryen. There he met, most likely in passing, Lady Asarya. Desyrk was handsome and charming. She was attractive. Then Demykalon became marshal, and Chesyrk was no longer a favorite and possibly felt he might not even be promoted to commander.

"I can only surmise that the two brothers, with prompting by Lady Asarya, told Petayn that they'd capture the anomen, not try to destroy it, and remove Lorien as rex. They'd make Ryentar regent for young Charyn, and Petayn would continue as marshal."

"That wasn't the real plan at all," said Alyna.

Alastar shook his head. "Desyrk wanted his brother to be rex. He would have liked that for himself, but egotistical as he was, he knew that wasn't possible. The next best thing was for Chesyrk to take over the army. The use of Antiagon Fire in the anomen to kill both Lorien and Chelia—that's what they had in mind—would point the finger at the Collegium, and the army would be able to hunt down imagers—or drive any survivors into hiding, or into becoming a hidden adjunct to the army, the way Desyrk had become, and that would have made Chesyrk, as the marshal of the army, the most powerful man in Solidar and the rex little more than a puppet . . ." Alastar paused, letting the impact of what he had said sink in before continuing. "When Taryn, Shaelyt, and I saved Rex Lorien and Lady Chelia, and when we all destroyed Chesyrk, Desyrk, and the troopers attacking Imagisle, Lady Asarya did not know that we had survived the Antiagon Fire in the anomen, and she immediately announced Lord Ryentar as regent for young Charyn."

Obsolym's mouth dropped open.

"When we returned to the Chateau D'Rex yesterday and confronted her, she admitted that she had wanted Ryentar to be rex all along. Rex Lorien was merciful, and wise, in not ordering more killings. He disinherited his brother, but created him as High Holder Regial in Montagne, but forbid him ever to return to L'Excelsis on pain of death. Lady Asarya is accompanying him under the same strictures. The only surviving senior officer of the armies, although he has a broken arm and a broken leg, is Marshal Wilkorn. He is providing a company to escort the lady and the High Holder to Montagne. They should be out of the Chateau D'Rex by eighth glass. Oh . . . and Rex Lorien has signed the tariff proclamation and sent it to the High Council. They will accept it."

Alastar was well aware that he had bent the truth in places and that he had left out the worst parts of Asarya's treachery, but he'd told enough, and bringing in what Ryel had done would only damage Chelia and weaken Lorien. Certainly what he had told was true in spirit, if not in every single fact, as far as he'd been able to determine, because the ability to determine some of those facts died with those who had lived them.

For several moments, the dining room was silent.

"Ahem . . ." Obsolym cleared his throat. "As the oldest, if not most senior maitre in ability, I'd like to say that Maitre Alastar has managed to guide us through a most dangerous situation. He deserves our support and thanks."

"He does indeed," added Akoryt.

Several others murmured what appeared to be approving words, although Alastar could not make them out. As the words died away, he spoke again. "We have a Collegium to rebuild, and, as before, Maitre Alyna will be in charge of that . . . starting in about two quints."

Alyna glanced at him.

"Oh . . . and there's one other thing." Alastar found he didn't quite have the words at hand, not the eloquent ones he'd planned. "Maitre Alyna has consented to marry me. As soon as practicable."

"About time for both of you," said Obsolym.

Alastar found himself blushing and tongue-tied.

EPILOGUE

Alyna held a large leather case in her hands as she stepped into the private study that had become both of theirs. She looked toward the study desk.

"You can put it there," said Alastar. "What is it?"

"You'll see." After lifting the top of the case and easing it back, she drew out a finely worked brass instrument of some kind, consisting of a small brass telescope slightly over a third of a yard in length, set above a circular brass plate. That plate was in turn mounted so that it could swivel both up and down, with brackets set on each side of another brass plate, this one a half circle. At the bottom of the half circle was some form of mounting bracket.

"What is it? Where did you get it?"

"It's a very good telescope diopter. Zaeryl sent it." She smiled. "There was a note saying that if I was going to survey avenues that he'd have to pay for, I needed better tools." She smiled more broadly. "He also said it was my belated wedding gift, since I'd proved I had no interest in jewels or finery."

"Quite a gift." *Especially since it likely cost more than jewels or finery.*

"The note was the best part."

"Oh? What did he say?"

"Quite a number of things, some of which you can read . . . a little later." She smiled broadly. "Actually, you could read them now, but I'll make you wait . . . a glass or two, anyway. He said that I'd proved I didn't need a husband and then went and married the most powerful man in Solidar to spite everyone. He also said that Vaelora would have been proud."

"I thought he said you weren't supposed to speak about her," Alastar teased.

"To others. That doesn't include family, and since you're family . . ." She slipped her arms around him.